D0297738

CRYSTAL GARDENS

Jayne Ann Krentz is the critically-acclaimed creator of the Arcane Society world, Dark Legacy series and Rainshadow series. She also writes as **Amanda Quick** and **Jayne Castle**. Jayne has written more than fifty *New York Times* bestsellers under various pseudonyms and more than thirty-five million copies of her books are currently in print. She lives in the Pacific Northwest.

The historical novels she writes as Amanda Quick all feature her customary irresistible mix of passion and mystery, and also have a strong psychic/paranormal twist.

Visit her website at www.jayneannkrentz.com

www.facebook.com/JayneAnnKrentz | www.twitter.com/JayneAnnKrentz

Arcane Society Novels:

By Jayne Ann Krentz
writing as Amanda Quick

Second Sight
The Third Circle
The Perfect Poison
Burning Lamp
Quicksilver

By Jayne Ann Krentz

White Lies
Sizzle and Burn
Running Hot
Fired Up
In Too Deep

By Jayne Ann Krentz
writing as Jayne Castle

Dark Light
Obsidian Prey
Midnight Crystal

Dark Legacy Novels:

By Jayne Ann Krentz

Copper Beach

Other titles by Jayne Ann Krentz writing as Amanda Quick:

With This Ring
I Thee Wed
Wicked Widow
Lie By Moonlight
The Paid Companion
Wait Until Midnight
The River Knows
Affair
Mischief

Other titles by Jayne Ann Krentz

Light in Shadow
Truth or Dare
Falling Awake
All Night Long

CRYSTAL GARDENS

Amanda Quick

piatkus

PIATKUS

First published in the US in 2012 by G.P. Putnam's Sons,
A member of Penguin Group (USA) Inc., New York
First published in Great Britain in 2012 by Piatkus

A CIP catalogue record for this book is available from the British Library.

ISBN 978-0-7499-5652-3 [HB]
ISBN 978-0-7499-5647-9 [TPB]

Printed and bound by CPI Group (UK) Ltd, Croydon, CR0 4YY

Papers used by Piatkus are from well-managed forests
and other responsible sources.

Piatkus
An imprint of
Little, Brown Book Group

For my husband, Frank,

with all my love

CRYSTAL GARDENS

One

The muffled thud of the shattered lock echoed like a thunderclap in the deep silence that drenched the cottage. Evangeline Ames recognized the sound at once. She was no longer alone in the house.

Her first, primal instinct was to go absolutely still beneath the covers. Perhaps she was mistaken. The cottage was old. The floorboards and the ceiling often creaked and moaned at night. But even as the commonsense possibilities flitted through her head, she knew the truth. It was two o'clock in the morning, an intruder had broken in and it was highly unlikely that he was after the silver. There was not enough in the place to tempt a thief.

Her nerves had been on edge all afternoon, her intuition flickering and flaring for no obvious reason. Earlier, when she had walked into town, she had found herself looking over her shoulder again and again. She had flinched at the smallest rustling noises in the dense woods that bordered the narrow lane. While she was shopping in Little Dixby's crowded high street, the hair had lifted on the back of her neck. She had felt as if she was being watched.

She had reminded herself that she was still recovering from the terrifying attack two weeks ago. She had very nearly been murdered. Little wonder her nerves were so fragile. On top of that, the writing was not going well and a deadline was looming. She dared not miss it. She'd had every reason to be tense.

But now she knew the truth. Her psychical intuition had been trying to send a warning for hours. That was the reason she had been unable to sleep tonight.

Cool currents of night air wafted down the hall from the kitchen. Heavy footsteps sounded. The intruder was not even bothering to conceal his approach. He was very certain of his prey. She had to get out of the bed.

She pushed back the covers, sat up quietly and eased herself to her feet. The floorboards were chilly. She stepped into her sturdy, leather-soled slippers and took her wrapper down off the hook.

The assault on her person two weeks earlier had made her cautious. She had considered all possible escape routes when she had rented the cottage. Here in the bedroom, the waist-high window was her best hope. It opened onto the small front garden with its lattice gate. Just outside the gate was the narrow, rutted lane that wound through the dark woods to the ancient country house known as Crystal Gardens.

Out in the hall a floorboard creaked under the weight of a booted foot. The intruder was moving directly to the bedroom. That settled the matter. He had not come for the silver. He had come for her.

There was no point trying to silence her movements. She pushed one of the narrow casement windows wide, ignoring the squeak of the hinges, and clambered through the opening. With luck the intruder would not be able to fit.

"Where do you think you're going, you bloody stupid woman?" the harsh male voice roared from the doorway. It was freighted with the accents of London's tough streets. "No one slips away from Sharpy Hobson's blade."

There was no time to wonder how a London street criminal had found his way to Little Dixby or why he was after her. She would worry about those questions later, she thought, if she survived the night.

She jumped to the ground and stumbled through the miniature jungle of giant ferns that choked the little garden. Many of the fronds were taller than she was.

To think she had come to the countryside to rest and recuperate from recent events.

"Bloody hell, come back here," Hobson howled from the bedroom window. "Make things difficult, will ye? I'll take my time with ye when I do catch you, just see if I don't. You'll die nice and slow, and that's a promise. Bloody little bitch."

A string of savage curses told her that Hobson was finding it impossible to squeeze through the casement window. A tiny whisper of hope swept through her when she did not hear the pounding of footsteps behind her. Hobson would be forced to use one of the two doors in the cottage. That meant she had a little breathing room, time enough, perhaps, to make it to the only possible sanctuary.

There was no escape through the woods that bordered the lane. The moon was nearly full but the heavy canopy of summer leaves blocked the silver light that should have dappled the forest floor. Even if she'd had a lantern, she would not have been able to make her way through the thick undergrowth. She knew just how impenetrable the vegetation in the vicinity of the old abbey was because she had attempted to explore it during the day. The trees and undergrowth around the ancient ruins flourished in what the locals whispered was an unnatural manner.

She found the graveled garden walk and flew down it, the hem of the wrapper flapping wildly. She paused long enough to unlatch the gate and then she was out in the moonlit lane, running for her life. She knew that Hobson would see her as soon as he emerged from the cottage.

Heavy footfalls thudded behind her.

"I have ye now, ye silly bitch. Ye'll soon get a taste of Sharpy's blade."

She risked a quick glance over her shoulder and saw the dark figure bearing down on her. She would have screamed but she would have been wasting her breath. She ran harder, heart pounding.

The ancient stone walls that protected the vast grounds of Crystal Gardens appeared impregnable in the moonlight. She knew from previous explorations that the massive iron gate was locked.

There was no point trying to run the length of the long wall to the front door of the sprawling country house. There was no time. Hobson was gaining on her. His footsteps were closer now. She could hear his harsh breathing, or perhaps it was her own labored gasps that she heard.

She reached the back wall of the ancient abbey and raced toward the mound of overgrown foliage that concealed the jagged hole in the stone barrier. She had discovered the opening a few days ago and had decided to indulge in some discreet exploration before the new owner arrived to take up residence. She could not help herself. Her sense of curiosity was linked in some ways to her psychical talent and the mystery of Crystal Gardens had fascinated her from the start. It was the reason she had chosen to rent Fern Gate Cottage instead of one of the other properties available in the countryside around Little Dixby.

The fact that the rent on the cottage was considerably cheaper than it was for the other suitable lodgings in the area had also been a factor. But she had discovered soon enough why the little house was a bargain. The locals feared the abbey and the woods around it.

She slammed to a stop in front of the concealing foliage and pulled aside a curtain of cascading greenery. The jagged opening in the stone was about two feet above ground level. It was large enough for a person, even a man the size of Hobson, to squeeze through. But if he did pursue her onto the grounds she might have a chance.

She looked back one last time. Hobson had not yet rounded the corner of the wall, but he would at any second. She could hear him—his thudding footsteps and his ragged breathing—but she could not yet see him. She had a few seconds.

She put one leg over the broken stone and then the other and then she was inside the grounds of Crystal Gardens.

She caught her breath, transfixed by the eerie scene that surrounded her. She had seen enough of the strange gardens by day to know that there was something bizarre about the energy inside the walls and that the vegetation was not normal. But at night the paranormal elements were unmistakable.

The foliage on the vast grounds glowed with an eerie luminescence. In the very center of the gardens, where the ruins of an ancient Roman bath were said to be located, the psychical light was as dark and ominous as a violent storm at sea.

She knew from the guidebooks that she had purchased from Miss Witton, the proprietor of the bookshop in Little Dixby, that Crystal Gardens was divided into two sections. The outer region in which she stood was called the Day Garden on the maps. It surrounded the walls of an elaborate maze, which, in turn, encircled the interior portion of the grounds, known as the Night Garden.

In the nearly two weeks that she had resided in Fern Gate Cottage she had not ventured much farther into the gardens than where she was tonight. But she knew intuitively that the peculiar nature of the atmosphere inside the walls would provide her with her best chance of escaping Sharpy Hobson's knife.

There was a steady stream of curses as Hobson yanked and clawed at the foliage.

"No little whore gets away with making Sharpy Hobson look the fool. I'll teach you to show some respect, see if I don't."

She looked around, summoning up a mental image of the layout of the gardens. The maze was the obvious place to hide. Her talent would very likely ensure that she did not get lost inside. But on a prior expedition she had discovered that a locked gate blocked the entrance to the labyrinth.

She started toward the gazebo. The graceful domed roof and the pillars glowed with a faint blue light that seemed to emanate from the very stone of which it was constructed. She hurried but she did not run. She wanted Hobson to see her.

He finally scrambled through the hole in the wall, grunting and swearing. She stopped and looked back, wondering how much of the paranormal light he could perceive. There was a shocked silence as Hobson took in his surroundings.

"What the flamin' hell?" he growled. He rubbed his eyes.

Then he saw her and promptly forgot about the strangely luminous landscape around him. He yanked a knife out of the leather sheath at his hip and lunged toward her.

"Thought you'd get away from me, did ye?" he growled.

She whirled back toward the gazebo. Her goal was the darkly gleaming pond in front of the structure. With luck Hobson would not be able to see it until it was too late. Her senses told her that if he tumbled into the gleaming black pool he would quickly lose interest in her. There was something nightmarish about those waters.

She was so focused on her plan to lure Hobson to the pond that she was unaware of the presence of the man in the long black coat until he walked out of the shadows and into the moonlight. He stopped directly in front of her, blocking her path.

"Is it the custom around here for visitors to call at such an unusual hour?" he asked.

His voice was as dark as the obsidian surface of the pond and charged with a similar chilling power. It stirred all of her senses. In the strange moon-and-energy-lit shadows it was difficult to make out the man's face clearly, but there was no need to see him. She recognized him immediately. Indeed, she thought, she would know him anywhere. Lucas Sebastian, the mysterious new owner of Crystal Gardens.

She stumbled to a halt, trapped between Lucas and Sharpy Hobson.

"Mr. Sebastian," she said. She was breathless and her heart was pounding. She struggled to identify herself, afraid he would not recognize her in the darkness, dressed, as she was, in her wrapper and nightgown, her hair falling around her shoulders. They had met only the one time, after all. "Sorry to intrude like this. Evangeline Ames, your tenant at Fern Gate Cottage."

"I know who you are, Miss Ames."

"You did say to call upon you if I had a problem. As it happens, I do have one."

"I can see that," Lucas said.

Hobson pulled up short. He made a slashing motion with the knife. "Get out of my way and ye won't get hurt. I just want the little whore."

Lucas regarded him with what could only be described as detached curiosity. "You are trespassing. That is a very dangerous thing to do here at Crystal Gardens."

"What's going on in this place?" Hobson looked around uneasily.

"Haven't you heard the stories?" Lucas asked. "Everyone around here knows that these grounds are haunted."

"Sharpy Hobson ain't afraid of no ghosts," Hobson vowed. "Won't be hanging around long enough to meet one. All I want is this bitch."

"What do you want with Miss Ames?" Lucas asked.

Evangeline was floored by Lucas's matter-of-fact tone. It was as if he was only casually interested in Hobson's reasoning.

"None of yer bloody business," Hobson snarled. "But I can tell ye she's worth a nice bit of blunt dead and I'm not going to let anyone get in my way."

"You don't seem to comprehend the situation," Lucas said. "The lady is my tenant and therefore under my protection."

Hobson snorted. "I'm doing you a favor taking her off your hands. The way I heard it, she's a lying little bitch."

"Someone hired you to kill her?" Lucas asked.

Hobson was starting to appear uncertain. Matters were evidently not proceeding the way they usually did when he went about his business.

"I'm not wasting any more time talking to you." Hobson leaped toward Lucas, knife ready to slash. "Yer a dead man."

"Not quite," Lucas said.

Energy, dark and terrifying, flashed in the atmosphere. Evangeline had just time enough time to realize that Lucas was somehow generating it and then Hobson was shrieking with raw, mindless panic.

"No, get away from me," he shouted. He dropped the knife and clawed at something only he could see. *"Get away."*

He whirled and fled blindly into the gardens.

"Damn it to hell," Lucas said quietly. "Stone?"

A second figure glided out of the shadows. "Here, sir."

The voice sounded as though it emanated from the depths of a vast underground cavern and, like Sharpy Hobson's voice, it carried the accents of the London streets.

In the strange light provided by the subtly glowing foliage Evangeline could see that Stone suited his name. He was constructed like some ancient granite monolith and looked as if he would be just as impervious to the elements. The moonlight gleamed on his shaved head. The shadows and the eerie luminescence around them made it difficult to estimate his age but he appeared to be in his early twenties.

"See if you can grab Hobson before he blunders into the maze," Lucas said. "Whatever you do, don't try to follow him if he gets that far."

"Yes, sir."

Stone broke into a run, moving with a surprising lack of noise for such a large man.

Lucas turned back to Evangeline. "Are you all right, Miss Ames?"

"Yes, I think so." She was still trying to calm her rattled senses and rapid pulse. "I don't know how to thank you."

A high-pitched, keening scream echoed from somewhere deep in the gardens. The unearthly cry iced Evangeline's nerves. She stilled, unable to breathe.

It ended with horrifying suddenness. Evangeline was shivering so violently it was all she could do to remain on her feet.

"Sharpy Hobson," she whispered.

"Evidently Stone did not get to him in time to prevent him from entering the maze," Lucas said.

"Is he—?" She swallowed and tried again. "Is he dead?"

"Hobson? Probably or he soon will be. It's unfortunate."

"Unfortunate?" she managed. "That's all you can say about the man's death?"

"I would like to have questioned him. But as that does not seem likely to happen, you and I will talk, instead."

She tried to compose herself. "Mr. Sebastian, I'm not at all sure what to say."

"There will be nothing complicated about our conversation, Miss Ames. You will come inside with me now. I will pour you a glass of medicinal brandy for your nerves and you will tell me what you are doing here in my gardens at this hour of the night and why a man with a knife was trying to murder you."

"But that's what I'm trying to tell you. I have no idea why Hobson attacked me."

"Then we must reason it out together."

He shrugged off his coat and draped it around her shoulders before she could summon up further protest. When his fingers brushed the nape of her neck a thrill of awareness stirred her senses. The heavy wool garment was still warm from the heat of his body. She caught a trace of his masculine scent. It caused her senses to flare in a way that she had never before experienced.

Stone appeared. "Sorry, sir. He saw the open gate and ran straight inside. Probably assumed it was a way out of the gardens."

"I'll deal with the body later," Lucas said. "I wish to speak to Miss Ames first and then I will escort her back to the cottage."

"Yes, sir. Will you be needing anything else?"

"Not at the moment."

"Yes, sir."

Stone moved into the shadows. Evangeline watched him disappear. She was starting to wonder if she was caught up in some bizarre dream. Perhaps she was hallucinating. It was not beyond the realm of possibility, she thought. Her employers and her friends were convinced that her nerves had been badly strained by the attack two weeks earlier. Perhaps they were right.

Lucas's powerful hand closed around her arm. The shock of the physical contact made her flinch. Her talent was still flaring wildly and it was linked to her sense of touch. She could perceive Lucas's aura now quite clearly. The fierce bands of ice-and-fire energy took her breath.

"Relax, Miss Ames," he said. "I will not hurt you."

There was nothing in his aura to indicate that he was lying. She was safe enough, she decided, at least for the moment. She pulled herself together and lowered her psychical senses.

"This way, Miss Ames." He steered her around a large bush. "Watch your step. There are a number of hazards on the grounds, including those roses."

The power she had glimpsed in Lucas's aura warned her that he was probably a good deal more dangerous than anything in his strange gardens.

Sharpy Hobson had stopped screaming, but she knew that she would hear the echoes of his last, horrified cries in her nightmares for a long time to come.

Two

Evangeline perched tensely on the edge of one of the well-worn chairs in the library; the lapels of Lucas's coat clutched at her throat. She watched him pour two glasses of brandy.

The glary gaslight from the wall sconces revealed a massive mahogany desk, two large reading chairs and two end tables. The furnishings, along with the frayed and faded carpet and the heavy draperies that covered the windows, had gone out of fashion decades earlier. The shelves were crammed with leather-bound volumes. A variety of scientific instruments including a microscope and a telescope were scattered about the room.

Lucas Sebastian was a mystery not only to her, but also to the people of Little Dixby. He had arrived to take up residence at Crystal Gardens three days ago and he had immediately become the source of speculation and gossip.

She had met him for the first time yesterday in Chadwick Books, the only bookshop in town. Lucas had entered the premises shortly after she had gone through the door. He had introduced himself to her and to the proprietor, Irene Witton.

Irene was new to the bookselling business, having purchased the shop from the widow of the previous owner a few months earlier. But she was ambitious and it was clear that she was delighted to have Lucas as a customer. There was nothing better for business than having word get around that the owner of the largest country house in the district shopped at her establishment.

Evangeline, however, had not been able to sort out her own reactions to Lucas so neatly. Her senses had flared briefly when he walked into the shop. It had been an instinctive, intuitive response. Although he had not touched her she had sensed what she knew was a strong psychical talent. Indeed, it had been impossible to ignore the subtle shift of energy in the atmosphere. The knowledge had lifted the hair on the back of her neck. A strange mix of excitement and wariness had twisted through her.

"It appears I am your tenant, Mr. Sebastian," she said.

"So you are, Miss Ames." He smiled. "My uncle's man of business informed me that you had rented Fern Gate Cottage for the month. He was very pleased. Evidently he has not been able to attract a tenant to the property in the past two years. I trust you are enjoying your stay here in Little Dixby?"

It had been on the tip of her tongue to tell him that, aside from the occasional highly illicit thrill of trespassing on the grounds of the old abbey, she had never been more bored in her life. In that moment, however, she discovered that was no longer true. But she could hardly say that her perception of the pleasures of country life had done a complete about-face when he had walked through the door of Chadwick Books.

"I find the countryside quite . . . invigorating," she said instead.

His dark brows rose a little. Something that might have been amusement glittered in his gem-green eyes. "Excellent. You will send word to the Gardens if you need anything in the way of repairs at the cottage?"

"Yes, thank you, but I'm sure that won't be necessary."

"One never knows," Lucas said.

He had selected some old maps and a guidebook to the local ruins, paid for his purchases and made his farewells. Evangeline and Irene had watched him walk out onto the street and disappear into the crowds of visitors that thronged Little Dixby in the summer. The town was within a three-hour train trip from London and had long been an attraction due to the remarkably well-preserved Roman antiquities in the vicinity.

Irene had folded her arms on the glass counter with a speculative air. She was a spinster in her late thirties. Evangeline was sure that Irene's failure to marry had nothing to do with her looks. She was an attractive, well-educated woman with an excellent figure, dark hair, blue eyes and a fine sense of style. The fashionable silver spectacles chatelaine she wore at her waist to hold her eyeglasses was decorated with delicately engraved butterflies and lovely turquoise stones.

Irene would have been nothing short of ravishing at the marriageable age of eighteen or nineteen, Evangeline thought. But looks and intelligence were not always sufficient when it came to the business of marriage, because marriage was a business transaction and everyone knew it. Social status and money mattered far more than true love and the metaphysical connection between lovers that the sensation novelists celebrated in their stories.

"So that's the new owner of the Gardens," Irene said. "Not quite what everyone expected. At least he did not appear to be mad like his uncle."

Evangeline blinked. "What on earth do you mean?"

"You're new around here," Irene said. "But surely you've heard some of the tales and legends about the Gardens?"

"Yes, but I wasn't aware that the former owner was mad," Evangeline said. She hesitated. "Well, I must admit that my daily maid did say that Chester Sebastian was notoriously eccentric."

Irene chuckled. "A polite word for mad as a hatter. Chester Sebastian was, however, a brilliant botanist and I, for one, will sorely miss him."

"Why is that?"

"He was a very good customer. I was able to locate several rare volumes and prints of botanical subjects for him. Price was no object. However, not everyone here in Little Dixby took such a charitable view of Chester Sebastian. I have been assured by no less an authority than Arabella Higgenthorp, the director of the local gardening club, that Sebastian conducted all sorts of what she calls unnatural horticultural experiments in the Gardens."

Evangeline thought about the strange energy she had sensed on the grounds of the abbey. "What do you think Mrs. Higgenthorp meant by unnatural?"

"People claim that Sebastian mixed the occult arts and the science of botany with disastrous results."

"Oh, for heaven's sake. What nonsense."

"Don't be so certain of that." Irene widened her eyes in a mockingly melodramatic manner and lowered her voice to a stage whisper. "The locals are convinced that Chester Sebastian's death was caused by some of the dark supernatural forces that he unleashed in his gardens."

"Ridiculous," Evangeline said. But she had sensed some dangerous currents of power on the grounds of Crystal Gardens. It was not beyond the realm of possibility that Chester Sebastian had been done in by one of his psychical botanical experiments.

Irene smiled. "Of course it's all nonsense but the story fits in nicely with other local legends. Visitors love that sort of thing."

Evangeline was amused. "And they tend to purchase guidebooks and maps that feature those thrilling local legends?"

"Yes, indeed. The tale of the lost treasure of Crystal Gardens in particular has been especially good for business."

"What treasure is that?"

"A hoard of Roman gold is said to be buried somewhere on the grounds of the old abbey." Irene wrinkled her nose. "But if you want my opinion, it was most likely discovered years ago, if it ever existed."

"No doubt." Evangeline looked out the window again but Lucas was nowhere in sight.

Irene followed her gaze. She stopped smiling. "In all seriousness, they do say there is a strain of madness in the family."

"Indeed?"

"According to the local gossip Chester Sebastian claimed to have paranormal talents." Irene made a dismissive movement with one hand. "One would have to be either delusional or a complete fraud to make such a claim, don't you agree?"

Evangeline chose her words carefully. "It certainly makes one wonder."

But she could not believe that Lucas was mad—exciting and perhaps dangerous, yes, but not insane.

Inspired, she had rushed back to Fern Gate Cottage to make detailed notes about the hero of her new book. She was on chapter four and John Reynolds was about to make his appearance. His features and demeanor had eluded her but she now knew precisely how he looked: Exactly like Lucas Sebastian—dark-haired and green-eyed with a hard face and an aura of raw power. In short, the type of man who would break society's rules when it pleased him to do so.

The problem was that until that moment she had intended John Reynolds to be the villain of her story.

"TRY THIS." Lucas handed her one of the glasses of brandy. "It's good for the nerves."

"Thank you." She took a cautious swallow. The stuff burned a little on the way down but the heat felt good, fortifying. She thought about Sharpy Hobson's dying scream and the glass trembled in her hand. "Shouldn't we send for the police?"

Lucas carried his brandy to the chair across from hers and sat down. "I'm sure the local police are reasonably discreet, but under the circumstances I doubt that the gossip could be contained, not in a town as small as Little Dixby. Among other things, there is the matter of your reputation to consider."

She felt the heat rise in her face. This time the warmth was generated by the politely veiled expression in his eyes, not the brandy. She gripped the lapels of his coat more securely.

"Yes, of course," she whispered.

"If it gets out that you were found in the Gardens dressed in your nightclothes at two-thirty in the morning, it will be assumed that you came here for an intimate rendezvous with me."

"But that man with the knife—"

"The fact that we were interrupted by a knife-wielding intruder will only add to the sensation elements of the story. The news will be all over Little Dixby by morning. I estimate that it will appear in the London papers within twenty-four hours. The publishers of the penny dreadfuls will be hawking their version of events shortly after that." Lucas swallowed some brandy and lowered his glass. "The extra time will be required for an artist to create an appropriately lurid illustration, you see."

"Good grief."

But he was right, she thought. The press would go to great lengths to enhance the titillating aspects of the story, even though none existed. It was all very predictable and it explained why so many women chose not to report crimes against their person to the police. In her case the notoriety could easily destroy her budding career as a novelist. The first chapter of *Winterscar Hall* was set to appear this next week in six of Mr. Guthrie's newspapers, including the *Little Dixby Herald*. If it got out that the author had been involved in a crime involving attempted murder and an illicit rendezvous with a wealthy gentleman, Guthrie would no doubt cancel the contract. She recalled a rather vague morals clause.

Under the circumstances, Lucas Sebastian's gallantry was surprising; stunning, actually. She made her living as a professional paid companion. She had no family or social connections. Like other women in her situation she clung to respectability by her fingernails. It would take very little to cause her to lose her grip. In her experience men of Sebastian's rank and wealth rarely concerned themselves with the reputations of females in her position.

She reminded herself that Lucas might have his own reasons for not wanting the police on the grounds of Crystal Gardens, starting with the dead man in the maze.

"I comprehend your reasoning, Mr. Sebastian," she said, "and I sincerely appreciate your thoughtfulness. But we can hardly pretend that nothing occurred here tonight."

"I disagree, Miss Ames." Lucas smiled a slow, cold smile. "You would be amazed by how simple it is to do precisely that. Even if you are willing to sacrifice yourself on the altar of local gossip, I am not."

"Sorry?"

"Come now, Miss Ames, use your head. You are not the only one in this little drama who would become the object of much speculation if this story appears in the press. I am involved, as well."

So much for assuming that he was concerned for her reputation, she thought. Whatever had she been thinking? Her romantic imagination had temporarily gotten the better of her common sense. Lucas was protecting himself, not her. No gentleman wanted his name dragged through the gutter press.

"Of course," she said briskly. "I quite understand. Forgive me, I didn't consider your position."

"As it happens, I require privacy while I am in residence here in Little Dixby. I would prefer not to become entangled in a police inquiry, to say nothing of having to deal with the so-called gentlemen of the press."

"You have made your point, sir," she said. "There is no need to elaborate."

She could hardly argue with his decision, she thought. She had made the same decision two weeks ago. She and Lucas both had secrets to conceal.

"You will understand that I must ask you some questions, Miss Ames. While I am committed to avoiding both the police and the press, I would like to know what I have become involved in tonight."

"Yes, of course, but I'm afraid I cannot give you an answer."

Lucas's eyes heated a little with a cold fire. Or perhaps that was just her imagination, Evangeline thought. Her nerves were still very much on edge.

"Were you acquainted with that man, Sharpy Hobson?" he asked.

"I'm quite certain I have never seen him before in my life," she said. "But I confess that this afternoon I had the unpleasant sensation that I was being watched. I could not sleep tonight, which was why I was awake when he broke into the cottage."

"Which raises another matter," Lucas said. "I'm very glad that you were able to escape, but it was a rather remarkable feat. How did you manage it?"

"I went out through the bedroom window. Hobson tried to follow but he did not fit. He had to use the kitchen door. That gave me a decent head start."

"You ran here to Crystal Gardens."

"It's not as if I had a great deal of choice. You are my nearest neighbor, sir."

He nodded once, just slightly, acknowledging that fact, and sipped his brandy in a thoughtful silence.

"I would have knocked on your front door to ask for help but there was no time to run to the front of the house," she added. "Hobson was gaining on me. That is why I made for the gardens."

Lucas regarded her very steadily. "You knew how to get through the wall."

She sighed. "I admit that I engaged in some exploration before you arrived to take up residence, sir."

"Trespassing," he corrected. He did not sound annoyed, though.

"Well, it is not as if there was anyone living here at the time. I could hardly ask permission to view the gardens."

"Those gardens are extremely dangerous. You saw that for yourself tonight."

"Yes." She shuddered and downed some of the brandy. "But I did not know just how dangerous until now. I had heard the local legends and stories but I did not believe them."

"They made you curious, though, didn't they?"

"I'm afraid so."

"Tell me, Miss Ames, do you always indulge your curiosity?"

She hesitated, sensing a trap. "Not always. But there seemed to be no harm in this case."

"You were drawn into the gardens not simply because of the legends but because you sensed the paranormal energy here."

It was not a question. Her uneasiness with the direction of his questions was growing stronger. There was always some risk in claiming psychical talent but she could not see the harm in doing so tonight with this man. She was very certain that Lucas also possessed paranormal abilities.

"Yes," she said. "The energy of this place is compelling."

He smiled a little. "I was quite certain that you possessed a strong psychical nature yesterday when we met in the bookshop. Your ability makes me very curious about you, Evangeline Ames. But, then, I have been interested in you since my uncle's man of affairs informed me that the new tenant at Fern Gate Cottage made her living as a paid companion."

Her uneasiness grew stronger. She was now certain that she was sailing into dangerous waters but she could not see any way to avoid the rapids.

"Why did that fact make you curious?" she asked, very cautious now.

"Granted, the rent on the cottage is quite cheap. That said, I have never encountered a professional companion who was able to afford a monthlong holiday in the countryside, even with a bargain lease thrown in."

"My employers are very generous," she said coolly. She was on firmer ground now. It was, after all, extremely rude to question a person's financial situation to his or her face. It was simply not done. "Those of us who are fortunate enough to be associated with the firm of Flint and Marsh enjoy very satisfactory commissions for our services."

"I see. That explains the expensive gown and attractive hat that you were wearing yesterday when I met you in the bookshop, as well as your ability to afford the rent on the cottage."

She could see that he was not satisfied with the answer she had given him. She braced herself for his next query.

"There are a number of other things about you that I find intriguing, Miss Ames."

"Indeed, sir? How very odd. We are scarcely acquainted."

He smiled his cold smile. "The events of this night have given us a much closer connection, don't you agree? Indeed, one could almost call it an intimate connection."

She was suddenly intensely aware that she was in her nightclothes. She glanced toward the door. The urge to flee was instinctive but she knew it would be useless to try to escape.

"As I was saying, there are several things about you that I find riveting," Lucas continued. He gave no indication that he had noticed her growing anxiety. "But the one that comes to mind tonight is the fact that in your last post you were employed as a companion to Lady Rutherford."

Evangeline discovered she was holding her breath. She gulped some brandy. The shock of the fiery liquor made her gasp. At least she was inhaling again, she thought. Breathing was important.

"What of it?" she managed.

"Nothing, really. It is just that it strikes me as rather odd that within days after you left your position in the Rutherford household, a gentleman who had recently made an offer for the hand of Lady Rutherford's granddaughter—an offer that was turned down, I might add—was found dead at the foot of a staircase. As it happens the staircase was located in a vacant building situated in a shabby street near the docks."

Shock slammed through Evangeline. "You know about that?"

"Mason's death and the location of the incident were in the papers," Lucas said. He sounded almost apologetic at having to remind her of such a simple fact. "As was the gossip that his suit had recently been rejected out of hand by the young lady's father."

"Yes, of course." She pulled herself together and assumed what she hoped was an air of polite bewilderment tempered with a hint of impatience. "Forgive me, sir, it's just that I'm rather surprised to hear that you pay attention to that sort of social gossip."

"Ah, but I do, Miss Ames, especially when I discover that my new tenant had some connection to the Rutherford household and that she was let go from her post the day after Mason was shown the door."

"It was understood from the start that the post was temporary." She looked at the tall clock and affected a small start of surprise. "Good heavens, just look at the time. I really must return to the cottage."

"By all means, but not before you finish your nerve tonic."

She looked down at the glass in her hand and saw that there was some brandy left. She raised the glass and downed the remaining liquor in a single swallow, a very large swallow as it turned out.

She did more than gasp for air this time. She choked and sputtered in a thoroughly embarrassing manner.

"Are you all right, Miss Ames?" Lucas sounded genuinely concerned.

"Yes, yes, I'm fine." She set the glass down hard on the nearby table and made a weak, fluttery motion with her hand, as if trying to fan herself. "But I fear you are right to be worried about the state of my nerves, sir. Indeed, I believe they have been quite shattered. I need my bed and my vinaigrette."

"Something tells me that you have never used a vinaigrette in your life."

"First time for everything." She got to her feet. "Forgive me, Mr. Sebastian. I am very grateful for all that you did for me tonight but I must return to the cottage now."

"Very well, I will see you home." Lucas set his own glass aside and stood. "We shall continue this conversation tomorrow."

"Terribly sorry, I'm afraid that won't be possible," she said smoothly. "I'm expecting friends from London tomorrow. They will be staying with me for two days."

"I see."

She thought quickly. The last thing she wanted to do was find herself alone in the cottage when Lucas came around to continue the conversation.

"Probably much longer," she said. "A fortnight no doubt. We plan to explore the local ruins. Very scenic, you know."

"So I have been told."

He took her arm and guided her out of the library and down a long hall. Her curiosity was aroused once more.

"My daily maid mentioned that you have not hired any staff," she ventured.

"Stone is all I need."

"This is a very large house for one person to keep in order."

"Stone and I are the only ones in residence and I intend for matters to remain that way. We will not be staying long. All we require are the kitchen, the library and a couple of bedrooms. The rest of the house is closed up—has been for years. When Uncle Chester was alive he and his housekeeper, Mrs. Buckley, kept only a few rooms open."

"I see. You are here to settle your uncle's affairs, then?"

"I am here to do a bit more than that, Miss Ames. I intend to find out who murdered him."

Three

Evangeline was shocked into what Lucas was certain would be a very temporary silence. While she grappled with the ramifications of his announcement, he eased her out the front door and into the night. They started down the moonlit lane toward the cottage.

"I was under the impression that your uncle died of a heart attack," Evangeline said at last.

"So I'm told."

"You don't believe that?"

"No, Miss Ames, I don't. What is more, I think there is a possibility that Mrs. Buckley, the housekeeper, was also murdered."

"Good heavens." She glanced at him very quickly and then turned her attention back to the lane. "May I ask if you have some reason for believing that his death was due to foul play?"

"At the moment all I have is suspicion."

There was another short silence from Evangeline.

"I see."

He knew then that she had already heard the rumors of madness in the Sebastian family line. It was only to be expected, he reminded himself. The gossip was rampant around Little Dixby. Chester had lived at Crystal Gardens for nearly thirty years, certainly long enough to impress the locals with his odd behavior.

I should have expected that she would think me delusional, Lucas thought. Even though she possessed considerable talent herself, it did not follow that she would ignore the gossip.

Having learned at an early age that his own paranormal talent made others uneasy and often fearful, he had gone to great lengths to conceal his true nature. But it had been impossible to hide his abilities from his relatives. He was well aware that some of the whispers of madness in the Sebastian bloodline came from the very heart of his family.

"No, Miss Ames, I am not delusional," he said evenly. "And for all his eccentricities, neither was Uncle Chester."

"I see," she said again. She fell silent.

He realized that under other circumstances he would have savored the moonlight walk to the cottage. Even the knowledge that she was not altogether certain what to make of him could not detract from the intense thrill of being so close to her. He sensed that she was aware of the energy between them, as well. But he suspected that she was telling herself that the edgy, overstimulated sensation had been caused by the recent excitement.

A short time ago in the library he had taken pleasure in watching the way the gaslight turned her hazel eyes to gold and the soft waves of her hair to a rich, dark shade of amber. Taken individually her features lacked conventional beauty but they melded together into a striking face animated by intelligence and strong character. Any man who sought to seduce her would first have to win her trust and respect. Afterward he would very likely discover that he was the one who had been seduced.

Logic and common sense suggested that he focus on the questions that surrounded Evangeline Ames, not his attraction to her. And there were a great many mysteries linked to her.

It could not be sheer coincidence that a lady who just happened to possess some strong psychical talent had chosen to rent a cottage that no one had wanted to rent in years—a cottage located a short distance from ancient ruins that reeked of dark paranormal energy. Her remarkably well-paid career as a professional companion raised more questions. Then there was the matter of her connection to the Rutherford household, which was, in turn, linked to a man who had died under mysterious circumstances. Last but not least, it was asking too much to believe that it was mere happenstance that a knife-wielding killer had tried to slit her throat tonight.

Whatever Evangeline Ames was involved in, coincidence had nothing to do with it. But the mysteries swirling around her only made her all the more intriguing.

"You're certain that you have no idea why that man attacked you tonight?" he asked.

"None." Evangeline concentrated on keeping her footing in the badly rutted lane. "I suppose he must have discovered that I was a woman living alone in the cottage and concluded that I would be an easy victim."

"His accent is straight from the streets of London."

"Yes, I did notice that."

"In my experience, the members of the criminal class who ply their trade in the city rarely venture into the countryside."

Evangeline looked at him. He sensed her curiosity and smiled a little.

"Why is that?" she asked.

"It is an alien environment to them," he explained. "They flourish in dark alleys, hidden lanes and abandoned buildings. They are urban rats. They don't know how to survive outside their native habitat. What is more, they tend to stand out in the countryside."

"I see what you mean." Evangeline sounded intrigued. "Their clothes and accents would mark them as outsiders."

"Yet Sharpy Hobson pursued you all the way to Little Dixby."

"Well, it isn't as if he had to travel to the ends of the earth or even to Wales."

He smiled. "No. London is only a few hours away by train."

"True." She exhaled a small sigh. "Although I must admit at times it feels as if Little Dixby is located on the far side of the world or perhaps in another dimension."

"Yesterday in the bookshop you gave me the impression that you were enjoying your stay in the countryside, at least until tonight."

"Let's just say that, until tonight, it has been restful to the point of boredom."

"You are from London," he said.

"Yes."

"Like Hobson."

"Are you implying that there is some connection between me and that villain?" she asked, her tone sharpening.

"It seems a likely possibility."

"I understand your logic but I honestly cannot imagine what it would be. I told you, I have never before encountered Sharpy Hobson. Believe me, I would have recalled such a meeting."

"There are some mentally unbalanced men who sometimes develop unwholesome fixations on a certain woman. They follow their victims, at first trying to frighten and control them. Eventually they become violent."

"I am not naive, Mr. Sebastian, and I have not lived a sheltered life. I am aware that such men exist. But even if I did unwittingly manage to attract the attention of such a deranged individual, why didn't he attack me in London? And why wait so long to follow me to Little Dixby? I have been living here for nearly two weeks."

She was truly bewildered, he concluded.

"There is no way to fathom the thinking of a madman," he said.

"No," she agreed. "But you will admit that Sharpy Hobson did not appear to be unbalanced tonight. He claimed that I was worth money to him."

"Hobson may not be the one who is deranged. The unbalanced person in this mystery is possibly the one who sent him here to find you."

Evangeline tightened her grip on the lapels of his coat. "Good heavens, yes, you are right. But that logic does not hold, either. I cannot think of anyone who might want to kill me, let alone pay someone to do the deed."

He listened to the dark murmurings and sighs of the dense woods on either side of the lane and considered what he knew of murder. There were those who believed that he knew far too much about the subject. They were right.

"A discarded lover seeking revenge might hire a villain off the streets to kill the woman who had rejected him," he offered.

"A lover?" The words were uttered on a half-choked squeak of pure disbelief. Evangeline hastily composed herself. "Good grief, sir, I assure you that is not the case."

Her response was interesting, he thought. It was as if she found the notion a complete impossibility. But he, in turn, found that difficult to swallow. Evangeline Ames was far too interesting, too compelling.

"Perhaps the person who commissioned the murder is not a man. Is there a woman who might have cause to be jealous of you?"

"Your imagination is certainly quite creative, sir. Do you write novels, by any chance?"

"No, Miss Ames. Nor do I read them."

She shot him a cool look from the corner of her eye. "Do you have something against novels, Mr. Sebastian?"

"I prefer to take a realistic view of the world, Miss Ames. Novels by their very nature are anything but realistic, with their scenes of overwrought emotions and the ridiculous happy endings."

She gave him a chilly smile. "They call it fiction for a reason, sir."

"Yes," he said, "they do."

"Some people find that reading novels is very therapeutic precisely because it does allow one to view reality from an entirely different perspective."

"I will take your word for it. Let us return to our mystery."

"I told you, I don't have any answers," she said.

"Then let us go back to the beginning."

"The beginning?"

"Why do you remain here in Little Dixby? You have made it plain that you are not altogether charmed by country life."

She pondered the question for a few seconds. In the moonlight, he could not make out her expression but he sensed that she was deciding just how much of the truth to tell him.

"As you know, I am a professional hired companion," she said.

"A very well-paid professional companion, judging by your clothes and the fact that you can afford to rent my cottage."

"I explained that I work for an exclusive firm." Her voice was crisp with impatience now. "But as it happens, I have other aspirations. Do not mistake me, I take great satisfaction from my work with the Flint and Marsh Agency but I am determined to move on to another career."

"What other career?"

She angled her chin. "One that I'm certain you will not approve of. I hope to be able to make my living as an author of sensation novels."

He was surprised by his own crack of laughter. "I should have guessed."

"I have, in fact, recently signed a contract with a gentleman who publishes a number of newspapers, Mr. Guthrie. Perhaps you have heard of him?"

"Certainly I'm aware of the Guthrie newspaper empire. He has made a fortune selling society gossip, accounts of lurid crimes and serialized sensation novels." Lucas broke off, realizing what he had just said. "Oh, I see."

"He will be publishing my first novel in serialized form." Evangeline said. "The first chapter of *Winterscar Hall* will appear next week in six of his smaller country newspapers. If I prove popular in the regional press, he will publish me in his London paper."

"Congratulations," Lucas said.

"You needn't pretend to be polite about it. You have made your opinion of sensation novels quite plain."

"It's true I do not read novels but I applaud your determination to take command of your life. You are a fascinating woman, Evangeline Ames. Indeed, I have never met anyone like you."

"Yes, well, I assure you that I find you one-of-a-kind, too, Mr. Sebastian."

"You have not answered my question," he said gently.

"The reason I am in Little Dixby?" There was amusement in her tone now. "You are not easily distracted, are you, sir?"

"Not when I want something very much."

"And you want answers."

"Yes." *And I want you, as well*, he thought.

"I do understand, you know," she said. "I have a great sense of curiosity myself."

"Ah, yes, those forays into the gardens before I arrived."

"You will admit they proved useful," she said.

"Because tonight when you were attacked you knew you could hide from Hobson if you could get inside the walls."

"I was not certain if he would follow me through the wall, of course, but I sensed that if he did, he probably would not be able to navigate those gardens as well as I could."

"You appeared to be aiming for the gazebo. What was your plan?"

"The pond," she said. "There is some sort of strange energy in that water. I hoped that if Hobson stumbled into it he would become disoriented, perhaps quite panicked."

"Very good, Miss Ames. You were right. The paranormal currents in the pond induce great confusion in most people, especially at night."

"I thought so."

"You still have not answered my question. What brought you to Little Dixby?"

"My writing," she said. "I thought you understood. Mr. Guthrie is publishing my story in chapters but I have only got the first three written. To meet Guthrie's schedule, I must complete a chapter a week, and the contract stipulates that each chapter must be about four thousand words. I cannot afford to miss a single deadline."

She was telling the truth, he decided. She was also lying through her teeth.

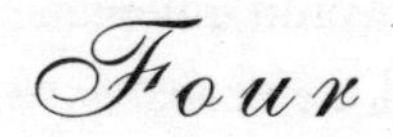

Four

Lucas brought Evangeline to a halt in front of the entrance to the small cottage. The little wooden gate was unlatched. It hung on its hinges, partially open. The mute evidence of Evangeline's wild flight sent a jolt of anger through him. *If Hobson were not already dead . . .*

Lucas cut the thought off abruptly. Emotional thinking invariably obscured logic.

He pushed open the gate and ushered Evangeline into the fern-choked garden. The graveled path was barely visible amid the thick sea of moonlit fronds.

"My uncle did not pay much attention to the cottage," Lucas said. "But he did run a few experiments with ferns, as you can see."

"I noticed." Evangeline gestured toward the thick woods that surrounded them. "Everything seems to grow so lushly near the abbey."

"It's the energy from the hot spring at the center of the gardens. The paranormal currents are not nearly so strong outside the walls but they nevertheless affect the foliage in the vicinity."

He did not add that the power of the spring had been growing in the past two years.

"How did Hobson get into the cottage?" he asked.

"The kitchen door," Evangeline said. "He forced the lock."

"Let me take a look."

They walked around to the back of the cottage and made their way through the kitchen garden. There were no vegetables or lettuces in the ground. The small space, like the front garden, was a miniature fern jungle.

When they reached the open door Lucas struck a light, heightened his talent a little and examined the broken lock.

The dark miasma of Hobson's anticipation of the kill seethed in the atmosphere.

Lucas shut down his senses before the psychical residue could cause his own talent to flare in response.

He straightened and moved into the kitchen. "He was not even trying to silence his approach."

"No," Evangeline said. She followed him across the threshold. "He was very sure of himself. Looking back, I think he wanted me to hear him."

"The bastard wanted you to have time to be afraid."

"How did you know that?"

"It's there in his prints." He gestured back toward the broken lock.

Evangeline looked at the muddy boot prints on the floor. "You can sense his intentions in his footprints?"

"Not his footprints. I can read the psychical residue that he left here."

Evangeline turned back to him, eyes widening. "The ability is an aspect of your talent?"

"Yes."

She thought about that for a few seconds and then nodded, once, accepting the explanation. "In the end, he was the one who knew great fear." She shivered. "I heard it in his final scream."

"He very likely pricked himself on one of the Blood Thorns," Lucas said absently. He turned up the wall sconce. The gaslight illuminated the small kitchen. "According to my uncle, the poison induces terrifying hallucinations and panic. Hobson probably started running. That is never wise inside the maze."

Evangeline gave him an odd look. "I'll try to remember that."

"You won't be going into that maze," he assured her. "No one will enter it except me. It is far too dangerous. Usually the gate is locked. The only reason it was open tonight is because I was inside when you and Hobson arrived." He glanced back at the door. "I'll send someone around to repair that in the morning."

"Thank you."

"Wait here," he said. "I'll have a quick look around before I leave."

"I'm sure I am quite safe now that Hobson is dead." Evangeline paused. "At least for tonight."

"I agree. But I will send Stone down here to keep watch until dawn. That is not far off."

"Oh, really, that is quite unnecessary."

"There is no cause for concern about Stone. He is utterly reliable. In any event, he will have instructions to remain outside the cottage."

"Mr. Sebastian, I am trying to tell you that there is no reason to post a guard on this cottage." There was a steely edge on the words. Evangeline did not take orders well, he noted.

He smiled. "Have you considered that I might be doing it for my own peace of mind?"

"I don't understand."

"I would like to get some sleep tonight myself. That will not be possible if I am worrying about your safety. As your landlord, I am responsible for you."

"For pity's sake, sir, this is ridiculous."

"Not to me. I would like to get some rest. I will not be able to do that knowing that you are down here all alone."

She opened her mouth but immediately closed it again. Her eyes narrowed faintly. Evidently she realized that further protest was useless.

He moved through the tiny parlor and went along the short hall past the bath. When he reached the bedroom the sight of the tumbled bedclothes and the open window sent another flash of ice-cold fury through him. *The son of a bitch had gotten so damn close.* If Evangeline had not been awake, if she had not heard the sound of the kitchen door being forced, if she had not been a spirited, quick-thinking woman with a measure of talent—so many ifs. He could not allow himself to dwell too long on what had almost happened.

This time he did not raise his talent. He did not dare. He knew what he would find, knew what it would do to his senses. He could not afford to lose his control, not now, not with Evangeline only a few steps away. He could not risk letting her see that side of him.

Besides, the bastard was dead.

Lucas stayed very still for another heartbeat or two, one fist locked around the edge of the door. When he was certain that he was in full command of himself he turned back toward the kitchen.

He did not question his reaction to the scene in the bedroom but he was more than a little surprised by the fierceness of it. He had, after all, known what to expect. After Evangeline's description of the attack, he'd had a very good idea of what he would see at the scene. The important thing to keep in mind was that she was unhurt. She was safe, at least for the moment. That was all that mattered.

Still, the intensity of his reaction was unsettling. It was not as if he had not encountered other far more horrific crime scenes. But for some reason the graphic evidence of the attack on Evangeline had slammed through all his carefully erected psychical barriers and struck him at his core. He barely knew the woman and yet here he was reacting as if the two of them were intimately connected, as if she belonged to him. *As if it was his right to protect her.* One thing was certain: From now on he intended to do a better job of taking care of her.

He turned away from the bedroom and went back down the hall to the kitchen. Evangeline was waiting.

"Satisfied?" she asked.

"All is well," Lucas said.

"I was sure it would be," she said. She gave him a sheepish smile. "Nevertheless it was kind of you to make certain."

"Try to get some sleep."

"An excellent notion. As I told you, my visitors from London arrive tomorrow. I shall be very busy entertaining them."

"I am glad to know that you will have company for the next couple of days," he said.

She searched his face in the glary light of the kitchen sconce. "You are concerned that whoever sent Hobson to kill me will make another attempt, aren't you?"

"Under the circumstances, I think we must assume that will be the case. However, I think we have some time before the person who commissioned your death makes his next move."

"Because he will not know immediately that Hobson failed?"

"Right. And even after he realizes that his hired killer is not coming back for his pay, it will take time to concoct another plan. It is not as if one can just walk down to the street and find that sort of talent loitering about on the corner."

She looked amused. "That sort of talent?"

He grimaced. "A poor choice of words. In addition to the difficulty of hiring a professional killer who is willing to travel to the country, the fact that you escaped the first attempt will make whoever is after you more careful the next time."

She tilted her head slightly and regarded him with acute attention. He could have sworn that her eyes heated a little, whether with interest, alarm or simple curiosity, he could not say.

"No offense, sir," she said, "but it strikes me that you seem to know a great deal about how this sort of business is conducted."

"One could say that the nature of my talent has compelled me to make something of a study of the criminal mind." He stopped and then decided to tell her the rest. "Much to my family's dismay, I occasionally consult for a detective inspector who is an old friend of mine at Scotland Yard."

"Your family does not approve?"

He smiled. "I think the twins, my brother and sister, find it rather intriguing but their mother does not."

"Their mother? Not yours?"

"Legally speaking, Judith is my stepmother. My mother died when I was fifteen. Judith has gone to great lengths to keep my work for the Yard a deep, dark family secret."

"I see. I must say, I agree with your brother and sister. Your consulting work sounds fascinating."

He thought about it. "I'm not sure 'fascinating' is the correct term to describe it. 'Compelling' comes closer."

A knowing look came and went in her eyes. "I understand. Something to do with the nature of your talent?"

"Unfortunately, yes."

It seemed to him that the atmosphere in the room was becoming more highly charged with each passing moment. He should be on his way, he thought. The longer he stayed here alone with her, the harder it would be to leave.

"I'll be going now," he said.

She slipped out of his coat and held it out to him. "Here, you mustn't forget this."

He took the coat from her. Unable to think of an excuse to linger, he went out onto the step. He stopped, one foot on the second step, and looked back at her.

"I suggest that you brace the door with one of the kitchen chairs for the rest of the night," he said.

"That is a very good idea. I'll do that."

He waited until she closed the door. The scrape of wood chair legs on the floorboards and a soft thud told him that she had taken his advice on a makeshift lock.

Satisfied, he shrugged into his coat. The garment was still warm from her body and carried her scent, a sweet, spicy, feminine perfume that was unique to Evangeline. The fragrance carried the essence of the woman and was somehow infused with her energy. He knew that he would never forget it.

Five

Stone was waiting for him in the kitchen. He had made a pot of coffee.

"That smells very good," Lucas said.

"Reckoned you wouldn't be bothering with sleep for a while yet," Stone said. He poured coffee into two thick mugs. "Not with that body waiting for you in the maze."

"You're right. I'll have to find it before dawn if I want to examine it. Bodies don't last long in the maze, or the Night Gardens, either, for that matter. To those plants, Sharpy Hobson is just so much fertilizer."

He sat down at the old kitchen table. Stone sat down across from him. They drank their coffee in a comfortable silence. They were employer and employee but they were also friends who had saved each other's lives on more than one occasion. Stone was one of the very few people in the world whom Lucas trusted. But, then, Stone was one of the very few who knew Lucas's secrets and was not nervous around him.

"When you finish your coffee I want you to go down to the cottage and keep an eye on it until morning," Lucas said after a while. "I'm sure there is nothing to be concerned about tonight but I want Miss Ames to have some peace of mind. She has been through an ordeal."

"I'll watch her for you." Stone put down his mug and got to his feet. "Are you sure you won't be needing any help with the body?"

"No. I'll examine it but I don't have much expectation of learning anything useful. Still, you never know."

"I'll be off then."

Stone walked out of the kitchen and went down the hall. Lucas waited until he heard the side door open and close. Then he put down the mug, got to his feet and went outside.

He walked across the terrace, went down the steps and started along the narrow path framed by two towering, faintly luminous hedges. Bizarre flowers, unnatural in size and color, glowed in the night. Chester Sebastian had transformed Crystal Gardens into a living botanical laboratory. The results of the paranormal experiments he had performed over the decades had taken on a life of their own. In recent years, they had run dangerously out of control.

It was no accident that the curious hybrids that Chester had developed flourished on the grounds. He had chosen the old abbey for his laboratory because of the paranormal aspects of the waters from the hot spring.

Unlike the waters that had made the town of Bath a popular destination for both the Romans and modern-day visitors, the spring that fed Crystal Gardens had acquired a far more sinister reputation.

The local townsfolk were not the only ones who were convinced that Chester had been killed by one of his own unnatural specimens. Most of the members of the Sebastian family believed that as well.

It did not take long to find the body in the maze. Hobson had collapsed face up, his expression frozen in a mask of horror. A few creepers and vines were already starting to twine around the dead man's legs and arms.

Lucas pulled on a pair of leather gardening gloves and wrenched the body free from the tenacious grip of the creepers. It was not easy.

He went quickly through Hobson's clothing. There wasn't much to find, a rather impressive amount of money, a couple of ticket stubs and two concealed knives. One of the tickets was for a cheap seat in a London theater where a melodrama titled *Lady Easton's Secret* was playing. The train ticket indicated that Hobson had arrived in Little Dixby on the afternoon train that day. The timing fit with Evangeline's estimate of when she started to feel that she was being watched.

Lucas tucked the knives and the ticket stubs into the pocket of his coat, kicked the body back to the hungry plants and walked out of the maze.

Six

Beatrice Lockwood angled her fashionable frilled parasol against the warm afternoon sunlight.

"Who could have guessed that the countryside would be so dangerous?" she asked. "It is quite pretty here in Little Dixby but it does appear rather dull. Not exactly a hotbed of criminal activity."

"And to think that Mrs. Flint and Mrs. Marsh banished you here so that you could recover from your case of shattered nerves," Clarissa Slate added. "Wait until we tell them of how you were attacked in your own bed by a man armed with a knife."

"Make certain they realize that I was not actually in the bed when the villain got to the bedroom," Evangeline said. "No need to alarm them any more than necessary. By the time Hobson arrived I was halfway out the window."

"As if that will reassure them," Clarissa said. "You know that they have both been very concerned about your nerves since the events of the Rutherford affair. They packed you off to the country to recover and just see what happens."

"I did try to tell Mrs. Flint and Mrs. Marsh that I was not suffering from shock as a result of the incidents that followed the Rutherford case," Evangeline said.

It was mid-afternoon and they were walking along the lane that would take them into Little Dixby, where they planned to have tea and tour the ruins. Earlier, Evangeline had met her two friends at the station with a hired carriage. Mayhew, the owner of the town's only cab, had driven the women and their luggage to Fern Gate Cottage. After unpacking, Clarissa and Beatrice had declared themselves eager to see some of the antiquities.

Evangeline was feeling a great sense of relief now that her friends had arrived. Although she was certain that her nerves had not been shattered by the events of the night, the truth was that this morning she had discovered that she was far more shaken than she cared to admit. The assault had revived all of the fearsome emotions she had experienced two weeks ago when Douglas Mason had lunged out of the bedroom doorway and held a knife to her throat. Really, she thought, how many such violent attacks should a lady have to endure in a month?

She was very glad that Clarissa and Beatrice were planning to stay for the next two nights. With luck she would get some sleep. If she had been obliged to spend the next two evenings alone in the unnervingly quiet countryside, she was certain she would have spent the long hours of darkness lying awake, listening for the sound of footsteps in the hall and watching for shadows at the bedroom window.

She had met Beatrice and Clarissa shortly after joining the firm of Flint & Marsh. The bonds of friendship had sprung up very quickly among the three of them, in part because each of them was alone in the world and each was facing a lonely future.

There were few options for women when it came to obtaining respectable employment. With marriage out of the question due to their poor finances and lack of social connections, they had each faced the gloomy prospect of making their livings as governesses or paid companions. Both professions were notoriously ill paid. After twenty or thirty years in either career, a woman was likely to find herself as impoverished as she had been when she started out. The only hope was that somewhere along the way a generous employer would remember to provide a tiny bequest in the will. It was a hope that was often cruelly crushed.

When Evangeline had begun making the rounds of the agencies that supplied governesses and companions to the wealthy, she had heard rumors of a most exclusive firm. The Flint & Marsh Agency in Lantern Street, it was said, placed their employees in the most elegant households. And unlike their competitors, they were rumored to pay exceptionally generous fees. Evangeline had hastened around to Lantern Street. After an intensive interview with the proprietors of the firm, she had been hired on the spot.

It transpired that there were two reasons for the superior fees. Flint & Marsh was no ordinary hired companion agency. The firm provided unusual services to its wealthy clients. And although the agency exercised every precaution, there was occasionally some danger involved. Not everyone was suited to the work, Mrs. Marsh had explained.

The second reason the agency paid well was because it demanded an unusual characteristic in the women it employed—a degree of paranormal talent.

The combination of psychical abilities and their determination to survive on their own terms in a world that was hard on women had bonded Evangeline and her friends as securely as a shared bloodline would have done. *Perhaps even more so*, Evangeline thought. In her work for Flint & Marsh she had seen enough of the intimate side of some of the most exclusive families to know that appearances were often deceiving. It never failed to astonish her how much jealousy, anger, bitterness and even violence could seethe at the heart of the most outwardly respectable families.

By the time Evangeline arrived on the doorstep of Flint & Marsh, Beatrice and Clarissa had been employed there for a few months and had already agreed to pool their resources to lease a small town house. They soon invited Evangeline to join them. She had accepted the offer with gratitude.

The prospect of sharing a house—to say nothing of expenses—held great appeal and not only because of the financial aspects. She savored the simple pleasures of taking meals with her newfound friends, sharing the news of the day and discussing the interesting work they did for Flint & Marsh. She had lived alone in the months following her father's death and she had not enjoyed the experience. Not that Reginald Ames had provided much in the way of company when he was alive, she often reminded herself. He had been consumed by his obsession to invent mechanical devices powered by paranormal energy.

She never saw a great deal of him but he had always been there in the background of her life. To be more precise, he was usually to be found in his basement workshop. Nevertheless, as long as he was alive, there was, at least, someone else in the house besides the housekeepers and daily maids, none of whom stayed long. Reginald's experiments and unpredictable moods ensured a steady turnover in the small household staff.

Evangeline had been lonely at times when her father was alive but she'd had her dreams of writing and her imagination to keep her company. She had not discovered what it was to be truly alone in the world until she had found Reginald dead in his basement workshop, a pistol on the floor beside him, a farewell note on the workbench.

Although they had much in common, Evangeline was well aware

that she and her friends were very different in appearance. Beatrice, with her red-gold hair and lagoon-blue eyes, possessed an air of fey innocence that caused others to underestimate her intelligence and her insight into others. The impression of innocence and naiveté served her well in her career at the Flint & Marsh Agency but it could not have been more false.

Beatrice had lived a very different life before she had found her way to the Lantern Street agency, a life that had stripped away all traces of innocence and naiveté. Her experience as a clairvoyant in Dr. Fleming's Academy of the Occult haunted her still.

Dark-haired and amber-eyed, Clarissa peered out at the world through a pair of gold-framed spectacles that gave her a prim, scholarly air. Few people saw beyond the stern appearance to the spirited woman underneath. That was fine by Clarissa. She used her strictly tailored clothes, tightly pinned hair and the eyeglasses to conceal the secrets of her past, secrets that could get her killed.

"If you ask me," Beatrice said, absently twirling her parasol, "the real problem is that the conclusion of the Rutherford affair came as a dreadful shock to our employers' nerves. They underestimated the danger involved in that assignment. It always upsets them when they make a mistake of that sort."

"I think you're right," Evangeline said. "But to be fair, they could not have foreseen what happened after the case was closed."

"Very true," Beatrice agreed, "but it does not mean that they do not feel the weight of responsibility. After all, if they had not sent you into the Rutherford household, you would not have encountered that dreadful man."

Clarissa's dark brows crinkled in a concerned frown. "The thing is, we simply cannot attribute two attacks within two weeks to coincidence. It defies logic."

"The first incident is easily explained, of course, given the nature of our profession," Beatrice said. "But this second assault makes no sense whatsoever."

Evangeline clenched her hand around the handle of her parasol. "The long odds against the two attacks being a coincidence have already been pointed out to me."

Beatrice's expression sharpened with curiosity. "By the gentleman who saved you?"

"Mr. Sebastian, yes," Evangeline said.

"You say he appears to possess some psychical abilities?" Clarissa pressed.

Evangeline thought of how Sharpy Hobson had fled, screaming, to his death. She shivered. "Trust me, there can be no doubt about it. Furthermore, Mr. Sebastian admitted his talent and recognized my own psychical abilities. Like us, he accepts the paranormal as, well, normal."

They walked in silence for a time, contemplating that observation.

"I must say," Beatrice said after a while, "Mr. Sebastian's presence on the scene strikes me as yet another stunning coincidence."

Evangeline and Clarissa looked at her.

"What do you mean?" Clarissa asked.

Beatrice swept out one gloved hand to indicate the landscape around them. "What is the likelihood that, out of all the picturesque country towns in England that Evangeline might have chosen for her retreat, she happened to pick the one spot on the map where she encounters a gentleman endowed with considerable psychical talent?"

Evangeline smiled. "You know very well that my choice was hardly a matter of random chance. When Mrs. Flint and Mrs. Marsh informed me that they were going to banish me to the country for a month, I immediately decided that I would come here to Little Dixby, if you will recall."

"Yes, I remember," Clarissa said. Her parasol bobbed impatiently in her hand. "Something about having come across a reference to it in that old journal of your father's."

"Papa was convinced that there are places dotted across England, indeed, the world, where the paranormal forces of the earth appear to be exceptionally strong," Evangeline said. "I have always wanted to explore some of them."

"I understand," Beatrice said. "But there were several other locations that you could have chosen."

"All of which are even more remote than Little Dixby," Evangeline pointed out. "At least this town has a train station and a bookshop as well as some interesting ruins. I had hoped that the energy in the area would prove inspirational to my writing."

Clarissa narrowed her eyes behind the lenses of her spectacles. "Has that proved to be the case?"

"No," Evangeline admitted. "At least not until recently. I'm sorry to report that I have written very little since I settled in at the cottage. I have been having some problems with my plot."

"That's not good news," Beatrice said. "What is wrong?"

"It was as if I struck a wall. Fortunately, all is not lost. I am making progress. Two days ago I finally realized that I had made a dreadful mistake."

"What mistake?" Beatrice asked.

"I discovered that I had selected the wrong character to be the hero," Evangeline said. "I now realize that the villain, John Reynolds, is actually the hero. The handsome gentleman who appears to be the hero in the first chapter will turn out to be the fortune hunter."

"Good heavens," Clarissa demanded. "How on earth could you make such an error?"

Evangeline waved one hand. "It's hard to describe how that sort of thing can happen to a writer. It just does."

"How odd," Beatrice said.

"It is very inconvenient, I assure you," Evangeline said. "But now that I have fixed the problem I'm sure I can finish the next chapter easily enough and post it to Mr. Guthrie."

Beatrice smiled. "That sounds encouraging. What about the local ruins? Have they given you inspiration for your story?"

"Not those of the old Roman villa that you will see in town," Evangeline said. "Unfortunately, the most interesting antiquities around here are locked away on the grounds of Crystal Gardens. They are not accessible to the public."

Clarissa looked intrigued. "But now you are acquainted with the new owner. Do you think Mr. Sebastian might give you a tour?"

Evangeline smiled. "I intend to try to persuade him to do precisely that."

Beatrice frowned uneasily. "Evie, I realize that you are very curious about mysteries. We all are, for that matter, or we would not be employed by Flint and Marsh. But, frankly, the old abbey sounds like a very dangerous place and from what you have told us, Mr. Sebastian may be as dangerous as his gardens."

Clarissa looked at her. "Why do you say that? Mr. Sebastian saved Evie last night."

"Don't you find it rather convenient that Mr. Sebastian appeared so quickly on the scene?" Beatrice said, her voice very neutral.

"Oh," Clarissa said. "I see what you mean."

Evangeline glared at both of them. "I don't see what she means. Whatever are you talking about, Bea?"

Beatrice raised her delicate red brows. "You say you fled into the grounds of Crystal Gardens at two o'clock in the morning?"

"Approximately," Evangeline said.

"And you encountered Mr. Sebastian and his man, this person named Stone, almost immediately."

"Yes."

"They were both fully clothed?" Beatrice persisted.

Evangeline hesitated. "Yes. What are you getting at?"

"Both men just happened to be wandering about in what you say are very dangerous gardens at two in the morning?" Beatrice asked pointedly.

"Good question," Clarissa said. "It does not sound as if they were roused from their beds by a commotion and dashed out into the gardens to investigate. If that were the case, they would have been partially undressed."

"They were already outside," Beatrice said. She paused for emphasis. "Rather an odd hour for a stroll in the garden, don't you think?"

"I see what you mean," Evangeline said quietly. She was annoyed with herself for not having made the observation. "I should have thought to question Sebastian's presence in the gardens at that hour, but, to tell you the truth, there was a great deal of excitement and commotion at the time and I was very happy to have him appear when he did. I must admit I was a bit rattled."

"Understandable," Beatrice said.

"Perfectly," Clarissa murmured. "After having endured two violent attacks in two weeks anyone would have been unnerved."

"I would appreciate it if you two would stop patting me on the head and speaking to me as if I was a victim of a case of shattered nerves." Evangeline twitched the parasol in a somewhat violent manner. "I assure you, my nerves are in excellent condition."

"Of course," Beatrice said gently. "We never meant to imply otherwise, Evie dear. It is just that we are worried about you."

"You know that is true," Clarissa added.

Evangeline stifled her irritation. She was fortunate to have such good friends, she reminded herself, even if they could be irritating at times.

"In hindsight, I seem to recall that Mr. Sebastian asked most of the questions," she said. "I felt he was entitled to some answers, under the circumstances. I was the one who was trespassing inside his gardens, after all."

Clarissa narrowed her eyes. "What questions did he ask?"

"He had done some research on his new tenant," Evangeline admitted. "In the process he learned that my last post was in Lady Rutherford's household and he was aware of Douglas Mason's death. He was curious about the coincidence."

"Oh, my," Beatrice murmured. "Mrs. Flint and Mrs. Marsh won't like that. You know how keen they are on discretion."

"It's not my fault Mr. Sebastian made some inquiries about me," Evangeline said, defensive now.

Sunlight glinted on Clarissa's spectacles. "How much did you tell him about the Rutherford affair?"

"Nothing that need concern Mrs. Flint and Mrs. Marsh, I assure you. As far as Mr. Sebastian knows, I was merely hired as a companion to Lady Rutherford for a short period of time. That's all." She hesitated. "But Mr. Sebastian appears to have some knowledge of Mason's true character."

"Yes, well, Mason's career as a fortune hunter was in the papers," Beatrice said. "It's the fact that Mr. Sebastian noticed a connection between your post in the Rutherford household and Mason's accident that makes one uneasy."

Evangeline said nothing.

"It's interesting, but I don't see that it's a reason for concern," Clarissa said with her customary logic. "After all, there was absolutely nothing in the press to indicate that Mason's death was anything but an accident."

"No," Beatrice said quietly. "Nevertheless, I think Sebastian knows far more than he ought to know about you, Evie. Do you think he believes that Douglas Mason's death was an accident?"

"I cannot say," Evangeline replied. "But of one thing I am certain."

"What is that?" Clarissa asked.

"Mr. Sebastian was not overly concerned with the fact that Mason is dead," Evangeline said. "Only with the possibility that there is some connection to the attack on me last night."

Clarissa and Beatrice considered that briefly.

"It is not as if we can ignore the possibility, is it?" Clarissa said at last. "I do not like it that you are living here alone, Evie."

"Neither do I," Beatrice said. "Perhaps you should return to London."

An unexpected jolt of alarm twisted through Evangeline. She found herself searching for reasons why leaving Little Dixby would be a very bad idea.

"Not yet," she said. "My imagination has finally been reinvigorated. Indeed, Little Dixby has inspired me. I must seize the moment. I dare not leave here until I have written a few more chapters of my book."

IRENE WITTON WAS behind the counter, concluding the sale of several postcards featuring photographs of the local ruins, when Evangeline led Beatrice and Clarissa into the bookshop. She looked up and peered at them over the tops of her spectacles.

"Ah, Miss Ames. How nice to see you again."

"Allow me to introduce my friends from London," Evangeline said. She made the round of introductions quickly. "They are interested in guidebooks to the antiquities."

"Yes, of course, I have an excellent selection of books and maps as well." Irene plucked her glasses off her nose and inserted them into the silver chatelaine case at her waist. "Let me show you."

She swept out from behind the counter and crossed the room to a bookcase. She pulled one of the volumes off the shelf.

"This is Samuel Higgins's *History of Roman Antiquities in the Vicinity of Little Dixby.* I believe it to be one of the finest accounts of the local ruins."

"I would like to examine it, if I may," Beatrice said.

"Yes, of course." Irene gave her the book and reached for another volume.

Clarissa pushed her eyeglasses higher on her nose and studied Irene's chatelaine. "That is a very elegant spectacles case. I have been looking for one of my own. So handy to have one's eyeglasses close at hand. Do you mind if I ask where you purchased it?"

"My spectacles case?" Irene touched the silver case at her waist. She smiled. "Thank you. It is new. I lost my old one some time back. I was quite pleased when I discovered this one in a shop in London recently. I will write down the name of the establishment before you leave."

Clarissa brightened. "I would appreciate it. My friends tell me that I am rather dull and boring when it comes to matters of fashion. I am determined to become more stylish."

Beatrice raised her eyes to the ceiling. "For heaven's sake, Clarissa, Evie and I never called you dull and boring, did we, Evie?"

"Not once," Evangeline declared.

"I regret to inform you that telling me that I dress as if I were an instructor in a girls' boarding school is the same thing," Clarissa said.

Half an hour later, their purchases secured in brown paper and string, the three crossed the street to the tea shop.

Evangeline waited until the pot of Assam and a small plate of insipid-looking tea sandwiches had been set on the table before she looked at Clarissa.

"Do Beatrice and I really imply that you are somewhat staid in your dress?" she asked gently.

"'Dowdy' might be the more appropriate word," Clarissa said. She helped herself to a tiny sandwich. "But it's all right. You are my friends and I forgive you."

Beatrice bit her lip. "Truly, we never meant to make you feel unfashionable. It is just that there are times when Evie and I feel you might enjoy dressing in a more cheerful manner. It is bad enough that the three of us must dress as hired companions when we are working. There is no reason to go about in such attire the rest of the time. It is not good for the spirits."

Clarissa wrinkled her brow. "My spirits are fine, thank you."

Evangeline picked up her cup. "If that is so, why did you inquire about Miss Witton's pretty spectacles chatelaine?"

Clarissa munched her sandwich and swallowed. "I was merely curious. It is a very stylish case, don't you think?"

Evangeline exchanged a knowing look with Beatrice and was very sure they were both thinking the same thing. Clarissa's birthday was coming up next month. A lovely silver spectacles chatelaine would make the perfect gift.

Seven

"That's it?" Clarissa said. Incredulous sympathy rang in her words. "That is all there is to do here in Little Dixby? Tour a few ruins, have tea and a few tasteless sandwiches and stop in a bookshop?"

"I'm afraid so," Evangeline said. "The most interesting sites around here are locked away behind the walls of Crystal Gardens."

They were walking back to Fern Gate Cottage. It was only four-thirty and there were hours of summer sunlight left in the day. But the shadows in the narrow lane through the dense woods were already long and dark. There was no more need for the parasols. Evangeline closed hers. Beatrice and Clarissa did the same.

"However have you managed to survive for the past two weeks?" Beatrice asked. "No wonder you have been bored to tears."

"I certainly was until last night," Evangeline said.

Clarissa made a tut-tutting sound. "Nothing like being attacked by someone who wants to slit one's throat to save one from succumbing to acute ennui, I always say."

Evangeline was about to respond but a shiver of awareness raised the hair on her nape. Instinctively she looked down the lane and saw Lucas Sebastian walking toward them. She stopped.

Beatrice and Clarissa halted beside her. They all watched Lucas. He was dressed for a country walk in an informal coat, trousers and boots. His head was bare. He moved through the shadows in near silence.

"Let me hazard a guess," Beatrice whispered. "Would this by any chance be Mr. Sebastian?"

"Yes," Evangeline said just as softly. She felt energy shiver in the atmosphere and knew that her friends had slipped into their other senses.

Clarissa became very serious. "Oh, my. You were right when you said that he possesses a great deal of psychical talent. I can see it in his aura, even from this distance. Very dark. Very powerful. He could, indeed, be very dangerous, Evangeline. You must be careful."

Beatrice's fey eyes widened slightly.

"No," Beatrice said. "Evie will be safe with him."

Clarissa glanced at her. "Are you certain?"

"I'm sure of it," Beatrice said.

"I agree that he is unlikely to do her any physical harm," Clarissa said. "The energy of his aura does not show any taint of the murky light that one sees in men who abuse those who are weaker than themselves. But we all know that there are other ways a woman can be hurt. When it comes to matters of the heart, a woman must always be on guard."

"Matters of the heart?" Evangeline yelped, outraged. "Have you gone mad? There are no matters of the heart involved here. Someone tried to murder me last night. I assure you that had nothing to do with my heart. Believe it or not, discovering who would want to do such a thing is my chief concern."

"Yes, of course," Beatrice said.

This time she actually did reach out one gloved hand and pat Evangeline—not on the head, but on the arm. Evangeline sighed and reminded herself that her friends meant well.

"Under the circumstances, I am hardly likely to lose my heart to Mr. Sebastian," she said very quietly. "And even if I were so foolish as to do such a thing, I am quite sure he would return it immediately."

"Mmm," Beatrice said. But she was still watching Lucas and she did not look convinced.

There was no more time to try to correct the wrong impression, Evangeline realized. Lucas was almost upon them. Hastily she summoned up a smile.

"Mr. Sebastian," she said. "How nice to see you again. Allow me to present my friends, Miss Slate and Miss Lockwood. I have told them of the events of last night."

Lucas stopped in front of them and inclined his head. "Miss Ames. Ladies."

"A pleasure, Mr. Sebastian," Clarissa said.

"Mr. Sebastian," Beatrice murmured politely.

Evangeline felt another shiver of energy in the atmosphere and knew that Beatrice and Clarissa were both taking a closer look at Lucas. She could tell by the glint of amusement in his eyes that he was aware of the psychical scrutiny. *This is awkward*, she thought.

Frantically she searched for a distraction. "What of the body, Mr. Sebastian?" She leaned down to unlatch the garden gate. "Were you able to recover it from the maze and examine it for clues?"

Lucas's mouth kicked up at the corner. "Do you know, Miss Ames, no other lady of my acquaintance has ever begun a conversation with a question like that."

"Pay no attention to Evie," Beatrice said. "She is a writer. Their conversations can take very odd turns."

"Yes, I'm discovering that," Lucas said.

Evangeline flushed and pushed open the gate. "Sorry, the question has been on my mind all day."

"The other problem in dealing with writers," Clarissa said in her most academic fashion, "is that they tend to view even the tiniest of incidents as grist for the mill, so to speak. They are always looking for inspiration for their plots and characters, you see. They collect such material the way some people collect stray bits of string."

Lucas did not take his attention off Evangeline. "I appreciate the warning, Miss Slate."

"That is quite enough," Evangeline announced. She went briskly along the graveled path through the fern forest. "I am attempting to have a serious conversation with Mr. Sebastian. The least he can do is answer my questions."

"The answer to your inquiries," Lucas said, "is that I did find the body but I learned very little about Sharpy Hobson that we had not already guessed. He appears to have been a professional criminal who traveled here on the train from London. I found a couple of knives and a train ticket and a theater ticket stub. Hobson was evidently fond of melodramas."

He stood politely aside, waiting for Clarissa and Beatrice to enter the garden. He followed them and paused to latch the gate.

"That's all you were able to discover?" Evangeline asked.

"There was a large sum of money," Lucas said. "The first half of his fee, I believe."

Beatrice glanced back at him. "His fee?" Understanding dawned. "Oh, I see, for murdering Evie. Good heavens."

Evangeline went up the steps. "How much am I worth, Mr. Sebastian?"

"A great deal, as it happens." He told them exactly how much money he had discovered on the body.

Evangeline was shocked. "Good grief."

"How odd that he would risk traveling with so much money," Clarissa mused. "It sounds quite dangerous, what with all the thieves and pickpockets around at the train stations."

"What else could he do with it?" Lucas asked. "He came from the criminal underworld, probably born and bred on the streets. He would not have trusted any of his associates and no legitimate bank would have accepted him as a customer. He likely concluded that his money was safer on his person than anywhere else. After all, he was Sharpy Hobson, a feared knifeman. Who would be so foolish as to try to steal from him?"

Beatrice was impressed. "You seem to have some familiarity with the criminal mind, Mr. Sebastian."

"He has made a study of it," Evangeline said, before Lucas could respond.

Clarissa's eyes widened. "Really? How fascinating."

Lucas was looking amused again, Evangeline noticed. That was probably not a good sign.

"Never mind Mr. Sebastian's obvious expertise," she said. "The point is that the money Hobson was carrying on his person appears to be another bit of evidence indicating that someone did indeed hire him to murder me."

"There was never any doubt in my mind," Lucas said mildly.

"Well, there was in mine," Evangeline said. "I suppose it is still possible that this is a ghastly case of mistaken identity."

"I don't think so," Lucas said.

She removed her key from her small chatelaine purse. "I just cannot imagine—"

The door opened before she could get her key into the lock. Molly Gillingham, the young daily maid, stood in the opening. Her cheeks were flushed with excitement. She darted quick glances at Lucas, while she greeted Evangeline.

"Welcome home, Miss Ames," she said. Her accent was uncharacteristically formal.

"Thank you, Molly." Evangeline waited. When Molly failed to step back, she smiled. "Perhaps you might remove yourself from the doorway?"

Molly turned red and hurriedly got out of the way. "Yes, right, I beg your pardon, Miss Ames." She cast another quick glance at Lucas. "Will you be wanting tea, miss?"

It was on the tip of Evangeline's tongue to inform Molly that she and Clarissa and Beatrice had just had tea in town but it occurred to her that Lucas presented a dilemma. There was nothing for it but to offer him tea.

"Please, Molly." She untied the strings of her bonnet. "We will take it in the parlor."

"Yes, Miss Ames." Molly dipped an unpracticed curtsy and rushed off to the kitchen.

Evangeline waited while her friends removed their bonnets and gloves and then she waved Clarissa, Beatrice and Lucas into the parlor. "Please be seated, Mr. Sebastian. I'll just go and have a word with Molly."

She ushered the three into the small space, closed the door and went quickly into the kitchen. She found Molly bustling about in a state of great excitement.

"It's Mr. Sebastian himself, right here in this very house," Molly said, speaking in a loud whisper.

"Yes, I did notice."

"Wait until I tell Ma and Pa that I served tea to the new owner of Crystal Gardens."

"Try to contain yourself, Molly," Evangeline said.

"They say in town that Mr. Sebastian is very likely as mad as his uncle but he doesn't look the least bit deranged to me."

"He certainly doesn't look deranged to me, either," Evangeline said briskly. "And I think it would be best if you did not pay any attention to such gossip."

"No, miss."

"I just wanted to make sure you could deal with tea for so many people."

"Never fear, miss, I help my ma make breakfast and supper for my family, all ten of us, every day. During the harvest I'm in the kitchen with the other women cooking from dawn until dusk for the men in the fields. Tea for the four of you is nothing."

It was clear Molly was thrilled at finding herself in such close proximity to the mysterious new owner of the old abbey. Evangeline did not have the heart to quash her enthusiasm. Pretty and rosy-cheeked, Molly was eighteen years old. She was an intelligent, irrepressible young woman who loved to read the serialized novels in the newspapers. When she had discovered that Evangeline was writing such a story, she had begged to be allowed to read the chapters being sent off in small batches to the publisher at the end of every week. Evangeline had been reluctant at first but in the end she had relented. Molly's delight with each new scene in *Winterscar* had been gratifying.

It was a pity Molly was fated to marry one of the local farmers, Evangeline thought. Molly possessed a great curiosity about the world beyond the borders of the village where she had been born and raised. She talked often of saving her money for a trip to London. But Evangeline knew that the reality was that the girl was unlikely to travel any farther than the neighboring town to see a traveling circus or take in a fair. She would probably never get to London.

Molly's future was not altogether dreadful, Evangeline reminded herself. There was, in fact, much to be said for life in a small, safe village, far removed from the dangers of London's streets. But that life promised to be filled with a great deal of sunup-to-sundown work on a farm and very little in the way of mental stimulation. She sensed that sooner or later the endless routine and the drudgery would dampen even Molly's bright spirits.

"Go on back to your guests, Miss Ames," Molly said. "I'll bring the tray in straightaway." She used both hands to swing the heavy iron kettle onto the stove. "Oh, I almost forgot to tell you that my uncle came by while you were out and fixed the lock on the kitchen door. Good as new now."

Evangeline glanced at the new lock. It looked very sturdy. "Please tell your uncle that I am grateful."

"It was no problem." Molly opened a cupboard and began taking down cups and saucers. "He says it looks like someone broke the lock when you went out for an evening stroll. The burglar must have been scared off before he could steal anything."

She had not gone for a stroll, Evangeline thought; she had been running for her life.

"Perhaps a dog barked," she said, "or one of the neighbors went past in the lane and frightened him off."

"None of the people who live around here are likely to drive along the lane to Crystal Gardens at night," Molly said. "Everyone thinks the woods are haunted. My uncle wanted me to tell you that he's certain that none of the local lads would have done something terrible like kick in your door."

"I never considered for a moment that it was someone from Little

Dixby," Evangeline said. And that, she thought, was nothing less than the truth.

"My uncle says it was probably one of the ruffians from that traveling circus over in Ryton. You know how it is with those circus folk. Everyone says you've got to keep an eye on them."

When freshly washed clothes disappeared off the line or a tool went missing from a gardening shed, it was common practice in the countryside to blame the theft on the members of a traveling circus or carnival. It was certainly the simplest explanation in this case, but Evangeline was reluctant to let the innocent take the blame.

"I don't think so," she said. "At the time the break-in occurred the circus folk in Ryton would have been busy packing up for the move to the next town. No, I'm convinced that it was some villain from London who arrived on the train in search of criminal opportunities. Perhaps one who was recently obliged to leave the city to avoid the police."

"Well, whatever the case, he's long gone now." Molly poured the hot water into a pot. "I'll put some of my fresh tea cakes on the tray. A strong, healthy gentleman like Mr. Sebastian needs his food."

Evangeline smiled. Obviously she was not the only female in the vicinity who had noticed that—speculation on the state of his mental health aside—Lucas was a strong, healthy male.

"Thank you, Molly." She started to turn in the doorway.

Molly took the cover off the dish that held some dainty little cakes. "Oh, Miss Ames, I wanted to tell you that last night I stayed up late after Ma and Pa went to bed and finished the second chapter of *Winterscar*. It was very thrilling."

Evangeline warmed with pleasure. "Thank you, Molly."

"I can hardly wait to see what happens now that Patricia is trapped in an upstairs bedroom with that dreadful John Reynolds, who plans to compromise her so that she will be forced to marry him. The way you left the ending, it appears that Patricia's only choice to save her honor is to jump out the window and break her neck on the rocks below the cliff."

"Which would not be wise because it would conclude the story a bit too soon, don't you think?"

"Yes, miss." Molly dimpled. "I'm sure Patricia will find a way to escape the villain's clutches without losing her virtue or breaking her neck."

"I think it's safe to say that you are right." *Because John Reynolds is no longer the villain,* Evangeline added silently. "You may go home after you bring in the tea."

Molly was crestfallen. "Are you sure, miss? I don't mind staying for a while. You will want help washing up after Mr. Sebastian leaves."

"I appreciate the offer but we'll muddle along without you."

"Yes, miss. Just so you'll know, I should tell you that my brother, Ned, delivered the eggs, milk, butter and cheese you ordered. And I made a lovely salmon-and-leek pie for you and your London friends to eat tonight."

"Your salmon and leek pie is the best I've ever eaten," Evangeline said.

Molly's smile held pride and satisfaction. "Thank you, miss. Just wait until I tell my ma that Mr. Sebastian called on you today."

Evangeline wondered what Mrs. Gillingham would say if she knew that the only reason Lucas Sebastian was taking up space in the parlor was his tenant had been chased onto the grounds of Crystal Gardens sometime after two in the morning by a knife-wielding murderer. Then, again, those details would not cause nearly as much breathless gossip as the news that the tenant in question had arrived at the abbey attired only in her nightclothes. There were some things best left unexplained.

"Go along to the parlor, ma'am." Molly motioned toward the door.

"You don't want to keep a fine gentleman like Mr. Sebastian waiting. It's a great honor to have him here for tea."

"Thank you for reminding me of my duties as a hostess," Evangeline said.

But the irony was lost on Molly, who was fussing very earnestly with the tea things.

Muffled voices drifted down the hallway. Alarmed, Evangeline rushed back to the parlor. She yanked open the door, nipped inside and hastily shut the door behind her.

"For heaven's sake, keep your voices down," she said in a loud whisper. "If Molly hears you talking about Sharpy Hobson or the events of last night, the gossip will be all over town before the sun goes down."

Lucas gave her a benign smile. He lounged with easy masculine grace, one shoulder propped against the wall near the window. His arms were folded across his broad chest.

Clarissa and Beatrice were sitting on two of the spindly chairs, the skirts of their walking gowns draped around their high-button boots. They both chuckled.

"You may be surprised to know that we had already deduced that for ourselves," Beatrice said. "As a matter of fact, we were discussing farming matters."

"Farming?" Evangeline sank back against the door, both hands behind her wrapped tightly around the knob. "Why on earth would you want to talk about agriculture at a time like this?"

"I was explaining to Miss Lockwood and Miss Slate that the farms around Little Dixby have always been extremely productive," Lucas said. "Crops thrive here. The villagers will tell you that you can grow anything on these lands and they have done so for generations. The roses in local gardens are extraordinary."

"Oh, I see." Evangeline frowned, thinking about what he had said.

"I expect the fact that this place is a vortex has something to do with the success of the local farms and gardens."

Lucas's brows rose. His beast-of-prey eyes heated a little. "You are aware that Little Dixby may be a paranormal vortex?"

"Yes, and if my father was correct, the focal point is Crystal Gardens," Evangeline said. "That's why I'm here, you see."

"No," Lucas said deliberately, "I do not see."

"Never mind, it's not important." She heard the rattle of cups on a tray. "That will be Molly."

She whirled about and opened the door. Molly walked into the room, moving very carefully with the heavily laden tray. Lucas straightened away from the window.

"That looks heavy," he said. "Let me take that for you."

Molly blushed a bright pink. "It's no trouble, sir."

But Lucas had already removed the tray from her hands. He set it on the small table.

"Thank you, sir," Molly said. She gave Evangeline a hopeful look. "Shall I pour, ma'am?"

"No, thank you, Molly." Evangeline smiled and sat on the sofa, automatically twitching her skirts into the proper folds. "I'll take care of it. Run along home."

"Yes, ma'am. Thank you, ma'am." Molly dipped another stiff little curtsy and went back out into the hall. She closed the door quietly.

Evangeline picked up the teapot and began to pour. Everyone paid a great deal of attention to the tea service until they heard the muffled thud of the kitchen door closing. A moment later Molly could be seen through the front window hurrying away down the lane.

The news that Lucas was taking tea with the new tenant at the cottage and her fashionable London friends would soon be common knowledge in the neighborhood, Evangeline thought. It was fortunate that Clarissa and Beatrice were here. Their presence ensured an aura of respectability.

The social rules that governed relationships between the sexes were more relaxed in the country than they were in London, but there were limits and it took so little to start people talking in a small town such as Little Dixby. Evangeline was well aware that there had been much speculation about her in the past two weeks. A single woman who lived alone was always watched closely. A single woman from London who dressed in a fashionable manner and who was rumored to be writing a sensation novel was even more interesting.

"We can talk now," Evangeline said.

"It's a great pity this dreadful Hobson person is dead," Clarissa said. "It would have been useful to question him. I don't quite understand how he died. Evangeline said something about thorns."

"Unfortunately, Mr. Hobson blundered into one of the more dangerous portions of the gardens," Lucas said. "His death was in the nature of an accident." He munched a small cake. "Not unlike Douglas Mason's accident."

Evangeline froze. Clarissa and Beatrice became very busy with their tea.

Predictably, it was Clarissa who recovered her composure first. "The thing is, why on earth would anyone send a criminal to murder Evangeline?"

Lucas gave Evangeline a considering look. "All I can tell you at the moment is that someone was willing to pay Sharpy Hobson a considerable sum to do so. Someone wants you dead, Miss Ames, and if you're certain there is no jealous lover lurking in the background—"

Evangeline choked on her tea. She sputtered and grabbed a napkin. "I am certain of that much."

Beatrice pursed her lips. "I agree. We can exclude the notion of a rejected lover. There simply isn't one in Evangeline's case."

"And her death would benefit no one," Clarissa added helpfully, "so money cannot be a factor."

"Always nice to know one's worth," Evangeline said into her teacup.

"It appears we have only one option open to us," Lucas said.

He polished off the last of the tea cakes and brushed crumbs from his hands. It seemed to Evangeline that his eyes heated a little. Not with desire, she realized. It was lust of a very different sort she sensed in him—the dangerous aura of the hunter who is setting a trap for prey. She was sure that this was not the first time he had done so.

Beatrice also detected the charged atmosphere. She watched Lucas with an expectant air. "What option is that, sir?"

"Men like Hobson, who can be hired to commit murder, are not actually as common on the ground as one might believe," Lucas said. "Those who are skilled at that particular sort of work have reputations in the criminal world."

Clarissa shuddered. "I can well imagine that is true."

"We must find out who employed Hobson," Lucas continued. "Fortunately, we have Stone."

Evangeline looked up from her tea. "What does Mr. Stone have to do with any of this?"

"He has connections on the streets of London." Lucas looked out at the dark woods. "He knows people in that world. This morning he took the train to the city where he will make inquiries about Hobson. With luck Stone will discover some information that will lead us to the person who hired Hobson."

Evangeline stilled. She was aware that Beatrice and Clarissa had gone equally quiet. They looked at one another. Evangeline saw the questions in their eyes. She raised her brows. "I did tell you that Mr. Sebastian has studied the criminal mind."

"Yes, you did." Beatrice sat up very straight and put her cup and saucer down with a determined air. "We are fortunate to be able to take advantage of his knowledge and connections. The problem here is that we are dealing with members of the professional criminal class. That is not our area of expertise."

Clarissa drummed her fingers on the arm of the chair, her serious face pinched in a worried expression. "No, that is quite true."

Lucas surveyed the three of them with a thoughtful expression. "It would be rather extraordinary if you ladies did have some practical experience with the criminal class. That is usually the province of the police."

"Mmm," Beatrice said politely. She sipped her tea.

"Yes, of course," Clarissa murmured. "The thing is, when you call in the police, you often find yourself dealing with the press. The police have their talents but they are not known for discretion."

Evangeline cleared her throat. "As it happens, Mr. Sebastian and I discussed that very point last night."

"When you were standing in his garden dressed only in your nightclothes?" Clarissa's brows shot upward. "Yes, I expect that you did have a conversation about whether or not to summon the authorities."

"For heaven's sake," Beatrice chided. "This is hardly the time to speak of such matters."

"Nonsense," Clarissa said. "Everyone in this room knows the facts of the situation. Evangeline and Mr. Sebastian made the right decision. One can only imagine the scandal that would have ensued if the story had landed in the London newspapers."

"If the attempted murder had its origins in the incident which occurred shortly after I left my last post, as Mr. Sebastian believes, I doubt that the police would have been of much help in any event," Evangeline said. "Mr. Mason's death was just an unfortunate accident."

"True," Beatrice said neutrally.

There was a short silence. Evangeline realized that Lucas was once again studying the three of them with keen attention.

"I think," he said after a moment, "that it is time you told me what it is that you ladies do to make your livings. And in particular, Miss Ames, I would very much like to know a bit more about what happened in the course of your last post."

Evangeline looked at Clarissa and Beatrice.

"I think we can trust Mr. Sebastian," Beatrice advised.

"I don't see that we have much choice," Clarissa said. "Evangeline's safety, perhaps her very life, is at stake here."

Evangeline sat back, cup and saucer in hand. "I did tell you, Mr. Sebastian, that my friends and I work for an agency that supplies paid companions to a very exclusive clientele."

"You mentioned your profession last night," Lucas said. "But it has become clear to me that none of you is typical of the sort of unfortunate women who are obliged to pursue that particular career."

"Really, sir?" Evangeline looked at him over the rim of her cup. "And just how many paid companions have you been personally acquainted with?"

Lucas's mouth quirked at one corner. "You have me there, Miss Ames. I must admit that you are the first professional paid companion I have spoken to for more than thirty seconds. They tend to be the retiring sort, always sitting in the shadows, working on their knitting or reading while their employers go about their lives. One tends not to notice them."

Evangeline gave him a cool smile. "Which is precisely why we are so very, very good at what we do, sir. No one ever takes any notice of us when we are at work."

"And the nature of your work?" Lucas asked.

"We are private inquiry agents," Evangeline said.

She waited for the inevitable signs of astonishment and disbelief to appear on Lucas's face. She knew that Clarissa and Beatrice were waiting, too. They were all doomed to disappointment.

"Interesting," Lucas said. He sounded oddly satisfied. He swallowed some tea and set the cup down on the saucer. "That certainly explains a few things."

Clarissa narrowed her eyes. "Such as?"

"Miss Lockwood's comment about the criminal underworld not being your area of expertise, for one thing. You deal in crimes in high society."

"With the utmost discretion," Evangeline added.

He smiled. "Obviously, or the firm of Flint and Marsh would have gone out of business a long time ago. Your professional work also explains your daring and resourcefulness last night. It was obvious that you've had some experience keeping a cool head when confronting danger."

"I assure you that we rarely experience actual physical danger in the course of our work, sir," Evangeline said. "Our employers take great care not to place us in such situations. We are not, after all, the police. Generally speaking, our clients are ladies who want discreet inquiries made into the character and finances of gentlemen who are attempting to become involved with a family's finances."

Lucas's eyes gleamed with icy understanding. "You expose fortune hunters."

"And those who are not above attempting to defraud widows and spinsters," Clarissa added.

"But you are correct, sir," Beatrice said. "One way or another, the business of unmasking fortune hunters constitutes the majority of our commissions. More often than not we are asked to investigate the backgrounds of men who wish to marry either a young heiress or a widow with some money of her own to protect."

"How do you attract clients?" Lucas asked. "I can't envision the firm advertising such services in the papers."

"Mrs. Flint and Mrs. Marsh acquire clients by referral," Evangeline said.

Lucas was clearly intrigued. "And their employees? How do they find unusual women such as the three of you?"

"In the same way," Beatrice said. "Word of mouth. Not everyone is suited to the work. It requires a certain . . . aptitude."

Lucas considered that with a thoughtful expression. "This aptitude for the work that you speak of. Would it by any chance include a measure of psychical talent?"

Clarissa and Beatrice looked at Evangeline.

"I did tell you that Mr. Sebastian takes the paranormal quite seriously," she said. She looked at Lucas. "I have a question for you, sir. There were obvious reasons for not summoning the authorities last night. But sooner or later you must report the death. How do you intend to explain a dead man in your gardens to the police?"

"There won't be any need for explanations," Lucas said. "Bodies don't last long in Crystal Gardens."

Eight

Lucas watched the three women with great interest as they dealt with the news of how he had disposed of the body in the garden. Their shock was plain on their faces. Eyes widened, jaws dropped slightly, teacups froze in midair.

Evangeline swallowed hard. But of the three she recovered first, most likely because she knew how Hobson had died, Lucas decided.

"I see," she said. "Well, I suppose there is no need to make a fuss over Hobson. He was trying to murder me, after all."

"My thoughts, precisely," Lucas said.

Clarissa got her mouth closed. She nodded, satisfied. "Under the circumstances it sounds like a very convenient way of handling the problem."

"I certainly thought so," Lucas said.

Beatrice eyed him with some suspicion. "Are you serious, Mr.

Sebastian? You intend for Sharpy Hobson's body to simply disappear into your gardens?"

"Hobson won't be the first to do so, Miss Lockwood. The deeper one goes into the Gardens, the more aggressive the plants become. In the maze and the Night Garden, nature works very swiftly, especially at night."

Clarissa looked interested at that information. "The time of day makes a difference?"

"I have observed that paranormal energy of any sort is often enhanced by darkness," Lucas said. "But the currents that emanate from the natural forces of the earth are invariably more powerful at night. My uncle's theory is that sunlight interferes with the wavelengths at the far ends of the spectrum or, more likely, makes it difficult for those of us with some psychical ability to sense those currents."

"My father also came to the same conclusion," Evangeline agreed.

Lucas looked at her. "You mentioned that your father had an interest in the science of the paranormal, Miss Ames."

"Yes," she said. "He possessed some psychical ability himself, you see."

Lucas did not take his eyes off her. "It is a trait that is often passed down through the bloodline."

"It is because of his interest in the paranormal that I decided to spend the month here in Little Dixby," Evangeline said. "In one of his journals he wrote that he considered this region to be a vortex."

Lucas nodded in a thoughtful manner. "A place where paranormal forces in the earth come together in such a way as to generate a great deal of energy. Fascinating. Uncle Chester was convinced of the same thing. He believed that Crystal Gardens was the center of the Little Dixby vortex." He paused. "So it was your interest in science that led you to rent the cottage, Miss Ames?"

"Well, no, not exactly," Evangeline admitted. "I am not especially keen on scientific matters. But when I made the decision to spend a month in the countryside, I recalled what I had read in my father's journal. I came here seeking inspiration for my writing. I thought the paranormal elements in the area might give me some ideas for my plot."

Lucas grimaced. "I should have guessed."

She fixed him with a cold look. "We writers are a sensitive lot, Mr. Sebastian. We are inspired by all manner of things, including the energy in the atmosphere around us."

"Right. I must remember that in future."

Her jaw tightened. "What is this about the plants on the grounds of the old abbey becoming stronger and more aggressive? What on earth is happening at Crystal Gardens, sir?"

"Damned if I know," Lucas said.

It said something about the seriousness of the situation and the fortitude of the three ladies sitting in the parlor that none of them paid any attention to his rough language, he thought. But, then, he had a feeling it would take a great deal to shock the three women from the firm of Flint & Marsh.

Evangeline tilted her head very slightly to one side and narrowed her eyes. "You really don't know what is happening?"

"I can only assume that my uncle's experiments are somehow to blame," he said. "The forces at work inside the walls are generated by an underground hot spring. The waters were sacred to the ancients. When the Romans arrived, they constructed a bathhouse on the site because they were convinced the spring waters had invigorating, even healing properties. Later the abbey was established on the same spot. It was believed that the spring waters enhanced the power of prayer and encouraged religious visions. Eventually, however, the abbey was abandoned. My uncle purchased the property about thirty years ago and began to conduct his botanical experiments. Still, things appeared to be more or less under control until the past two years."

Clarissa tapped one fingertip against the rim of her cup. "What sort of experiments did your uncle carry out?"

"He was well intentioned," Lucas said. "He created a number of hybrids in an attempt to develop plants with various psychical properties. He was searching for new sources of medicine and faster-growing, more productive crops. But at some point, things began to go wrong. The vegetation is taking over. The gardens have become a dangerous jungle. Some areas are almost completely inaccessible."

"No wonder there is talk of the occult," Beatrice said.

"In the past two years at least three intruders have managed to get as far as the maze and perhaps all the way into the Night Garden," Lucas continued. "Uncle Chester could not be certain because the bodies disappeared."

"Why on earth would anyone take the risk of trespassing into such a dangerous place?" Beatrice asked.

Lucas looked at Evangeline. "Perhaps Miss Ames would like to take that question."

She flushed, looking rather like a girl who had been caught sneaking out of the house to meet a boy, he thought.

"I was bored and I got curious," she said with a touch of cool defiance. "That's the only reason I went into the gardens. I wasn't reckless. I just did some exploring. I certainly did not attempt the maze."

"Most likely because it was locked," Lucas said.

Evangeline's face turned a brighter shade of red but she pretended she had not heard the implied accusation.

"Miss Ames's curiosity aside," Lucas continued, "the chief reason a few adventurous souls have attempted to enter the maze and the Night Garden is the legend of the treasure."

Clarissa brightened. "Yes, Miss Witton at the bookshop mentioned it today. A hoard of Roman gold is believed to be buried somewhere on the grounds."

"There is nothing like the prospect of finding a chest of golden objects to attract treasure hunters," Lucas said. "But for the most part the forces in the Night Garden frighten off would-be trespassers."

"Those who do get inside are rarely seen again," Clarissa concluded.

"Generally speaking, no," Lucas said.

"I have heard the tales of ghosts and demonic forces," Evangeline said. "But I discounted most of the more dramatic gossip. The thought of people vanishing into the gardens and being consumed by the plants is actually a good deal more chilling than explanations that involve the supernatural."

Clarissa frowned. "She's got that look, Bea."

"Yes," Beatrice said. "I recognize it."

Lucas studied Evangeline's thoughtful expression. "What look?"

"Evangeline always gets that expression when she is contemplating a new plot idea for her story," Clarissa explained. "I believe your talk of carnivorous plants has inspired her."

Lucas suppressed a groan. "I assure you, that was not my intent."

"Never mind," Beatrice said. "One grows accustomed to Evangeline's odd little habits. Back to the subject of the maze. You were obviously able to enter it if you found Hobson's body inside."

Reluctantly he dragged his attention away from Evangeline. "Yes. My uncle could navigate it as well. It is possible to make one's way through the maze if one possesses a fair amount of talent. But even then there are any number of dangers, such as the poisonous thorns and vines that can lock around a wrist or an ankle and chain a man as securely as an iron manacle."

Evangeline brightened. "Would you mind if I took a moment to fetch a pen and some paper? I'd like to make some notes."

"Yes, I would mind, Miss Ames." Lucas put some steel into his voice. "In case you have not noticed, we have other priorities here."

"Right." Evangeline picked up her cup and got a faraway look in her eyes.

Lucas set his teeth. She was making notes in her head, he thought.

"Evie told us that your uncle died in the gardens," Beatrice said. "Did he fall afoul of one of those dreadful plants?"

"Actually he died at the breakfast table. That is where his housekeeper, Mrs. Buckley, found him."

Evangeline frowned. "But I understood that he collapsed somewhere on the grounds."

"The gossips never get the facts straight," Lucas said. "The locals prefer to believe that he was killed by supernatural forces. Make no mistake, I'm convinced he was murdered, but not by demons or spirits from the Otherworld."

Evangeline exchanged looks with Clarissa and Beatrice. Lucas sensed the woman's curiosity and gathering excitement. They all loved the thrill that accompanied a mystery, he thought. Something to do with their talents, no doubt.

"Have you got a motive for your uncle's death?" Clarissa demanded.

"Not yet," Lucas said. "But I suspect it is connected to his recent discovery in the Gardens."

Beatrice was enthralled. "What discovery was that, sir?"

"I don't know," Lucas admitted. "All I got was a short, very cryptic telegram telling me that he had discovered something of great importance in the Night Garden. He died before I could make time to come here to see for myself."

"Weren't you curious, sir?" Evangeline asked.

"You must understand that Chester was always sending word of new botanical discoveries and the results of his latest experiments," Lucas said. "If I had come to Crystal Gardens every time I got a message from him telling me of some fantastic new hybrid, I would have been here every week."

"But this time he may have stumbled onto something truly valuable or important, is that what you believe?" Evangeline asked.

"It seems a likely explanation but there are others," he said.

"Did your uncle have any enemies?" Beatrice asked.

"None that I know of," Lucas said. "Most people considered him a crackpot. But there are a handful of other botanists engaged in similar experiments. Not many, of course, given the paranormal nature of the work. But some of those whom he considered colleagues could more properly be classified as rivals."

"So professional jealousy might have been a factor," Evangeline said.

"This is all quite fascinating," Clarissa mused.

"I should dearly love to see your Gardens, Mr. Sebastian," Beatrice said.

"As would I," Clarissa said.

"I would also like to take a proper tour of Crystal Gardens." Evangeline brightened.

"I will be happy to show all of you the sections that I feel are still safe," Lucas said.

"Wonderful," Beatrice exclaimed.

"How exciting," Clarissa added.

Evangeline smiled. "Thank you, sir. As you can see, there is a great deal of enthusiasm for a tour."

"The grounds are most interesting after dark," Lucas said. He did not take his attention off her. "I shall arrange a tour tonight on one condition."

Evangeline made a face. "You want more details about my last case, don't you?"

"As I am now involved in whatever is going on as a result of that situation, I think it's important that I know more about it," he said.

Evangeline hesitated. "We still don't know if the attempted murder is linked to the Rutherford affair."

They all looked at her. No one spoke.

She sighed. "But you are right. It is too much to believe that there is no connection. For the life of me, I cannot imagine what it would be. I will tell you the story tonight when we view the Gardens."

Nine

That night the three of them stood with Lucas on the terrace of the country house and watched the gardens and the gazebo glow in the moonlight.

"Spectacular," Clarissa breathed. "Absolutely beautiful."

"But one can certainly feel the ominous undercurrents in this place," Beatrice added. "They are detectable even to my normal senses." A visible shudder went through her. "I can well understand why your uncle did not have a great many problems with intruders, Mr. Sebastian."

"No," Lucas said. He looked at Evangeline. "Most could not get as far as you did, Miss Ames."

"Well, I do have some talent," Evangeline said coolly. "And I find this place quite fascinating."

He smiled. In the silvery radiance her face was shadowed and mysterious.

"Yes," he said. "I can see that." He paused a beat. "I would remind you that we had an agreement."

"You may as well tell him the story," Clarissa said.

"I agree," Beatrice said. "I think we can trust Mr. Sebastian. He will not gossip."

Evangeline folded her arms beneath her breasts. "There is not much to tell. It was a routine case. The client was an elderly woman, Lady Rutherford, who had developed some suspicions about the man who wished to marry her granddaughter. The girl's parents would not listen to her. They believed it to be a brilliant match and the young lady herself thought her suitor very handsome and charming. Mr. Mason could be . . . quite convincing."

"The press made that point," Lucas said.

"I took the post of companion to the client. In that guise I accompanied the lady to several affairs at which the suitor was also present, a garden party, a reception, a ball, that sort of thing. I knew the first time I saw him that Mason was a fraud, of course. The problem was proving it."

Lucas frowned. "Your talent allowed you to perceive his deception?"

Evangeline hesitated a beat too long before she answered. "In a manner of speaking. Naturally he never looked twice at me."

Lucas smiled. "Because you were just the grandmother's companion."

"It is amazing what a pair of spectacles, a gray wig and an unfashionable gown will do to alter a person's appearance," Beatrice said.

"I am well aware that most people see only what they expect to see," Lucas said. "Go on with your story, Miss Ames. I presume you informed your client that her suspicions were correct."

"Yes, and she tried to persuade the girl's parents to look more deeply into Mason's finances. But, as I said, he was very clever when it came to concealing his true nature. Lady Rutherford was beside herself with anxiety. So I set out to find proof."

Lucas realized he was fascinated, as if he were gazing into a crystal ball. "You obtained this evidence?"

"Yes." Evangeline moved one hand slightly. "That is my talent, you see. I am very, very good at finding things. It's just a knack, really, an occasionally useful knack, mind you. But it was nothing more than a parlor trick until I joined the Flint and Marsh Agency."

"I can see where it might be a useful talent in your career as an investigator," Lucas said.

"To make a long story short, I was able to locate some documents that made it plain that Mason was a fraud. The young lady's father was shocked and outraged. He immediately sent Mason packing. Lady Rutherford dismissed me quietly and paid her bill. That should have been the end of the matter and the conclusion of the case."

A whisper of dark knowing iced Lucas's senses. "But it was not the end of the matter, was it? Mason somehow discovered that you were the one who had exposed him."

Evangeline turned her head in sharp surprise. Clarissa and Beatrice were equally startled.

"How did you—?" Evangeline stopped. "Never mind. I should have known you would guess the truth. You are correct, of course. He must have watched me after I left Lady Rutherford's house. He set a trap. I received what I thought was a message from one of my father's old friends. Something to do with the discovery of some old shares of stock that Papa had owned that had suddenly become valuable. I immediately went around to the address that I had been given."

"The deserted building near the docks where Mason's body was later found," Lucas said. "You met him there."

Evangeline tightened her folded arms. "Yes."

Beatrice sighed.

Clarissa stirred. "You are very intuitive, Mr. Sebastian."

"Please continue, Miss Ames," Lucas said.

"When I arrived at the address I had been given I had to go up a steep flight of stairs. Mason had concealed himself in a room at the top of the landing. He put a knife to my throat."

"Just as Hobson attempted to do last night." Lucas suppressed the dark fury inside him with an act of will. "Damn the bastard to hell," he said very softly.

He became aware of the crystalline silence that had enveloped the terrace. All three women were staring at him, he realized. He reined in the unfocused energy that he was generating.

It was Clarissa who spoke first. "He came so close. It chills me even now to think about it."

"You may as well tell me the rest of the story, Evangeline," Lucas said.

Out of the corner of his eye he saw Beatrice and Clarissa exchange glances. It dawned on him that he had used Evangeline's first name. The small act of familiarity had not passed unnoticed. Under the circumstances, Evangeline's friends very likely found the implied intimacy more shocking than the strong language he had employed a moment earlier to describe Mason.

"Mason emerged from what I had assumed was an empty room," Evangeline said. Her voice was unnaturally even and far too steady. "He put his arm around my throat. The knife was in his other hand. He said he was going to punish me for what I had done. He said that if I did not cooperate in my own rape, he would kill me. I knew that he intended to kill me regardless so I concluded I had little to lose. We struggled. He lost his footing and tumbled down the stairs. He broke his neck. I fled the scene."

Without a word Clarissa touched Evangeline's arm in a small gesture of comfort. Beatrice moved closer to both of them.

Lucas stood very still. The darkness roared and thrashed within him. There was nothing he could do, he reminded himself. Mason was dead. But the black energy howled silently at the loss of prey. He concentrated on controlling his talent.

It took him a few seconds to realize that Evangeline, Clarissa and Beatrice were all watching him warily. He sensed their tension and knew that he was the source. He worked harder to restrain the prowling hunger.

"You are quite certain that Mason is dead?" he asked.

The question broke the unnatural stillness of the atmosphere. Evangeline relaxed first. Clarissa and Beatrice took deep breaths.

Now I've done it, Lucas thought. *I've terrified all three of them.*

But Evangeline, at least, did not seem fearful, just cautious.

"I'm absolutely positive that Douglas Mason died that day," she said. "There can be no doubt."

"Yet someone has gone to the trouble of hiring a man to kill you," Lucas concluded. "The only logical assumption is that there is a connection between the two incidents. But even if I am wrong, it is obvious that someone has some extremely unpleasant intentions toward you."

Clarissa's mouth tightened. "Mr. Sebastian is correct, Evie. Hobson came from the streets but we must assume this crime has its roots in the Rutherford affair. That is a world Flint and Marsh knows well. Beatrice and I will return to London tomorrow morning and inform our employers of what has happened."

"We shall commence an investigation immediately," Beatrice said. "Between Mr. Sebastian's efforts in the criminal underworld and our own knowledge of society, we will discover who is behind this."

"I will return to London with you," Evangeline said. She unfolded her arms and made to go back into the house. "We must return to the Cottage and start packing at once."

"I do not think that would be wise," Lucas said.

Evangeline and the others looked at him.

"Why not?" Evangeline said. "This is my affair. I know more of the particulars than anyone else. I can assist in the inquiries."

"Consider this from the point of view of whoever is after you," Lucas said patiently. "In the city you will be far more vulnerable than you are here in the country."

"Why do you say that?" she asked. "I am at home in the city. I know it well."

"Perhaps, but it appears that the villain is equally at home there. Otherwise he would not have known how to do business with the likes of a criminal such as Sharpy Hobson. What is more, he will find it easier to get close to you in an urban environment. Here in the country strangers wandering around the neighborhood are noticed."

"I would remind you, sir, that I was attacked here, not in London," Evangeline said.

"At night," Lucas pointed out. "When you were certain to be alone in the cottage. Sharpy Hobson did not try to kill you during the daytime because there was far too much risk that someone would have noticed him either coming to or going from the scene."

"Are you suggesting that Evangeline continue to stay alone in the cottage?" Clarissa asked. "Given what has occurred, I hardly think that is a sound idea."

"I agree," Lucas said. "Therefore, I suggest that she move here to Crystal Gardens."

There was a moment of dumbfounded astonishment. Then all three women started to speak at once.

"That is quite impossible," Evangeline said. "I realize that you feel a sense of responsibility for me because I am your tenant, and I do appreciate that. But surely you must see that I cannot move into this house."

"Let's not be hasty," Clarissa said. "You may be an experienced inquiry agent but you have never been faced with a situation like this."

"Clarissa is right," Beatrice said. "For heaven's sake, Evie, someone is hunting you. Don't you understand? Whoever this villain is, he clearly means to harm you, very likely murder you. You have been lucky enough to survive one attack, two if you count Mason's attempt to kill you. You may not be so fortunate the next time."

"Assuming there will be a next time," Evangeline said.

"There will be," Lucas said.

Evangeline must have sensed his certainty because she gave a resigned sigh.

"Yes," she said. "I suppose that is a distinct possibility."

"Listen to your friends," Lucas said. "You know they have the right of the matter."

"It's not that," Evangeline said. "It's just—"

"The proprieties of the situation," he said. "I understand. Believe it or not, I did consider the matter of your reputation, Evangeline. I have a sister, if you will recall. I am well aware that a lady cannot move into a house occupied by a single man and his male servant. This afternoon I sent a telegram to my aunt Florence. She will arrive on the noon train tomorrow. I can assure you that she will make an ideal chaperone."

Evangeline opened her mouth but she evidently could not think of what to say. Clarissa gave a small gasp of astonishment. Beatrice shook her head in disbelief.

Evangeline finally found her tongue. "It is obvious that you have given the problem considerable thought, sir."

"After I brought you back here last night I spent a great deal of time contemplating both you and your situation, Evangeline."

And he would spend even more time wondering why she was not telling him the whole truth about what had happened that day when Douglas Mason had died on the staircase.

Ten

The following morning Evangeline saw Clarissa and Beatrice off to London on the eight-fifteen train. As they stood together on the platform, Evangeline was aware of Lucas waiting a short distance away.

"You will be careful, won't you, Evie?" Clarissa asked for the hundredth time.

"Yes, of course," Evangeline said. "Try not to worry about me. I'm sure I will be perfectly safe with Mr. Sebastian. You and Beatrice must promise to keep me informed by telegram of anything that you discover, even the smallest clue."

"Yes," Clarissa said. "By the same token, let us know whatever news Mr. Sebastian turns up in the course of his inquiries."

"What he learns from his man, Stone, and Stone's associates on the streets may be of use to us in our investigations," Beatrice said.

"I will send word of whatever Stone has to report when he returns from London," Evangeline said.

Beatrice looked unhappy. "I do not like leaving you here alone, Evie. I feel there is a great risk in doing so."

Evangeline smiled. "You saw for yourself, Crystal Gardens is built like a fortress. I shall be safe there. Mr. Sebastian's aunt will arrive this afternoon. Her presence will take care of the proprieties and I am convinced that the gardens will provide wonderful material for my novel."

"The risk that Beatrice is concerned about is of a more personal nature, Evie," Clarissa said bluntly. "When Mr. Sebastian looks at you there is a certain energy in the atmosphere."

"I'm sure you're imagining things," Evangeline said quickly.

Clarissa shook her head. "No, Bea is right. You must be careful, Evie."

Evangeline looked at Beatrice and then turned back to Clarissa.

"Why?" she asked, careful to keep her voice very low. "Let us be blunt about the matter. We have discussed this before and we have agreed that none of us are likely to have a great many opportunities to experience passion. I thought we had all vowed to seize the chance if it came along."

"Yes, but this is different," Beatrice insisted.

"I don't see why," Evangeline said. "If Mr. Sebastian is interested in a romantic liaison, why should I be concerned so long as we are discreet? And one could hardly ask for a more discreet location for an affair than here in Little Dixby. For goodness' sake, after I return to London I will never see anyone in this place again."

Clarissa and Beatrice looked at each other, uncertain.

"When you put it like that," Beatrice said, "I cannot argue. I would just add that it is not your virtue I am worried about."

"I'm very glad to hear that," Evangeline said, "because I have decided that it is no longer worth worrying about, myself."

"It is your heart that concerns us," Beatrice concluded.

"Oh, for pity's sake," Evangeline said. "At my age I am hardly likely to fall in love. That is for romantic eighteen-year-olds. I promise you, I know what I'm doing."

"But what if you make the mistake of falling in love with him?" Clarissa asked. "We do not want to see you hurt, Evie."

Evangeline looked around to make certain that none of the other passengers had wandered within hearing distance and that Lucas was still safely beyond earshot.

"The thing is," she said, "I have come to realize that my lack of experience in such matters may be hindering my writing."

Beatrice's brows shot up. "Whatever are you talking about?"

"I have concluded that I must experience passion firsthand if I am to write about it in my novels. But clearly one does not want to tumble into bed with just any man purely for the sake of research. I would much prefer to study the subject with a gentleman to whom I am attracted and who finds me attractive."

Relief flashed in Beatrice's eyes. "Is that why you are contemplating an affair with Mr. Sebastian? For the sake of your writing?"

Evangeline flushed, very aware that Lucas was watching her. She knew he could not overhear them above the rumble of the steam engine and the general commotion on the platform, but she was horribly self-conscious nevertheless. One did not, after all, usually discuss such matters at a train station.

"I am trying to explain that there is no reason for the pair of you to worry about my heart," she said.

"If you're sure you know what you are doing," Clarissa said.

"I am absolutely positive," Evangeline said, lying through her teeth.

The whistle sounded, announcing the imminent departure of the train.

"Come, Clarissa, we must go aboard," Beatrice said. She looked at Evangeline. "Promise that you will be careful."

"I promise," Evangeline said.

She watched Clarissa and Beatrice go up the steps of the first-class car. Lucas came to stand beside her.

"You have interesting friends, Evangeline," he said.

"Yes," she said. "I am fortunate in that regard."

Fortunate, indeed, she thought, because regardless of whether or not she engaged in an affair with Lucas, she was probably going to lose her heart to him. She would need her friends very badly when she returned to London.

"LOOK AT THE WAY he is standing with our Evie," Beatrice said. She raised her senses and studied Evangeline and Lucas through the window as the train pulled away from the station. "It is as if she belongs to him in some fashion. I can see the heat in their auras. It is as if they were already lovers."

Clarissa looked at the pair on the platform. "One can sense the energy that surrounds them when they are together. For all Evie's talk of sacrificing her virtue for the sake of her writing, I fear she is wading into some very deep waters."

"He is going to break her heart."

"Most likely." Clarissa clasped her gloved hands. "But it can't be helped. The three of us have accepted that possibility. A woman of spirit can survive a broken heart."

"Evie has plenty of spirit."

"Yes," Clarissa said. "But on the positive side, I think that, even while he is in the process of breaking her heart, Mr. Sebastian will keep her safe."

"Assuming he is capable of protecting her."

Evangeline and Lucas disappeared. Clarissa sat back in the seat and looked at her friend.

"There is much we do not know about Mr. Sebastian but I am sure of one thing," she said. "He knows a thing or two about violence. Evie could not have a more capable bodyguard."

Eleven

"Extraordinary." Lucas stalked into the library and slung his coat over the back of one of the chairs. "I'm trying to save your neck and all you seem to care about is putting this monstrosity of a house in order."

Evangeline followed him into the room and shut the door firmly behind her.

"Not the entire house," she said. "Just this wing. It appears that most of the abbey has been closed up for years. And to make matters crystal clear, I do appreciate your efforts to protect me, sir. I just do not see any reason for us to live as if we were on a camping expedition in the American West."

There was a series of faint, muffled thuds. Lucas glanced up at the ceiling. Evangeline's daily maid, Molly, and an assortment of Molly's relations were working on the floor above. In addition to the furious activity overhead, it sounded as if a battle between ranks of armored knights were taking place in the kitchen. The clash and clang of iron pots and steel cutlery reverberated down the long hallway.

"I thought I explained to you that my uncle and his housekeeper were the only people in residence," Lucas said. "They had no need to keep more than a few rooms open."

"According to Molly, your uncle rarely employed anyone from the village. Mrs. Buckley was the only servant in the household. No wonder she shut most of the rooms."

"Uncle Chester did not entertain and he didn't encourage visitors," Lucas growled. "He was devoted to his research and he did not like interruptions. I am not in a mood for them, either. I need to stay focused on the problems at hand."

"I understand," Evangeline said. "But don't worry, the bulk of the heavy cleaning will not take more than a couple of days."

"A couple of *days*? Damnation, woman, I want everyone out of this house by the end of the day, is that clear?"

"Perfectly clear, sir," Evangeline said. Her tone was suddenly quite chilly.

I'm growling at her, Lucas thought.

Annoyed with his own bad temper, he went to the desk and turned up the lamp. Although the sun was shining outside and the curtains were open, the library was cloaked in deep shadows. The windows faced into the gardens. The glass was almost entirely covered by the thick mat of twisted, tangled vines. The heavy vegetation effectively cut off most of the light. It was the same with all of the windows on that side of the house.

Lucas angled himself onto the corner of the old desk, one foot braced on the floor, and looked at Evangeline. A deep prowling thrill of awareness whispered through him. He was growing accustomed to the sensation. It struck every time he was in Evangeline's presence. But while he had become familiar with the urgent ache of desire, he was not finding it any easier to suppress or ignore it. *And maybe that is why I am so short-tempered with her today.*

It wasn't her fault that having her so close aroused his senses and left him feeling edgy, he thought. He had convinced himself that he would feel more in control and more focused once he knew that she was safe within the walls of Crystal Gardens. Evidently he had miscalculated. Not that he'd had any choice. He would not have gotten any sleep at all if he had left her alone at night at the cottage while the unknown bastard in London plotted to kill her.

Evangeline looked quite different this afternoon than she had this morning. The fashionable blue walking dress, matching gloves and bonnet and the high-button boots she had worn to see her friends off at the station were gone. She was dressed for the grimy work she was overseeing in a severely plain housedress and an apron. Both were outdated and much too large, especially in the bosom. He wondered which of Molly's more buxom female relatives had loaned them to her. Evangeline's amber hair was tightly pinned beneath a white cap. The apron was stained with what looked like dirty water from a mop bucket and there were sooty smudges on her cheeks. She gripped a feather duster in one hand.

She looked altogether entrancing, he thought.

"From what I can tell, your uncle did not even bother to use the dining room," Evangeline said. "It appears he took his meals in the kitchen, if you can believe it."

"That is precisely what Stone, and I have been doing since we arrived," Lucas said. "The arrangement has worked quite well. Stone does the cooking. He finds it more efficient to eat in the kitchen."

"That is all very well for Stone, but you can hardly expect your aunt to dine in the kitchen and you certainly cannot tell her that she must sleep in a bedroom that has been shut up for years." Evangeline pointed one finger toward the ceiling. "There's an inch of dust on everything up there. Thankfully the furniture and carpets in all the rooms were well draped and your uncle's housekeeper appears to have taken care of the linens. Nevertheless, there is a great deal to be done before your aunt arrives later today. Thank goodness Molly's relatives were available to help out."

Lucas folded his arms. "Do you know, Evangeline, I thought I had accounted for even the smallest details when I concocted the plan to move you here, but it never occurred to me that you would insist on scrubbing the house from top to bottom."

"Only a few rooms, not the whole house." Evangeline walked halfway across the room and stopped. "You sound as if you are annoyed, sir. No one is asking you to pick up a mop bucket."

"Now why would I be annoyed? Perhaps because I have been forced to take refuge in this room while my house is turned upside down by strangers? Maybe because I had your safety in mind, not a spring-cleaning, when I brought you here today? Or do you think it might just possibly have to do with the fact that I don't like being confronted by someone wielding a broom every time I go around a corner? I'm trying to solve one murder and prevent another, yours, to be specific. Damn it, I don't have time to dodge people armed with mops and buckets."

"Ah, so that's it," she said calmly. "I thought so."

"You thought what?"

"I'm sure that you long ago learned to take a well-run household for granted. However, like a piano, a house must be properly tuned if it is to function smoothly and efficiently."

"This particular household does not have to function at all. With any luck we will not be here more than a few weeks at most."

"That is far too long to sleep on pallets, eat cold meals and go without a fire in the evenings. You are welcome to do all those things, if that is your preference, but as long as I am living here I must insist on the basic trappings of civilization. Those include, at a minimum, a clean kitchen, a well-stocked pantry, a proper bath and fresh linens on the beds. I'm sure your aunt will agree with me."

"No offense, Evangeline, but given your current predicament, I'm surprised you are so obsessed with maintaining such high standards."

She gave him a cool smile. "Where would we be without standards, Mr. Sebastian?"

"An excellent question. Never mind, it is obvious that I've lost this battle. What's done is done. Just see to it that none of Molly's relations wander outside beyond the terrace, is that clear?"

"Yes, of course, but I really don't think there will be a problem in that regard. The Gillinghams, like the rest of the good people of Little Dixby, are terrified of your gardens."

"With good reason," he said. "And speaking of the Gillinghams, I want every last member of the family gone by sundown. As I have explained, the gardens are more dangerous after dark."

"I understand. Trust me, no one except Molly seems to have any inclination to remain on the grounds at night. Molly had considerable difficulty persuading her relatives to come here to clean during the day. I had to promise that you would pay double the usual wages."

"Did you, indeed?" He raised a brow. "Spending my money rather freely, aren't you?"

"Nonsense, you know perfectly well that as the owner of Crystal Gardens you are expected to contribute to the local economy. Hiring workers is one way to do that."

"I will not argue the point."

Evangeline frowned. "Why are you so set against having any servants in the house at night? I'm sure I could persuade Molly to stay. She is much more adventuresome than her relatives."

"I plan to carry out my investigations of the gardens after dark, when the energy is at its height. The last thing I need is for young

Molly or one of her relatives to see me wandering around outside at midnight. There are already too many rumors of occult activities circulating about this place as it is."

"Oh, dear, I do see what you mean." Evangeline gave him a sympathetic smile. "But I'm afraid it may be too late to convince the locals that you are not eccentric like your uncle."

Lucas winced. "I was afraid of that."

"Is that why you happened to be outside the night before last when I arrived in the gardens at two in the morning? You were conducting your investigations?"

"Yes."

"I see. Well, that explains it then."

He frowned. "Explains what?"

"Clarissa and Beatrice asked me why you happened to be so conveniently at hand when I needed help. I was forced to tell them that I was so rattled at the time that I had neglected to inquire why you and Stone had more or less magically appeared, fully dressed in the gardens, at such a late hour."

"There is no great mystery involved. As I told you, we were outside already and heard you enter the grounds."

"Speaking of Stone, have you had any word from him yet?"

"He sent a telegram saying that he will be arriving on the same train as Aunt Florence. He indicated he had some news to report."

Excitement flashed across Evangeline's expressive face. "That sounds hopeful."

"We shall see."

Evangeline looked toward the vine-covered window and then turned back to him. "Please understand that I am grateful for your offer of protection, sir, but I cannot help but feel that I should be in London with my friends."

"No," he said.

"I do not like the idea of them conducting inquiries into this matter without me. After all, I am at the heart of this problem. I should at least be working on my own behalf. I feel utterly useless loitering about here in Little Dixby while the others are investigating."

"You are hardly loitering about. You have been working like a demented housekeeper all morning."

She exhaled a wistful little sigh. "Trying to keep busy, I suppose. The activity takes my mind off what may be happening in London."

He came up off the corner of the desk and walked toward her. "If it makes you feel any more useful, I can assure you that we are far more likely to obtain results with you here in the country."

"Why do you say that?" Her expression cleared. "Oh, I see. You think that the person who hired Hobson will make another attempt and that it will be easier to catch the villain if that attempt is made here in the country. Yes, I understand your logic. But what if you are wrong? What if the killer decides to simply wait me out? Sooner or later I will have to return to London. I cannot remain here forever. He must know that."

Lucas stopped in front of her. "I feel certain that we are dealing with a desperate individual, Evangeline. Desperate people are not good at waiting."

Take me, for example, he thought. *How much longer can I wait for you?*

He was growing more desperate for her by the hour. Something deep inside him had stirred and was now fully awake and hungry. The need would not be satiated until he had claimed Evangeline.

The realization that he wanted her so intensely should have alarmed him more than it did. Under most circumstances he was very good at waiting. He had long ago mastered the art of self-control. He had been forced to do so, not because of any outward compulsion but because of his need to control his talent.

He had comprehended early in life that if he did not master the psychical side of his nature, it would overwhelm him, just as it had the handful of others on the family tree who had been cursed with his kind of talent. He had vowed that he would be the one to break the cycle—had even dared to convince himself that he had achieved his goal.

Now Evangeline was making him question his self-assured assumptions. Her very energy was a potent drug to his senses. When he was around her he felt reckless in ways that he knew were dangerous, but he could not bring himself to keep his distance.

She looked at him, sharp interest in her eyes. "You do seem to know a great deal about how villains think. I know you said that you had studied the criminal mind, but how, exactly, did you go about that task?"

"It's a long, dull and rather complicated tale."

"In other words you are not going to tell me."

He smiled. "Perhaps someday."

She straightened her shoulders. "Very well, sir, you are entitled to your secrets. Can you at least tell me how you go about your consulting work for Scotland Yard?"

I'm doomed, he thought. In that moment he did not give a solitary damn. He embraced his fate. More specifically, he wanted to embrace Evangeline. He ached to pull her into his arms and drag her down onto the cushions of the old sofa. He wanted to feel the gentle swell of her breasts against his bare chest and grip her thighs in his hands. He wanted to drown his senses in her intoxicating energy and lose himself in her.

You're a fool, Sebastian, and sooner or later you will pay the price.

"I mentioned an acquaintance at the Yard," he said, selecting his words with great care.

"A detective inspector, yes."

"Donovan has some talent himself. He understands that psychical energy is real and that there are often traces of it at the scene of a crime. Criminals who possess a powerful talent are often difficult to catch."

"Yes, I can well imagine," Evangeline said.

"When Donovan concludes that he may be chasing one who possesses paranormal abilities, he sometimes asks me to give my opinion."

"I see." Her brow furrowed a little as she considered that information. "What can you tell about the criminal from the energy left at the scene?"

He had come this far, he might as well tell her a bit more—not the whole of it, but some of it. With her own strong talent she might at least comprehend the compulsion he felt to employ his other senses.

"Mostly I am called to investigate murder, Evangeline." He watched her steadily, steeling himself for the first hint of shock and revulsion. "That is usually the crime that lays down the most intense emotions."

"You *sense* the killer's emotions?"

"Yes. They can often tell me something of his or her personality and supply clues to the motive. Those are the kinds of facts that Donovan can use to conduct his investigations."

The brilliant energy in her eyes did alter, but not as he had anticipated. There was shock but no revulsion or horror. What he saw and sensed was comprehension—true recognition—of what he went through at the scene of a crime.

"You catch a glimpse of the killer's mind," Evangeline said softly.

"In a way, yes."

"I see." She shivered. "I hadn't realized."

Finish it, Sebastian.

"Murder is always a disturbingly intimate act, involving the darkest emotions," he said evenly.

"Your investigations must be dreadful experiences for you."

"I would like to tell you that is true," he said, "because it would at least make me appear decent in your eyes. But the reality is that I find the hunt a thrilling challenge. I find it satisfying, even gratifying in ways that no *decent* gentleman ought to acknowledge."

"I understand what you are saying," she whispered.

"Do you?"

"Yes, of course," she said. "The fact that you find the hunt for a killer deeply satisfying does not mean that you are not a decent, honorable man. It simply means that you are doing what you were born to do—find justice for the victims."

He smiled humorlessly. "You really were born to write romantic fiction, weren't you?"

Anger heated her eyes. "Do not mock me, sir. You hunt killers. That is noble work."

He shook his head. "You are very naive, Evangeline."

"I don't think so."

"It is not a wholesome thing, this business of hunting killers." He looked out into the dark gardens. "And those who kill by paranormal means are the worst of their kind."

"I do not doubt it."

"The intimacy of the experience is impossible to describe." Now that he had started he could not find the will to stop. He wanted her to know what it was like for him. He needed her to know. "In the case of a murder by paranormal means the killer's aura must resonate with that of the victim right up until the last beat of the heart. That is how it is done, you see. The killer must find the vulnerable currents in his victim's energy field and dampen them until the heart stops." He looked back at Evangeline. "He *experiences* the victim's death in the most intimate manner possible. What makes it a thousand times more dreadful is that such killers usually enjoy the kill. For some, it is an intoxicating drug, the ultimate sensation of power."

She clenched her fingers in her apron. "Yes."

He turned back to the vine-draped window. "It takes a great deal of energy to stop the heart of another person. That is why there are invariably traces of psychical residue left at the scene."

"And that is what you sense," she said quietly. "It must feel as if you are actually in the killer's mind at the moment when she inflicts death. How terrible that must be for you."

. . . *When she inflicts death*. An odd turn of phrase, he thought. Most people would have used the masculine pronoun when speaking generically of such matters.

"Fortunately, I am not summoned often to such murder scenes," he said. "Murder by paranormal means is rare for the simple reason that there are very few killers around endowed with enough talent to commit the act."

"I can only hope you are correct, but I fear there may be another reason why you are not summoned to such scenes very often." Evangeline sounded very thoughtful. "I suspect that in many cases the crimes go unnoticed. Death by paranormal means would be like the perfect poison, impossible to detect."

He turned around to face her. "That, Evangeline, is an excellent observation. You are correct."

She looked him in the eye. "You are summoned to a hard but honorable and, yes, decent calling, Lucas."

"Stop it." He took two strides toward her and clamped his hands around her shoulders. "Do not make me out a hero, Evangeline."

She stunned him with a knowing smile.

"You are too late, sir. I have already recast John Reynolds."

"Who the hell is John Reynolds?"

"He was supposed to be the villain of my story, but fortunately I realized in the nick of time that he is actually the hero. I am modeling him on you."

"Damn it, Evangeline—"

She put her fingertips on his lips to shush him. "To return to the business at hand—"

"*You* are the business at hand."

"I was referring to your deductions concerning the mental and emotional state of the person who hired Sharpy Hobson to murder me," she said. "He was nowhere on the scene last night. How can you conclude that he is desperate?"

Lucas called on his patience.

"It doesn't always require psychical talent to analyze a criminal's mind," he said evenly. "Common sense and logic work just as well, if not better. I can assure you that no one commissions a murder and sends the hired killer all the way to Little Dixby unless he is exceedingly determined. Failure combined with Hobson's disappearance will only make whoever is behind this more frantic. I sincerely hope that having lost his paid killer, the person who wants you dead will come after you himself. Then we will have him."

"I see. Yes, that makes sense." Evangeline raised her brow. "Not exactly a cheery thought, though. Nevertheless, I can't help wishing I could take a more active part in the investigation."

"You look like a child who has been told that her friends are going to the fair without her. I can see that you would rather be investigating, but it is for your own good that I insist you remain here in the country."

"'*For your own good*' are the four most irritating words in the English language."

A flicker of amusement whispered through him. "Yes, I have been told that on a number of occasions."

"By whom?"

"Beth and Tony, my brother and sister. As it happens, I'm inclined to agree. But do not think that you are being denied a useful role in this affair."

"Making certain that the furniture is dusted and the floors are mopped here at Crystal Gardens is a useful role?"

"I thought I made it clear," he said. "I do not like it but you are the bait we will use to draw the killer out into the open."

"Of course." Evangeline perked up immediately. "I hadn't thought of things in those terms. So I'm the bait, am I? That does sound at least somewhat useful."

He shook his head. "A very odd statement from a lady who in the past two weeks has confronted two killers, one of whom attacked her in her own bed."

She wrinkled her brow. "As I keep reminding everyone, I was not in the bed when the villain got to the bedroom."

"Yes, I know." He captured her chin on the edge of his hand. "You were already out of the window and running for the safety of a very dangerous garden. You are a remarkable woman, Evangeline Ames. I believe I have said something to that effect before."

She blushed and gave him a tremulous smile. "I find you equally remarkable, sir. Unique. You are in fact the ideal model for John—"

He clamped a hand across her mouth. "Do not, I beg you, mention your character's name again."

"Very well," she said.

His palm muffled the words. Cautiously he took his hand away from her lips. She watched him with her fascinating eyes and her mouth twitched a little as if she was suppressing a smile. But she did not say another word.

Energy shivered in the atmosphere between them, heating his blood. It would probably be a mistake to kiss her, he thought.

He kissed her.

It was meant to be a fleeting brush of his mouth against hers. He told himself that he would take only a small taste. But the flash of hot elation that slammed through him when his mouth closed over hers stunned his senses.

Evangeline went very still. He realized that for all her self-possessed ways, she was shocked by the kiss. Fair enough. So was he.

Evangeline made a soft, husky little sound and dropped the duster. She wrapped her arms around his neck and pressed herself against him. Her mouth opened a little beneath his. He locked her close against him and abandoned himself to the kiss.

Energy sang in the atmosphere, igniting all of his senses in ways he had never known. Delight, need and hunger swept through him. The kiss was not merely seductive and arousing, but shatteringly, breathtakingly intimate. He was a man of the world. He had been with other women but he had never experienced this sense of psychical and physical passion. It dazzled his senses.

He fitted his hands to Evangeline's waist. Mercifully she was not wearing a corset under the plain gown. He could feel the sleek, sensual shape of her waist and the curve of her hips through the heavy fabric. Her fingertips touched the back of his neck. Her scent clouded his mind.

The thud of a bucket hitting the floor on the other side of the door and the sound of voices in the hall shattered the spell. He raised his head and looked into Evangeline's slightly dazed eyes. She did not look outraged or fearful, he concluded. Astonished, perhaps. She was not the only one.

"Evangeline," he said. Very gently he scraped his knuckles across her flushed cheek. He stopped because he had no idea what to say next.

"You must excuse me, I want to see how things are getting on in the kitchen." She was as breathless as if she had just dashed up a flight of stairs. "Your aunt and Mr. Stone will be arriving soon."

"Have I offended you?"

"Don't be ridiculous, sir—Lucas. It is hardly the first time that I have been kissed."

"I see." He tucked a strand of her amber hair beneath the little cap. "I hope this kiss stood up to comparison."

"Yes, absolutely. It was quite thrilling. Indeed, I'm not sure that I will be able to find the words to describe it."

A chill crackled through him. He set his jaw. "If a description of what just happened between us shows up in your novel, I will not be pleased, Evangeline."

She blinked and then, to his chagrin, she gave him a teasing smile.

"As you do not read novels, sir, you will never know how I describe the kiss between my hero and heroine, will you?"

"Damn it, Evangeline—"

"You must excuse me. There is work to be done if I am to make certain that Molly and her relatives are out of here by sundown."

Evangeline bent down, seized the duster, yanked open the door before he could open it for her and whisked herself out into the hall, skirts flying behind her.

He stood in the doorway, watching until she disappeared around the corner. When she was gone he closed the door.

He crossed the room to the window and stood looking out into the gardens through a narrow crack created by the thick vines. It was, he thought, like peering through the bars of a monk's cell.

He was no monk but he knew then that, thanks to his talent, he had been living in a psychical version of a cell most of his life.

He was very certain that he had met the woman who held the key.

Twelve

Evangeline was with Molly, making up the bed in the room that was intended for Lucas's aunt, when she heard the rumble and clatter of carriage wheels. The windows on the side of the house where she and Molly were working faced the drive. She looked out and saw the village cab. Mayhew, the owner of the vehicle, was on the box. Stone sat beside him, his shaved head covered with a low-crowned cap.

"I believe Mrs. Hampton has arrived," Evangeline said.

"Good timing, if you ask me." Molly joined her at the window. "We are finished with her room."

They watched Stone vault easily down from the box to open the door of the carriage. He swept his hat off his head in a respectful manner. The sunlight danced on his hairless skull.

"Oh, my," Molly whispered. "Is that Mr. Sebastian's man?"

"Yes," Evangeline said. "His name is Stone."

"Oh, my," Molly said again. "Someone said that he was a big man. And he is, isn't he? Strong as an ox, I'll wager. But a good deal more handsome."

The feminine approval in her voice made Evangeline smile. She glanced to the side and saw that Molly was gazing down at Stone with rapt attention.

"Is this the first time you've seen him?" Evangeline asked.

"Yes, ma'am, but I heard some talk about him in the village."

"For what it's worth, I don't think Mr. Stone knows much about farming. He was raised in London."

"Fine by me," Molly said. "I've no interest in marrying a farmer. I know the life and I'd just as soon avoid it."

Evangeline laughed. "Good grief, listen to you. You haven't even met Mr. Stone and already you're talking about marriage."

"A girl has to think about such matters when she's still young enough to have some choice, miss. Wait too long and suddenly you're all alone in the world."

"Yes, I know."

Molly was horrified. "I beg your pardon, miss. I never meant to say that you're too old to marry—that is, you're not a spinster, Miss Ames."

"It's all right, Molly. We both know that's exactly what I am. In London women who reach my age and are still single rarely marry, not unless they have some money."

"It's no different here in the country. The farm goes to my brothers so I must make my own plans and they don't include becoming a farmer's wife. I am going to open a tea shop here in Little Dixby. It will be a very elegant shop with cakes and sandwiches that will be much finer than the poor-quality food Mrs. Collins serves in her tea shop. There will be lemonade and ices in the summer. With so many visitors coming to view and sketch the ruins these days, I know I could make it work."

Evangeline pondered her response. The last thing she wanted to do was quash Molly's dreams. Opening a tea shop would cost money and it was obvious that the Gillinghams did not have a great deal of it. But Molly had spirit and energy and intelligence. With luck, those attributes would prove to be sufficient to achieve her goals.

"That sounds like a fine plan," she said.

"Thank you, miss." Molly turned back to the view of the drive. "Look, that must be Mrs. Hampton. Very impressive, isn't she?"

Evangeline studied the woman Stone was assisting down from the carriage. Florence Hampton was tall for a woman. She carried herself with the authority and bearing of a ship's captain. A small gray velvet hat trimmed with white feathers was perched atop a tightly coiled chignon of silvered hair. She wore a fashionable dark gray carriage gown and gray leather walking boots. In one gray-gloved hand she gripped a silver-handled walking stick.

Evangeline started to turn away from the window. "I must go downstairs to greet her."

"Wait, miss, someone else is getting out of the carriage," Molly said.

Evangeline paused in the doorway. "Mrs. Hampton probably brought her personal maid. I'm not surprised. That's one of the reasons I thought it best to open up this entire floor."

"That is no maid, miss. It's another fine lady. Will you look at that pink and green gown? It's the most beautiful dress I've ever seen."

"What on earth?"

Evangeline hurried back to the window. She looked down and saw an attractive young blonde who looked to be nineteen or twenty stepping down from the carriage.

"You're right," Evangeline said. "Definitely not a maid."

"Look, there comes the lady's maid."

The last person to step down from the carriage was unmistakably in service. She was middle-aged and clearly experienced. She immediately took charge and began issuing instructions to Stone and the driver, who set about unloading the luggage.

"That makes three new people we shall have to feed," Molly said. "I'd best see about ordering more salmon. We'll be needing another two dozen eggs as well."

"Something tells me that Mr. Sebastian is in for a surprise," Evangeline said. "I'm quite certain he was not expecting anyone except his aunt. I'd better alert him."

She hurried down the back stairs because they were the closest to the library. But she was too late to warn Lucas of the change in his plans. She arrived in the doorway of the library just in time to see him greet the visitors.

"What the blazes is going on here?" he asked. His voice was stone cold. "I sent for you, Aunt Florence. I did not intend for you to arrive with Beth and your staff."

"Lovely to see you again, too, Lucas," Florence said. "To clarify, I did not bring my entire staff, just Rose. You could not possibly expect me to travel without her."

Florence had the sharp, stern face of a hawk and a voice to match. A formidable woman, Evangeline thought.

"Why are you here, Beth?" Lucas demanded. "You're supposed to be in London selecting a husband."

"I have made my decision," Beth said coolly. "I wish to marry Mr. Charles Rushton. When I told Mama, she declared him unsuitable. I have therefore decided that I shall not marry anyone at all."

Elizabeth Sebastian was an attractive young woman, Evangeline mused, and one endowed with a strong will reminiscent of her much older brother. It would be interesting to see how Lucas dealt with her.

"Rushton?" Lucas scowled. "Is that the archaeologist? The one who studies dead languages and has no money?"

"Mr. Rushton is a very brilliant gentleman," Beth said. "Furthermore, he comes from an eminently respectable family. On the one occasion that you had a conversation with him, you commented afterward that he seemed quite intelligent and well read."

"What of it? You know your mother as well as I do. Intelligence and respectability are not enough. She is right to be concerned about Rushton's finances. They are almost nonexistent."

"Charles doesn't need money," Beth declared.

"How convenient for him," Lucas said far too politely.

"I will have enough to support both of us. Mama says that I am entitled to a generous portion of the family money when I marry."

Florence snorted. "Don't be ridiculous, Beth. You cannot marry a penniless man like Rushton. You are an heiress. Your mother has every right to be wary of fortune hunters."

An angry flush stained Beth's cheeks. "Charles is not a fortune hunter."

"You can't be certain of that," Florence said. She caught sight of Evangeline in the doorway. Her expression tightened in disapproval. "We will have this conversation some other time, not in front of the servants."

Evangeline decided that was her cue. She glanced back over her shoulder at Molly who was hovering directly behind her. "Tea, Molly. A large pot."

"Yes, miss." Molly hurried off in the direction of the kitchen.

Evangeline moved into the room. "Good afternoon, ladies."

Florence and Beth looked at her.

"You must be the housekeeper," Florence said. "You seem rather young for the position, but I suppose my nephew did not have much choice out here in the country. Never mind. My maid, Rose, will tell you my requirements. But I'll warn you now that I am most particular about breakfast. I want it served in my bedroom at precisely eight o'clock. I trust you have coffee? I never drink tea in the mornings."

Thirteen

"I do apologize, again, for the misunderstanding, Miss Ames," Beth said.

Evangeline laughed. "No need. I was wearing an old dress, a dirt-stained apron and a cap and I was wielding a duster. Your aunt's conclusion was perfectly logical."

They were sitting together on the small terrace overlooking the vine-draped gazebo and the black water pond. Florence and her maid, Rose, had vanished upstairs. Lucas had retreated to the library.

"I must say you are being very gracious about it," Beth said. "Lucas, I fear, did not see the humor in the situation. He was furious because we had insulted you."

"I assure you, I was not insulted."

"I'm relieved to hear that but I suspect Lucas will be fuming about the incident for some time."

Lucas had been surprisingly annoyed by the small case of mistaken identity, Evangeline reflected.

"Your brother has a number of pressing issues to deal with," she said. "He is a trifle short-tempered at the moment."

"Which is so unlike him," Beth commented.

Evangeline blinked and then took another look at Beth. "You're not joking, are you?"

"Heavens no. I assure you, my brother is the most even-tempered man in the world. He can occasionally be very cool and reserved. He is also inclined to be stubborn and inflexible. But he rarely displays the edge of a temper. I can't recall the last time he actually looked and acted as irritated as he appears to be today."

"I'm afraid you and your aunt have overset his plans. He did not expect three new arrivals this afternoon."

"I insisted upon accompanying Aunt Florence and one can hardly blame her for bringing Rose," Beth said. "We were not at all sure what to expect in the way of staff here. We had no notion of what was going on. Lucas's telegram was terribly cryptic, which is absolutely typical of him. Something about needing a chaperone for a lady who would be staying at Crystal Gardens. It was quite mysterious and rather intriguing since the family was unaware that Lucas had any romantic attachment at all at the moment."

Alarm and something that might have been panic jolted through Evangeline. It was amusing to be mistaken for the housekeeper. It was another matter entirely to be mistaken for a potential bride.

"Heavens, is that what you and your aunt concluded?" she gasped. "That Lucas sent for Mrs. Hampton because he was romantically involved with me and wanted to protect my reputation?"

"It was the obvious conclusion," Beth said. She frowned. "Oh, dear, I've gone and ruined the surprise, haven't I? I do apologize yet again."

"You traveled here on the train with Mr. Stone. Didn't he explain things?"

Beth chuckled. "Stone rarely speaks to anyone except Lucas, and when he does engage in conversation he employs very short sentences, I assure you. In any event, he rode in the second-class car. Aunt Florence and I were in first class. We didn't even see him until we arrived in Little Dixby."

"I see. In that case I must tell you—"

"It was something of a shock, of course."

"What was a shock?"

"Learning that Lucas had developed a serious interest in a lady at long last. Until now he has shown no indication that he is even considering marriage."

"Beth, please, if I may interrupt—"

"He enjoys female companionship. Tony and I are certain of that much. But his liaisons have always been conducted in the most discreet manner imaginable. Generally speaking he favors independent widows who have even less interest in marriage than he does. Of course, we all knew that sooner or later he probably would marry."

"I understand." In spite of herself, Evangeline felt a definite sinking of her spirits. Naturally Lucas would someday wed. She was acquainted with the facts of life as they pertained to a gentleman in Lucas's world. "A man in your brother's position is expected to marry for the sake of the family name."

"Yes, although in Lucas's case, it is not, strictly speaking, a necessity. There is my twin brother, after all. We both recently turned nineteen. I think Mama had begun to hope that Lucas would choose not to marry, in which case the responsibility for carrying on the family name and overseeing the fortune would eventually fall to Tony. She would have liked that outcome very much. Indeed, it is her fondest dream."

"I see."

Beth's brows came together in a delicate frown. "My mother and Lucas have never enjoyed a cordial relationship, I'm sorry to say. They tolerate each other but that is all. Lucas was fifteen years old when his mother died. His father remarried almost immediately, of course."

"That is what most widowers do," Evangeline said. "Society expects it of them." The only reason her father had not remarried after her mother's death was he had been too busy with his inventions in his basement laboratory to notice that his wife of seventeen years was gone.

"Mama was barely eighteen at the time of her marriage," Beth explained, "only three years older than Lucas. I'm sure it must have been awkward for both of them. In addition, Lucas's psychical nature was just beginning to manifest itself. She confided in me that, as a young bride, she was quite frightened of him. He still makes her uneasy. Mama does not believe in the existence of the paranormal, you see. Even after all these years, I think she still suspects that Lucas is delusional and possibly quite dangerous."

"Good grief," Evangeline said. She paused. "I gather that you do not have a problem with your brother's talent?"

"No, not at all." Beth moved one hand in a graceful wave. "I find it fascinating. So does Tony. We have begged Lucas to allow us to study and test his psychical powers but he refuses. He has always been very generous and indulgent with us. Indeed, he was more of a father to Tony and me than our own father, who died when we were three years old. But on the matter of submitting to scientific experiments, Lucas has always stood firm."

Evangeline considered the problem briefly and shook her head. "I'm not sure it would even be possible to conduct tests on his talent. How does one prove the existence of paranormal energy? There are no instruments that can detect it."

"Not yet, but Tony is working on the problem. He and I are both very interested in the paranormal because of our relationship to Lucas. We would like to try some experiments if only to prove that his talents are genuine."

"What good would that do?"

Beth leaned forward in an earnest manner. "Tony and I think that if we can prove Lucas's abilities are real and that the paranormal is normal, so to speak, he would not have to conceal his talent from the world."

"I see."

Beth looked back toward the vine-covered house, making sure that no one was about to intrude on them. She lowered her voice. "Between you and me, I'm sure Lucas's talent explains why it has taken him so long to find himself a wife."

"Indeed?"

"Mama agrees with me but for different reasons. It is my theory that Lucas has never been fortunate enough to find a woman who could accept him and his talent. Mama, however, is convinced that respectable, well-bred ladies are afraid of him, even though they don't know why. She says their intuition warns them of what she insists on calling his eccentric nature and it makes them uneasy."

"I suspect that you and your mother are both right," Evangeline said, trying for a diplomatic approach. "Paranormal talents are not well understood."

"Yes, exactly, that is what Tony and I have been saying for years." Beth's face lit with enthusiasm. "How long have you been acquainted with my brother?"

"Only a few days," Evangeline admitted. "But I am aware that he possesses a very powerful gift."

"He does not think of it as a gift, I assure you." Beth's mouth tightened. "Nor does anyone else in the family."

"Why do you say that?"

"Lucas is not the first man in the Sebastian family to exhibit a strong psychical talent." Beth grimaced. "There are those who believe that the bloodline is somehow tainted by the paranormal, but they don't call it that, of course."

Evangeline tightened her fingers around the arm of her chair. "They call it madness."

"Yes. Take Uncle Chester, for example." Beth waved a hand to indicate the ominous gardens. "Mama and just about everyone else who knows about his experiments here at the Gardens are convinced that he was quite mad and that in the end he was the victim of his own creations."

"Are you aware," Evangeline said carefully, "that your brother believes that your uncle might have been murdered?"

"No, really?" Beth's elegant brows shot up. "That explains why he is staying here at the Gardens. Tony and I did wonder about that. But it makes perfect sense now."

"What do you mean?" Evangeline asked, wary now.

"When it comes to a sudden death, Lucas would naturally be inclined to assume the worst, at least until proven otherwise. It is his nature."

Evangeline frowned. "Yes, of course, because of his work for the police."

"Aha, so he has told you about that, has he?" Beth looked pleased. "How interesting. Wait until I inform Tony."

"Why do you find it so odd that Lucas mentioned his consulting work to me?"

Beth gave her a knowing look. "Because he tells very few people about it. Almost no one outside the family is aware that he consults on crimes of murder, let alone that he employs his talent when he does so. But I had a feeling that he might have told you."

"Why?"

"There is something about the way you and Lucas are when the two of you are in the same room together." Beth made another vague motion with one hand. "Some sort of awareness that only you and he share. It is as if you are communicating with each other in a silent, secret code. Sorry. I can't explain it. I just knew that Lucas had very likely told you about his police investigations. It is one of his most closely guarded secrets."

"I see." Evangeline smiled. "Perhaps you have some psychical talent yourself."

Beth laughed. "I wish that were true. Sadly, neither Tony nor I have displayed any hint of paranormal ability." She grew more serious again. "I do not know how Lucas can bring himself to do what he does. It is hard on him, I am certain of it. But when his acquaintance at Scotland Yard summons him, he always responds."

"Perhaps it is something he feels he must do," Evangeline said, choosing her words with care.

"I think that you are right. The crimes he is asked to investigate are almost always the most dreadful of murders. Mama says normal, respectable people do not get involved in such affairs. She has always feared that if Lucas's fascination with terrible crimes becomes known outside the family, it will prove a terrible embarrassment. She is afraid that Tony and I might no longer be received in polite society. Ha. As if Tony and I care a jot about the social world."

"What of Mr. Rushton?" Evangeline asked. "Would he be concerned if he learned about Lucas's true nature?"

"I'm sure he would not. Charles Rushton is a very modern-thinking man with a great interest in science and absolutely no interest in society. If and when he learns of Lucas's talents, I'm sure he will want to study Lucas, just as Tony and I hope to do."

"You haven't told Mr. Rushton about Lucas's abilities?"

"Heavens no." Beth winked. "It's a family secret, you see, which makes it all the more intriguing that you know of his talent. But, then, I suspect you have some psychical ability of your own."

"Yes," Evangeline said, "I do."

"I was sure of it. Tony and I have been convinced for some time now that Lucas would not fall in love until he found a woman who understood him, a woman who possessed some talent herself."

It was time to put things straight, Evangeline decided.

"You are mistaken," she said. "Your brother did not bring me here because he is contemplating marriage to me."

Beth looked skeptical. "Why, then?"

"Because someone is trying to murder me."

"Good heavens." Beth's shock was plain. "Are you serious?"

"Very serious." She decided to give Beth an edited version of events. "I rented Fern Gate Cottage for the month, you see. The night before last I was attacked by a man with a knife, a common street criminal who was hired by an unknown individual."

"I do not know what to say. This is absolutely horrible. I had no idea."

"I managed to flee here to the Gardens. Your brother saved me and now he feels a responsibility to protect me until we can find the person who hired the killer. That is why Stone traveled to London. To make inquiries on the streets."

Beth absorbed that information in a surprisingly thoughtful silence.

"Hmm," she said at last.

"What?" Evangeline asked, wary.

Beth's eyes gleamed with speculation. "I may lack psychical talent, Miss Ames, but even I can see that what Lucas feels for you goes far beyond a landlord's sense of responsibility for a tenant."

"I really don't think so."

"What happened to the man who attacked you with the knife?" Beth asked.

Evangeline cleared her throat and looked out toward the gazebo. "He ran off when Lucas appeared, straight into the gardens. Met with an accident."

"Ah, so the plants got him." Beth looked eminently satisfied. "Lucas did mention on one or two occasions that there were some interesting carnivorous hybrids developing here at Crystal Gardens. Tony and I expressed a desire to study them but Lucas said the foliage was becoming much too dangerous."

"Forgive me, Beth, but you seem to be taking these rather bizarre events in stride."

"It is my scientific nature, I suppose." Beth winked. "In addition, I have known Lucas all my life. He thinks he has hidden most of his secrets from Tony and me but we are his brother and sister. We know far more about him than he realizes."

Fourteen

What on earth is going on, Lucas?" Florence sailed across the library like a battleship coming into harbor and docked in one of the chairs. She thumped the silver-handled cane on the carpet. "I think I am entitled to some answers."

Lucas sat down behind his desk. "You spent over two hours on the train with Stone. I'm sure he gave you a summary of events."

"No, he did not. Stone was in the second-class car. He is not the most talkative of men, in any event. I doubt he would have told us a thing if he had been sitting directly across from us."

"Very well, in short, on the night before last Miss Ames was attacked at Fern Gate Cottage."

Florence stared at him, dumbfounded. "Good Lord."

"She survived the assault unhurt, as you can see, but I am keeping her here where she will be safe until I can track down the individual who hired the killer."

"Good Lord," Florence repeated. "This is . . . astonishing." She blinked and then contemplated him with her raptor gaze. "But why do you feel it is your responsibility to protect her? Surely this is a matter for the police."

"I thought I made it clear. Miss Ames was renting Fern Gate when she was attacked."

"Yes, I know." Florence frowned. "Oh, I see. You feel an obligation to protect her because she is a tenant? That's a bit of a stretch, isn't it?"

"The police are not bodyguards. There is no one else who can keep her safe until this affair is concluded."

"I should have known this situation would be a good deal more complicated than one would have assumed."

"I needed a chaperone here at the Gardens to provide an air of respectability."

"Yes, yes, I understand." Florence thumped the cane on the carpet a couple of times. "And to think that Beth and I rushed here today because we believed that you had found yourself a fiancée at long last."

"Aunt Florence—"

"Really, you are so unpredictable, Lucas. Have you any notion why someone would want to murder Miss Ames?"

"Not yet. I am hoping Stone will have some news for me. He traveled to London to make inquiries. I intend to talk to him as soon as I have finished explaining matters to you. Why the devil did you bring Beth with you?"

"I had no choice. When I mentioned your telegram and told her that I was packing to take the train here, she insisted on coming along. You know how stubborn she can be."

"Damn." But he was more resigned than angry. "She can be difficult when she fixes on an objective."

"Not unlike her older brother," Florence observed. "However, in this case I believe she was compelled only in part by her sense of curiosity. There were, I'm afraid, other forces at work."

"Judith."

"She has become obsessed with finding Beth a husband. Your sister is, after all, nineteen."

"In her dotage. How sad."

"That is not amusing," Florence shot back. "It would not be wise to wait much longer. Next season she will be facing stiff competition from the new crop of young ladies who will be making their debut."

"From the sound of things, Beth has already made her decision. I've met Charles Rushton. He's a solid young man. Intelligent, modern-thinking and clearly head over heels in love with Beth."

"He may be all those things, but he hasn't got a penny to his name," Florence said flatly. "Judith will never allow Beth to marry him. Let us return to the subject of Miss Ames."

"What about her?"

"I don't suppose she is related to Lord and Lady Ames of Pemberton Square?"

"I'm quite certain she is not. As far as Evangeline knows, she is alone in the world."

Florence frowned. "She has no family at all?"

"Evidently not."

"I see. How unfortunate. Well, judging by the gown she put on after she changed out of the housekeeper's dress and apron, she appears to have some income. Someone must have left her some money. Most young ladies facing her prospects end up as governesses or hired companions."

Lucas smiled. "Evangeline does, in fact, make her living as a paid companion."

"You are joking, of course. There is no way she could afford clothes like that, let alone the rent on the cottage, not on a companion's income."

"Evangeline is a very resourceful woman."

Too late he realized how Florence might interpret his words.

Her eyes widened in horror. "Lucas Sebastian, surely you are not trying to tell me that she is *that sort of female.* I cannot believe that you are so lost to common decency as to keep your mistress here under your own roof."

"Not another word, Florence." Lucas was on his feet, rage slashing through him. He flattened his hands on the desk. "I will allow no one, not even you, to insult Miss Ames. Is that clear?"

"Really, Lucas, this is a bit of an overreaction, don't you think? I apologize if I mistook the situation but surely you can understand—"

"Is that clear?" he repeated through set teeth. "If not, I will have Stone arrange to escort you into Little Dixby immediately. You can stay at an inn there until you take the train back to London tomorrow."

Florence stared at him, the handle of the cane gripped very tightly in one gloved hand. "Lucas, please, you are frightening me."

He closed his eyes and summoned his self-control. It took him a heartbeat or two but he got the fire inside extinguished. When he was certain he was in full command of himself he opened his eyes and sat down very deliberately.

"Perhaps it would be best if you went back to London, in any event," he said coldly. "Beth's presence in the household is sufficient to protect Miss Ames's reputation."

Florence said nothing for several seconds. Finally she cleared her throat.

"It won't be necessary to send me back to London," she said. "I will remain here. I apologize again for the misunderstanding."

"Please yourself," Lucas said. "But if you stay, it must be clearly understood that there will be no more insults, veiled or otherwise, of Miss Ames."

"You have made your wishes on that score quite clear." Florence got to her feet. "If you will excuse me, I will go upstairs to make certain that Rose has got matters under control. Your young housekeeper seems eager enough but she is obviously not very experienced."

Lucas stood again. He walked around the end of the desk, crossed the room and opened the door. Florence started past him. She paused and eyed him closely.

"Does Miss Ames really make her living as a hired companion?"

"Yes."

Florence frowned. "No offense, but she does not strike one as your average paid companion."

"No," Lucas said. "She is not your average companion."

"*Hmmph.* I expect one of her clients left her a handsome bequest. That would explain the expensive gown."

Florence sailed out the door into the hall. Lucas thought about calling her back and explaining that Evangeline was actually an investigator for a private inquiry agency and that she had started a second career as a writer of sensation novels. He decided against it. Sometimes it was simpler and more efficient to let others come up with their own explanations.

Fifteen

An hour later Evangeline marched into the library to confront Lucas. When she saw that he was propped against the desk, talking to Stone, she hesitated in the doorway. Both men looked grim.

"I see you are busy, Mr. Sebastian," she said. "I will come back later."

"It's all right," Lucas said. "Stone has concluded his report. It appears we know a little more than we did before. Stone has employed one of his old acquaintances on the street to continue making inquiries."

Evangeline looked at Stone. "Is that all?"

"No, Miss Ames," Stone said. He looked at Lucas and waited.

Lucas took over. "Stone did discover that Sharpy Hobson grew up on the streets, as we assumed. Evidently he was a member of a small gang of three boys who survived in the traditional way, picking pockets and fencing stolen goods. They later moved on to more violent crimes. However, at some point two of the young men disappeared from the streets. No one knows what happened to them."

"Everyone knows that the criminal underworld is a violent place," Evangeline said. "Perhaps the two boys met bad ends. It would not be surprising."

"Stone was able to discover that there are rumors that Hobson's two associates managed to better themselves. They were brothers and the other street boys considered them both very clever. Evidently they were smart enough to get themselves off the streets. Hobson, however, lacked the desire to move up in the world." Lucas folded his arms. "Word is he liked the kind of work he did on the streets."

Evangeline turned back to Stone. "You hope to find Sharpy Hobson's two former partners, don't you?"

"Yes, miss," Stone said.

"Why? What good will that do?"

Stone looked at Lucas, who answered the question.

"According to the rumors Stone picked up, Hobson recently accepted a commission for a job that required him to buy a train ticket. Someone asked him why he was leaving London. Hobson said that he was going to do a well-paid favor for one of his old partners."

Excitement splashed through Evangeline. She smiled at Stone. "Brilliant work, Mr. Stone. If your inquiry agent can find Hobson's old partner, we will have the man who hired him to kill me."

Stone turned a dull red. "We'll find him, Miss Ames."

She smiled. "Thank you, Mr. Stone. I am very grateful for your efforts."

Stone ducked his head and left the room with his usual cat-footed grace, closing the door quietly behind himself.

Lucas smiled. "I do believe you made Stone blush."

"Yes, well, I didn't mean to embarrass him. He really did do excellent work in London. At last we have a lead."

"So it seems. What was it you wanted to see me about?"

Evangeline straightened her shoulders. "I realize it is none of my affair, but I feel you were somewhat curt, to say the least, with your aunt and your sister. They have both gone to considerable trouble to rush here to Little Dixby to accommodate you. The least you could do is be polite to them."

"Having my sister show up as well as my aunt was not part of the plan. I am trying to conduct an investigation here, not host a house party."

"I understand. But that is no excuse for rudeness."

He groaned. "You don't know my family, Evangeline. Trust me when I tell you that my relations must be managed with a firm hand."

She lowered herself onto a chair. "And you are the one who manages them?"

"For my sins, yes." Lucas unfolded his arms, went behind the desk and sat down. "After my father died my grandfather saddled me with the task. It wasn't as if he had a great deal of choice. Tony was too young and my grandfather didn't much care for any of his nephews."

A whisper of knowing flitted through her. "But given a choice in the matter, you would have preferred to pursue another path in life."

"Few of us have a choice when it comes to our responsibilities. They are what they are."

"Yes," Evangeline said, "but not everyone accepts that."

"I do not live in a fantasy world, Evangeline. And as it happens, I am very good at making money."

She smiled. "I do not doubt that for a moment."

"It turns out that making sound investments has a great deal in common with hunting killers. Similar skills and talents are required."

"What skills and talents?" she asked.

He met her eyes. "The ability to find and predict patterns, a streak of ruthlessness and a strong will to survive."

"I will remember that in the event that I ever have enough money to invest."

Sixteen

The gardens glowed faintly in the night. The luminous light came from the vegetation and the darkly shimmering surfaces of the ponds.

Evangeline stood at the window of the bedroom, clad in her wrapper and slippers, and looked out over the eerie scene. The vines and creepers that draped the lower walls of the old house did not grow so thickly on the upper floors. It was as if the higher it climbed away from the source of its paranormal nourishment, the less the strange foliage flourished. She could not see the whole expanse of the gardens from her bedroom, but a far greater portion of the grounds was visible from her window than from any of the ground-floor windows.

A short time earlier she had sensed, rather that heard, Lucas moving past her door. She knew that he had gone downstairs and was no doubt going out into the gardens to start his investigations.

She had not been able to sleep in spite of the clean room and the fresh linens. The kiss in the library that afternoon had thrown her off balance. Once she found herself alone in her room she had not been able to stop thinking about it. The memory of it sent another shiver of icy-hot energy through her. It was not as if she had never been kissed, she reminded herself. But with Lucas everything was different.

A glary light appeared down below in the gardens. Lucas walked out of the house and onto the terrace. He was carrying a lantern and he was alone. Stone was also out there somewhere in the night, patrolling the great wall that surrounded the gardens. Earlier in the evening she had heard Lucas talking quietly to him, telling him to keep watch on the sleeping household. *To keep watch over me*, she thought.

Lucas paused on the terrace steps. The fiery illumination of the lantern briefly revealed the hard, determined cast of his face. In that moment the steel in the man was clearly marked. Evangeline caught her breath. This was a man who would do whatever he felt was necessary to fulfill what he considered to be his responsibilities. Now he was preparing to enter the dangerous green Hades that was the Night Garden to find the truth about his uncle's death.

She watched him go down the steps, circle the obsidian-dark pond and enter the gleaming, vine-draped gazebo. He stepped off the stone floor on the far side and disappeared almost immediately into the thick, luminous foliage.

She knew that he was going toward the entrance of the maze. For a moment or two she was able to track his progress by the occasional flashes of lantern light that sparked deep inside the greenery.

Abruptly the last sliver of light winked out. She suspected that Lucas had turned down the lamp, preferring to rely on his para-senses to navigate the darkest regions of the grounds.

She turned away from the window long enough to seize hold of the small dressing table chair. She carried the chair back to the window and settled down to wait for Lucas to emerge from his midnight quest. She knew that she would not sleep until he was safely back inside the house.

A weak flicker of light at the corner of her eye made her glance toward the Day Garden. She expected to see Stone making his rounds. The glow of a lantern turned down very low flickered into view near the high wall. The man who held the light was no more than a dark silhouette in the moonlight, but she could see at once that he was not nearly large enough to be Stone.

An intruder had entered the grounds.

She jumped to her feet and gripped the window ledge, waiting tensely for Stone to appear and confront the newcomer.

Seconds passed. A second man joined the first. The lantern winked out but there was enough moonlight to allow Evangeline to watch the two dark shadows. They were moving toward the gazebo and the entrance to the Night Garden.

There was no sign of Stone. Something was very wrong. Her intuition flared, sending her already jangled senses into a frenzy of alarm.

She struck a light and lit the bedside taper. Candlestick in hand, she went out into the hall and down the stairs. At the foot of the staircase she hurried toward the rooms near the kitchen that Stone had claimed. Perhaps he was not outside after all, she thought. Perhaps he was still asleep.

She rapped sharply on the door. There was no response.

"Mr. Stone," she called softly. "Mr. Stone, are you in there?"

Silence reverberated.

She wrapped one hand around the doorknob and twisted tentatively. The door opened easily. She hesitated. Both she and Stone would be equally horrified and dreadfully embarrassed if it transpired that he was still in bed.

There was nothing for it. She could not waste another moment. Holding the candlestick, she peeked around the edge of the door. The flickering light of the flame revealed the empty, still-made-up bed. Stone was gone.

Her first reaction was relief. He was outside in the garden after all. He would surely spot the intruders. He and Lucas were more than capable of taking care of themselves.

But what if Stone didn't realize that the two men were on the grounds?

The feeling that something very bad was about to happen out in the gardens got stronger and more disturbing.

She closed the door to Stone's room and went swiftly along the hall to the kitchen. Blowing out the candle, she opened the door and moved outside onto the terrace. The cool night air flirted with the hem of her wrapper.

The luminous gazebo loomed in the moonlight. She looked around for Stone and saw no sign of him. Searching for him would take precious time, but he was her best hope. Stone would know how to protect Lucas.

There was no alternative. She was very good at finding that which was lost. Tonight Stone had gone missing. She summoned up her psychical impressions of the man and focused her senses on the search.

When she looked down she saw a faint fog of energy stirring at her feet. She knew in a way she could not explain that this was what she was searching for, Stone's psychical trail.

Senses raised, she circled the pond, taking care not to look directly into the moonlight-silvered water. The disturbing energy tugged at her but she suppressed the urge to walk to the edge and look down into the depths.

She hurried along the path between two towering hedges, ignoring the massive night-blooming flowers that glowed on the green walls.

She exited the hedge path and rounded a wildly overgrown rosebush. The flowers radiated an iridescent light. She was in the Day Garden, not the more dangerous Night Garden, but her intuition told her it would be unwise to brush up against the small thorns or pause to inhale the scent.

She was concentrating so hard on staying well clear of the roses that she did not notice the pulsing energy currents on the ground until her slipper-clad foot collided with a large, immovable object. She tumbled and went down, landing hard on her hands and knees. Jolted, she gasped for breath. It took her a second or two to realize what she had tripped over.

"Stone."

She crouched and studied Stone's too-quiet form with all of her senses. The strong, steady currents of energy around him assured her that he was alive, but the subdued heat in some of the key wavelengths indicated that he was deeply, unnaturally asleep. Her fingers shook a little. Stone would never fall asleep on patrol and certainly not so profoundly.

She struggled to her knees and searched his body for signs of a wound. To her relief there were none, but something traumatic had happened to Stone. He lay face up in the moonlight, eyes closed. He did not stir.

"Mr. Stone," she whispered.

Gingerly she shook one massive shoulder. When she got no response, she pressed her fingertips to his throat. Relief surged through her when she discovered that his pulse was steady and strong. It was clear, however, that he was not going to be of any use to Lucas tonight.

There was no point wasting time going back into the house to summon Florence and Beth. Neither of them could go more than a few steps into the gardens at night without becoming disoriented.

She went back along the hedge path, past the rim of the pond, and pushed through a curtain of orchids and creepers to enter the gazebo. Her senses were flung wide, focusing on the new search. She had to find Lucas.

She had no difficulty detecting the cold, fiery energy of his prints on the glowing stone floor.

She stepped off the far edge of the gazebo and followed the trail of prints to the entrance of the maze. The iron gate stood open. The interior of the maze was lit with dark energy.

She moved cautiously into the luminous passageway formed by the living walls of plants. In her heightened state of perception she could have sworn that she heard the foliage breathing and whispering around her. She knew it was impossible but she could not shake the sensation that the maze was somehow aware of her presence.

She paused just inside the entrance, listening for footsteps or voices. But she heard nothing. The atmosphere was oddly hushed, as if the paranormal foliage absorbed and muffled normal sound.

The floor of the maze was composed of a carpet of oddly shaped green leaves. The ceiling and walls were formed by thick foliage that bristled with red-tipped thorns and blooms that resembled gaping mouths.

No moonlight penetrated the maze, but the paranormal luminescence of the leaves and the ominous flowers that studded the walls provided enough light to allow her to see where she was going.

She followed Lucas's hotly seething prints deeper into the labyrinth, following the trail through an impossibly complicated pattern of twists and turns. There was no sign of the intruders.

A short time later she arrived at yet another intersection and saw that Lucas had gone left. She followed, hurrying more quickly now. Her slippers made no sound on the green carpet.

She rounded the corner and crashed into Lucas. He clamped an arm around her waist and put a hand over her mouth before she could cry out in surprise.

"What the devil do you think you're doing?" he said into her ear.

At least she could hear him now that he was so close. She tried to respond but that proved impossible with his palm covering her lips.

"Mmmph," she said.

"Keep your voice down," he warned. "Sound doesn't carry far in here, but if they come close enough they will be able to hear us."

Cautiously he took his hand away from her mouth.

"You know about the two men who followed you in here?" she whispered.

"I sensed them a few minutes ago. What are you doing here?"

"I saw the men enter the garden. I came to warn you."

"You should have sent Stone."

The irritation in his voice was more than a little annoying.

"Believe it or not, I thought of that," she said coolly. "Unfortunately Mr. Stone is incapacitated."

"What?"

The question was asked in a rather absent manner. She realized that he was focused on listening for the intruders.

"Stone is lying unconscious out in the Day Garden," she said quietly.

"What?"

She had Lucas's full attention now, she thought.

"I think those two men must have done something to him," she added. "That is why I'm the one who came to warn you."

"Hush." Lucas put his hand across her mouth again. "Here they come. It didn't take them long to realize that they made a wrong turn a while ago."

She nodded to show that she understood the need for silence. Lucas freed her mouth. Now she could hear the ghostly voices in the maze. There was an eerie distortion, as if the men were conversing in another dimension. It was impossible to tell how close they were, let alone estimate their position in the labyrinth. But as they drew nearer, their words became more distinct.

"What if the guard is dead?" The voice was masculine and laced with anxiety. "There will be a search in the morning when he is found."

"There is nothing to be done about it now. If he is dead, it will no doubt appear that he died of a heart attack or a stroke."

The second man spoke with impatience and authority. He was the one in command.

Evangeline realized she had been expecting to hear the unpolished accents of street criminals. But the intruders sounded like respectable, educated men.

"I told you it was dangerous to come here tonight," the nervous man said.

"It is not as if we have a choice. It was one thing to wait a few days in hopes that Sebastian would not stay long. But they're saying in town that he has opened up an entire wing of the abbey. Damnation, three women and a lady's maid are now in residence. He has hired day help. It is obvious that he means to settle in for the summer."

"We can wait until he leaves," the anxious man said hopefully.

"We cannot take the risk. There is every indication that he is planning to make the gardens his country house and the locals are saying that he is as mad as his uncle. We must find the gold before he starts looking for it himself. At the rate he is accumulating houseguests and increasing staff, it will soon be impossible to obtain access to the grounds. We were fortunate to get past the guard tonight. There may not be another chance."

"I understand, but we must be away from here as soon as possible."

"I'm no more eager to remain here than you are, believe me."

"Nothing in these gardens is natural," the anxious man warned, "especially this maze."

"Be grateful," the other man said. "If not for the paranormal energy in the vicinity and Chester Sebastian's botanical experiments, the gold would likely have been found and removed long ago."

The pair would come around the corner in a few seconds. There was nowhere to hide, Evangeline realized. That left two options. They must either confront the intruders or flee deeper into the maze.

Lucas's hand closed around her upper arm. He drew her toward another intersection in the maze and around the corner.

"Stay here," he whispered into her ear. "Do not touch any of the foliage."

She nodded again to show that she understood the instructions.

He moved to the entrance of the passageway and stood just to the side of the opening. She knew then that he intended to confront the pair. Her intuition spiked.

"I do not think this is a good plan," she whispered.

He ignored her. Perhaps he had not heard her. There was no time to say anything else. The ghostly voices were coming closer.

She watched one of the intruders walk past the entrance. In the otherworldly illumination of the maze he was little more than a silhouette. She saw enough of him to note that he was tall and thin with a sharp, narrow profile. He held an oddly shaped miniature lantern in both hands, carrying it before him like an offering. The device emitted a narrow beam of paranormal light. The man's entire attention was on the beam. He did not even glance into the intersecting passage.

Lucas let him pass.

"Hold on." The nervous man sounded as if he were succumbing to panic. "If I lose sight of you I will never be able to find my way out of this damned maze."

"Then you'd best hurry, Horace," the other man said.

"I'm coming. I don't dare move quickly in here. The thorns, you know."

The one called Horace hurried past the opening. He was a head shorter than his companion and on the plump side. Light sparked on the lenses of the spectacles perched on his nose. He was evidently sweating profusely, because he kept dabbing at his brow with a handkerchief.

Lucas glided out into the passageway behind Horace. Evangeline felt the sudden heightening of ominous energy—not the foliage, she realized. Lucas was generating the dark currents of power. She shivered even though the waves of energy were not focused on her. Nightmares stirred in the atmosphere.

"What the bloody hell?" Horace's voice rose on a crescendo of fear. "Burton, wait, there's something here, something dreadful—"

The words were cut off abruptly. They were followed by a solid-sounding thud. Evangeline knew the intruder had just collapsed on the floor of the maze.

"Son of a bitch, you must be Sebastian." Burton's voice echoed eerily. "I had hoped to avoid using this again tonight, but you have left me no choice."

"I do not encourage treasure hunters," Lucas said. "I should let the gardens deal with you, but these damn plants don't need any more food. They are flourishing too well as it is."

A sharp, intense beam of green paranormal energy flashed in the passageway. Evangeline realized it was a more powerful version of the ray given off by the odd lantern device. Simultaneously, Lucas's nightmarish energy roiled the atmosphere.

Psychical fire exploded in the passage. Shock waves reverberated through the heavy foliage. There was a fearsome rattling of leaves and vines, as if long-quiet skeletons had awakened and started to dance.

Ghostly winds began to howl.

Evangeline ran to the entrance of the passage. A dark storm was coalescing, filling the green corridor.

"Lucas," she screamed. But her voice was lost in the thunder of the rapidly evolving paranormal tornado.

A dark figure moved through the churning gale. A second later Lucas emerged from the shrieking storm. He stumbled into the passage where she stood. A searing rainbow of energy enveloped him. *His aura,* she thought. He had somehow used it to protect himself from the violent forces. But she sensed that the psychical shield would cost him dearly. He had to be employing a vast amount of energy to maintain it.

"Lucas." She could not even hear her own voice above the crashing winds of power. She grabbed his arm. He stumbled and went down hard on one knee but managed to stagger back to his feet.

A small object rolled through the entrance behind him. She recognized the lantern that the intruder had carried. Without thinking about it, she stooped and seized the handle.

Lucas clamped his powerful fingers around her other hand and hauled her upright. His palm was warm against her skin. *Too warm,* she thought. At least the hot rainbow had disappeared.

"Run," he ordered.

She needed no urging. He drew her toward the far end of the passage and around the corner into another avenue of the maze. She thought she heard a panicked shout behind her but she did not turn around to look. She could feel the energy of the storm at her back now. The violent winds were being channeled into the intersecting corridors of the maze. The foliage writhed like nests of snakes on all sides.

Lucas pulled her swiftly around another intersection.

"Whatever you do, don't prick yourself on any of the red-tipped thorns," he said. His voice was harsh, as if it required enormous effort just to speak.

"Trust me, I'm doing my best to avoid touching anything in this place. What happened back there?"

"I think those two were using the energy of that lantern to navigate the maze. But when one of them turned it on me he did something to intensify the beam. It became a weapon. But there is a great deal of unstable energy in the atmosphere in here. I suspect that the lantern beam touched off the paranormal firestorm."

She realized that the hand he had wrapped around her wrist was growing warmer, as if a high fever were heating his blood.

"Lucas," she gasped, stumbling to keep up with him, "are you all right?"

"We can't go out through the gate because of the storm. We need to get to the baths in the Night Garden."

"You were injured in the explosion, weren't you? I can feel the fever in you. Tell me what is happening, I beg you."

"I don't know what happened back there," he said. "It felt as if my psychical senses were being seared." He shook his head and blinked several times, as if trying to focus.

"We must get you back to the house."

"Not tonight," he said.

"What do you mean?"

"We're trapped in here until morning. I told you, that storm is blocking the only exit. Given the amount of energy in this place and the fact that the forces in here are so powerful at night, it will take hours for things to calm sufficiently to allow us safe passage."

"Dear heaven."

He yanked her around another intersection. The lantern she was carrying rattled.

"What is that sound?" Lucas asked.

"The weapon that man used against you. He dropped it and it rolled into the passage where I was waiting for you. I thought we might want to examine it."

"What the devil?" Lucas glanced down at the lantern. "Have a care with that thing. We don't know how it works or what it can do."

"Of course I'll be careful," she said very coolly. "I'm not a fool, Lucas. I grew up in the household of an inventor. I am always cautious around unknown devices."

Lucas's jaw tightened. He plunged down another narrow passage, hauling her with him. "My apologies. I will, indeed, want to take a closer look at it after we get out of here."

"No apologies are necessary. I do comprehend your concern. And I realize that you are not accustomed to working with a woman who is also a trained investigator."

His mouth twisted into a grim smile. "I appreciate your making allowances for me."

"Do you have any idea who those two men were?"

"No. Never met either of them. Treasure hunters from the sound of it. I think it's safe to assume that they were involved in my uncle's death."

Evangeline was about to ask more questions, but at that moment they rounded one last corner and emerged into the jungle that was the Night Garden.

"Good heavens," she whispered. "This is an incredible place."

The thick canopy of massive leaves and twisted branches shut out all traces of moonlight, but the garden glittered with iridescent energy. The glow was much brighter than the midnight light of the Day Garden. The atmosphere was warmer, as well. But she knew intuitively that it was the surging, crashing waves of paranormal power that made this section of the grounds so dangerous.

The energy tides ebbed and flowed around her in unpredictable currents. She sensed that some of the rivers of power could drag a person under, drawing the victim down into the paranormal depths that waited just beneath consciousness.

A pool of dreams waited there in the darkness, dreams of wondrous worlds and endless pleasures, dreams in which she would know power and passion beyond anything she had ever imagined.

"Evangeline." Lucas gave her a quick shake. "Wake up."

"But I am awake." Startled, she blinked a couple of times and pushed her jangled senses higher. The subtle trancelike sensation faded. She caught a faint, delicate whiff of a compelling, exotic perfume. "Do you smell something?"

"The Dream Rose." Lucas urged her through a cluster of radiant ferns. "One of my uncle's last creations. He hoped to produce a variety that could be used to induce sleep. Like so many of the rest of his experiments, it went awry. Try not to breathe deeply until we are inside the bathhouse."

"What can possibly be so terrible about a flower that smells so good?"

"From a distance it exerts an alluring effect on the senses. As you get closer, the effect becomes hypnotic, irresistible. Even one bloom releases enough perfume to put a person into a trance. But it is not a true sleep. One dreams, however, and the dreams are nightmares."

"You sound as though you have experienced the effects of the blooms."

"I did on one occasion. Believe me when I tell you that once was more than enough."

"I'll take your word for it." She looked down and saw a cluster of spectacularly luminous blooms. "Look at those flowers. They are incredible."

"Whatever you do, don't touch them, especially not now, not at night."

"They are dangerous, too?"

"Everything in this place is dangerous. I thought I'd made that clear. That particular plant is carnivorous. The young ones eat insects. The larger version attracts and kills mice and rats."

"Good heavens."

"Another botanical experiment that was supposed to have a practical application." Lucas was sweating now. He scrubbed the perspiration from his eyes. "My uncle was convinced that a few pots of the plants placed inside a house would control vermin. His theory was correct. Has it escaped your attention that even though a large portion of the house has been closed for years, there are no mice or spiderwebs?"

She shuddered. "Now that you mention it, I was very relieved to discover that there were no signs of vermin in the kitchen and the pantry. I attributed it to the diligence of the missing housekeeper."

"The vermin are drawn into this garden by the perfume. Very few escape."

"I have met any number of housekeepers and wives who would pay dearly to acquire such plants. But surely you are not saying that the rat-eating plants would devour a living person?"

"No, but the flowers produce a toxic substance that is powerful enough to produce a chemical burn of sorts. The injury takes days to heal." Lucas shook his head, as if to clear it. "Not much farther now. The entrance to the bath is just ahead. Once we are inside you will be safe while I sleep off this confounded fever."

She tore her attention away from a beautiful array of darkly glittering orchids and saw the entrance to the ancient bathhouse. Her heart sank at the sudden realization that the interior seemed to be filled with a dense, endless night.

"Lucas, I know you mean to protect me from the dangers of the garden," she said, "but I must tell you that I cannot endure the thought of spending the rest of the night in that place. Not without a lantern."

She looked down at the small lanternlike device in her hand. "I do not think this will do. I would rather take my chances out here where there is some light."

"The unlit entrance is deceptive," he said. "You will see what I mean once we are inside. In any event, I cannot allow you to stay out here. Brace yourself. Going through the gate can be disturbing. My uncle designed it to keep out the animals and insects that do manage to survive the garden. He also intended it to discourage any intruders who might get this far."

"That pair we encountered tonight certainly seemed to know their way around these gardens," Evangeline said.

"Yes," Lucas said in a flat voice. "They did."

Reluctantly she followed him through the dark opening. It was like walking through a small storm of energy, albeit a much less intense version of what was sweeping through the maze. The hair lifted on the back of her neck. Her senses reacted as if they had been struck by several tiny shocks of electricity.

She sucked in a quick breath. Lucas tightened his grip on her hand.

"One more step and we're in," he promised.

And then they were on the other side of the gate. Lucas stopped and released Evangeline's wrist. She looked around in wonder.

The interior of the room in which they stood was gently lit by a crystal-clear pool of water. It took her a moment to realize that it was the energy in the water that illuminated the vaulted chamber. Unlike the wildly unsettling currents out in the gardens, however, this was a gentle, soothing energy. Wisps of steamy vapor rose from the surface of the ancient bath, filling the space with a pleasant, humid warmth.

"This is astonishing," she said, enchanted. "Beautiful. And it feels very good in here. Please don't tell me that the sensation is deceptive and that it conceals some form of dangerous energy."

"The pool in this room and the one in the next chamber are safe. It is the third that is dangerous."

She looked down a passageway into the next chamber and saw another glowing pool. "I do not see a third pool, just two."

"The third bath is in a chamber off the second one. But Chester secured it with a locked door. Although he never expected an intruder to get this far, he took extra precautions with that pool."

"What is so dangerous about the bath in the third chamber?"

"I will explain some other time." He led the way down the passage into the second pool chamber. "Not tonight. The fever has exhausted me. I was barely able to make it through the gate a moment ago. I cannot put off sleep much longer."

She was getting more worried by the second. "I understand."

She followed him into the second chamber and examined him in the fluctuating currents of paranormal light. His hard face was drawn taut with the effort he was exerting to stay on his feet. Tight, grim lines etched the corners of his feverish eyes. She touched his arm, opened her senses and focused on his aura. Her breath caught in her throat when she saw the raging heat in the darker wavelengths.

"This fever," she said. "It appears to be of a paranormal nature."

"I am well aware of that." He yanked off his coat and tossed it down onto a stone bench. "So bloody hot. Feels like I'm on fire."

"Perhaps you could cool off in one of the pools?"

"No." He ripped at the buttons of his shirt with uncharacteristically clumsy fingers. "Too warm. I can't take any more heat."

He got his shirt open halfway down his chest and abandoned the task. He started unsteadily toward a small alcove.

She trailed after him. "Wait. Where are you going?"

He paused, one hand clenched around the edge of the alcove opening. His knuckles were white.

"I'm going to use the privy," he said evenly. "As it happens, the Romans were excellent plumbers."

She was mortified. "Oh, right."

She turned away very quickly.

He emerged a short time later, scooped up his coat and sat down on the stone floor, his back against a wall. He looked at her with his hot eyes.

"You were able to follow those two men and me into the maze," he said. "I assume that ability is an aspect of your talent?"

"Actually I followed you. If I need to find something badly enough and if I focus, I can usually locate it."

"In other words you could find your way back out of the maze?"

"Yes, I think so, but why are you asking?"

"If I do not awaken from this fever, you will need to make your own way out."

"For heaven's sake, do not say such a thing."

"If I do not awaken by dawn," he continued with grim determination, "or if I do not seem to be myself when I do wake up, you will have to go back to the house alone. The Night Garden will be much safer in the morning, but be careful regardless. As soon as you get out of the maze, find Stone. Tell him what happened. He will keep you safe."

"Lucas, are you trying to warn me that you don't expect to recover from this fever?"

"Damned if I know." He wiped his face with one hand. "I've been burned before but never like this."

She went toward him slowly. "I'm not at all certain, but it's possible that I might be able to help you."

"There is nothing anyone can do," he said quietly. "With luck I will sleep it off. Promise me that whatever happens, you will not leave this place until dawn."

"I give you my word. But, please, let me try to lower the fever."

He surprised her with a faint, wicked smile. "My dear Miss Ames, don't you know that I have been burning since the moment I met you?"

"This is not a good sign," she said. "Your fever is so high that it is causing you to hallucinate."

"I have been enjoying this particular hallucination." He stopped smiling. "But unfortunately, it appears to be fading. I seem to be slipping into some sort of night. I must rest."

He crumpled his coat into a makeshift pillow and more or less collapsed onto his side. He looked up at her, squinting a little as if he was having trouble perceiving her.

"I am sorry, Evangeline," he said. "I meant to protect you but I have placed you in danger. This is my fault and I shall die with that knowledge on my conscience."

"Lucas, no." She crouched beside him and gripped his hand. "I will not allow you to talk like that."

His fingers tightened convulsively around hers. "I have complete confidence in you, Miss Ames. You are the most resourceful woman I have ever met. You will find your way out of here. And Stone will protect you from whoever is trying to kill you."

Lucas closed his eyes. She sensed that he was plummeting downward into a deep sleep. He needed rest but she knew that she could not allow him to fall too far into the darkness. The heat was coming off of him in violent currents. His hand was hot in hers.

She had only a vague, intuitive notion of what had to be done. The one thing she was absolutely certain of was that she had to be so very careful. The physical connection between them would enhance the effects of whatever she tried to do to cool the fever. If she went too far she would kill Lucas as surely as the fire that blazed in his aura.

She opened her senses cautiously and started to focus her talent on the overheated currents. The shock of the flashing energy pulsing through Lucas was so intense it was all she could do to hang on to his hand. For a few seconds it suppressed the breath in her lungs. She feared it might actually stop her heart.

She fought back instinctively, dampening the flaming wavelengths with her own soothing, cooling energy. She worked cautiously, afraid of going too far. The searing memory of what she had done the last time she had used her talent in this fashion was still very vivid.

But Lucas was not Douglas Mason. His energy field was far more powerful. Perhaps it was his talent that made him psychically strong, she thought, or maybe it was the self-mastery he had developed to control the paranormal side of his nature. Whatever the explanation, her fear of accidentally freezing Lucas's aura began to fade. It would take a great deal of power to extinguish the strong currents of energy that he radiated, she thought, perhaps even more than she could exert.

The realization that she was not going to hurt him filled her with an exhilarating sense of relief. She grew bolder, increasing the intensity and tightening the focus. The fever began to subside. Lucas grew cooler to the touch. The hand she gripped was no longer burning hot. Lucas was no longer sweating profusely.

The seconds ticked past into an eternity.

After a time she was satisfied that the energy of his aura once again felt normal and stable. Lucas slept but he no longer hovered on the abyss of what could have been a permanent state of unconsciousness or even death. He was exhausted but he was now getting the healing rest that he so desperately needed.

She sat on the stone floor, gripping his hand and monitoring his aura to make certain that the fever showed no signs of spiking again. After a while, satisfied that he was no longer in danger, she got to her feet.

She walked to the edge of the second pool and looked down into the luminous waters. The ancient stone floor of the bath, the steps and the submerged benches could be clearly seen. The subtle, invigorating energy stirred her senses.

She kicked off her damp slippers, hiked up the hem of her nightgown and wrapper and crouched at the edge of the pool. Tentatively she dipped her fingers into the water. A delightful sensation of well-being tingled through her.

She sat down on the stone rim, dangled her feet in the pleasantly warm water and thought about what had happened when she had calmed the fever in Lucas.

Ever since the day she had encountered Douglas Mason on the staircase, she had lived with the terrible knowledge that she could kill with a touch.

But thanks to Lucas, she now knew that she could also heal.

Seventeen

He came awake with the sure and certain knowledge that the unexpected had occurred. He was still alive.

Not only alive, Lucas thought, but he was feeling strong and vital once more. The fever was no longer inflaming his senses. By some incredible stroke of good fortune, he had survived the devastating burn.

Memory slammed back and with it his last fevered vision of Evangeline kneeling beside him, holding his hand. He remembered the gentle heat in her eyes.

It was Evangeline who had saved him, not fortune. He knew that as surely as he knew that he was again in full possession and control of his talent. He had no notion of how she had calmed the psychical burning inside him, but there could be no doubt that she was the reason he still had all of his senses—the reason that he was still among the living.

He opened his eyes and turned his head, searching for her. She was sitting on the edge of the pool, her arms braced behind her, feet gliding slowly back and forth in the water. The chintz wrapper and nightgown were crumpled up above her knees. Her hair cascaded down her back. She seemed lost in contemplation of the glowing bath, a nymph at her forest pond. He was half afraid to speak for fear of startling her out of some magical dream.

And quite suddenly he was not merely present among the living, he was fully, achingly, ravenously aroused.

He sat up slowly, letting the rustling of his clothing announce that he was awake.

She turned her head very quickly, smiling with relief and, he thought, another emotion as well. He raised his talent a little and could have sworn that he saw the heat of sexual desire in her eyes. A fantasy, he thought, brought on by his hunger for her.

"How do you feel?" she asked.

"Much better than I expected, given what happened back in the maze." He thought about it. "I feel very good."

"I'm glad to hear that."

He got to his feet, trying to come up with something intelligent to say. He became aware of the fact that his shirtfront was hanging open. Evangeline was gazing at his bare chest with great interest. He also noticed that she had made no effort to draw her feet out of the water or cover her knees with her clothing.

He reached into the pocket of his trousers and took out his watch. The hands were frozen on midnight, about the time he had entered the maze. He closed the case.

"My watch has stopped," he said. "The energy in these gardens is so strong that it often affects delicate mechanisms like clocks. I don't suppose you have any idea of how long I was asleep?"

"Sorry, no. A couple of hours, perhaps." She splashed her feet in the water and leaned back on her hands, smiling a mysterious smile. "I have noticed that the currents from the waters tend to lull one into a very relaxed state of mind. Time doesn't seem to mean very much in here."

"No." He looked down the stone passage toward the entrance of the baths. The energy gate was still pitch-black. There was no sign of light on the far side. "It can't be more than another few hours until dawn."

"No." She raised her eyes from his chest to his face and studied him as though he were some rare and intriguing curiosity.

His fingers did not seem to be working properly so he stopped trying to refasten his shirt.

"Evangeline, we must talk," he said.

"Now?" she asked with a wistful expression.

"It will be dawn soon."

She splashed her feet a little in the water. "Yes, you have already mentioned the time." She raised one hand in a restless gesture and lifted her hair away from the back of her neck. "It is rather warm in here, isn't it?"

He was riveted by the delicate, vulnerable curve of her neck. "The pools give off a great deal of heat," he said. His voice sounded a little thick, even to his own ears.

"And energy," she said, smiling as if at some secret joke.

"Yes." He put the coat down on the stone floor and walked slowly toward the pool where she sat. "Energy, too."

"It is quite exhilarating. And sparkly. Like champagne, although I admit I have not had an opportunity to drink a great deal of champagne. It's quite expensive. Generally speaking, paid companions stick to sherry. Although I have met one or two who have gone on to gin. Most professional companions endure a great deal of boredom, you see."

"But not you."

"No, not me. I am rarely bored. I enjoy my work for the agency and when I am alone I have my writing. It is an endless source of fascination. But I will admit that there are times when I have felt very much alone."

He was torn between frustration and amusement. "I think that at the moment you are feeling a little tipsy as well, are you not?"

She giggled. "Yes, as a matter of fact. But I assure you, my head is quite clear."

"Is it?"

"Oh, yes, in fact I don't believe that I have ever been able to perceive things so clearly in my life. I feel free, Lucas, and it is because of you."

"I set you free?"

"You did, indeed."

"How did I do that?"

She tipped her head to one side. "It's complicated. I really do not want to go into it just now."

"How long have you been dangling your feet in the waters of that pool?"

"I have no idea." She kicked her feet again. "My turn to ask you a question. How many women have you brought here to this bathhouse, Mr. Sebastian?"

He smiled. She was flirting with him and he was enjoying it. A dangerous pastime, he thought. But what the hell, the die had been cast. Evangeline would soon be his. She knew that as surely as he did. That was why she was practicing her feminine wiles on him—why she said she felt free. The exhilarating aspect of the whole thing was that he, too, felt as if he had been released from his own self-imposed prison.

They were made for each other, he thought. Perhaps it was, indeed, fortune or fate or karma that had led them both to this moment. He did not believe in any of those supernatural forces, and what had transpired tonight out in the gardens was not the method he had intended to employ to win her. But what was done, was done. Their future was sealed by the events of the night.

"I have never invited any other lady into the Night Gardens, let alone this bathhouse," he said. He hunkered down on his heels at the side of the pool. "I'll tell you a secret."

"Good." She giggled. "I adore secrets."

"The reason I never invited anyone to join me in this pool is because I have never encountered a woman I believed could enjoy the experience with me, a lady of talent."

"What do you mean?"

"It is clear from the old records that the pool waters have the most pronounced effect upon people like us, Evangeline."

"Those with paranormal abilities?"

"The stronger the talent, the more powerful the effect."

"I suppose that makes sense." She leaned over and trailed her fingers through the water. "If the properties of the spring are paranormal in nature, it stands to reason that those who possess strong psychical abilities will be more affected than those who do not simply because they will be able to sense the energy more acutely."

He smiled, savoring the anticipation. "That was always my uncle's theory."

Evangeline gave him another tantalizing smile and looked at him from beneath her lashes. "If your uncle was correct, then a romantic liaison conducted in this chamber would most probably be experienced in a very intense manner by two people who possessed strong psychical abilities."

This was, indeed, the best of all possible worlds, Lucas concluded. Then again, perhaps he had not recovered from the paranormal fever after all. Maybe he was hallucinating. Whatever the case, his future wife was attempting to seduce him. If this was a dream, he could only hope that he would never awaken.

"That would be the obvious assumption," he said. "Shall I tell you another secret?"

"Yes, please."

"My uncle tested that assumption with his housekeeper, Mrs. Buckley. You see, she had a measure of talent, too."

"What?" Evangeline's eyes widened. Then she gave a lilting laugh. "Never say that your uncle and Mrs. Buckley were lovers."

"For years. It was, of course, a family secret. But I suspect they spent a number of nights in this place."

"Well, well, well." Evangeline leaned forward and swished her hand through the water again. "But what about you, sir? I cannot believe that you never found a lady you wanted to bring to this place."

He reached out and brushed a wave of silken hair off her shoulder. "You are the first."

"Excellent." Evangeline smiled somewhat smugly and winked. "I am delighted to hear that."

She splashed some water onto the side of the pool. The droplets sparkled like liquid diamonds. They dampened his boots and the cuffs of his trousers.

"You are bathing in dangerous waters, Miss Ames," he warned softly. "Quite literally."

"I thought that we were on a first-name basis, Lucas."

He smiled. "Thank you for reminding me, Evangeline."

"I believe that life was meant to be experienced with all the senses."

"Do you?"

"Most definitely."

She hoisted the skirts of the wrapper and nightgown and stood up on one of the submerged benches. The water came midway up to her elegantly curved calves. She put out a hand and regarded him with an expectant air.

He straightened slowly and took her hand. The instant her fingers touched his a euphoric flash of knowing swept through him. It was, he decided, as if all the forces of the universe had conspired to make this night, this moment, happen.

Evangeline stepped daintily out of the pool, released his hand and shook out her clothing. The folds of her nightclothes fell about her wet ankles. He wondered if she realized that the sash of her wrapper had come undone.

"I think I know the real reason why you have never brought a lover with you to this place," she said.

"Is that so?" He traced the curve of her jaw with one finger. "What is the real reason?"

"In a word, control." Smiling, she stepped away from him and pirouetted in a small circle. She stopped and faced him once more. "You do not like the notion of losing your own self-control, and you are far too noble to take advantage of a lady who might be made somewhat inebriated from the atmosphere of this place."

He moved closer until the bottom of her damp wrapper and gown brushed the tops of his boots. He caught her chin on the edge of his hand.

"You are right in part," he said. "Self-control is important to me because my ability to control and focus my talent depends on it. But you give me far too much credit when it comes to my chivalrous nature."

"Ha. I stand by my verdict, sir. You would never take advantage of a lady."

He smiled slowly. "Watch me."

He took her mouth in a slow, deliberately provocative manner. He told himself that he intended to teach her a small lesson, one she would remember in the morning when the effects of the pool had worn off. He was in control, he thought. He could keep matters in hand.

But he had not made allowances for the electrifying effects her response might have on him.

"Lucas," she whispered against his mouth. "Dear heaven, Lucas."

She wound her arms tightly around his neck and leaned into him, kissing him back with a feminine passion and energy that set fire to his senses. He had been partially aroused ever since this reckless scene had begun, but he had been fully in command of himself. It was clear now that he had miscalculated badly. He was straining against his trousers and starting to sweat again. But this fever was of an altogether different kind, he thought.

He crushed her close, deepening the kiss. Evangeline's fingers moved up through his hair. A euphoric energy swept through him. He was not just more physically aroused than he had ever been, he felt stronger, more powerful, more *aware* on every level. It was as if Evangeline's feminine fire were somehow resonating with the currents of his own life force, enhancing his senses.

She shivered in his arms and tightened her hold on him. Her mouth opened beneath his and for the first time in his life, he comprehended the astonishing metaphysical power of passion. Until he had met Evangeline he had been convinced that he knew all there was to know of desire. He controlled his lusts, they did not control him.

But Evangeline changed everything. With her he could be free.

He raised his head, opened his eyes and saw that hers were closed. Her head was tipped back, exposing the curve of her throat. He abandoned the seductive nectar that he had been drinking from her lips, wrapped his hands around the nape of her neck and kissed the delicate spot just behind one ear. Her nails dug into his shoulders. She made a soft, hungry little sound.

"I would walk through any circle of hell to have you tonight," he said against her throat.

"Yes, I know, but there is no need." She opened her eyes. "I am here and this is not hell. It is heaven. I vow, I cannot think about anything else except this sensation. It is so thrilling. I have always wondered how one could lose oneself utterly to passion. Now I know."

The provocative challenge in her eyes made his blood sing. He laughed. The sound was hoarse and husky, more an aching groan of need.

"As it happens, I have just had a similar revelation," he said.

Her scent was intoxicating, exhilarating, compelling. He moved his palms slowly downward until the soft weight of her breasts rested on the edge of his hands. He used the pads of his thumbs to stroke her tight little nipples through the thin fabric of the wrapper and nightgown.

Evangeline flattened her palms against his chest and kissed his shoulder. He lowered his hands to her waist and slid them beneath the edges of the chintz wrapper. With a tiny sigh, she tangled her fingers in the curling hair that covered his chest.

It was too much. He could bear no more of the sweet torment.

He scooped her up in his arms, moved to the nearest stone bench and sat down with her draped across his thighs. Her wrapper fell away. He bent his head to kiss her and moved one hand beneath the hem of the nightgown. He slid his palm up the inside of her leg, pausing to savor the incredible softness of her skin.

Evangeline clung to his mouth for a moment and then, with a tiny, breathless moan, she tore free and buried her face against his shoulder. He could feel the sensual tension, both physical and metaphysical, that held her in thrall. His senses were ablaze with the need to give her pleasure. He wanted to watch her face when she found her release.

He moved his hand higher. When he reached the secret little

hot spring at the juncture of her thighs he found her wet and ready. The exotic perfume of her aroused body alone was enough to make him climax. It was all he could do to maintain the last vestige of his control.

He stroked the small bud at the top of her sex. Evangeline closed her eyes very tightly. Her fingers crushed the fabric of his shirt.

"Lucas," she gasped. "I can't stand it anymore. Something is happening to me."

"Let it happen, my sweet. Let go. Fly for me."

He eased a finger into her passage. She was tight and slick. He could feel the small muscles at the entrance, gripping him snugly even as they resisted the intrusion. He hooked his finger gently upward on the inside of her channel and at the same time continued to excite her delicate clitoris.

He knew when her climax was upon her even before she did. One moment she was tight and rigid, clenching again and again around his finger, and in the next her release shivered through her in small, convulsive waves.

Her muffled cry, laced with shock, astonishment and wonder, echoed in the stone chamber.

"Lucas."

The knowledge that it was his name on her lips when she came was almost as satisfying as taking her completely. Almost.

He opened the front of his trousers.

She was just starting to relax into the aftermath of her climax when he eased himself cautiously into her tight core. She gasped and stiffened in surprise.

"Lucas." She blinked a few times, confused and alarmed. "Something is wrong."

"Do you still want me, love?"

"Yes, certainly, but I'm not sure—"

"Raise your senses again," he instructed.

Energy flared in the atmosphere. Her eyes heated once more. His own aura flashed higher in response.

He wrapped one hand around the back of her head, brought her mouth down to his and thrust quickly past the delicate barrier.

She wrenched free of the kiss and uttered a small shriek. Her fingers raked his shoulders. He knew there would be marks come dawn. The knowledge thrilled him. But there was suddenly a lot more crashing energy in the chamber and it was coming from Evangeline. Her eyes were no longer glowing gently with feminine desire. They burned.

He sensed that the currents of their auras were suddenly on fire and resonating together. The exquisite, almost unbearably intimate sensation took his breath away.

He forced himself to hold off a moment longer, intensely aware of Evangeline's rapid breathing and the quick, excited beat of her pulse. He kissed her jaw, her cheek, her mouth.

When she had adjusted to the sensation of him buried so deep inside her, he began to move. He had intended to thrust slowly and carefully but the snug, wet, hot feel of her was too much. The last thread of his control snapped. He sank himself to the hilt, his climax crashing through him.

He was lost in the storm but it did not matter. Evangeline was here with him.

Eighteen

Sharpy Hobson had failed. That much was now maddeningly evident.

Two days had passed since the blade man had taken the train to Little Dixby. Hobson had not come around for the remaining portion of his money and there had been no reports in the press of violent murder done in the countryside. Nor was there any news of a London criminal having been arrested in a small town.

There was only one explanation. Hobson had not been able to carry out the contract. He had likely returned to London and was even now swilling gin in his favorite tavern, reluctant to face his old partner with the bad news.

Garrett Willoughby paced the small dressing room. He was still wearing his stage makeup and costume. The house had been less than half full tonight. *Hardly surprising*, Garrett thought. The ridiculous melodrama with its cheaply staged excitements—the fake fire and the train wreck—had run its course after less than a month. The theater manager would soon be closing down the play.

Garrett came to a halt in front of the mirror and contemplated his reflection. He had been an actor long enough to know when it was time to seek another role. But it was not supposed to have come to this. The scheme had been damn near perfect. If it had been carried out the way they had planned it, Douglas would have been engaged to the Rutherford heiress by now. In a few months he would have married the young lady.

The heiress had been fated to die in a tragic accident soon after her wedding day, leaving her grieving husband a wealthy man. Garrett and Douglas had shared everything all their lives. They had intended to split the girl's money as well. It had all seemed so simple and straightforward. But the plan had gone wrong. It was Douglas who was dead and Evangeline Ames was to blame. Garrett did not know how a mere woman had overcome his street-hardened brother, but somehow she had done so. Perhaps she had managed to trip Douglas at the top of the stairs. Whatever the case, it was her fault that Douglas had been exposed, her fault he was dead, her fault the scheme had come to naught.

Her fault, Garrett thought, that he would soon be forced to find another ill-paying role in another cheap melodrama instead of living the life of a gentleman.

The rage churned inside him like a terrible poison. The only cure was vengeance.

He had hired Hobson because the three of them, Douglas, Sharpy and himself, had known one another most of their lives. They had grown up on the streets together. But while he and Douglas had been able to take advantage of their looks and brains to climb out of the criminal underworld, Sharpy had been too slow-witted to follow them. Not that Sharpy had cared. He had been content to rule his own little corner of hell, taking satisfaction in his reputation as a throat-slitter for hire. He never failed.

How had Ames survived? Garrett wondered. True, Sharpy was not the smartest criminal in London, but he was skilled at what he did and he was ruthless. He savored the work, especially when the victim was a woman. It was hard to believe that he had been unable to deal with Evangeline Ames.

But this was the same bitch who had somehow managed to send Douglas hurtling down a flight of stairs to his death, Garrett reminded himself. The wave of fury rolled through him.

He seized the small pot of stage makeup and hurled it into the mirror. The glass cracked, shattered and rained shards on the dressing table.

When he could breathe again, he opened the small drawer in the dressing table and took out the pistol.

Nineteen

It took her a few minutes to catch her breath and collect herself. When Evangeline opened her eyes she saw that Lucas was watching her with an unsettling expression. It was shatteringly intimate and tender but there was masculine possessiveness in the look, as well. It was as if he had learned her deepest, most closely held secret and that he wanted her to know that he knew it.

She raised her head from his shoulder, still slightly dazed. What on earth did a woman say at a time like this?

"Lucas," she whispered. She traced the strong angle of his jaw with her fingertips, lost in the wonder of what had just happened.

He caught her fingers in one hand and kissed them. His eyes met hers. "Are you all right?"

She smiled. "I think so. That was . . . extraordinary."

"Yes," Lucas said. "It was extraordinary." He smiled. "But you are an extraordinary woman, Evangeline Ames."

She realized with a start that she was still draped across his thighs in the most wanton manner imaginable. The wrapper had fallen open and the hem of her nightgown was crumpled above her thighs.

Mortified, she scrambled off his lap and got to her feet. She was not the only one who was partially undressed. Lucas's shirt had come undone and the front of his trousers was still open. It required an act of will not to stare at the broad expanse of his sleekly muscled chest, but she dared not drop her gaze any lower.

"I don't know what to say," she said.

"There is no need to say anything." Lucas leaned down and pulled off his boots. "You are a passionate woman. Passion is a normal emotion. It does not require words. Except, I suppose, in sensation novels."

She glared. "I am not a naive young girl, sir. I have read a great number of sensation novels and I am an author of such stories, if you will recall. I am an expert on the subject."

"Of course." He stood up and stripped off his shirt. "My apologies."

She straightened her shoulders. "It is not as though I was unacquainted with desire before our"—she fluttered a hand, searching for the right word—"our *encounter*. I have been kissed any number of times." She frowned, trying to recall the exact figure. "At least three times, I believe."

"Ah, yes, that would account for your expertise."

She frowned. "Although I must admit that until tonight I was obliged to use my imagination when it came to describing certain sensations. This experience tonight has been very educational, I must say. Enlightening, actually."

"Happy to have been of service, my dear author." He gave her a lazy smile, the sort of smile a lion might wear after dining on a plump gazelle. "In future, rest assured that I will be delighted to make myself available for additional research. I hope you will consider me a source of inspiration."

She made a face. "Now you are laughing at me."

"Never, Miss Ames." He stepped out of his trousers. "Well, perhaps a little."

It finally dawned on her that he was undressing in front of her. She was shocked, almost—but not quite—speechless.

"Whatever are you doing?" she gasped.

"Preparing to bathe in that pool directly behind you. Would you care to join me?"

She was aghast. At least she ought to be aghast, she told herself. "You expect me to *bathe* with you?"

"It seems to me that after the intimate connection we have just enjoyed, a bath together is hardly an outrageous suggestion. Sounds quite pleasant, in fact. We are already naked."

He was certainly naked, she thought. It was instructive to look at him. The only other nude males she had seen had been marble statues. The real thing was far more interesting. The sleek, powerful muscles of Lucas's shoulders and thighs made her want to touch him.

"Only one of us is nude," she pointed out.

"An oversight on my part." He walked toward her. "Next time we must try to find a bed. It would be a good deal more comfortable than a stone bench, don't you think?"

Next time. The words rang in her head, echoing endlessly. He was talking about a next time. That was both thrilling and unnerving. Clarissa and Beatrice's warning flicked at the edge of her awareness. *We do not want to see you hurt, Evie.*

Lucas came to a halt directly in front of her and grasped the lapels of her wrapper.

She cleared her throat. "I have been thinking about what you said earlier concerning the properties of the pools in this room."

"Yes?" He pushed the wrapper off her shoulders and let the garment fall to the floor. "What did I say? I seem to have forgotten."

"Something about how the currents distort finely tuned mechanisms like pocket watches and one's sense of time."

"What of it?" He brushed his mouth across hers.

She felt the dazzling heat rise within her again just as it had earlier. She struggled to hang on to common sense. But it was hopeless. He was kissing her throat. She was vaguely aware that he was pulling her nightgown upward, above her hips.

"You mentioned that the pool in this room was known to induce a peculiar sort of excitement."

He got the nightgown off over her head and flung it aside. "I did try to warn you."

"Yes, you did." She heaved a small sigh. "Perhaps I was somewhat overstimulated by the currents in this chamber."

"Evangeline—"

"No need to apologize, sir." She swept one hand out in a silencing gesture. "What's done is done and I must admit that my only regret is that I took advantage of you."

"Let us get one thing clear between us. You did not take advantage of me."

He picked her up in his arms.

She clutched his shoulder. "Are you quite certain? I behaved in what can only be described as an extremely forward manner."

"I assure you that I would be delighted to have you behave in such a manner at any time in the future."

"You are teasing me again, Lucas."

"Perhaps." He walked to the edge of the pool. "But only because you are stirring up a great deal of melodrama over nothing."

"Nothing?"

"Nothing," he repeated.

A tiny whisper of dread roiled her senses. Perhaps the passionate embrace had meant little to him, she thought. He was, after all, an experienced man of the world.

He started down the steps into the sparkling waters. She rallied swiftly. She, too, had experience of passion and desire now, she thought. Thanks to Lucas she had known the ultimate connection with a man. Her writing would be all the better for it.

"Perhaps you are right," she said. "I am making too much out of this, aren't I?"

"I think so," Lucas said. "But that is no doubt because you are an author and therefore given to dramatic turns of phrase."

"No doubt," she agreed.

He descended deeper into the warm bath with her in his arms. There would never be another night like this one, she thought. She would regret it until her dying day if she did not allow herself to savor it to the fullest.

With a soft sigh, she abandoned herself to the moment and the silken caress of the bath.

Lucas sat down on one of the submerged pool benches, Evangeline cradled in his arms. The warm, intoxicating waters swirled gently around them.

"How did you alleviate the fever in my blood tonight?" he asked after a while.

"I can't explain it," she admitted. "Not entirely. I sensed the unnatural heat in your aura and I . . . cooled the currents until they felt normal."

"Have you done such a thing before?"

"Not exactly." This was the last thing she wanted to talk about, she thought. Only Beatrice and Clarissa knew her dark secret. What would Lucas think of her if he knew what she had done—what she was capable of doing? "Well, yes, in a manner of speaking. But only one other time and the effect was quite the opposite. I did not know I could do what I did on that occasion, either. Not until the moment was upon me."

"Whose fever did you quench on that occasion?"

Suspicion sliced through her. He was interrogating her.

"Why do you want to know?" she asked.

Lucas smiled. "Perhaps I am jealous."

She shuddered. "There is no need for jealousy, I assure you."

"Who was he, Evangeline?"

"A gentleman who once claimed to love me. He asked for my hand in marriage. On the surface he appeared to be everything I had ever hoped to find in a husband. Intelligent, courteous, thoughtful. He brought me flowers and wrote poetry to me. He admired my writing."

"Did he?"

"He told me I had a gift for describing the metaphysical sensations of the darker passions as well as the transcendent nature of love. He was convinced, he said, that only rare individuals could experience the ultimate heights of passion."

"Rare individuals such as you?"

"*Mmm*. Yes."

"Yet you never went to those heights with him," Lucas said. "After tonight I know that for certain."

"I did tell you that I had been kissed before. Indeed, Robert was very expert."

She was talking much too freely, she thought. If she had any sense she would stop. Vaguely she wondered if the waters of the bath were affecting her like too much champagne, making her chatty.

"This Robert actually used words like 'the transcendent nature of love'?" Lucas demanded.

"Yes." She swept one hand absently back and forth in the water. "He was very charming. He always knew what to say. We laughed together. And we had so much in common. We toured museums and art galleries."

Lucas's eyes heated, but not with passion. "He was your ideal lover?"

"Not quite perfect, as it turned out." She took one hand out of the water and held her thumb and forefinger half an inch apart to illustrate. "But close, very close. You see, in those days I could not perceive the energy in a person's aura as clearly as I can now. I was only able to view a very limited range of light. So I missed the darkness in Robert entirely."

"What happened?" Lucas asked.

"In hindsight, one could say that there were a couple of clues that revealed his true character."

"What clues?"

Her wariness intensified. "You are starting to sound very much like a police detective, Lucas."

"What was it that gave away Robert's true character?" Lucas said, obviously forcing himself to at least sound more patient. The effort was not entirely successful.

"The first occurred when he disappeared after learning of my father's suicide and financial losses," she said. "I told myself that he had every right to end the courtship. After all, he had been under the illusion that I would have a respectable inheritance."

"But his actions did spoil your image of him as a romantic, is that it? They made it plain that he was more interested in your money than he was in you."

"Yes, but that would hardly make him unique among suitors, would it?"

"No," Lucas said. "What of the second hint?"

The warm, effervescent energy of the water was distracting her, making it impossible to concentrate.

"Sorry?" she said.

"You said you got a second hint of Robert's true nature."

"Oh, right. I discovered the second indication of his rather flawed character when he tried to murder me."

Lucas watched her with a dark, unblinking gaze. "Douglas Mason, the fortune hunter you exposed in the Rutherford affair?"

"Yes," she said. She held herself very still, half afraid of what would happen next and yet wanting Lucas to know the truth about her. "He called himself Robert when he wooed me."

"Bastard," Lucas said very softly.

"I couldn't believe it when I realized that he was the man my client wanted me to investigate. Soon after I assumed my role as Lady Rutherford's companion we attended a reception at a photo gallery with the Lady's granddaughter. I was stunned when Robert walked into the room. He was not only using a different name, he had even given himself a title."

"Did he recognize you?"

"No." She smiled wryly. "I was wearing spectacles and a very plain gown. My hair was covered by a large hat and a widow's veil. I was using an assumed name, too. It is my customary disguise. Mason never looked twice at me. I was, after all, just an elderly lady's companion."

"It's amazing how unobservant most people are."

"Those of us who are employed by Flint and Marsh depend on that fact. As you know, I continued my investigation and discovered the proof Lady Rutherford was able to use to expose Mason."

"Who later discovered that you were to blame and then tried to murder you."

"Yes."

"I know the memories are difficult, but can you recall anything he might have said that would help us identify his brother?" Lucas asked.

"No. I've thought about that a great deal ever since Stone brought you the information from London. But I never knew that Robert—I mean, Douglas—had a brother. He never mentioned him when he was courting me."

"Tell me what happened the day he tried to kill you."

"When he confronted me at the top of the stairs he was in a rage. It was as if he had gone mad. All he talked about was the terrible things he intended to do to me before he slit my throat."

"Bastard," Lucas said again, very softly this time. He tightened his arms around her. "I'm very glad that he is dead, of course. My only regret is that his death was an accident. I would have taken a great deal of satisfaction in assisting him on his way to the next world."

For a few seconds she was too stunned to find her voice. No one had ever wanted to protect her.

"That is . . . very chivalrous of you," she whispered.

To her horror, she pressed her face against his shoulder and started to weep.

Lucas held her for a time, letting her cry. He did not say anything. It was as if he knew there were no words.

Eventually she sniffed a few times, raised her head and splashed some water on her face.

"My apologies," she said. "I assure you I am not in the habit of turning into a watering pot at the slightest provocation."

"Oddly enough I was already aware of that."

She pulled herself together with an effort. "Yes, well, there you have it, the whole, sordid story of my one great romance. As you can see, it did not end well. Heavens, I expect it must be nearly dawn. We will be able to leave this chamber soon."

"One more thing before we leave the subject of Douglas Mason," Lucas said.

"Yes?"

"He did not trip and fall down those stairs, did he? You did something to his aura, something similar to what you did to mine but you went further. You iced his aura."

The certainty in his voice told her there was no point trying to lie. Nor did she want to prevaricate anymore. She needed him to know the truth about what she could do with her talent; needed him to either accept or reject the real Evangeline Ames.

"I stopped his heart," she whispered.

Lucas smiled his predator's smile. "That is a very handy psychical ability you have, Miss Ames."

She was shocked by his casual acceptance of her lethal power.

"Lucas, I killed a man with my talent," she said, wanting to be very certain that he understood. "I swear to you that I did not realize what would happen when I started to dampen the rage in his aura, at least not at first, but in those last few seconds I knew what I was doing and I did not stop."

"No, I'm sure you didn't comprehend the full power of your talent until you had occasion to employ it. It is not exactly the sort of skill one can practice, is it? In your moment of desperation all of your senses would have been aroused to the fullest extent and focused utterly on survival. That was when you intuitively realized what you could do."

"I'm still not sure exactly what I did. All I know is that when he put his hands on me I could feel the heat of his killing fury. I could perceive the distortion in the wavelengths. I knew that I could dampen those currents with my own mental energy. So I did. And I kept on doing it until he just . . . collapsed there at the top of the stairs."

"Whereupon you gave him a little shove that sent him to the bottom of the staircase, thereby making it look like an accident and thus avoiding both a police inquiry and a lurid scandal involving attempted rape and murder charges."

"It seemed the most convenient way to handle the situation," she admitted.

He kissed her briefly, a quick, possessive kiss that set her senses tingling. When he raised his head, admiration and dark desire gleamed in his eyes.

"Nicely done, my sweet. Where have you been all my life, Evangeline Ames?"

"The thing is, something changed in me that day. It was as if using so much energy opened up a new channel of psychical vision. Afterward I could see more of a person's aura." She shuddered. "Much more than I wanted to see in most cases. It is unnerving, to tell you the truth."

"Whatever you have seen, remember that I have seen far worse."

"Yes, I don't know how you do what you do, Lucas."

"The only thing that matters to me is that you are not unnerved by what you see in my aura."

"No, never." She eyed him with growing uncertainty. "But doesn't it concern you that I am capable of killing a person with my talent?"

"No." His eyes darkened. "I have driven men to their deaths with my talent."

She pondered that briefly. "Nevertheless, I am certain that there are any number of men who would be quite appalled by the knowledge that they had just had a . . . a sexual encounter with a woman who was capable of such an act. I'm sure the notion would induce visions of black widow spiders in your average gentleman."

"Do I strike you as an average gentleman?"

She smiled. "No, Lucas. You are anything but average. You are the most extraordinary man I have ever met."

"The only thing that appalls me, Evangeline, is that I have enjoyed only one such sexual encounter with you." He moved his hand under the water, covering her breast. "I would very much like to have another."

She was suddenly aware that he was once again fiercely aroused. His erection pressed urgently against her hips. When he turned her in his arms she realized his intention.

"Here?" she asked, both startled and intrigued. "In the pool?"

"Here," he said. "In the pool."

"Oh, my. I had no idea that this sort of thing was possible."

"I did say that I would be only too happy to assist you with your research."

Twenty

How could it all go so bloody wrong?" Horace Tolliver asked. "All the planning, all the research, all for naught. On top of everything else, the device has been lost."

But he was talking to himself. He looked down at his taller, older brother who was sprawled on the sweat-soaked sheets. Burton had always been the strong one. Now he was lying at death's door.

Horace still did not know precisely what had happened in the maze, but he had managed to piece together most of the story from his own memories and what little Burton had told him before collapsing from the fever.

Horace crossed the small bedroom to the dressing table. He soaked another cloth in the bowl of cold water he had placed there, squeezed out the excess moisture and went back to the bed. He removed the cloth he had placed on Burton's hot brow a few minutes earlier and replaced it with the cool one.

He dropped the used cloth into the bowl and went to the small chair beside the bed. He sat down with a weary sigh and remembered the harrowing events of the night.

"Everything went wrong right from the start, Burton. But, then, how could we have known that Sebastian was able to navigate the maze, let alone that he was already inside it when we entered?"

His recollection of what exactly had transpired inside the maze was blurry. He remembered turning around to see Sebastian standing behind him in the passageway, and then he had been overcome with waking nightmares so terrible his mind had sought refuge in unconsciousness. He had awakened some time later to find himself on the cold, damp ground of the lane, looking up at the moon. Burton was calling his name.

"Wake up, Horace. You must wake up. I cannot carry you any farther. Something is happening to me. I feel weak and feverish. That damn energy storm affected my senses. You will have to walk the rest of the way back to the cottage."

Horace had stumbled to his feet, vaguely astonished to find himself alive. Burton, however, had been barely able to remain standing. Horace had pulled his brother's arm around his own shoulders and together they had managed to stagger nearly half a mile to the end of the lane. There Burton had collapsed.

Somehow Horace had summoned the strength to sling Burton over his shoulder and carry him the rest of the way back to the small cottage. By then, the fever was raging.

Horace had applied cold compresses all night but there was no sign of improvement. Shortly before dawn, desperate now, he had walked into town and awakened the doctor who, for double the usual fee, had agreed to attend the sick man.

The doctor had taken himself off very shortly thereafter, shaking his head. *"I've never seen a fever like this"* had been his parting words. *"I cannot help your brother, sir."*

He had advised continuing with the cold compresses and gave Horace a bottle of laudanum in the event that Burton showed signs of great pain. But it was clear that he did not expect the patient to recover.

"I failed you, Burton." Horace dropped his head into his hands. "You were always the one who looked after me, right up until the last. You carried me out of that maze and out of those damn gardens. But now you need me and there is nothing I can do."

Burton stirred, lost in some fever dream. He did not open his eyes.

Twenty-one

Lucas made love to her again there in the sparkling waters of the bath. Afterward he carried her up the steps and used his shirt as a towel to dry both of them. He was reluctant to see this night end, he thought. He would have been happy to spend another day or two or the rest of his life in this idyllic place with Evangeline. But that was not possible.

When he finished wiping the last of the glittering droplets off of Evangeline's soft, delightfully flushed body, he crumpled the shirt into a wet heap and set about getting dressed. Evangeline quickly donned her nightgown and wrapper and looked down the long hall toward the entrance.

"It must be dawn by now," she said.

"Yes." Lucas fastened his trousers and sat down on a stone bench to pull on his boots. "Now to find out what happened to Stone and our two uninvited guests."

"I do hope Mr. Stone is all right," Evangeline said.

"It would take a lot to kill him."

"Do you think that the intruders might have survived the explosion in the maze?"

"We did," he reminded her. He picked up the miniature lantern and took another look at it, wondering again how to work it and what it was designed to do. "But if they needed this device to navigate the maze, then it's possible that they are still wandering around somewhere inside. If so, they'll keep for a few more hours. I'll deal with them after I get you back to the house."

"What will we do if that energy storm has not yet dissipated?" Evangeline asked.

He contemplated the possibilities and gave her a slow smile. "If that is the case we may be obliged to spend another night here."

Evangeline looked alarmed. "Good grief."

"Is the thought so terrible?"

She wrinkled her nose. "You are teasing me again."

"Yes, I am." He walked to her and kissed her brow. "Sadly, I'm afraid that the storm will have died out by now and, much as I would enjoy spending another night here with you, I strongly suspect that I will have no excuse for doing so."

She blushed furiously and became very busy tying the sash of her wrapper. "Yes, well, do hurry, Lucas. We must get back to the house before anyone awakens. It would not do for your aunt and your sister to see us returning from the gardens at this hour, to say nothing of the servants." She looked at his naked chest. "Certainly not in this condition."

He grew serious once more. "I do not want you to be embarrassed."

"Then for heaven's sake, hurry."

Evangeline stepped into her slippers, turned smartly on one heel and started down the hall toward the entrance of the baths. It occurred to Lucas that they had not yet talked about what must happen when they emerged. He had meant to have the discussion before they exited the maze but now did not seem to be the appropriate time. There were other priorities.

Evangeline stopped and looked down the stone passage to the third pool chamber.

"What is it?" Lucas asked.

"There must be a great deal of energy inside that room," Evangeline said. "I can sense some of it from here."

"You're no doubt picking up the currents of the energy gate that bars the entrance. It's very powerful. As far as I know, Uncle Chester never found a way through it, although he was obsessed with getting into that room."

"Why?"

"According to the old records it is the strongest of the three pools. Very few people have ever been able to enter the chamber."

Evangeline changed course and went along the passage. Lucas followed her to the door of the chamber.

"The door is new."

"Chester installed it. But the real barrier is the energy storm on the other side."

Evangeline flattened her hand on the door. "The energy behind it feels old."

"It is. That storm gate was in place when Uncle Chester bought the property."

Evangeline took her hand away from the door and looked at him with haunted eyes. "I think there is something important hidden in this chamber, but I have no idea what it is. It may be simply the raw power of the pool in that room."

"We do not have time to deal with it now. We will come back some other time."

Evangeline studied the door. "Soon, Lucas."

"Soon."

He took her hand and drew her away from the Vision Pool chamber.

Once through the veil of energy he discovered that dawn had, indeed, arrived. In fact, the sun was already well above the horizon. The disorienting effects of the energy in the baths, combined with the broken pocket watch, had caused him to miscalculate the hour, he thought.

But that excuse did not hold. He smiled to himself, aware that he had no one but himself to blame for the delayed departure. He had been unable to resist making love to Evangeline one last time.

The Night Garden was a different place by day. The phosphorescent effect was almost imperceptible unless he raised his talent a few degrees. The night-blooming flowers had folded their petals against the sun. They would not open again until full night had descended. But the dark, ominous currents of energy that seethed in the atmosphere were still there, lurking just below the surface.

"Be careful," Lucas warned. "Just because things look safer in daylight, it doesn't mean that they are. If anything, this place is actually more dangerous by day precisely because the hazards are less obvious to the senses."

Evangeline gave a cluster of orchids a wary look. "Don't worry, I'm not going to pick any flowers to take back and press between the pages of a book of poetry."

"Have you ever in your life pressed any posies between the leaves of a book of poetry?"

"Well, no," she admitted. "But the heroine in my novel does so."

"Why?"

"Because the villain, whom I had intended to make the hero, gave her flowers after a stolen embrace. She thinks she will never see him again so she preserves one of the roses in the book of poetry that he also gave her. But recently I realized I had picked the wrong man for the hero."

"You got the hero and villain of your own story mixed up?"

"Things like that happen to a writer," she said. "All part of the creative process."

"I see."

"Luckily I got matters sorted out before I finished chapter four. That is the problem when one writes for the newspapers, you see: One is always stuck with the facts as they were set down in the previous chapters. There is no going back and revising because the earlier chapters are already in print."

"It sounds stressful," Lucas said.

"Not nearly as stressful as almost getting murdered at the top of a staircase."

He smiled. "Good point."

The energy storm in the maze had receded. The currents of power were still disorienting but they felt normal once again. Lucas led the way back through the labyrinth to the corridor where the explosion had occurred.

Evangeline looked around apprehensively. "I don't see any bodies. Surely the vegetation in this place could not have been able to consume two people by now."

"No. It takes two or three days to digest a creature the size of a rat. It would require a longer period of time for two bodies to vanish. Either the intruders are still blundering around somewhere inside this place or they escaped."

"You rendered the shorter man unconscious. He would not have awakened in time to flee."

"The other man could have carried him away from the scene," Lucas said.

"Wouldn't he have been overcome by the effects of the explosion as you were?"

"Yes, but perhaps not immediately. You will recall that I managed to make it to the bathhouse."

"But that was as far as you could go," she said. "I cannot imagine the tall man could have gotten more than a short distance away from the gardens, especially if he was carrying his companion."

"In which case, we may find one or both men somewhere nearby, perhaps still on the grounds."

They emerged from the maze a short time later. There were no bodies near the entrance. There was, however, a sizable crowd milling around on the terrace. Stone, Florence, Beth, Molly and a large number of Molly's Gillingham relatives had gathered, many of them armed with picks, axes and scythes.

Molly saw them first. Relief lit up her face. "Mr. Sebastian, Miss Ames. You're alive."

Stone turned swiftly. His dour expression lightened. "Mr. Sebastian."

"Lucas," Florence exclaimed. "Thank heavens you are both safe. I feared the worst."

"I did not," Beth said. She smiled at Lucas. "I knew that you would emerge safely and that you would bring Miss Ames with you. I told everyone that you would wait until the sun was up before you attempted to leave the Night Garden. But Stone wanted to be prepared to go in after you if you didn't show up."

Lucas studied the crowd. "What were you intending to do? Tear apart the maze?"

"It was either that or try to burn it down and I didn't think we could get much of a blaze going in that solid mass of greenery," Stone said.

"No," Lucas said. Relief whispered through him. It was a very good thing Stone and the others had not tried to burn down the maze or hack it to pieces. The foliage had far too many ways of protecting itself. He looked at Molly and the rest of the Gillinghams. "I thank all of you for coming out to rescue us. I'm glad for everyone's sake that it was not necessary to try to destroy the maze, but I will not forget that you were willing to take on the task. I am fortunate to have such fine neighbors. Please know that if I can repay any of you in any way you have only to ask."

There was a round of *"Think nothing of it, Mr. Sebastian,"* and *"Happy to be of service"* and *"Glad you and the lady are both safe."*

And then an awkward hush fell on the crowd. Lucas realized they were all trying very hard not to stare at Evangeline who stood beside him in her nightclothes.

Florence reacted first. "Beth, you will take Miss Ames up to her room. I'm sure she is quite exhausted."

"Yes, of course." Beth gave Evangeline a sympathetic smile. "Let's go inside."

"Thank you," Evangeline said.

Clearly relieved at the prospect of escape, she started to walk toward the house with Beth.

"Yes," Lucas said, raising his voice just enough to make certain that all of the Gillinghams could hear him. "My fiancée has been through an ordeal, as I'm sure you can imagine. Please see to it that she is properly taken care of. She'll be wanting tea and some rest."

For an instant everyone, including Evangeline, froze. She was the first one to break free of the trance. She whirled and looked at Lucas as though he had just pronounced her doom.

"What have you done?" she said softly.

She whirled and fled toward the house as if all of the hounds of hell were at her heels.

Twenty-two

I failed you, Mr. Sebastian." Stone stood stiffly in front of the library desk. "You assigned me to keep watch last night and instead I let those bastards put me to sleep like a baby."

"Not quite like a baby." Lucas picked up the small lantern and held it to the light of the gas lamp that hung over the desk. "This weapon generates paranormal radiation of some sort. You had no way to shield yourself from the effects of the currents."

Stone scowled at the device. "It was just a bloody lantern. I remember that the light was greenish. But when I looked directly at it, I suddenly couldn't move. And that's the last thing I remember."

"The light was generated by this crystal." Lucas opened the small glass door of the lantern and took a closer look at the dull gray crystal inside. "I can sense the power in it but I'm not sure how to activate it. Unfortunately, I don't have time to run proper experiments. We have priorities at the moment. Identifying the intruders is at the top of the list."

"Yes, sir."

Lucas set the lantern aside. He waved at a nearby chair. "Sit down and tell me everything you can remember about what happened last night."

"Yes, sir." Stone sat awkwardly on one of the chairs and frowned in concentration. "I was making my rounds, keeping an eye out for signs of intruders, listening for voices and the small sounds that everyone makes when they move about."

Lucas walked to the vine-shrouded window. "Go on."

"I remember hearing a bit of rustling in the shadows on the other side of the wall near the old gate. I think I saw a small flash of light. Then I heard the grating of the hinges."

Lucas turned his head to look at Stone. "They got through the gate?"

"Yes, sir."

"Huh. I thought the lock was impregnable."

"It sounded like they used a key. I heard it turn in the lock."

"Interesting. Continue."

"Not much more to tell." Stone hunched his massive shoulders and slumped dejectedly in his chair. "I went to see about the open gate. I got there in time to catch two men slipping onto the grounds. I'm very sure they didn't hear me coming, not until I challenged them."

"Then what happened?"

"The smaller man got very nervous when he saw me." Stone closed one big hand into a fist and glared at the small lantern. "I think he would have tried to flee if the taller one hadn't stopped him."

"Which one used the lantern on you?"

"The tall one. He grabbed it out of the other man's hands and aimed it at me like it was a pistol. I saw the light beam and the next thing

I knew I was waking up just before dawn. I went in search of you straight off. When I couldn't find you or Miss Ames I feared the worst. Figured you were trapped inside the Night Garden. By that time, Molly had arrived to cook breakfast. She had one of her cousins with her. The cousin ran for help and I roused your aunt and your sister. You know the rest."

"Yes."

Curiosity stirred in Stone's expression. "D'ya think we could have hacked and chopped our way into the Night Garden?"

"I don't know," Lucas said. "It's safer during the day but those plants have a lot of unknown properties. At the very least it would have taken days to get through the foliage, and the process would have been extremely dangerous for everyone who came in contact with the greenery."

"Like I told ye, I thought about setting fire to the maze, but I wasn't sure it would burn properly."

"You were right. Furthermore, a fire might well have triggered an explosion of paranormal energy that could have proved hazardous for people in the vicinity."

Stone's brow furrowed. "If you can't chop down the gardens and you can't burn 'em down, how will you destroy them?"

"Damned if I know." Lucas went back to the desk. "But first things first. We learned a couple of important facts last night."

"What facts?"

"The intruders were treasure hunters who were after some Roman gold that is said to be concealed in the Night Garden. They were not the first who have trespassed in search of the hoard. But these two got a lot farther than most because of their psychical abilities, that little lantern and a key to the gate."

"Yes, sir." Stone's frown darkened. "What else did ye learn?"

"The fact that they knew their way around and possessed a key makes that pair the most likely suspects in my uncle's murder."

Stone's brow cleared. "Think they'll be back?"

"Perhaps," Lucas said. He picked up the lantern again and thought about the howling storm that had roared through the maze. "Assuming they managed to survive the effects of the explosion. Treasure hunters don't give up easily. They tend to be obsessive."

"If they got out of the maze, I'm sure they escaped the grounds," Stone said. "I walked every inch of the old wall this morning and there were no bodies."

"They may have escaped the grounds, but that does not mean they were not affected by the storm. I barely survived, myself."

"What are you saying?" Stone raised his head, shocked. "I didn't realize you were injured, sir. You looked fit and hearty when you came out of the maze this morning."

"I owe my good health and my undamaged senses to my fiancée," Lucas said.

"Miss Ames saved you?"

"Yes," Lucas said. "She did."

"Well, then, if the intruders didn't have a Miss Ames of their own handy, they might be in bad shape this morning."

Lucas smiled slowly. "That, Stone, is an excellent observation. Please send one of Molly's relatives in here immediately."

"Yes, sir." Stone shot to his feet and started toward the door. He paused midway across the room. "Which relative do ye want, sir?"

"I'm not feeling particular. I just need someone who can go into town and discover if by any chance the doctor was called out during the night to attend two men who were stricken with a high fever."

Twenty-three

At eleven o'clock that morning, Evangeline paced the library, seething with a frustration that bordered on panic. She was so tense that she flinched violently when the door opened. She spun around and saw Lucas.

"Have you lost your mind, sir?" she said. It was all she could do to keep her voice low so as not to be overheard by anyone who happened to be passing by in the hallway.

Lucas closed the door and watched her warily. "I don't think so. But, then, I'm not certain one would know if one lost one's mind. The question is complicated, isn't it? Madmen usually believe themselves to be sane."

"This is not a joking matter, Lucas. You have brought disaster down on our heads."

"Calm yourself, my sweet." Lucas crossed the room to where she stood. He tipped up her chin and gave her a quick kiss. He released her before she could protest and continued on to his desk. "If I didn't know you better, I'd swear you sounded as if you were about to succumb to a bout of female hysteria."

"I am not hysterical."

"No, of course you aren't." He looked at her across the width of the desk. "I thought you were upstairs, recovering from your ordeal."

"I have recovered quite nicely, thank you very much." She spoke through her teeth. "Your sister has plied me with tea. Molly sent up a tray of poached eggs and toast. And your aunt informed me that after I have recovered from my *ordeal*, she wishes to speak to me in private."

"I am sorry to hear that," Lucas said. "But I am confident that you can hold your own with Aunt Florence. Whatever you do, don't allow her to browbeat you."

Evangeline drew herself up. "Just what do you suggest I say to her?"

"I'm sure you'll think of something." He went to one of the bookshelves and removed a leather-bound volume. "Since you obviously have bounced back rather nicely from your ordeal, I suggest that we move on to a more pressing topic."

She folded her arms. "Just what subject do you consider to be more pressing than the current disaster, Mr. Sebastian?"

"I had a thought while I was upstairs shaving and changing into fresh clothes." Lucas carried the volume to the desk. "It occurred to me that it might be useful to go through my uncle's journals, especially the ones he kept in the months before his death. If he was acquainted with those two men we encountered in the gardens last night, which I believe is a distinct possibility, and if they visited him prior to the murder, there is a strong likelihood that he mentioned them in his notes. He kept close track of the handful of other botanists who studied the paranormal. There aren't that many, after all, and I'll wager that Uncle Chester knew them all."

Distracted, Evangeline looked at the rows of journals on the shelves.

"You do not have time to do that sort of research. Why not let Beth do it for you?"

He frowned. "Beth?"

"I'm sure she would be thrilled to assist you with the investigation."

"That is a very good idea. I'll send for her at once." He reached for one of the velvet bell pulls that hung next to the desk.

It was too much. Evangeline flew to the desk, skirts whipping furiously around her ankles, and slapped both hands, palms down, on the surface.

Lucas looked up from the journal, frowning first in surprise and then in concern. "What the devil?"

"Damn it, Lucas, your uncle's murder can wait."

"I don't think so. Not after what happened last night."

"We have a crisis on our hands because of what happened last night and you are the one who caused it. The least you can do is discuss it with the appropriate degree of concern."

"Very well." Lucas closed the journal. The small lines at the corners of his eyes tightened a little. "But first be good enough to tell me what crisis we are talking about if it is not the matter of the murder."

"How can you ask such a question? You know the answer to that."

He relaxed slightly. "Ah, so that is the problem. It is your own situation that concerns you. Perfectly understandable. Don't worry, I have not forgotten that someone is after you, my dear. But you are safe here at Crystal Gardens. It is just a matter of time before we have more news from London. As soon as we know the identity of the man who hired Sharpy Hobson, I will inform you immediately."

"Not *that* crisis, you cork-brained man. I refer to the one we are facing at this very moment. What is more, you cannot blame this situation on a London villain. The villain of this piece is right here in this room."

Lucas raised his brows. "Cork-brained?"

"I apologize for the language." She straightened, taking her hands off the desktop. "But it is not my fault that you have driven me to distraction."

"Let's start back at the beginning." There was a new edge in Lucas's voice. "Define this crisis that has you so overset."

"You gave that crowd out in the gardens the impression that we are now engaged, for heaven's sake. How could you do that?"

"I thought I handled it rather smoothly, if I do say so."

"What?"

"I'm certain that everyone understood me. Do you think I left any room for confusion?"

"Stop making light of this utter catastrophe," she wailed.

Lucas's jaw tightened. "I regret that I was not able to make the announcement in a more formal manner, but you will admit that under the circumstances there were not a lot of alternatives."

She stilled. "What do you mean?"

"It was just after dawn. It was obvious that we had spent the night together in the gardens. I was not wearing a shirt and you were in your nightgown and wrapper. We had an audience. I had to make the announcement immediately. Bloody hell, woman, did you really expect me to post a notice in the newspapers and send out announcements to our engagement ball first?"

"I was afraid of that."

"An engagement ball?"

Something inside her crumpled. "I know you meant well, Lucas, but you have made everything so much more complicated."

"Is that so? I fail to see the problem. It all looks quite simple and straightforward to me. Unlike, say, identifying the person who wants you dead and solving my uncle's murder."

"Please don't misunderstand. I realize that you were trying to protect my reputation. It was very kind of you, but—"

"Kind?"

She raised her chin. "You are an honorable man, Lucas, a true gentleman."

"Why do I get the feeling that this conversation is not going well?"

She ignored that. "You were attempting to protect me and I appreciate it more than you will ever know." She blinked away the incipient tears. "But don't you see? We are now living a lie. Sooner or later you will have to tell your family the truth. What will they think?"

Ominous energy heated the atmosphere. Lucas walked around the end of the desk and started toward her.

"Are you asking me what they will think of you?" he said. "Because I give you my word that anyone who dares to question your virtue will answer to me."

The manner in which he was advancing on her made her unaccountably nervous. Instinctively she retreated a few steps.

"Don't be ridiculous," she said. "It doesn't matter what your family and the locals will think of me after the truth comes out. I can simply disappear as I always do after a case. What concerns me is what they will all think of you when our so-called engagement is ended. You have put your own reputation at stake to save mine. I can't let you do that."

"It's done, Evangeline. And just to be clear, I knew exactly what I was doing when I made that announcement this morning."

He did not stop. He was moving toward her with the deliberate pacing stride of a large beast of prey. She took another step back and then another and came up hard against one of the bookcases. Lucas closed in on her. He put out his hands on either side of her head and gripped the shelf behind her, trapping her, not just physically but psychically as well.

"Lucas?"

"As far as I am concerned we are not living a lie," he said. "We are engaged. As for my reputation, let me worry about it."

She was suddenly wary but her alarm was rapidly metamorphosing into excitement. The wavelengths of his aura crashed and roared around her, demanding a response. She could feel her own currents seeking resonance. She tried to resist but it required a great deal of energy. The effort made her breathless.

"I suppose that when the truth comes out we can explain that our engagement was merely an act that we both put on in order to trap your uncle's killers," she said, struggling to hang on to her composure and her powers of logic. "We can tell people that you hired me to play the part of your fiancée and that we wanted to give a convincing performance."

"I have news for you: The performance was extremely convincing. My sister, my aunt and the villagers will never believe that last night was an act. What's more, you and I know that it was all quite real." He paused. His eyes heated. "Don't we?"

"Lucas—"

"Did we or did we not make love last night?"

"Well, yes, but that is not the point."

"What is the point?"

"Last night we were under the influence of all that energy emanating from the bathhouse pools," Evangeline said, breathless now. "And there is no knowing how that explosion in the maze affected our senses."

"You and I are not the type to resort to excuses. We made love because we both wanted to and I, for one, do not regret it. Do you?"

The power of his aura was overwhelming her. She simply did not have the strength to fight him off any longer. *No, the truth is that I do not want to struggle against this glorious sensation*. She might have other lovers in the long, lonely future that awaited her, but she knew in her heart that she would never experience this incredibly intimate connection with any other man.

"You're trying to confuse me," she whispered.

"Am I?"

"Oh, bloody hell," she whispered. "You're right, I'm overreacting. You are more than capable of looking after yourself, Lucas Sebastian. If you are not concerned about your own reputation, why should I fret about it?"

"My thoughts precisely."

"It is not as if engagements are not terminated from time to time," she added, trying for a positive note. "Generally speaking, it is only the woman's reputation that is shattered when that happens." She brightened. "Unless, of course, she is the one who ends the engagement." Her spirits drooped again. "But that only works if her family is of equal or higher social status."

"Evangeline—"

"But that doesn't apply in our situation. The thing is, a wealthy man from a good family has nothing to fear, socially speaking. As for me, I can go back to my old life with no one the wiser."

Lucas tightened his grip on the shelving behind her. "I think it's time you stopped talking, Evangeline. You did say that you were getting confused."

"Yes, I did say that, didn't I? I can't seem to think clearly just now."

"Neither can I. Maybe it's time we both ceased trying to make intelligent conversation."

He kissed her before she was obliged to come up with a response. His mouth closed over hers in a ruthless assault that sent shock waves through all of her senses.

Why was she fighting him? she wondered. The recklessness that had taken possession of her last night once again rose to the surface, pushing aside common sense and logic. She clutched his shoulders and abandoned herself to the embrace. Heat and energy shimmered in the atmosphere.

She did not hear the door open. But Lucas evidently was aware of it because he reluctantly broke off the kiss. He did not release his grip on the bookshelves but he turned his head to look over his shoulder.

"What is it, Molly?" he asked, icily impatient.

Horrified, Evangeline peeked around Lucas's shoulder. Molly stood in the opening. She looked petrified. An attractive lady dressed in a fashionable traveling gown and hat stood behind her. A young man who looked a great deal like Beth was at her side.

"I'm s-s-sorry, sir," Molly stammered. "I did knock. There's a Mrs. Sebastian and a Mr. Sebastian here to see you, sir."

"This day just keeps getting more and more irritating," Lucas said. But he said it very quietly. He let go of the bookshelves and turned around. "Evangeline, allow me to introduce Judith Sebastian, my stepmother, and my brother, Tony."

Twenty-four

An hour later Lucas confronted Judith alone in the library. She sat, rigid with tension, in one of the reading chairs. He faced her from behind the desk. It was not the first time the two of them had met like this, Lucas thought. The encounters never ended well for either of them.

"What are you doing here, madam?" he asked. "I was under the impression that you detested Crystal Gardens."

"I hate this place." Judith glanced toward the vine-covered windows and shuddered. "Your uncle's dreadful botanical experiments should be destroyed. Those gardens are unnatural in the extreme."

Shortly after her arrival Judith had been shown upstairs to one of the bedrooms. She had changed into a dark green gown. Her blond hair was pinned into an elegant chignon that emphasized her delicate features and blue eyes.

"Crystal Gardens is not Kew Gardens," Lucas said. "I'll allow you that much. Nor would I suggest holding a garden party on the grounds. But the plants and flowers out there are entirely natural. It is just that they thrive on the paranormal elements in the waters here."

Anger and an old, familiar look of fear flashed in Judith's eyes.

"You know I do not believe in the paranormal," she said.

He smiled coldly. "Which is one of the reasons you and I have never had much in common to talk about."

Judith flushed. "I did not come here to quarrel with you, Lucas."

"Then why did you arrive unannounced? And why drag Tony with you?"

"I didn't send a telegram because I knew you would probably send one straight back telling me that I would not be welcome. When Tony learned that I was coming here, he insisted on traveling with me. He finds this dreadful place quite interesting, I'm afraid."

"I am not here to entertain a houseful of guests. I am engaged in two very serious projects here at the abbey. Believe me when I tell you that I would prefer no guests at all. But I seem to be acquiring a houseful of relatives, all of whom travel with a great deal of luggage and a maid or two. At this rate Molly will have to open up another wing."

"You're the one who sent that cryptic telegram to Florence. It is not my fault that Beth chose to accompany her to the Gardens."

"And you're here because of Beth, is that it? You don't approve of the young man who has caught her fancy."

"Yes, I did come to discuss Beth's future with you," Judith said. "But before we get to that subject, I must ask you what on earth is going on around here. Florence told me that last night you had a tryst somewhere on the grounds with Miss Ames and that the two of you were caught coming back to the house at dawn. You were both in a state of dishabille and now you claim to be engaged."

"Miss Ames and I *are* engaged."

"Surely you cannot mean to marry the woman. Florence says she makes her living as a paid companion, for heaven's sake. I comprehend that you feel there is a matter of honor involved. Nevertheless, the proprieties would hardly seem to apply in this situation. It is not as if Miss Ames moves in society."

"When have you ever known me to give a damn about the proprieties?"

"Are you saying that you actually do intend to marry her?"

"In a word? Yes."

"I cannot believe that. I know you too well, Lucas. You are involved in some complicated scheme."

He picked up the sterling silver letter opener and balanced it on two fingers. "I strongly suggest that you tell me why you came here today. If you do not get to the matter at hand, you will find yourself on the next train back to London."

Judith pressed her lips tightly together. "Very well, I suppose your engagement is your business."

"Yes, it is. A word of advice: You will treat Miss Ames with respect. Is that understood?"

Judith clasped her hands tightly together. Her jaw twitched. "Of course."

"Say what you feel you need to say. You can stay the night and return to London tomorrow."

Judith's mouth curved bitterly. "Gracious, as always."

He called on his willpower and managed to control his temper. "Come now, there is no need for false politeness between us, Judith. We have both understood each other very well, right from the start."

The blood drained from Judith's cheeks but she held on to her composure. "You are right. I came here because of Beth. The very last thing I want to do is plead with you, Lucas, but I will get down on my knees if it will do any good."

"What do you want from me?"

"You know as well as I do that she has refused three very fine young men of good families in the past year."

"What of it?"

"She has declared that if she cannot marry Charles Rushton, she will not wed anyone."

"She did say something to that effect. I believe he is an expert on antiquities and dead languages. You know she has always been interested in such matters."

"Beth is interested in a great many subjects. What does that signify?"

"I believe Beth feels she and Mr. Rushton are intellectually compatible and that they have a great deal in common."

Judith's hand tightened into a small fist. "Such things have nothing to do with marriage."

"I realize that you feel that marriage is a business arrangement."

"Don't you dare patronize me. For a woman that is precisely what it is, a business arrangement."

It was pointless to try to conduct a civil, rational conversation with Judith, Lucas reminded himself. He should know that by now. Nevertheless, he had to make some attempt, if only for Beth's sake.

"Beth is an intelligent, sensible young woman," he said. "I suggest that you let her make her own decision because I am sure that she will do so, regardless."

"Young women are rarely sensible when it comes to marriage."

"Is there something specific about Charles Rushton that you find objectionable?"

"For heaven's sake, he hasn't got a penny to his name," Judith said, exasperated.

"Are you certain of that?"

"Yes, of course I'm certain. I had Miller look into his finances when I realized that Beth was starting to spend far too much time in museums in Rushton's company. The man is barely squeaking by on a small income from some investments left to him by his grandfather. He can scarcely support himself, let alone a wife, and he has no prospects whatsoever. It is obvious that he is a fortune hunter."

"Even if what you say is correct, what do you expect me to do about it?"

"You must make it clear to Beth that you forbid the marriage."

"Do you really think that would stop her? If anything, it would probably have the opposite effect. She is far more likely to make a runaway marriage if she concludes that we are all against her."

"Then you must speak to Rushton." Judith rose from the chair. "You control the money in this family. He knows that. If you make it clear that you are opposed to the marriage and that Beth will be cut off if she marries against your wishes, I'm sure he will disappear."

Lucas got to his feet. "What if you are wrong about Rushton, Judith? What if he does love Beth and she loves him?"

"I doubt very much that I'm wrong. But even if it transpires that I am, it makes no difference. Love is a frail, fleeting and unreliable thing. It cannot be relied upon to sustain two people for a lifetime. I do not want Beth to discover that the hard way."

"As you did?" he asked.

Fury mixed with old pain glittered in Judith's eyes. "How dare you, Lucas?"

Regret welled up inside him. He found it difficult to feel deep sympathy for Judith, but there were lines that should never be crossed. He had just done that and he did not like himself very much for it.

"I'm sorry," he said quietly. He crossed the room to open the door. "That was uncalled for."

"Yes, it was," she said. "It is quite unnecessary to remind me of my own past. You may believe me when I tell you that I have never forgotten it. Indeed, I think about it every day of my life."

"I am well aware that your marriage to my father did not bring you much in the way of happiness. But do you really want to force Beth into the same sort of loveless match?"

"No, of course not. But with her advantages there will be other suitors. She will find another, more suitable young man. Unlike me, she will have a choice."

Judith swept past him through the doorway and out into the hall.

He closed the door and went back across the room to contemplate the gardens through the vine-clad windows. Judith's words seemed to echo in the silent room. *Unlike me, she will have a choice.*

He stood there for a long time, thinking of what he had done that morning. By announcing the engagement to the crowd that had awaited them outside the maze, he had effectively taken away Evangeline's right to make her own choice. Now it seemed that she was in something of a panic. She had gone through an extraordinary series of dangerous events in the past few days, events that had taken a toll on her nerves.

She needed time, he thought, time to see that marriage to him was the right thing for her, for both of them.

He ought to woo her. She deserved that much. But how did a man accomplish a proper courtship when he was trying to keep his lady from being murdered?

Twenty-five

Evangeline was in the parlor, finishing a cup of tea with Beth and Florence and enjoying the afternoon sunshine that streamed through the windows, when Judith arrived in the doorway.

The parlor was situated on what Evangeline had come to think of as the sunny side of the house, the side that faced away from the walled gardens. The warm light would not last much longer. In another hour the sun would begin to disappear behind the dense woods, creating an early summer twilight around the abbey.

"Miss Ames," Judith said. "I was hoping to find you here."

"Mrs. Sebastian," Evangeline said. "Please join us."

Beth picked up the teapot. "Do sit down and have some tea, Mama."

"Yes, Judith, have some tea," Florence urged. "You look as if you need a bit of fortifying. I understand, believe me. I vow, the atmosphere of this place is very hard on the nerves. It was always unpleasant in the past, but now it is more distressing than it ever was."

"I know what you mean," Judith said quietly.

"Last night I took a double dose of my special sleeping tonic but I got very little rest," Florence continued. "I finally fell asleep just before dawn, only to be awakened a short time later by all the commotion caused by the discovery that Lucas and Miss Ames had vanished. Really, this entire visit has been too much."

"Aunt Florence has just told us that she intends to leave in the morning," Beth explained.

"It is clear I am no longer needed here and I really cannot take any more of this place," Florence said. She shuddered. "Rose is upstairs packing. We will take the morning train to London tomorrow."

"I wish to speak in private with Miss Ames," Judith said. She looked at Beth and Florence. "Do you mind leaving us for a time?"

Florence gave her a searching look and then glanced at Evangeline. Comprehension flickered in her eyes. She put down her cup.

"Not at all," she said. "I shall go upstairs and try to nap."

She rose and swept out of the room.

Clearly relieved to be dismissed, Beth set the pot down and jumped quickly to her feet.

"I'm off to the library," she said. "I was just taking a short break."

Judith looked blank. "From what?"

"Tony and I are assisting Lucas with some research."

Judith frowned. "What sort of research does he want you to do?"

"We are reading through Uncle Chester's last journals to see if we can find the names of any of his colleagues who many have visited here at the Gardens in recent months."

"What on earth for?"

Beth paused in the doorway. "Haven't you heard? Lucas thinks Uncle Chester was murdered."

Judith's frown turned to horror. "Dear heaven."

"Uncle Chester's housekeeper, Mrs. Buckley, might have been

another victim, as well," Beth said. "There were intruders on the grounds last night. Evie and Lucas encountered them in the gardens and were nearly killed. Mr. Stone was knocked unconscious."

"No, please." Stricken, Judith more or less collapsed onto one of the chairs. "Not more murders. Not here. What is wrong with that man? I swear, he is obsessed with death."

"Evie can explain," Beth said. "I must return to the library. Lucas is very impatient for the answers. Naturally he's afraid that the murderer might escape."

She rushed out into the hall. Evangeline waited until the patter of rapid footsteps had faded. Then she picked up the teapot and poured tea for Judith.

"Thank you," Judith whispered. She picked up the cup with a shaky hand, swallowed some tea and set the cup down with great care. "How dare he involve Beth and Tony in one of his dreadful investigations."

"To be fair, Lucas was not inclined to do so. It was my idea. Beth and Tony seem quite enthusiastic about the business, though."

"Of course," Judith said faintly. "The twins have always considered Lucas's dreadful little hobby exciting."

"There appears to be no danger involved," Evangeline said quickly. "They are simply reading the journals and making some notes."

"You do not understand. No one does." Judith sounded oddly weary.

"What don't I understand?" Evangeline asked.

"I knew from the start that he loathed me."

"Who? Lucas?"

"Yes, Lucas. He was only three years younger than me, barely fifteen when I married his father. "He terrified me from the beginning. Such a strange young man. I was convinced that he was mentally unstable. After the twins were born, I refused to let him anywhere near the babies."

"You can't possibly have believed that Lucas would have been a danger to you or the children."

"In those days I could not be sure that anyone was safe around Lucas. His behavior became increasingly bizarre. He was reclusive. He spent hours locked in his room with his books. On the occasions when he did emerge, he looked as if he had barely slept. When he was away at school I could sleep but whenever he was in the house I lay awake until he left the house at night to prowl the streets. He seldom returned before dawn. I was so relieved when he moved into lodgings of his own."

"I see."

"I learned that his midnight forays into the streets did not stop. I heard the servants talking. There were rumors that Lucas disappeared more and more often into the night and that sometimes he returned with blood on his clothes."

"How did the servants in your house discover such a thing?"

"Because he took Paul, one of the footmen, with him when he moved out," Judith said grimly. But after a month or two, Paul quit Lucas's service and asked my butler if he could have his old post back. After he was rehired he confided to some of the other members of the staff that he was afraid Lucas might be involved in black magic."

"Lucas was coming into his paranormal talents. His psychical powers are quite strong. They could have easily overwhelmed a young man. He was struggling to control his new senses and in the process he no doubt behaved in an unconventional fashion."

"Unconventional does not touch it, Miss Ames. *There was blood on his clothes*, I tell you."

"Because he had begun to investigate murders with his talent," Evangeline said gently. "I'm sure that crime scenes are often bloody."

"You speak of the paranormal so casually, Miss Ames." Judith's jaw clenched. "I realize it's fashionable to attend séances and psychical readings, but please bear in mind that to many of us that sort of thing is nothing but occult, superstitious nonsense."

"Paranormal energy has nothing whatsoever to do with the occult or superstition," Evangeline said. "It is just energy." But she knew that she was wasting her breath. "Did Lucas's father realize that his son was troubled and seeking answers?"

Judith made a soft little sound of disgust. "George was useless. He would not listen to my concerns about Lucas. Actually, he did not pay much attention to anyone, including his own son. He was rarely home and when he was, he secluded himself in his study with his books on ancient Egypt and Rome. Occasionally he wrote papers for journals no one read. But most of the time he was off excavating some archaeological site in a foreign land. Three years after our marriage he died on one of the expeditions. The walls of a tomb he was excavating collapsed on him."

"What of Lucas's grandfather?"

"He was certainly more of a father to Lucas than George ever was, but I know that Lucas's claims of paranormal talent alarmed him. He worried about the taint in the bloodline, you see."

Evangeline tightened her grip on her cup and managed to keep her voice steady with an effort. "Psychical talent is not a taint in the blood."

"That is your opinion. All I can tell you is that I was aware that Lucas's grandfather had some concerns about his grandson's mental stability. In the end, however, he acknowledged that Lucas was very shrewd when it came to managing the Sebastian investments. He made Lucas his sole heir. Lucas has had complete control of the family fortune for years."

"I have the impression that your marriage to Lucas's father was not what anyone would call a love match."

Judith's mouth twisted. "Is there any such thing? I married George

Sebastian for the usual reasons. My parents had no money. All I had to recommend me was my youth and my looks. George and my father were colleagues. Both of them were obsessed with archaeology. Shortly after Lucas's mother died, my father suggested to George that I would make an excellent wife. George considered that to be an extremely convenient solution to his problem."

"What problem?"

"George had discovered that he needed someone to oversee his household," Judith said, her tone very dry. "He was having some difficulty retaining housekeepers—in part, I suspect, because of Lucas. Whatever the reason, George and I were married within the month."

"So quickly?"

"George was not interested in an elaborate ceremony. He was occupied with plans for his next expedition. He departed for Egypt less than a week after we were married."

"I'm surprised you agreed to the marriage."

Judith looked toward the windows and then turned back. There was pain in her eyes but her voice was steady. "I told you, I had just turned eighteen. My parents insisted that I wed George. I had no choice. One does what one must. But that is all in the past. The only reason I am being so candid with you is because I wish to make it clear that I do comprehend your situation."

"What do you mean?"

"I realize that you have been presented with what appears to be a golden opportunity to marry into the Sebastian fortune. But speaking woman to woman, I would advise you to be careful what you wish for."

"As it happens, I am very much aware of the risks involved when one seeks to marry for the sake of fortune and social status," Evangeline said. "I assure you that I have no interest in making that mistake."

"I'm glad to hear that because I can promise you that such a marriage is sometimes a lifetime sentence."

"But your husband died years ago."

"His death changed nothing for me," Judith said. "Lucas controls the fortune, which means that I am still trapped in my lovely gilded cage. What is worse, my daughter and son are trapped with me."

"I don't understand. Surely your husband made provision for you and the twins."

"George never paid any attention to financial matters. The only provision he made for the twins and me was to stipulate that Lucas was obliged to support each of us unless or until we marry. That has never been an issue for me. I have never had any desire to remarry. But I fear what Lucas will do when the time comes for Beth and Tony to wed."

"Surely you don't believe that Lucas will cut them off after they marry?" Evangeline said.

"I told you, I know him as you do not, Miss Ames. I have always been aware that he would one day find a way to take revenge against me for what he perceives to be my crime of marrying his father."

"You can't be serious. Perhaps Lucas resented you when he was fifteen years old. He had only recently lost his mother, after all, and his father was bringing a new woman into the household. But that was years ago and he is no longer a boy. He understands such things now. He knows you are not to blame."

"You are wrong, Miss Ames. Lucas does blame me and he intends to punish me. What is more, he is going to do so in the way he knows will hurt me the most, through my children."

"No, I cannot believe that," Evangeline said. "Not for a moment. Even if he does harbor a grievance against you, he would never take it out on Beth and Tony. It is obvious that he is very fond of them."

"You do not believe me because you do not know him as I do, Miss Ames. Lucas is planning to cut off both Beth and Tony. But first he must see them wed. Nothing would enhance his vengeance so much as seeing my daughter run off with her penniless antiquities expert."

"I am certain that you have badly misjudged Lucas," Evangeline said. "I think that Beth has a much more accurate sense of his character. She certainly does not fear him."

Judith made a short, harsh, exasperated sound. "You need not point that out to me. Beth and Tony positively idolize Lucas. He was the closest thing to a father that they ever had in their lives. And I will give him credit for playing the role well. The twins are so naive, so innocent. They have no idea that Lucas has been biding his time, waiting until he can use them to exact his revenge against me."

"That cannot be true," Evangeline said. "I refuse to believe it."

"You have been acquainted with Lucas for only a few days. You know nothing about him."

"I know enough to be convinced that your fear of him is unwarranted. It is no doubt based on your personal fear of his paranormal talents. I understand that he made you anxious when you were a young bride. But surely by now you must realize that he is not unbalanced."

"Has he told you of his unpleasant little hobby, Miss Ames?"

Evangeline stilled. "You refer to the fact that he occasionally consults for Scotland Yard?"

"It is bad enough that he involves himself in police investigations. That sort of thing is hardly the province of a gentleman. But Lucas only consults on the most ghastly cases of murder, the sort of lurid crimes that appear in the penny dreadfuls. And now he has concluded that his own uncle was murdered when it is obvious that Chester Sebastian was very likely the victim of one of his own unnatural botanical experiments. I ask you, Miss Ames, does that not sound like a mentally unbalanced man to you?"

"You are looking at this from the wrong perspective."

Judith got to her feet. "Do not try to lecture me on the subject of Lucas Sebastian. I have been dealing with him in one way or another since I was eighteen years old. The knowledge that my son and daughter's future is in his hands terrifies me."

"Please listen to me. Or listen to Beth, for that matter."

"Only a very naive and foolish woman could convince herself that she was in love with Lucas," Judith said tightly. "Something tells me that you are neither naive nor foolish, Miss Ames."

"I trust not."

"Then you are an opportunist." Judith's smile was bitter. "I do not blame you in the least. But you are swimming out of your depth. I'm sure you think yourself a clever woman because you managed to get yourself thoroughly compromised by a wealthy gentleman who appears to feel obligated to do the honorable thing. But that is not what has happened. You are the one who is being used, Miss Ames."

"In what possible manner?"

"Do not be deceived into thinking that Lucas's notion of honor requires him to marry you because you were compromised. I assure you, he follows his own rules, not the social conventions. Nor should you delude yourself into believing that he has fallen in love with you. Lucas does not know the meaning of the word. If he has decided to marry you, it is because he has concluded that you will be useful to him."

Evangeline's temper flashed. She was suddenly on her feet. "How?"

"I do not pretend to know his plans. No one has ever been able to read Lucas. But I do know that he always has an objective and that he is quite ruthless when it comes to achieving it. You have been warned."

"Thank you." Evangeline made no attempt to conceal the ice in her words. "One more thing."

Judith paused. "Yes?"

"This hobby of Lucas's that you mentioned?"

"What of it?"

"As it happens, I am in need of his skills at the moment."

Judith frowned. "I don't understand."

"Someone is trying to kill me."

"Is this some sort of joke? If so, I must tell you that it is in very poor taste."

"The would-be killer has already made one attempt on my life. There is every reason to think he will try again. Naturally, I am hoping that Lucas will find the person who wants me dead before that individual is successful."

"Good Lord." Judith was dumbfounded. "I cannot help but wonder if you are as delusional and unbalanced as Lucas. I take back my warning to you about the risks of marrying him. From the sound of it, the two of you may be ideally suited."

Judith opened the door of the parlor and swept out into the hall. A short time later her footsteps sounded on the stairs.

Twenty-six

Evangeline sat quietly, drinking tea, for a time. Eventually she rose and went out into the hall. She walked to the library. The door was open. Lucas was standing at his desk, examining the lantern weapon in the glare of a gas lamp. When he saw her his eyes heated a little.

"Evangeline," he said. "Excellent. I was just going to send someone to find you. Come in and close the door. It has become almost impossible to have privacy in this place. Anyone would think I was hosting a damned house party. To think I once had it in mind to set up camp here in the library for a few days or weeks while I conducted a simple murder investigation."

Evangeline moved into the room and closed the door behind her. "Are there any simple investigations when it comes to murder?"

"A good question. It depends on one's definition of 'simple.' It is often easy enough to identify the killer. The difficult part is comprehending why he or she committed the act. People can come up with the most astounding explanations and excuses. But in my experience there are only a handful of reasons for murder."

"Such as?"

"Jealousy, vengeance, greed, fear and pleasure."

"Pleasure?"

"The more common term is 'madness.'" Lucas raised his brows. "Some killers enjoy the kill, Evangeline. For them it is a great game, and for the most part they are the ones I hunt."

"The mad killers."

"Yes."

She glanced at the lantern. "It does not appear that your uncle was murdered by a madman."

"I think we can look to one of the other traditional motives to explain Uncle Chester's and possibly Mrs. Buckley's death. Based on what we learned last night when we encountered the intruders, greed would seem to be the motivation." Lucas glanced at the lantern. "That may be the murder weapon."

"If so it would explain why there was no wound on your uncle's body."

"Murder by paranormal means leaves no obvious mark. The death usually appears to have been caused by a heart attack or a stroke."

"Good heavens, you have investigated such murders?"

"Yes, but they are quite rare." He set the lantern on the desk. "Very few people of talent are capable of committing murder in that manner."

Evangeline froze.

Understanding lit Lucas's eyes. "You are not a murderer, Evangeline. You killed in self-defense. That is a very different matter. Sit down and tell me why you came here to see me."

Evangeline sank down onto one of the reading chairs, absently twitching the folds of her skirts into place. "I have just concluded a rather uncomfortable conversation with Judith."

"Hardly surprising," Lucas said. "Most of my own conversations with Judith qualify as uncomfortable." He propped himself against the edge of the desk. "Several have ranked as seriously unpleasant. I expect she warned you that I was a dangerous, mentally unbalanced man who was given to the morbid pastime of investigating the most dreadful murders."

"I see you are aware of her deluded notions concerning your character."

Lucas folded his arms. "I appreciate that you refer to her as deluded. But I must admit she has her reasons for her opinions."

"She is frightened of you."

"Evidently."

"I understand how you might have made her very nervous when she was a young bride. You were dealing with the onset of your talents, after all, and she does not even believe in the paranormal. It is no wonder she thought you might be somewhat unbalanced."

"Her reaction to me was certainly understandable," Lucas said.

The perfectly neutral tone of his voice aroused her intuition. *There was more to the story,* she thought.

"You, on the other hand, no doubt resented her because you had recently lost your mother," she continued, moving cautiously. "Furthermore, you were on the brink of manhood. The last thing you would have wanted was a stepmother. The fact that Judith wasn't that much older than you would have made it all the more difficult for both of you."

"Yes," he said. He offered nothing more.

"Nevertheless, one would have thought that the hostility between the two of you would have softened somewhat over the years."

"One would certainly think so," Lucas agreed.

She recognized a conversational wall when she ran head-on into one, she thought. The strained relationship between Lucas and Judith was none of her affair. She was not a member of the family, after all. Nevertheless, she could not stop herself from pressing for answers.

"Judith said that when you were younger you were in the habit of going out into the streets at night and that you did not return until dawn. I assume that was when you began your murder investigations."

"Yes."

"But there was more to it, wasn't there?"

"You want to know what I was doing on those nights?"

"Something tells me it is important."

Lucas looked at her very steadily for a time, his eyes dark and unreadable. She knew that he was debating how much to tell her, *not because he doesn't trust me*, she thought. *He is hesitating because he does not know how I will react.*

When the silence lengthened, she sighed and sat back. "It's all right, Lucas. I understand that you do not wish to tell me. You are entitled to your secrets."

"You have confided your most closely held secrets to me. It is only right that I tell you mine."

He pushed himself away from the desk and went to the darkened windows. He stood quietly for a moment. She waited.

"I tried to talk about my paranormal senses with my father, but he soon made it clear that he considered them to be in the nature of a character flaw. He got angry and claimed that I had inherited my talent from my mother's side, which was demonstrably untrue. He warned me to keep silent about my abilities. I confronted my grandfather. He confirmed that my affinity for the darkest of psychical energy came from the male line. The talent did not appear frequently, but when it did show up, it often proved disastrous."

"In what way?"

Lucas gripped the windowsill with one hand. "Some of my ancestors could control their talents. Others could not. Those who failed often attributed their sensitivities to the work of demonic forces and so did others in the family. More than one of my predecessors ended their lives in private asylums for the insane."

"The paranormal was not well understood in the past."

Lucas glanced at her. "The paranormal is hardly better understood today, as we both know full well."

"True." She managed a small smile. "In the modern world psychical abilities are viewed as a kind of parlor trick. Indeed, we are overrun with fraudulent mediums and people claiming psychical powers."

Lucas turned back to the window. "The problem with assuming that all practitioners of the paranormal are frauds is that one can easily overlook the real thing until it is too late."

"What do you mean?"

"When I realized that my talents were growing stronger and that I was being drawn to the scenes of violent crimes, I knew that I had to learn to control my psychical nature. The alternative was to risk madness or perhaps something worse."

"What could be worse?"

"Becoming a human predator, one of the monsters."

"Never," she said fiercely. "That is not in your nature."

"I like to think that is true, but I came very close when I was nineteen, Evangeline."

"No, never."

He ignored that. "I went in search of a mentor, a guide, someone like me who could teach me what I needed to know to handle my talent. I visited every medium in London and attended every demonstration of psychical powers I could find. I immersed myself in the practitioners' underworld and after a time some of them began to trust me. The mediums were all frauds, of course, but some of the practitioners who claimed to possess paranormal abilities were genuine."

"I'm sure that's true."

"I began hearing rumors of an especially powerful talent they called the Master. The practitioners spoke of him in whispers. I set out to find him."

"Because he was believed to be so powerful?"

"No, because from the hints that I received, I was convinced that his particular talent was similar to mine."

"You found him?" she asked.

"It would be more accurate to say that he found me. He had heard rumors, too, you see. There were whispers on the streets about a young man who was drawn to the scenes of murder and violence, a young man who had arrived at the scene of a recent crime in time to stop the killer, who was later found dead in the alley, the apparent victim of a heart attack."

"Your doing?" Evangeline asked quietly.

"It was the first time I ever used my talent in that manner," Lucas said, "the first time I realized I could do so. The man charged me. He had the knife that he had planned to use on the woman. There was a struggle. I clouded his mind with unbearable horrors. The shock stopped his heart."

"You reacted instinctively in self-defense, just as I did when I encountered Douglas Mason at the top of the stairs."

"The man did not die instantly," Lucas said. "It . . . took a few seconds."

"During which time you were in physical contact with him. You felt the dreadful currents of death, the shock that I experienced when Mason died. I have known it only once but I suspect the sensation will haunt my dreams for the rest of my life."

"There is nothing else to compare with the terrible energy generated at the moment of violent death."

Knowing whispered through her. "I think that you have known that terrible sensation more than once."

"Too many times. It is not good for the spirit."

"No, I agree. But on that occasion you saved not only your own life but the life of the intended victim. She would have died if you had not interrupted the killer in time."

"And what of all the others before her, Evangeline? The ones I failed to save because it took me so long to learn the killer's pattern?"

"You cannot blame yourself for failing to read the mind of a madman. No one can do that. The point is that you did stop him. Like a doctor who loses patients, you must learn to concentrate on the people you have saved."

Lucas smiled his humorless smile. "An interesting analogy. How do you manage to remain such a thoroughgoing romantic after all you have been through?"

"But I am not romanticizing your actions. I merely pointed out that you have saved any number of people. By any definition, that makes you a hero."

"No, Evangeline, I do what I must because of the nature of my talent. You could say that I am driven to do it."

"You may feel compelled to save others and to destroy those who would prey on the vulnerable, but that is hardly a character flaw. For heaven's sake, Lucas, you are quite clearly the master of your talent and therefore of yourself."

His eyes heated a little. "Not entirely. Not around you, Evangeline."

She tensed. "If you refer to what happened between us last night—"

"I do, most certainly."

"Then I would remind you that I was the one who set out to seduce you, sir."

He smiled. "Is that how you remember it?"

"My memory is quite accurate on the matter," she said firmly. "Now, then, to return to the subject of your association with this man you called the Master."

"It was that case, the one in which I killed a man for the first time, that attracted his attention. He contacted me. We talked. In the end he took me under his wing and taught me many things. He showed me that hunting killers was the greatest challenge of all. For a time we hunted them together and we did so in secret."

"You hunted them?" She frowned. "Or you investigated murders?"

"Ah, yes, I see you grasp the distinction." Lucas's smile held no amusement, only sad regret. "I congratulate you, Evangeline. You understood the difference much more readily than I did."

"I'm sure the line between investigation and hunting is a very thin one, at times indistinguishable." She hesitated. "I think that perhaps it does not always matter."

"It matters." He began to prowl the library. "To return to my story, the Master was a wealthy gentleman who lived a double life. He moved in society and belonged to the best clubs. He kept his paranormal abilities and his interest in murderers secret. He taught me to do the same."

"That seems quite sensible to me." She smiled. "As we all know, gentlemen do not claim psychical talents and they do not dabble in murder investigations."

Lucas's cold smile came and went. "Yes, of course."

"Very well, you and this gentleman hunted murderers together for a time. I assume the Master had some connection with the police?"

"He never revealed his identity to the authorities," Lucas said. "But, yes, he often made certain that they stumbled upon evidence that led them to the killer. A few arrests were made."

She blinked. "Only a few?"

"Several of the killers simply disappeared from the streets." Lucas must have seen the way she was looking at him because he shook his head. "Not my doing."

"The Master set himself up as judge, jury and executioner?"

"In several instances, yes. But it took me a while to tumble to what was happening. The Master was very, very good at covering his own tracks. Mind you, the murderers he dispatched were evil. I felt no sympathy for them. But I soon realized I could not do what he did."

"You could not become a cold-blooded killer, even in the name of justice."

"What I eventually came to understand is that the Master enjoyed the business, not just the hunt, as I confess I do, but also the kill. Inevitably there was a confrontation between us. He said I was too soft, too weak to do what had to be done. I agreed that I was not cut out to be his true heir. We parted ways. A few months later the killings began."

"What killings?"

"This was over a decade ago, thirteen years back to be precise. The victims were all mistresses of men who moved in society. All of the deaths were made to look like bizarre accidents but it wasn't long before the police and the press realized that they were the work of a vicious murderer. The killer always left a token at the scenes. The newspapers ran wild with the story. They even gave the killer a name."

Evangeline did some brief calculations in her head. "Are you talking about the Courtesan Killer?"

"You remember the crimes?" Lucas frowned. "You would have been very young at the time."

"I was thirteen or fourteen. The accounts in the papers left a very strong impression on me."

"And on me, as well," Lucas said grimly. "They caught my attention immediately because they did not fit the patterns I had learned on the streets. The predators I had been trained to hunt usually chose victims who would not be missed, at least not by respectable society. They take prostitutes, beggars and street urchins for the most part."

"I see what you mean. These victims were prostitutes but they were very elegant prostitutes. Courtesans."

"It was as if the killer was challenging those who moved in the better circles. Several gentlemen packed their mistresses off to the Continent for extended vacations. Others hired bodyguards. But most left the women to fend for themselves. I went to the scene of the first two murders and realized that there was a pattern. Before I could work it out, however, there was a third murder. I managed to get to the scene of the fourth crime while the woman was still alive."

"I recall reading that the fourth courtesan survived and that the killer was found dead at the scene. The victim claimed that she had been saved by a stranger who happened to pass by and realized that she was in desperate straits. The stranger was never found. That was you, I assume?"

"It was all supposed to end somewhat differently. The killer had sensed that I was closing in on him. He planned to kill both the courtesan and me and leave evidence at the scene that would make it appear that I was guilty of the murders. But by then I knew the real identity of the killer. I arrived well before I was expected."

"You saved the fourth woman and you dispatched the murderer. I have forgotten the name of the villain who perpetrated the Courtesan Murders but I do recall that he was a gentleman who moved in the highest circles of society."

"Edward Cox," Lucas said. "My mentor and teacher. The Master who taught me how to hunt and how to kill."

Twenty-seven

Lucas stood over his desk, hands flattened on the large map of the abbey grounds that he had spread out and pondering the three odd marks that Chester had made. Something told him the marks were important but he could not see why. There were no notes.

Footsteps sounded in the hall. Two people, he concluded, a woman and a man. Both were almost running. He looked up as Beth and Tony arrived in the doorway.

Beth had one of Chester's notebooks clutched in her hands. She was alight with excitement. Tony looked equally exhilarated.

"We think we may have found something of great importance in Uncle Chester's last journal," Beth announced.

Her enthusiasm brightened the atmosphere around her. No wonder she did not want to marry one of the dull, stiff-necked men who were courting her, Lucas thought. She needed someone who could appreciate her intelligence and her bright spirit.

"Come in, both of you," Lucas said. "Tell me what you think you've discovered."

"We found a reference to two of Uncle Chester's colleagues who apparently visited him here at Crystal Gardens about a month before he died," Beth said. She walked to the desk and put the notebook down on the map. "Unfortunately, Uncle identified them only by their initials, not complete names, but the initials of the given names fit with the names that you heard them call each other last night, H and B."

"Horace and Burton," Lucas said quietly. Energy crackled across his senses, arousing the hunter in him.

"Yes." Tony came to stand next to Beth. He, too, was flushed and energized. "What is more, the last initial of each is the same, T."

"Meaning they may share the same last name," Lucas said. "They might be related."

"Exactly," Tony said. "It occurred to us that it may be possible to go through Uncle Chester's correspondence and discover names that match the initials and, with luck, the addresses of the two men. It is obvious that Chester invited the pair here to the gardens. There ought to be some record, a letter or a telegram."

"This is excellent news," Lucas said. "Well done, both of you."

Beth glowed. Tony grinned.

"Show me what you found," Lucas said.

"The first references to HT and BT are in early June." Beth opened the notebook to the place she had marked with a strip of paper and pointed to one of the handwritten entries. "Uncle Chester writes that he has invited the pair to view the results of his latest experiments. A few days later he says he received a telegram stating that the two men would arrive the following Friday. He mentions in passing that Mrs.

Buckley was not pleased at the prospect of guests, but he adds that she has been in a bad temper for some time. He sounds irritated with her."

Tony reached out to turn a few pages. "These notes are from the following week. HT and BT have arrived and are staying here in the house. Uncle Chester is very excited because the two guests have brought a new device that can be used to navigate the Night Garden. He says it looks rather like a small lantern and that it is powered by a crystal."

They all looked at the small brass-and-glass lantern that was sitting on a nearby table.

"Son of a—" Lucas began. He remembered that Beth was standing right in front of him and stopped abruptly. "That certainly gives us at least a partial answer to one of the questions we are dealing with. You're right, the next step is to identify HT and BT."

"If you have no objection Beth and I will start going through Uncle Chester's correspondence immediately. We have a good notion as to the dates. Shouldn't take long to find those names."

"There is one problem with that plan," Lucas said. "I have already gone through Chester's correspondence, what little there is of it. He was too impatient to write letters, for the most part, and he rarely kept the few he received."

Tony's eager expression was instantly transformed into disappointment.

"Damnation," he growled. "I was so certain we had found the answers."

Beth was equally downcast. "I suppose we should have known that it wouldn't be that simple."

"We may have another option," Lucas said. "Chester was a man of the modern age. When he did bother to communicate, it was generally by telegram. I suggest you go into town and have a chat with the telegraph operator. There should be records of telegrams sent and received by Chester. And while you're there, talk to the train station manager and old Mayhew who operates the cab. Little Dixby gets a lot of visitors at this time of year but most come to tour the ruins in town. There were never many visitors here at the Gardens. Someone may remember something of note."

Tony cheered instantly. "Should have thought of that myself."

"We shall walk into town immediately," Beth said. "With luck, we will have some answers within a few hours."

They rushed out of the library before Lucas could respond. He went back to the desk and contemplated the map. He was still at it a short time later when he heard more footsteps. He smiled in anticipation just before Evangeline appeared.

"Molly tells me that Beth and Tony are on their way into town," she said. "Did they discover something of interest?"

"They found two sets of initials in Chester's last journal that could very well belong to the two men we encountered in the maze. They are going to ask a few questions at the train station and interview the telegraph operator."

"That is very good news, indeed, but it may be unnecessary. Molly's cousin, Norris, just arrived with word that the doctor was called out early this morning to attend a gentleman who was running a strange fever. Evidently the doctor returned home fearing the worst."

Lucas came out from behind the desk and went swiftly toward the door. "Address?"

"A cottage on Willow Pond. According to Molly it is only about a mile from here if one takes the shortcut through the woods at the end of the lane."

"Within walking distance," Lucas said. The energy of the hunt whispered through him. "If they survived the energy storm, they might have made it back to the cottage."

"I'm coming with you," Evangeline said.

He paused in the doorway. "No. There is no telling what sort of reception we will get. If HT and BT are at the cottage, they may be armed."

"It sounds like one of them may be dying," Evangeline said. "If he is suffering from the same fever that you endured last night, you will need me."

Twenty-eight

Horace was removing yet another fever-heated cloth from Burton's hot brow when he heard the sharp, demanding raps on the front door. For a few seconds his spirits lifted. Perhaps the doctor had returned with some new medicine.

He dropped the cloth into the bowl on the dresser and rushed into the small parlor. He paused to peek through the curtains. When he saw Sebastian and the woman on the front step his heart nearly failed him. All was lost. There was no point trying to escape through the kitchen garden. He could not abandon Burton. The only hope was to bluff.

He opened the door. "Who would you be, sir, calling at such an hour?"

"Lucas Sebastian," Lucas said. "This is my fiancée, Miss Ames. We met last night when you and your associate trespassed onto the grounds of Crystal Gardens."

Horace fought to control his panic. "I have no notion of what you are talking about. There's a sick man in this house. He might very well be contagious."

"He's still alive, then?" Miss Ames asked quickly. "I might be able to help him."

Horace squinted at her through his spectacles. "The doctor has already been here. He said there was nothing to be done."

"We believe your associate is afflicted with a fever of the paranormal senses. It is unlikely the doctor has ever encountered such an illness."

"And you have, Miss Ames?"

"Yes," she said. "I have. Just last night, in fact. Mr. Sebastian suffered a similar fever shortly after the energy storm in the maze. As you can see, he is very much alive and in excellent health today."

"Because of you?" Horace asked. Suspicion warred with desperation.

"Miss Ames saved my senses last night," Sebastian said. "Where is the harm in letting her examine your associate?"

"He's not my associate," Horace said. "He's my brother."

Miss Ames whisked up her skirts and moved through the doorway. "Where is he?"

In spite of his panic, habit took over. Horace fell back, allowing her to sweep past him into the shadowed parlor. Sebastian crossed the threshold in her wake. Aware that he had lost the small battle, Horace closed the door.

"Burton is in the bedroom," he said.

But he was speaking to Miss Ames's back. She was already moving through the bedroom doorway.

Sebastian glanced briefly into the room. Evidently satisfied that Miss Ames was not in danger from Burton, he turned around and regarded Horace with flat, cold eyes.

"You and I are going to talk while Miss Ames determines if there is anything she can do for your brother," Sebastian said.

"I d-don't understand," Horace stammered. "My brother and I came to Little Dixby to sketch the ruins."

He knew he sounded weak and insincere. He had never been much good at lying. But there was an aura of menace around Sebastian that was quite terrifying. Indeed, the ominous energy saturated the atmosphere in the parlor. Sebastian's eyes appeared to be glowing a little. *Like the eyes of a demon,* Horace thought. He was a scientist, a modern thinker, but he had never been more frightened in his life. Burton could not protect him today.

Sebastian did not even bother to dismiss the flimsy explanation. "I assume you murdered my uncle because he would not allow you and your brother to search for the Roman gold said to be buried somewhere in the Night Garden."

"Murder?" Horace stopped breathing for a few beats. "See here, I swear we did not murder Chester Sebastian. It is well known that he died from the effects of some toxic plant in his gardens."

"That may be a popular theory here in Little Dixby, but I am convinced that he was the victim of foul play. I suspect you also killed his housekeeper, presumably because she could identify you."

"No, please, I swear. Burton and I haven't killed anyone."

"You and your brother visited my uncle last month, shortly before his death."

"How can you possibly know that?"

"There is a record of your stay in his last journal."

"His journal," Horace repeated dully. "Yes, of course."

"You brought with you a lantern powered by a crystal," Sebastian continued relentlessly. "The device allowed you to navigate the maze and, presumably, the inner garden. It also functions as a weapon. You will be relieved to know that my man, Stone, survived it, by the way."

Sebastian knew everything. Horace felt the floor starting to dissolve beneath his feet. A great black hole yawned beneath him. There was no point trying to prevaricate. The devil had come to drag him down into hell. He was shaking so badly he could no longer stand. He collapsed onto the nearest chair.

"The lantern was never intended as a weapon," he said. "The crystal can be used to generate a beam that allows one to find one's way in places where there is a great deal of energy clouding the senses. We hoped it could be used to locate the gold in the ground. But I realized soon after I perfected it that it could also focus a beam that would temporarily freeze all the senses, normal and paranormal. The result is a period of unconsciousness."

"Last night when your brother used it at full power in the maze, it triggered an energy storm."

"We had no idea it would do that," Horace said. "You must believe me. Burton intended only to render you unconscious. It's that bloody damn treasure, you see. He is obsessed with finding it."

"Obsession can drive a man to commit murder."

A great weariness came over Horace. Sebastian was about to have him arrested for murder and Burton was dying. There was no hope left.

"No, Mr. Sebastian," he said. "We did not kill your uncle."

"Why did you go after the treasure you believe to be in the Night Garden? There are Roman hoards buried all across England, just as there are ruins scattered about. Wealthy Romans often buried chests containing their valuables in the ground when they were forced to flee attackers or when they had to leave their estates for some reason."

"Yes, but they rarely left maps, you see. And the odds against accidentally stumbling over a chest of gold buried in a farmer's field centuries ago are slim, to say the least. But the legend of the gold on the grounds of the old abbey is much more specific. Burton's research indicates that the hoard is in the Night Garden. He believed that with our talent and with the aid of the crystal device, we would have an excellent chance of locating it."

"You knew the gardens are dangerous."

"Of course." Horace sighed. "I also reminded Burton that Chester Sebastian had been conducting his experiments at Crystal Gardens for decades and that if there were a treasure to be found, he would have discovered it. But my brother can be quite fixated on a goal."

"Neither of you is a botanist, I take it?"

"No, but we do have a great interest in the paranormal, so it was not difficult to coax your uncle into inviting us to visit the Gardens."

"He was always eager to talk to others who took his work seriously, but he was cautious," Sebastian said. "Some of his colleagues were opposed to his research. Others wanted to steal specimens, even though he warned them that none of the plants would survive long if removed from the source of the waters."

"We called on Chester and showed him my little lantern. He was very excited and agreed to conduct an experiment inside the maze. He said it was becoming increasingly difficult to get through it, even with his talent. He was convinced that the energy in the gardens was growing stronger."

"He was right."

"He gave us a tour of the grounds. Burton concluded that the lantern worked. We thanked your uncle and departed to make our plans. The next thing we know, Chester Sebastian was dead. We assumed that would give us plenty of time to explore the grounds in a logical fashion. We rented this cottage and began preparations. Then you arrived. Burton feared you intended to settle in at Crystal Gardens. He became desperate." Horace spread his hands. "You know the rest."

Miss Ames appeared in the doorway. "Your brother is resting comfortably. The fever has abated."

Horace shot to his feet, hardly daring to hope. "Burton will survive?"

"I believe he will recover, although there may be some permanent damage to his senses due to the duration of the crisis. I cannot say one way or the other because I have not had a great deal of experience with this sort of thing."

Horace hurried to the doorway and looked into the bedroom. Burton was sleeping peacefully. It was clear, even from a few feet away, that he was no longer wracked with the paranormal fever.

"I do not know how to thank you, Miss Ames," Horace said.

"You can do so by answering Mr. Sebastian's questions," she said.

"I have answered them all." He looked at Sebastian. "I give you my word there is nothing left to tell you. All we wanted was the treasure. We did not intend to hurt anyone and I swear we did not murder your uncle."

"What of the housekeeper? Do you know what happened to her?"

"No, I never paid much attention to her. She seemed a sullen sort." Horace pushed his spectacles higher on his nose. "Do you intend to have Burton and me arrested?"

"No," Sebastian said. "But I may want to ask you more questions at some other time. Do not leave Little Dixby until I give you permission. Is that clear?"

"Perfectly clear, Mr. Sebastian." Horace cleared his throat. "About my crystal lantern, I don't suppose you found it by any chance? It was one of a kind."

"It is safe enough for the moment but the crystal appears to be dead."

Horace considered that for a moment. "I expect it was the explosion inside the maze. It no doubt ruined the tuning of the crystal. It's very sensitive."

"My brother has a great interest in the science of the paranormal. He may wish to speak to you about your invention."

"Your brother?" Horace frowned. "I don't understand."

"It is not important now," Sebastian said. He took Miss Ames's arm and started toward the door. "We will deal with the matter some other time."

"Very well."

Sebastian paused at the door. "There is one thing I do not understand, Tolliver. Surely you saw enough examples of my uncle's botanical experiments to know how dangerous it would be to start digging anywhere on the abbey grounds."

"I did try to warn Burton but he wouldn't listen."

Sebastian shook his head.

"Treasure hunters," he said. "No common sense at all."

Twenty-nine

Evangeline untied the strings of her bonnet and handed it to Molly. "Mr. Sebastian and I are both in need of tea. Would you please bring a tray to the library?"

"Yes, Miss Ames," Molly said. But she hesitated, bonnet in hand. "May I ask if you found those two men you were looking for? The intruders?"

"Yes, Molly, we found them, thanks to your cousin," Evangeline said.

Lucas grunted in disgust. "For all the good it did."

"Are they going to be arrested?" Molly asked eagerly.

"No," Lucas said. He stalked down the hall toward the library. "They were treasure hunters, not killers."

Molly's eyes widened. She turned back to Evangeline. "What does he mean, Miss Ames?"

"It means he was mistaken," Evangeline said. She stripped off her gloves. "Mr. Sebastian is not accustomed to making errors of that nature. It annoys him."

"Oh, I see." Molly frowned. "Does that mean that his uncle and Mrs. Buckley were not murdered, after all?"

"No, it does not mean that there was no murder done here at Crystal Gardens," Lucas said very loudly from halfway down the hall. "It just means I have eliminated two of the possible suspects."

He vanished into the library. Evangeline smiled at Molly.

"Tea, Molly," she said.

"Yes, Miss Ames."

Molly hung Evangeline's bonnet on a peg and hurried off toward the kitchen. Evangeline dropped her gloves onto the hall table and went into the library. She eased the door closed behind her. Lucas was standing at the window, brooding on the cell door view of the gardens.

"You are still certain that your uncle and Mrs. Buckley were murdered?" she asked.

"I am still convinced that Uncle Chester's death was not from natural causes. I thought I made it clear that I have never been absolutely positive about what happened to Mrs. Buckley. All I know is that it would be helpful to find her, dead or alive."

"I agree." Evangeline sat down, absently adjusting her skirts.

"I was so certain those two men killed him, Evangeline."

"It did seem the most likely answer; in fact some would say it still does. Tell me, why did you believe Horace Tolliver?"

Lucas shrugged. "Damned if I know. I just did, that's all I can say. Why? Do you have a different opinion?"

"No, I'm inclined to agree with you."

"Now I must start over again from the beginning." Lucas turned away from the window. "I have been far too obsessed with finding Horace and Burton Tolliver."

"With good reason. They were the last visitors here at Crystal

Gardens, according to your uncle's journal, and they have psychical abilities. They intruded onto the grounds. They were armed with a paranormal weapon that they employed against both Stone and yourself. Everything pointed toward their guilt."

"But they are not guilty. I'm sure of it."

She nodded. "As I said, I agree."

Lucas clasped his hands behind his back. "We must examine the evidence from another perspective."

Evangeline hid a small smile of satisfaction. She liked it that he had referred to the two of them as a team. "We are assuming that there were no other visitors here at the Gardens after the Tolliver brothers. But we arrived at that conclusion based on your uncle's journal."

Lucas looked at her. "What are you thinking?"

"Beth mentioned that Chester used his journals primarily to record his botanical experiments and to make notes of a scientific nature. He kept track of visits from colleagues and other botanists, but Beth says there was no mention of your own visits here at the abbey."

Lucas went back to the desk and picked up the silver letter opener. "He would not have seen any reason to note a visit from a member of his family in a journal devoted to his botanical experiments."

"Perhaps he did not bother to makes notes of other visitors, either, because he did not consider them colleagues."

Lucas tapped the tip of the letter opener against one palm. "He would not have noted the visit of a neighbor or a deliveryman. Nor would he have bothered to record a visit from someone local, someone with whom he was well acquainted."

A peremptory rap was the only warning before the door slammed open. Beth and Tony rushed into the room. Excitement radiated from both of them.

"We have something very important to tell you, Lucas," Beth said, breathless.

"You learned the names of Chester's two visitors," Lucas said mildly. "Good work. But as it happens, we found them."

"Yes, we know that you discovered the identity of those two men and that you concluded they did not kill Uncle Chester," Tony said. "That is not what we hurried back here to tell you. While we were in town we stopped at the telegraph office, as you suggested."

Beth turned to Evangeline and waved a slip of paper. "As it happens, a telegram had just come in for you, Evie. It was sent by your friend Miss Slate. The telegrapher was making arrangements to have it delivered by Mr. Applewhite. Naturally Tony and I brought it back here with us."

"Clarissa and Beatrice must have discovered something important." Evangeline jumped to her feet and took the telegram. She read it quickly and looked up. "Douglas Mason had a brother."

"That fits with the information that we got from Stone's agent," Lucas said.

"Ah, but there's more," Evangeline said proudly. "Clarissa and Beatrice discovered that the brother is an actor named Garrett Willoughby who recently appeared in a melodrama titled *Lady Easton's Secret*."

"The theater ticket that I found on Sharpy Hobson's body was for a performance of that play," Lucas said. Energy shifted in the atmosphere. "This is excellent news. I will send Stone to London immediately."

"He may have some difficulty finding Mason's brother," Evangeline said. "According to the telegram the play closed last night. No one knows where Willoughby went. Clarissa and Beatrice are making further inquiries."

Thirty

Don't you ever sleep, Mr. Stone?" Molly asked.

"Slept too much last night, thanks to that damn lantern weapon the intruders used on me," Stone growled.

"Thank the Lord you survived, I say."

They were standing on the terrace overlooking the Day Garden. Moonlight silvered the scene. With the advent of the new arrivals and yet another maid, Mr. Sebastian had announced that Molly and at least one of her cousins would be staying at the abbey until further notice. The number of people in residence made it necessary to have some staff in the house at all times.

Molly had checked the hall clock before heading outside with the mug of freshly brewed coffee that she had poured for Stone. It was going on ten o'clock. The house was quiet. Miss Ames had vanished upstairs after dinner to work on chapter four of her book. Mrs. Sebastian and Mrs. Hampton had retreated to their bedrooms. Mr. Sebastian and the twins were working in the library.

Molly had waited until Stone slipped silently out the back door to take up his watch before she had followed with the mug.

"I thought you might like some coffee," she ventured.

Stone was momentarily surprised by the small gesture but he took the mug quite readily. She liked the feel of his big hand brushing against her fingers.

"Thank you," he said. He inhaled with evident appreciation. "Smells good."

"Freshly made."

"The roasted chicken you fixed for dinner was the best I've ever eaten," Stone said.

"Like I told Miss Ames, a man your size needs his nourishment. Are you sure you're recovered from that dreadful experience last night?"

"Don't worry, I won't fall asleep tonight." He sounded offended.

"What will you do if those intruders come back?"

"Mr. Sebastian and I talked about it earlier. We decided that if anyone tries to enter the grounds again I'm not to confront them alone. I'll wake up Mr. Sebastian and we'll deal with them together."

"I've never known anyone with paranormal talent until I met Miss Ames and Mr. Sebastian. Mind you, folks around here always knew there was something odd about Mr. Sebastian's uncle, Chester, but I never saw much of him. He kept to himself for the most part."

"Did you ever meet his housekeeper?"

"Oh, yes, a number of times. She wasn't what you'd call sociable, though. She used to go into town a couple of times a week to shop. She always complained to the shopkeepers whenever Chester Sebastian had houseguests. She said visitors were a lot of work for her because her employer wouldn't hire extra help."

"Any idea where she went after she found Chester Sebastian's body?"

"No, but I expect she retired. The Sebastians are rich. There would have been a pension."

"Mr. Sebastian says she would have been provided for but she never applied to him."

Molly struggled to comprehend that. "Do you mean that she never inquired after her pension?"

"That's what I've been told."

"That's very strange," Molly said. "Mrs. Buckley left town very soon after Chester Sebastian died—the next day, in fact. I'll wager I know what happened."

"What?"

"She probably pinched the silver and whatever household valuables she could stuff into her trunk before she got on the train. That's why she didn't go to Mr. Sebastian for money. She was afraid that sooner or later he would realize she was a thief."

"That's possible, I expect. But Mr. Sebastian made some inquiries and she's nowhere to be found."

"Because she doesn't want to be found," Molly said.

"Mr. Sebastian thinks something might have happened to her."

Molly peered at Stone. "Like what?"

"Who knows?" Stone looked out over the softly luminous scene. "Sometimes people vanish in these gardens."

Molly shuddered. "Those are just stories."

"Are you certain?"

"I don't believe in magic and demons."

"Neither do I. But after meeting Mr. Sebastian I do believe in the paranormal. There is a lot of strange energy in these gardens. Even I can sense it."

Molly looked out over the silvered foliage. "I just told you, Mrs. Buckley left town. Wherever she is, she's not out there in the gardens."

"You said she left in a great hurry. Maybe she just wanted everyone to think that she was gone."

"She was seen getting on the train."

"Maybe she came back," Stone said.

"Why would she do that?"

"I don't know. I'm not psychical like Mr. Sebastian. He says it's important to find out what happened to Mrs. Buckley and I expect he's right. He usually is."

"Must be a bit strange to have some psychical talent."

"Mr. Sebastian says most people have a little," Stone said. "They just don't recognize it. He says they call it intuition."

"My ma says I have good intuition. Sometimes I just know things."

"So do I," Stone said. "I knew the first time I met Mr. Sebastian that I wanted to work for him."

"That's how I felt when I took the post with Miss Ames. I told myself it might lead to something much better."

"Better than what?"

Molly smiled. "Better than spending the rest of my life on a farm. I'm not afraid of hard work, mind you, but milking cows and feeding chickens isn't very exciting."

"Do you want to go into service?"

"No," Molly said, "I'm going to open a tea shop."

Stone rocked a little on his heels. "That sounds interesting. You're a fine cook."

"Thank you, Mr. Stone."

Stone drank some coffee and lowered the mug. "Never met anyone who wanted to open a tea shop. You're an interesting woman, Molly Gillingham."

She admired the breadth of Stone's shoulders silhouetted against the moonlit gardens. "You're a very interesting man, Mr. Stone."

"Most people think I'm as dull as dishwater and about as stupid."

"It's the size of you," Molly explained. "People see a man as large and strong as yourself and they assume that you're naught but muscle. But obviously that's not true."

"And just how would you know that?"

"Oh, any number of reasons." Molly clasped her hands behind her back. "For starters, Mr. Sebastian is a very intelligent man. He would never have hired you if he thought you were a complete bonehead."

"Don't be so sure of that," Stone said. There was an edge of bitterness in his voice. "There are a great many rich and powerful men who are keen on the idea of employing a giant such as myself because it impresses their fine friends."

"You're not a giant," Molly said sharply. "You're a healthy, well-built man with a brain. There's a difference."

Stone smiled for the first time, embarrassed but pleased. "Think so?"

Molly gave him an approving, head-to-toe survey. "Oh my, yes, Mr. Stone. Tell me, how did you meet Mr. Sebastian?"

"He found me on the streets. Gave me a post as his coachman. I always figured it was luck that brought him my way."

Molly smiled. "Luck works both ways. Mr. Sebastian was fortunate to find you, Mr. Stone."

Stone said nothing. He finished his coffee in silence and handed her the mug.

"I'd best start making my rounds," he said.

"I'll set the coffeepot to keep warm on the stove," Molly said. She turned to go back inside the house. "I'll put out a couple of muffins, as well."

"I appreciate that." Stone started down the steps. He paused halfway. "Molly?"

She stopped just inside the doorway. "Yes, Mr. Stone?"

"I hope you get that tea shop you want."

"I will, Mr. Stone. Never doubt it."

His smile came and went in the shadows.

"I don't," he said. "Not for a minute."

"You're the first man I've ever met who believes I'm going to make something of myself."

"In that case, the others don't know you very well."

"No," she said. "They don't."

Thirty-one

He'd had enough of family for one day, Lucas thought. He needed to be alone for a while. No, not alone, he realized. He needed to be with Evangeline.

He closed the ancient herbal that he had been perusing and got up from behind his desk. Beth was curled on the small sofa, reading one of Chester's journals and making notes. Tony had a stack of old maps of the grounds spread out on a desk.

"You will excuse me for a time," Lucas said. "I'm going to take a walk. I need some fresh air."

"Enjoy your stroll," Tony said. He did not look up from the maps.

"Do be careful out there in the gardens," Beth said. She made another note. "It is night, after all."

"I did notice," Lucas said. He started toward the door.

"I don't suppose you found anything of interest in that herbal," Tony said.

Lucas paused, his hand on the doorknob. "No, the notes mostly concern the medicinal and metaphysical properties of various plants and flowers. I expect Chester used it for research."

"The herbal is quite old," Beth said. "No doubt very rare. I wonder where Chester acquired it."

"That I can answer," Lucas said. "Chadwick Bookshop in town. The receipt was still tucked inside. I also came across a large number of rare botanical drawings that Miss Witton, the shopkeeper, was evidently able to locate for him. But I didn't find anything that relates to whatever is going on out there in the gardens."

He went out the door and paused briefly in the hallway. The back stairs were closer. He took them two at a time to the floor above and stopped in front of Evangeline's bedroom. Aware that Florence and Judith had also retired to their rooms down the hall, he knocked very softly.

There was a soft rustling from inside the room. A moment later the door opened. Evangeline stood there. She had changed into one of the simple housedresses that she seemed to favor when she was occupied with her writing. She looked at him with an expectant air.

"Lucas," she said. "Did you find something of interest in those old books?"

"Not yet." He looked past her to the small desk near the window. Several sheets of paper and her pen lay on the surface of the desk. "I feel in need of a stroll in the gardens. Would you care to join me?"

She hesitated. He got the feeling that she did not quite believe him. She was a perceptive woman, he thought. It was not the fresh air he craved. He needed her.

Then she smiled and the slow-burning fever of desire heating his blood flashed into a roaring blaze.

"I'll just turn down the lamp," she said.

They went down the back stairs and out onto the terrace. The gardens glowed.

"It is really quite an eerie scene, isn't it?" Evangeline said. "I am having some difficulty describing it in my story."

He groaned. "Please do not tell me that you are using Crystal Gardens as a setting for your novel. We've had trouble enough with treasure hunters. I do not want to find myself dealing with a horde of your readers descending on the abbey to tour the inspiration for the setting of your story."

"Don't worry. I gave this place a different name and set it in a different location."

"I suppose I must be grateful for that much."

"A writer must take her inspiration where she can."

"I need to remember that. It keeps slipping my mind."

He took her arm and guided her down the terrace steps.

"Are we going into the Night Garden?" she asked.

"No," he said. "We are going to a place where we won't have to be on guard against every thorn and flower."

"Where would that be?"

"The drying shed. It was Mrs. Buckley's domain. She took great pleasure in growing and drying herbs. She made them into potpourris, pomanders, and sachets and the like. Some of the shops in town sold them to the visitors. There is also a stillroom where she concocted perfumes and soaps."

The drying shed was actually a room that opened off one of the old cloister walks. When Lucas opened the door, the heady scents of dried herbs drifted out.

"It smells wonderful in there," Evangeline said.

Unlike the gardens, the shed was steeped in shadows. The only light was the shaft of silver moon that slanted through the window.

"I assume these herbs came from the gardens," Evangeline said. "Why aren't they luminous?"

"Mrs. Buckley's herbs were all grown in the Day Garden," Lucas said, "not the Night Garden. Whatever paranormal light they might have given off at one time disappeared soon after the herbs were picked."

"Ah, yes, because the source of the energy, the water, was cut off. These plants are dead."

Evangeline turned to face him. She was standing in the moonlight. The silver gleamed on her hair. He could see the faint heat in her eyes. She wanted him. The knowledge was enough to send his fever higher.

"Evangeline," he said.

It was all he could say. Desire left him if not entirely speechless, certainly incoherent, he thought.

He walked to where she stood and took her into his arms. She came to him on the sweet, intoxicating scent of the herbs that surrounded them and her own vital feminine essence. He kissed her in the moonlight, drugging himself on the taste of her.

When she whispered his name and leaned more heavily into him he began to unhook the bodice of her gown.

"I cannot tell you how grateful I am that you are not wearing a corset," he said against her throat.

Her laughter was soft and lilting in the darkness. "I did not bring any corsets with me to Little Dixby because I knew I would not have anyone to assist me with the laces."

He laughed, too, a hoarse, husky laugh that turned into a groan when she undid the buttons of his shirt.

"I rarely wear one at all, except with my most fashionable gowns," she confided. She kissed his bare chest. "My friends and I are convinced they are not good for the health."

"I do not know if they are healthy or not, but I can assure you that they are a damn nuisance when it comes to this sort of thing."

"I'll remember that in the future," she said.

She was teasing him—he knew that—but the implication that she might one day be with another man froze him to the bone. He let the skirts that he had just unfastened fall to the floor and closed his hands around her shoulders.

"There will be no need to remember," he said, "because I will be around to remind you."

"Will you?" She touched the side of his jaw. Her eyes were fathomless.

"Yes," he vowed. He kissed her again, a sealing kiss to reinforce the promise.

He finally got her out of the gown. When she was left in nothing but a chemise, drawers and stockings, he drew her down onto a heap of fragrant herbs and looked at her as she lay there, limned in moonlight. Energy sparkled and flared in the atmosphere.

He knelt beside her and undid the front of his trousers. She reached for him.

"Lucas," she whispered.

He lowered himself alongside her and put one hand on her leg just above the garter that secured her white stocking. She made a soft little sound and reached inside his trousers. She circled him cautiously with her warm hand, exploring. He thought he would go mad. He opened the chemise and kissed her breast. Her hand tightened on him in what he knew was an instinctive response.

"You have no idea of what you are doing to me," he warned.

She smiled. "Are you trying to frighten me? Because it is not working."

"No, I can see that. Just as well because it is too late."

"For you or for me?"

"For me," he said. "I am lost."

"That makes two of us."

"Then I am not lost, after all. You have found me."

He kissed her and slipped his fingers inside the opening of her drawers. She was wet and full. He stroked gently, doing everything in his power to heighten the tension that he could sense building inside her. It became a contest of wills because she was doing the same to him.

In the end they surrendered to each other at the same moment. He lowered himself on top of her and thrust deep. She pulled him close and wrapped her stocking-clad legs around him.

He was braced for the shock of intimacy this time, but it dazzled his senses all the same. She gave a breathless cry. When she came the compelling energy of her release was more powerful than any force he had ever known. He could not resist, even if he had wanted to do so. He did not care.

Lost, he thought. And found.

Thirty-two

Sometime later, she stirred beside him. The shifting of her weight released more fragrant scents from the herbs. He opened his eyes and looked at her.

"How did you end up alone in the world?" he asked.

She sat up slowly, saying nothing at first. Her hair had come free of the pins. She ran her fingers through the tresses to shake out the bits and pieces of dried herbs.

"My father was an inventor," she said at last. "That sort tends to be very poor at managing finances."

"You have my sympathies. I know the breed. They are always in need of money for new equipment and materials."

"Sadly true." She looked down at him. "How is it you are aware of that?"

"One of my cousins, Arthur, fancies himself an inventor. I control the finances in my family so I hear frequently from him."

Evangeline's lips curved into a dry smile. "Well, in that case, perhaps you do understand. My mother died when I turned seventeen. She taught me how to handle the family finances and how to run a household. I took charge of both after her death. At least, I attempted to do so. That was when I realized just how difficult her task had been."

"Things did not go well, I take it."

"Overseeing the household was not a problem, but my father had no notion of economy. His only concern was having enough money to finance his inventions."

"Did he obtain any patents?"

"I'm afraid not. His inventions were not what most people would call practical."

"Inventing impractical devices is not an uncommon failing in inventors."

"The problem with Papa's inventions was that they could only be operated by those who possessed psychical powers."

Lucas winced. "He invented *paranormal* machines?"

"He *attempted* to do so. I fear he was not very successful. The market for such devices is quite small, you see."

Lucas folded his hands behind his head. "Because so few people possess the degree of talent required to operate machines that work on paranormal energy."

"Most people laughed at him or considered him to be a fraud. It was all quite complicated, but you may believe me when I tell you that my father's devices were extremely difficult to construct and almost impossible to demonstrate, let alone bring to market. There were other problems, as well. Each device my father designed had to be tuned to the wavelengths of the individual who planned to use it. Papa was not able to do the tuning. I seemed to have a talent for it but there wasn't much point because there were so few customers."

"But your father pressed on with his inventing," Lucas said, "and he kept requiring more money."

"As you say, it is the way of inventors. I simply could not control Papa's spending habits. Mama had intimidated him for years. That was how she kept us solvent. But after she died Papa acted as if he had been freed from prison. He went mad with our money. He purchased new equipment for his laboratory. He bought outrageously expensive artifacts and crystals to use in his experiments. I became increasingly desperate. I concealed the true state of our finances from him. I hid the records of our investments. But it was like trying to hide money from a gambler. He simply bought what he wanted on credit and then I was forced to pay the bills."

"I understand."

"I managed to hold things together for a few years," Evangeline said. "I kept things afloat until I was twenty-two. That was the year Robert—Douglas Mason—courted me. He was under the impression that I would have a handsome dowry. But that same year Papa succeeded in exhausting the bulk of our resources. In the end, all we had left was the house and a necklace that Mama had left to me. Before she died she made me swear that I would never tell Papa about the jewelry. It proved to be excellent advice."

"What happened?"

"I confronted Papa and told him that we were facing bankruptcy. I hoped to shock him into a full comprehension of the dreadful state of our affairs. I thought he would be forced to come to his senses."

"Your therapy didn't work, did it? Reason never does with that sort."

"You are right, of course. To my horror, Papa concluded that the only solution was to obtain a loan using our house as the collateral. He put the proceeds into an investment scheme that proved to be a fraud. I did not discover what he had done until I found him dead in his basement workshop. He had put a pistol to his head."

Lucas levered himself up on his elbows. "He left you to find the body."

"I doubt he was thinking about that aspect of the matter."

Probably not, Lucas thought, but it had added another layer of cruelty and pain to the whole business. He suppressed the anger that unfurled deep inside. Reginald Ames was not the first man to take his own life after a financial disaster and he would not be the last. But it never ceased to astonish and appall him that men who under other circumstances prided themselves on their honor could abandon their responsibilities in a way that devastated those they left behind. How did one pull the trigger in such a situation, knowing that one's wife or daughter would be left to cope with the financial and social ruin?

"What became of the necklace?" he asked quietly.

"Fortunately, I had never told Papa about it. I never told the creditors, either."

"A wise decision."

"After the funeral, I pawned it. I was able to obtain enough money to see me through until I obtained my position with Flint and Marsh."

"It must have been extraordinarily difficult for you."

"There have been a few rough patches," Evangeline admitted. "But in some ways, I have done much better on my own, thanks to the Flint and Marsh Agency, and now I have my writing. I am in control of my own destiny these days."

"There is a great deal to be said for that."

"Yes, there is."

Reluctantly he got to his feet and reached down to pull her up off the makeshift bed.

"We are both going to smell of herbs when we return to the house," Evangeline said. She shook out her skirts. "I must look as if I have been rolling around in the stuff. Which is only the truth, I suppose."

"We will use the back stairs again." He fastened his trousers. "No one will see us."

He shoved his shirttails into his pants, savoring the pleasant sense of relaxation and satisfaction that had come over him. A man could become accustomed to this sort of thing. *No*, he thought, *a man could become addicted.*

Evangeline did up the front of her bodice. "The scents in here are quite lovely. I can see why Mrs. Buckley enjoyed her little sideline."

"Her products were certainly popular with the visitors." Lucas motioned toward a doorway. "That was her stillroom."

"My mother had a stillroom." Evangeline went to stand in the doorway of the adjoining room. "I remember as a little girl I loved to watch her prepare tonics and remedies for sore throats, fever and the like. She was quite skilled. I think in a more enlightened era she could have been a chemist."

Lucas moved to stand behind Evangeline. He looked into the second room. Moonlight spilled through the window, illuminating a workbench littered with glass beakers, small pots and a burner. A chill of knowing aroused his senses. He heightened his talent.

Dark energy glowed on the workbench and on the floor.

"Lucas?" Evangeline stirred uneasily. "What is it? What's wrong?"

"I think I know how my uncle was murdered. She used poison. She concocted it here in this stillroom."

"Mrs. Buckley?"

"Yes."

"Are you certain?" Evangeline asked.

"It does explain why she left town in such a great rush and why she never came around for her pension."

"But why on earth would she murder your uncle after having worked for him all those years?" Evangeline asked. "You said they were lovers."

"I can't tell you why she killed him, not yet, but one thing is clear from the energy near the workbench."

"What?"

"Mrs. Buckley was in a great rage when she distilled the poison."

Thirty-three

"I realize that your relationships with your family are your own business and none of my affair," Evangeline said. "Nevertheless, I am compelled to offer you some advice."

"I have the impression that you are frequently compelled to offer your opinion to others," Lucas said.

"I think of it as one of my more endearing traits."

"'Endearing' would not be the first word that comes to mind to describe that particular characteristic. What is it you feel you need to tell me?"

They were sitting at the table on the terrace, drinking glasses of lemonade that Molly had brought out for them. It was mid-afternoon. Judith and Florence had retreated upstairs. Beth and Tony were in the library. Beth was scouring the household accounts that she had unearthed in Mrs. Buckley's old bedroom. Tony had found some tools in Chester's laboratory and was using them to take apart the lantern weapon.

"I am concerned about your strained relationship with Judith," Evangeline said.

"It is not your affair, Evangeline."

"I realize that, but you must see that Judith's primary concern is for her son and daughter. Beth is her priority at the moment because she feels she must get Beth safely married off this year."

"There shouldn't be any problem. Beth attracts suitors like flies."

"Judith has convinced herself that you will deprive your sister of her inheritance after she marries. She also fears that you are deliberately fostering Beth's connection to Charles Rushton precisely because you are aware of the sad state of his finances."

Lucas's mouth curved faintly in a grim smile. "In other words, I will crush Beth's future and leave her penniless in order to avenge myself on Judith."

"I do realize that is not your intention," Evangeline said. She sipped some lemonade and put down the glass. "But you might want to make that clear to Judith."

"Why bother? She won't believe me. She thinks I'm mad. She has from the beginning."

"The two of you certainly got off on the wrong foot all those years ago, didn't you?"

"There was no right way," Lucas said, "not for either of us."

"I don't understand."

"No," Lucas said, "you don't. And all I am going to tell you is that I won't let Beth make the same mistake Judith made."

"The mistake of marrying a much older man because of parental pressure?"

"Something along those lines, yes." Lucas put down his glass and got to his feet. "I think it's time to find out if we can get into the third pool room."

"You are trying to distract me."

"Is my cunning plan working?"

"It certainly is." She jumped to her feet. "But it is only three o'clock in the afternoon. You said that most of the garden's secrets are concealed during the daylight hours."

"That's true. But other things are sometimes more clearly revealed."

She glanced toward the house. "Should we tell someone what we are about?"

"No need. I informed Stone earlier that I intended to go back into the garden today. He will keep an eye on things."

"You are wondering if the Roman gold is hidden in that third room, aren't you?"

"You are the one who said that the secrets concealed inside are old."

"No, I said the energy sealing the entrance is ancient. I have no way of knowing what is inside the chamber because I had nothing to use to help me focus."

"You didn't know what you were looking for at the time," Lucas said. "Now you do."

"It doesn't work quite like that. If it did I would long ago have dug up my own hoard of Roman gold, believe me. I thought I explained, my psychical sensitivity is linked to my sense of touch. I need some connection to the object I am searching for, something to help me obtain a focus."

"Let's see what we can find." He walked toward the shed. "But first we'll pick up a few items that may prove useful."

The thrill of the mystery whispered to her senses. She rushed to follow him.

"There is only one more thing I would point out, Lucas," she said.

"I knew it." He did not pause. "You simply can't resist this compulsion, can you?"

"Sorry, no." She collected her skirts and broke into a brisk trot to keep up with him. "The one final point I wish to make is that at least you have a few relatives to contend with. I can tell you from personal experience that there are worse things than having a difficult family."

He stopped at that and turned back to face her, comprehension shadowing his eyes. "That would be having no family at all? You may be correct, although there are times when I would disagree with you."

"Come now, you know perfectly well that you are very fond of Beth and Tony."

"On occasion."

She smiled. "I have seen the three of you together. You are quite close."

He shrugged. "We are family."

"Exactly."

He frowned. "But I see now that I had not considered the matter from your perspective."

"Does that mean that you will now condescend to listen to my advice on how to deal with Judith?"

He raised a hand and smoothed a few stray tendrils of her hair back behind her ears. The energy of desire stirred the atmosphere around them. He kissed her forehead, a light, glancing, casually possessive kiss that marked her as his in a thousand indescribable ways.

"I will listen, but I will most likely ignore it," he said.

He moved on to the shed.

She followed quickly. "I was afraid of that. Has anyone ever told you that you are an exceedingly stubborn man?"

"I believe you yourself may have mentioned it on occasion. I recall the word 'cork-brained' was employed."

"I apologized."

"That does not mean that I will allow you to forget the remark." He stopped in front of the windowless shed, opened the door and moved into the dark space. When he reappeared he had two pairs of heavy leather gardening gloves in his hand. He gave her one pair. "Put those on. They'll provide some protection."

He went back into the shed while she did as he had instructed. The gloves were far too large and the thick leather made her feel clumsy.

Lucas emerged from the shed again, buckling a wide leather belt low on his hips. Two knife sheaths, one quite large, the other much smaller, hung from the belt. He must have seen the curiosity in her eyes.

"The small blade is for taking specimen samples," he explained. "The larger one is called a machete. Chester brought it back from one of his botanical expeditions. It can slice through some of the foliage in this place." He glanced at a nearby curtain of orchids. "At least it could the last time I was here."

"Too bad we did not have that large knife with us last night."

"I didn't take it into the maze because it is of little use after dark. The energy in the Night Garden is so powerful at that time that it is nearly impossible to hack through even something that appears as fragile as a cluster of daisies or a bank of ferns."

She studied the massive iron gate that guarded the entrance of the maze. "Would it be possible to destroy the Night Garden by day?"

"I think one could make some headway by day but it would be slow going." Lucas took a key out of his pocket and unlocked the gate. "And I'm afraid that what foliage was destroyed in sunlight would most likely regrow overnight."

"So quickly?"

"The only limitation on the growth of the plants now appears to be the proximity to the paranormal waters of the spring. That was always true, but for some reason, after centuries, the forces at work around the spring are growing more powerful. I must find the cause."

She watched the gate slowly swing open, revealing the yawning green mouth of the maze. "Would it perhaps be possible to use strong chemicals to destroy the foliage?"

"Uncle Chester conducted a few experiments to see if the plants could be destroyed with various acids but none were markedly successful."

"In other words, you may never be able to destroy the Night Garden."

"Not with any methods that have been tried thus far." Lucas entered the dark mouth of the maze. He disappeared almost immediately, fading ghostlike into the shadows. "Watch your step. The same rules apply in daylight as at night. Try not to brush against even the most harmless-looking leaf and, whatever you do, don't scratch yourself on a thorn."

She paused at the entrance. The currents of energy emanating from the labyrinth were different in the daylight, more subdued but no less ominous. The waves of paranormal power sparked frissons of shuddery awareness across her senses.

She heightened her talent and moved into the intense, primal energy of the maze. Her senses stirred. The foliage sighed and whispered around her.

"It is as if the plants are sleeping now," she said.

"But no less alive."

Lucas used the old key to lock the gate. "I don't want to risk Tony and Beth trying to follow us. They are both endowed with far too much curiosity and sense of adventure."

She smiled. "In that they take after their older brother."

Lucas gave her an unreadable look. "Do you think so?"

"Judith told me that you were the closest thing Tony and Beth had to a father. It is obvious you were a good one. They adore you and they admire you."

"Judith exaggerates," Lucas said. "She always does."

His tone was gruff but he sounded oddly pleased, Evangeline thought. There was a note of satisfaction in his voice, paternal satisfaction.

"You will make a very good father to your own children," she said before she could stop to think.

He looked startled. "I track monsters and sometimes I kill them."

"Speaking as a former child, I can assure you that is a fine trait in a father. It's very reassuring to know that Papa can take care of the monsters hiding under the bed."

Lucas startled her with a soft laugh. She had the feeling that he surprised himself, as well. He slipped the machete out of its sheath.

"Let us be off," he said.

Evangeline looked around and was relieved to discover that she could perceive the walls and ceiling of the maze as clearly as she had during the night.

"Oh, good," she said. "We won't need a lantern."

"No," Lucas said.

He walked quickly toward the far end of the corridor. She hesitated a few seconds. It occurred to her that last night she had been wearing only a nightgown and a wrapper but today she was dressed in a tailored shirtwaist gown and low-cut walking boots. The dress was styled with a fairly trim, narrow silhouette, the bustle small and discreet. The hem ended just above her ankles and there was no dust ruffle to sweep the ground. Nevertheless, she did not want to risk having the draped fabric accidentally snag against one of the poisonous thorns.

She collected her skirts in her gloved hands, pulled the folds more snugly around her legs and followed Lucas deeper into the maze.

The lush, verdant energy of the plant life around her sent frisson after frisson across her senses.

"I wonder if this is what it was like at the dawn of creation," she whispered, "when the world was new and awash in the raw power of life?"

"That is a question for the poets, not scientists," Lucas said. "But I'll agree that there is a lot of power here. You can surely sense how difficult it would be to destroy this garden, root and branch."

"Yes," she said. "Furthermore, I think it would be wrong to do so, even if it is possible. This is a wondrous place."

Lucas smiled faintly. "Perhaps I should set up a booth and sell tickets."

"That is an interesting notion. It is a pity that so many parts of the garden are dangerous."

They exited the maze into the Night Garden and made their way to the shadow gate that guarded the ancient bathhouse. Evangeline braced herself for the mild shocks of energy and followed Lucas through the entrance.

They moved through the first pool chamber and went along the vaulted corridor into the next. The waves of sparkling energy from the second bath rolled over her senses like liquid jewels. Hot memories of the night of passion briefly overwhelmed her. She was aware of the sudden warmth flushing her cheeks.

Lucas surveyed the chamber. A little heat kindled in his eyes.

"I don't know about you," he said, "but speaking for myself, I will never forget this room."

She cleared her throat and concentrated on the door of the stone passageway that led to the third chamber.

"I assume you have a key to the door of the third chamber?" she asked briskly.

His brows rose. "Are you attempting to change the subject?"

"We are here on an investigation. I hardly think this is the time to discuss unrelated subjects."

"Right." Lucas looked down the stone passage. "Back to the business of the third pool. The door itself will not be a problem. There is no key. The lock is an ingenious device that requires a code. One pushes a series of steel pins in a certain sequence and the door opens."

"You have that code, I assume?"

"Yes. Chester gave it to me years ago. The more difficult problem is dealing with the energy in that chamber. You will understand when I get the door open. Neither Chester nor I could get more than a few steps into the room. Believe me, we both tried on a number of occasions."

He walked down the hallway and stopped in front of the massive steel-bound door. Evangeline followed and watched him push several pins in the big lock.

There was a grinding rumble of the hinges but the door swung open slowly, revealing an arched doorway framed in large blocks of solid stone.

One of the stones glowed with an inner light, storm-dark and ominously radiant.

A cauldron of hot energy boiled in the doorway. Flashes of paranormal lightning pierced what appeared to be impenetrable chaos. The currents of power spilled out into the room, charging the already overheated atmosphere. Evangeline's senses flared in response. Her hair lifted, floating around her head. Excitement twisted with dread inside her. She was fascinated, thrilled, enchanted.

She moved forward slowly and came to a stop in front of the energy gate.

"Astonishing," she whispered.

Lucas looked at the gate. "Do you think you can work that kind of energy?"

"Yes," she said, very certain. "This gate was fashioned by a person, not by the forces of the earth."

"Not by my uncle, either, I can tell you that much. He installed a new door but the energy gate was here when he bought the abbey."

"This gate is old," Evangeline said. "Centuries, perhaps thousands of years old. But it was created with the power of a human aura, so dampening it with my own wavelengths should work. The pattern feels . . . female."

"You can tell that?"

"Yes. A very powerful woman crafted this gate. I think that only a woman could open it."

She studied the glowing crystal embedded in the doorway. "And I think I know exactly where to begin."

She took a step closer and then another and put out one hand. Gingerly she flattened her palm against the slab of crystal. It brightened immediately. Paranormal electricity crackled through her but she felt no pain, just a euphoric exhilaration.

Slowly she probed for the fierce currents of power radiating from the crystal. When she had identified the strongest waves of energy, she countered with a dampening force. At first nothing seemed to be happening, but after a few seconds the energy of the gate started to abate.

A moment later the storm winked out of existence like an extinguished candle flame.

"Incredible," Lucas said. "You are an amazing woman, Evangeline Ames. But I believe I have made that observation on previous occasions."

The admiration and respect in his voice warmed her. "Yes, you have, but I thank you."

"Now to see if the treasure is in there," Lucas said.

She laughed at the anticipation that shivered in the atmosphere around him. He was as caught up by the adventure as she was.

He moved through the doorway and stopped, looking at something that Evangeline could not see.

"I should have known this was not going to be simple," he said.

"What is it?" Evangeline walked swiftly into the room and followed his gaze.

"There is no treasure in here." He moved one hand to indicate the bare stone chamber. "So much for my theory."

The only thing in the room was the large, deep pool in the center. Unlike the two pools in the outer rooms, this one was rimmed with slabs of silvery crystals. The water glowed, just as it did in the outer baths, but the light was very different. The surface resembled a moonlit mirror.

"Well, it was an excellent theory," Evangeline said.

"Thank you," Lucas growled. "I certainly thought so."

Evangeline walked closer and looked down into the pool. The outer baths were crystal clear but this one was not. Lucas came to stand beside her. Their reflections flashed and sparked on the surface of the pool.

"It's like gazing into a liquid mirror," she said. "One can sense the depths but one cannot see beneath the surface."

"A trick of the light," Lucas said. "It's difficult to even look at the water." He turned away to survey the chamber.

Evangeline knelt on the rim of the pool and dipped her fingertips into the silvery water. She did not have any problem looking at the water. Energy shivered through her.

The mirrored surface brightened. Ghostly visions appeared. She glimpsed a woman in a white gown, her hair coiled and braided in a style that could be seen in the remains of ancient Roman wall murals.

She stirred the waters again and watched, fascinated, as other images came and went, floating across the surface of the pool—a woman wearing the habit of a medieval nun, another dressed in the style of the seventeenth century.

Over the centuries other women had unlocked the storm gate and entered this room to look into the pool, Evangeline realized. Somehow the mirrored surface had captured and retained some of their reflections. She wondered what the others had seen, what they had sought to discover in this place.

She stirred the dazzling waters with her fingertips, seeking the patterns of the currents of power. Another wave of exhilaration flashed through her when she found what she was looking for.

"What the devil do you think you're doing?" Lucas reached down and seized hold of Evangeline's shoulder. He started to haul her to her feet. "I told you, those waters are dangerous. According to the legends they induce hallucinations and visions."

"Look," she said quietly. She shook off his hand and put her fingertips back into the waters. "That is no vision."

Lucas kept his hand locked on her shoulder but he looked down into the pool.

"Damnation," he said. "The treasure."

The waters had cleared, revealing the bottom of the ancient stone bath and a single stone bench built into one side just below the surface. There was a heap of objects on the bottom. Earrings, necklaces, rings and delicate bracelets sat on the bottom of the pool and all of it gleamed dully with the unmistakable luster of ancient gold.

"So many valuable things," Evangeline said, awed by the staggering sight. "Whoever left this treasure here was extraordinarily wealthy by any standards."

"Perhaps this was a jeweler's hoard," Lucas said. "He may have stored his wares in this pool so that they could not be stolen."

"The owner of the objects may have been male but I am certain that only a woman could access this pool to retrieve the gold." Evangeline hesitated. "And she would have to be quite powerful."

Lucas looked at her. "To get through the storm gate, do you mean?"

"Yes, but I believe that is only the first obstacle. I am certain that the pool waters provide a second barrier."

"I understand that one would have to have the talent to clear the surface so that the bottom of the pool is visible, but I don't see why the water is an obstacle."

"Not every woman who could reveal the treasure would be able to enter the pool to retrieve it. The waters are deep. They would come up to my neck at the very least and I think they could be very dangerous, even lethal."

She pulled her fingers from the water. The surface shifted, once again becoming a liquid mirror. The treasure was no longer visible.

"What do you think would happen if I put my hand into the pool?" Lucas asked.

"I have no idea but I'm certain that there is considerable risk involved."

"What kind of risk?"

She looked at him. "I cannot say."

"I'm going to conduct the experiment."

She made a face. "I rather thought you might."

Lucas took off his coat and rolled up one sleeve. Carefully he dipped his fingers into the water.

And yanked them out again at once. His features tightened in agony.

"Damn it to hell." He clenched his jaw, gritted his teeth and gasped for breath. Hastily he shook the droplets of water from his hand.

"Are you all right?" she asked quickly.

"Yes, I think so," he rasped. He took a deep, steadying breath. "But I don't think I'll conduct any more experiments for the moment."

"What happened?"

"I'm not sure. Let's just say I had the distinct impression that I was about to fall straight into the fires of hell."

"Hallucinations?"

"More than just visions. I could *feel* the flames." He hesitated, frowning. "There was a soul-eating cold as well. It was indescribable."

"I think I can reach the treasure safely."

Lucas did not look convinced. "Are you sure?"

She put her hand into the water and sent a delicate charge of power into the gently shifting current. The surface cleared.

"Yes," she said. "I'm certain it would be safe for me. What now, Lucas?"

He got to his feet. "We have found the treasure but we are no closer to finding Mrs. Buckley or the answer to a number of other questions. We may as well leave the hoard here until I can make arrangements to transport it safely to London. This chamber has kept the gold safe for centuries. It can continue to do so for a while longer."

"You will need me to retrieve it for you."

He smiled. "Another excellent reason for keeping you close, my sweet."

She stirred the waters, savoring the exultant sense of feminine power that was sparkling in her blood. "Always nice to feel useful."

A thoroughly masculine, thoroughly wicked gleam lit his eyes. "Never doubt that I have innumerable uses for you, Evangeline. But we won't go into that here and now. Time for us to leave." He paused, growing more serious. "One more thing. We will not speak of this to anyone when we return to the house. Not yet."

"Not even to the members of your family?"

He shook his head. "I'm concerned that in their excitement they will accidentally let the secret slip out. There is always the risk that Molly or one of her relatives might overhear a conversation meant to be private. The news would soon be all over town. I do not want to have to waste time rescuing treasure hunters from the gardens."

"I understand." She started to pull her hand back out of the water but the sight of the object that had fallen on the submerged step gave her pause. She looked more closely at it. "Lucas?"

He turned back. "What?"

"Do you see that cylindrical case on the step?"

"Yes. What of it?"

"It appears to be silver, not gold like the other items in the treasure. After all these centuries it should be black with tarnish."

"I expect that the paranormal properties of the pool waters prevented tarnish from forming," Lucas said.

"There is something about the shape and the workmanship that is modern. I don't think it is part of the treasure."

Lucas crouched at the edge of the pool again and took a closer look. "You're right. Someone else did manage to access this chamber and quite recently. Whoever it was, he dropped that object into the water. It landed on the step but he was unable to retrieve it. I wonder if that belonged to my uncle."

"No," she said, "I don't think so. I must get it out of the water so that I can be sure."

"That step is nearly two feet below the surface."

"I can reach it if I lean far enough over the side. You will hold me to make certain I don't fall in."

"I don't think this is a good idea," Lucas said.

"I will be safe, I promise you."

"You're sure that object is this important?"

"I'm positive."

She was already unfastening the bodice of her gown. She pushed the top down to her waist, leaving just her chemise.

"At another time I could very much enjoy this," Lucas said. "But right now all I can think about is making certain you don't fall into the pool."

"I won't." She knelt again at the edge of the pool. "Hold my hand."

His fingers clamped around her wrist. She leaned forward and extended her bare arm into the water up to her shoulder. The energy of the pool caused her senses to spark and flash. The sensation was breathtaking. She had a sudden, almost irresistible impulse to undress entirely and bathe in the waters, to abandon herself to the mysteries and secrets locked in the pool.

"Evangeline."

Lucas's sharp voice shattered the spell.

"Right," she said. "Sorry. Got distracted."

She grasped the object on the step and brought it out of the water. Straightening, she held the silver case so that they could both see it.

"It's a chatelaine designed to carry a pair of spectacles," Lucas said. "Chester wore eyeglasses but he did not keep them in a case."

"This was made for a woman," Evangeline said. She turned the case in her hand and looked at the initials engraved on the back. "What is more, I know who she is."

Thirty-four

"You're certain the chatelaine belonged to Irene Witton, the owner of the bookshop?" Lucas asked. His other senses were tingling and the hair on the back of his neck was stirring.

"I can't be absolutely positive," Evangeline said, "but I can tell you that Miss Witton seems to know a great deal about the local legends. She stocks a variety of treasure maps. What is more, her initials are IW, the letters on the back of the case. And, last but not least, I distinctly recall that when Clarissa admired Irene's chatelaine, Irene mentioned that it was new and that it was a replacement for one she had lost. Under the circumstances, I cannot imagine that the case belongs to anyone else. Do you have a better idea?"

"No," he said.

The high street was busy. The shops were full, street vendors hawked their souvenirs and the purveyors of antiquities, real and fraudulent, were doing a brisk business.

But Chadwick Books was closed. A small sign hung in the window. The shades were lowered.

A chill of knowing iced Lucas's senses. "We are too late."

Evangeline glared at the CLOSED sign. "Irene Witton must have feared that we would become suspicious. She has packed up and left Little Dixby."

"Perhaps," Lucas said. "But it is also possible that she was not that fortunate."

"What do you mean? Surely you don't think—" Evangeline broke off because Lucas was already steering her down the street. "Wait. Where are you going?"

"To see if I can determine what happened to Irene Witton. I want to take a look around the inside of the bookshop."

"You're going to break into the shop, aren't you?"

"Hush." He angled his head to indicate the passersby on the street. "I'd just as soon not advertise my intentions. In some less enlightened quarters, breaking and entering is considered illegal. Although I have a feeling that no one will be complaining to the authorities on this occasion."

"What if you are wrong? Witton lives in rooms above the shop." Evangeline glanced upward at the shuttered windows. "She might be ill."

"If that proves to be the case, we will apologize and explain that we feared for her health when we saw the sign in the window."

Evangeline touched the small sack she carried. It contained the chatelaine. "That sounds like a reasonable answer. Always assuming that she is in a reasonable mood if she awakens to the noise of a burglar breaking into her shop."

"I promise you, there will be very little noise."

Lucas turned down a narrow lane that intersected the high street. Evangeline hastened to keep up with him. When they reached the alley that ran behind the row of shops, they both looked back to make sure they were not being observed. Then they made their way to the rear door of Chadwick Books.

Lucas knocked a couple of times, but when there was no response he tried the doorknob. It turned easily.

"So much for the necessity of breaking into the place," he said.

"If Miss Witton left in a hurry she might have neglected to lock the back door."

"In my experience it is often killers fleeing the scene of the crime who fail to lock up behind themselves."

"Of course, because they don't have a key."

"Sometimes that is the case."

He did not add that there were murderers who did not lock the door at the scenes because they wanted their terrible crimes to be discovered, murderers who lusted to see their handiwork portrayed in the press. But this would not be that kind of murder, he thought. There was motive aplenty in this situation. There was no need to posit a deranged killer.

He opened the door and moved into the back room of the shop. He did not require the currents of dark energy swirling in the atmosphere to tell him that violence had been done and done recently. The woman's body was sprawled facedown. Blood from the head wound soaked the wooden floorboards. The heavy iron bookend that had been used as a weapon was not far away. He could see bits of hair and flesh clinging to it.

Evangeline gave a soft gasp of dismay.

"You were right," she said. "We are, indeed, too late. But this makes no sense. We assumed that if we found a body here, it would be that of Irene Witton. That is not Miss Witton."

Lucas went down beside the dead woman and turned her just enough to allow them to see her face. Evangeline moved closer, careful to keep the toes of her walking boots and the hem of her skirts out of the blood pool.

"I do not recognize her," she said.

"I do." Lucas got to his feet. "This is the missing housekeeper, Mrs. Buckley."

"Good grief." Evangeline looked around uneasily. "The blood appears to be quite fresh."

"It is," Lucas said. "She has not been dead very long. In fact, the killer is still here on the premises."

There was a soft creak from the direction of the staircase that led to the rooms above the shop.

Evangeline stilled.

Lucas turned to face the narrow staircase. "You may as well come down, Miss Witton. We know what happened here. We are not armed."

There was another protesting creak from the wooden boards. Irene Witton appeared at the top of the staircase, a pistol clutched in both hands.

"But I am armed," she said.

Thirty-five

It was not supposed to end like this," Irene said.

Lucas watched her descend steadily down the stairs. "These things never seem to end the way they are supposed to end."

The pistol in Irene's hands did not waver. She kept the gun trained on Lucas. "Mrs. Buckley ruined everything. Now I have no choice but to leave on the morning train. I was packing my bags when I heard you break in a few minutes ago. I was so rattled after dealing with Buckley that I neglected to lock the door."

"That would not have stopped us," Lucas said. He did not look at the gun. He kept his attention on Irene's eyes.

"No, I can see that," Irene said.

Evangeline took a small step away from him. It was a subtle move. Lucas knew it was designed to put some distance between the two of them, thereby forcing Irene to shift her aim back and forth.

"Stop," Irene ordered. Her voice was cold and controlled. "Don't move, Miss Ames."

Evangeline obediently halted. But she raised the sack in her hand. "We found your missing spectacles chatelaine. You left it in the Vision Pool chamber."

"Impossible." For the first time Irene appeared shaken. "It fell into the pool. No one could reach that far into those waters."

"I did," Evangeline said.

"I don't believe you."

"Shall I prove it?"

"Yes," Irene snapped. "Empty the sack."

Evangeline slowly untied the cord that closed the small sack and turned the cloth bag upside down. The silver case fell into her hand.

Irene was stunned. "If you found the chatelaine, you must have seen the treasure."

"We did," Lucas said. "We left it in the pool for safekeeping."

"I think I know what happened," Evangeline said. "You came here to Little Dixby because you somehow learned about the treasure."

"My father was an expert on antiquities. He possessed a psychical talent that allowed him to make several remarkable discoveries in Egypt and Italy. Perhaps you have heard of him, Dr. Howard Witton."

"Witton is a legend in antiquities circles," Lucas said. "You are his daughter?"

"Yes. I inherited his talent but because I was a woman, I was not allowed to follow in his footsteps. It became clear to me at an early age that I would never be able to explore and excavate the important ruin sites. My father's colleagues refused to accept me as an equal. I was forced to content myself with being my father's assistant."

"As I recall, Witton died a few years ago," Lucas said.

"I was his sole heir." Irene smiled coldly. "His colleagues begged me to give his papers and the items in his private collection to one of the museums. Several offered to buy them. They are worth a fortune. You may believe me when I tell you that it gave me great pleasure to refuse all of their entreaties and their offers. I did not need the money, you see."

"I don't blame you for taking satisfaction in that manner," Evangeline said.

"It meant I could never marry, of course," Irene said.

"No," Evangeline said. "If you had wed, you would have very likely lost control of your inheritance. Most men would have been only too happy to sell off the most valuable antiquities."

"I have not regretted my choice, not for a moment." Irene's mouth twisted in a bitter smile. "It is not as if I have been deprived of male company. You would be amazed at how many gentlemen are attracted to a woman who possesses both money and talent, even if she is well beyond eighteen years of age."

"How did you learn of the Crystal Gardens treasure?" Lucas asked.

"Toward the end of his life my father grew too infirm to travel abroad," Irene said. "During that time he came across some records of the treasure that was said to be buried on the grounds of the old abbey in Little Dixby. According to the story, the hoard was protected by magical forces."

"Your father did not believe in magic," Evangeline said. "But he recognized the possibility that paranormal forces might be at work on the grounds."

"Yes, and he was intrigued," Irene said. "He contacted Chester Sebastian and asked permission to search for the gold. But Chester refused."

"All my uncle cared about were his botanical experiments," Lucas said. "He despised treasure hunters."

"After my father died, I became fascinated with the legend of the

Roman gold and the paranormal aspects of the story. But I knew that your uncle would never agree to allow me to search for it."

"You saw your opportunity when the owner of this bookshop died," Lucas said. "You purchased it from his widow and you set about seducing Chester with rare botanical prints and books."

"And my talent," Irene said. "I used it as deliberately as any courtesan employs her charms, dropping small hints about my abilities over a period of several months. Eventually Chester asked me to participate in some experiments. I let him see just enough of my psychical nature to make him want more. When he discovered that I could navigate the maze, he was enthralled. He soon realized that I was far more powerful than his housekeeper. She had been unable to gain access to the Vision Chamber."

"But it occurred to him that you might be able to do so," Lucas said.

"I refused at first. I was very coy about it. I told him that I doubted that I was capable of completing such a daunting task. But he insisted that I try. He even promised to give me the treasure if I could retrieve it. He didn't care about the gold. By then he was obsessed with finding the source of the paranormal waters. He had convinced himself he would find it in the Vision Chamber."

"When you proved you could access the chamber he must have been elated," Lucas said.

"He was elated," Irene said. "When I cleared the pool waters and we saw the gold, I thought he would faint from excitement. But all he could think about was finding a way to tap the energy of the pool for his damned botanical experiments. He was content to give me the entire hoard as thanks for my work."

"That was when you discovered that clarifying the waters was only the beginning," Evangeline said. "You soon realized that you could not submerge yourself in the pool."

Rage flashed across Irene's face. "I just needed time to learn how to control the currents in those waters. I was certain I could do it, but that's when *she* found us there in the chamber."

Lucas glanced at the body. "Mrs. Buckley?"

"Yes. The silly woman thought I was having an affair with your uncle. I had the bodice of my gown off, you see, in an attempt to reach into the waters. Mrs. Buckley went mad with jealousy."

"Not without reason," Evangeline said. "Mrs. Buckley and Chester were lovers for years until you came along. You were able to give him what she could not—access to the chamber and the pool. On top of everything else, your state of undress that day made it appear that you were sleeping with him."

"Buckley made a great scene. She flew at me, spitting and cursing. She grabbed my chatelaine and ripped it off my gown. It was all nonsense but the foolish creature was beyond reason. Chester tried to calm her down. He told me to leave so that he could deal with Mrs. Buckley."

"You fled the chamber but you forgot the chatelaine," Evangeline said. "In all the commotion it somehow got kicked into the pool and landed on one of the underwater steps."

"I dressed, made my way out of the maze and left Crystal Gardens. I assumed that Chester would deal with Mrs. Buckley and in the morning he and I would discuss how to go about making another attempt to get the treasure out of the Vision Pool."

"But in the morning, Mrs. Buckley summoned the doctor, who determined that Chester had collapsed from a heart attack and died at the breakfast table," Lucas said.

Irene made a short, disgusted sound. "She murdered him. I'm sure of it. I don't know how she made it look like a heart attack, but there is no doubt in my mind that she killed him in a jealous rage."

"I agree with you," Lucas said quietly. "She poisoned him with some potion that she created in her stillroom using lethal plants from the gardens."

Evangeline fixed Irene with an intent expression. "If you believed that she murdered Chester Sebastian, you must have wondered if she would try to kill you, as well."

"I was somewhat concerned for a short time," Irene said. "But the very next day she left town on the morning train. At first I thought that things would be much simpler with both of them out of the way."

"You went back into the gardens, didn't you?" Lucas asked. "You had the code to the door. You could get through the energy gate and you could clear the waters. But you discovered that you could not go down the steps into the pool. It was all you could do just to dip your fingers into the bath."

"I told you, I just needed more time to study the energy," Irene hissed. "But the next thing I knew, we heard that you would soon be arriving to deal with your uncle's estate. I assumed you would try to sell it. But instead you took up residence." Irene's voice rang with accusation. "Then Miss Ames and your relatives moved into the abbey. You hired some of the locals. There was talk in town that you intended to make Crystal Gardens your country house. People whispered that there was a giant of a man who stood guard over the grounds."

"There was nothing you could do but bide your time," Lucas said. "You hoped that eventually we would all leave."

"Only an obsessed eccentric like your uncle would want to live there permanently," Irene said. "The forces in the gardens are becoming more disturbing by the week. Chester knew that. He was convinced that the energy in the Vision Pool was the reason."

"Did he tell you why he thought the forces of the spring had become so strong?" Lucas asked.

"No, and I did not care. All I wanted was the treasure. Then Mrs. Buckley showed up at my back door this morning. She had the nerve to try to blackmail me."

"With what?" Lucas asked.

"She said that unless I paid her a large sum of cash, she would tell you that I was after the treasure and that I was responsible for your uncle's death. She thought she had it all planned out, you see. She was certain you would believe her because you had known her for years. You had no reason not to trust her."

"You waited until her back was turned and you cracked her skull with that bookend," Evangeline said.

"I decided that the only thing I could do was leave town until the excitement was over," Irene said.

"But we arrived before you could leave," Lucas said.

"The pair of you have complicated my life in every conceivable manner. There is nothing for it but to get rid of you. Believe me, I will not enjoy the business but you have left me no option."

Lucas found the focus that he needed and heightened his talent, sending the energy of terror into Irene's aura.

The pistol in her hands started to tremble.

Irene's eyes widened in horror. "What is happening? You are doing something to me. I can sense it. My heart. *I cannot breathe*."

She tried to pull the trigger but it was too late. She collapsed, unconscious.

Thirty-six

"The police arrested Irene Witton for the murder of Mrs. Buckley." Evangeline put down the morning edition of the *Little Dixby Herald* and picked up her teacup. "She is claiming to have paranormal powers and is telling everyone that she saw a nightmarish vision of demons and monsters guarding a silver pool that holds a hoard of ancient gold. When she recovered from the horrific visions she found the body. The general consensus of opinion in town is that the shock of killing Buckley has left Witton unhinged. Speculation is that she will end up in an asylum."

"Which may well be her goal," Lucas said. He forked up a bite of eggs. "Assuming she isn't actually insane."

Evangeline met his eyes and knew that he was considering the possibility that he might have pushed Irene over the edge of sanity by the force of his talent.

"She is not mad," Evangeline said. "I saw her aura when I checked her for a pulse. I did not see the taint of madness. But I can well believe that she has decided to fake a mental illness. She has no doubt concluded that it will be easier to escape from an asylum than it will be from prison."

Beth buttered a slice of toast. "You and Lucas speak very casually of the possibility that she might escape."

"From what little I know of her, I think it is safe to say that Irene Witton is not without resources." Lucas drank some coffee. "But at least she is no longer a problem for us. She was obsessed with the gold. If she ever manages to return to Little Dixby it will be too late. By then the treasure will be safely stored in a museum."

Tony appeared in the doorway. Evangeline stared at him, startled. His hair was standing up in spikes all over his head and his shirt and trousers were badly wrinkled. He had a long rolled-up map in his hand. His excitement was palpable.

"Are you well?" Evangeline asked. "You look as if you slept in your clothes."

"Actually, I didn't sleep much at all." Tony looked at Beth. "You were right about those crystals."

"Really?" Beth crumpled her napkin and tossed it on the table. "You found them?"

"I think so, yes." Tony rushed to the table, pushed aside the dishes and silverware that Molly had set out for him and unrolled the map.

Lucas got to his feet. "What did you find?"

Tony looked up from the map. "The crystals."

"What crystals?" Lucas asked patiently.

Beth was on her feet. "I remembered that you said you thought the energy in the gardens started to intensify about two years ago. I went back to Uncle Chester's journals for that period and I found notes about an experiment he planned to carry out."

Evangeline rose and came around the table to examine the map. "What kind of crystals?"

"Uncle Chester wasn't sure," Beth said. "He found them in a crate in an antiquities shop in London. There were three of them. According to his notes they were a dull, murky gray, not very interesting at first glance, but he could sense the power in them. The proprietor of the shop had concluded that the stones were not worth much. Chester got them at a very cheap price."

"He brought them back here and conducted some experiments on them," Tony said. "He was convinced that they could be made to resonate with the frequency of the spring waters."

"He tried various techniques but nothing worked," Beth continued. "Then it occurred to him that the crystals might need to be sunk into the ground in order to resonate with the natural forces in the area. He buried them in various locations."

"All three of which border the Night Garden," Tony said.

"Those marks I noticed on one of the maps," Lucas said.

"Exactly." Triumph gleamed in Tony's eyes. He stabbed a finger at the three marks he had circled on the map. "He noted the locations so that he could find them again if the experiment didn't work."

"Why didn't he dig them up when he sensed that something was wrong in the gardens?" Evangeline asked.

"Because it never occurred to him that the crystals were the problem," Beth said. "He was convinced the source of the trouble was the Vision Pool. He fixed his attention on that possibility and did not look for other answers."

"A classic mistake in any sort of investigation," Lucas said, "whether it is a case of murder or a scientific inquiry. We must locate those crystals and get them out of the ground as soon as possible. Then we will see if there is any change in the energy level."

Thirty-seven

The knock on the library door sent a chill of foreboding through Lucas. A woman's knock, he thought. Not Molly. Not Evangeline. Not Beth. Resigned, he got to his feet.

"Come in, Judith," he said.

She opened the door and walked slowly into the room. "You knew it was me. You always seem to know things like that."

"In this case it was a simple process of elimination. No psychical talent involved. What was it you wanted?"

She closed the door, walked halfway across the room and stopped. One gloved hand was clenched at her side.

"Miss Ames has advised me to confront you with my fears," she said.

"I should have known that Evangeline was somehow behind this." Grimly he indicated a chair. "You had better sit down because I suspect that I will soon find it necessary to do so. Something tells me this is going to be another difficult conversation."

Judith remained on her feet. "Our conversations have always been difficult."

He winced. "Oddly enough, I recall making a similar observation to Miss Ames. Are you going to sit down?"

"I would rather stand."

"As you wish." He had no choice but to remain on his feet so he faced her from across the desk. "I assume this is about Beth and Tony."

"Of course it is." Anger mixed with fear darkened Judith's eyes. "In a way it has been about them from the beginning, has it not?"

He rubbed his temples. "Judith, I think it would be best if you did not say anything else on the subject."

"What does it matter if we have the truth plain between us at last," Judith asked, very fierce now. "I know what you thought all those years ago when I married your father with such unseemly haste. I know what you thought when the twins were born almost two months early. You believed that I had ruined myself with another man, that I was pregnant when I married George and that is why my parents forced me into such a dreadful marriage. You never said a word but I could see the accusation in your eyes."

He lowered his hand. "It doesn't matter, Judith. Not then and not now."

She took a step closer, her shoulders rigid. "It does matter because you were right. I was pregnant by a married man twice my age. It was not even a matter of seduction. It was rape, but of course no one could say the word aloud."

"Enough, Judith."

"His name was Bancroft. Five years ago the bastard was found dead in an alley outside a brothel. The press ignored the location of the death, of course. There was a great outcry about the dreadful increase in street crime."

It had become clear that Judith was not going to sit down. Lucas went to stand at the window looking out into the dark gardens.

"What was the world coming to, everyone asked when a gentleman of Bancroft's rank in society could not walk the streets in safety," Judith continued, her voice unnaturally even. "But when I saw the accounts of his death in the papers I wanted to celebrate. The bastard was dead. A heart attack, according to the press. It was not the kind of justice I had thirsted for all those years, not true vengeance, but at least he was dead. For a time, I slept better at night."

"Are you finished?" Lucas asked. He did not take his eyes off the gardens.

"No." Judith's voice tightened in her throat. "I slept better until your grandfather died and left everything to you. It was bad enough that George had made no provision for the twins, but when I realized that your grandfather hadn't either, that you controlled the fortune, I began to know a kind of panic you will never understand."

Lucas turned his head to look at her over his shoulder. "Do you really believe that I would cut off Beth and Tony to punish you?"

"They are not related to you by blood," Judith said bitterly. "You know that."

"It doesn't matter."

"Because the law recognizes them as George's offspring? I am well aware of that. But you know the truth. You can cut them off without a qualm when they marry and tell yourself that you owe them nothing."

"That will not happen."

"You have waited all these years to have your revenge on me for the lies I have had to live all these years. Your father was away in Egypt when the twins were born. He never showed in any way that he was suspicious that the children were not his."

"Father had very little interest in any of his children," Lucas said.

"True enough. But your grandfather always suspected the truth. I could tell. I'm certain that is why he made certain that everything was left to you."

Lucas turned completely around to face her. "None of this matters. You can stop torturing yourself with your fears. Within a week after I inherited my grandfather's estate, I drew up papers to ensure that in the event anything happened to me, you and Tony and Beth would receive the bulk of the family fortune."

Judith looked at him in disbelief. "Why would you be so generous when you know they are not related to you by blood?"

"Because it doesn't matter," he said. "How many times must I repeat myself? Beth is my sister and Tony is my brother. They will always be my sister and brother. I assure you they have been provided for in my will. You have been taken care of as well. Trust me when I tell you that none of you will end up on the streets."

Judith looked disconcerted. After a few seconds a faint hope lit her face. "I want to believe you."

"I know you do not think highly of me, but have you ever known me to lie to you or to Tony or to Beth?"

Judith bit her lip. "No."

"Then, for the sake of your sanity and your nerves, I hope you will believe me now."

"I do not know how to thank you," Judith whispered.

"There is no need. You and Beth and Tony are family. That is all that matters."

"Miss Ames said that you would feel this way."

A brisk knock sounded on the door. Grateful for the interruption, Lucas went back behind his desk.

"Come in, Evangeline," he said. "I think Judith and I are finished." He looked at Judith. "Or was there something else?"

"No," Judith said. She rallied. "There is nothing else."

The door opened. Evangeline smiled. "Are you sure I'm not interrupting anything important?"

"Not at all." Judith gave her a tremulous smile. "I'm on my way upstairs to pack. I have decided to return to London with Florence in the morning. Our maids will accompany us, of course."

"Leaving so soon?" Evangeline said.

"Beth and Tony find the place fascinating, but neither Florence nor I have ever been comfortable here at Crystal Gardens." Judith went toward the door. "Beth's presence is quite sufficient to satisfy the proprieties. If you will both excuse me?"

"Certainly," Evangeline said.

Lucas hesitated and then made his decision. "Judith, there is one thing you might want to know."

Judith tensed, wary and fearful again. "What is it?"

"I investigated Bancroft's death. It may give you some satisfaction to know that the news accounts got it wrong. But, then, that is often the case."

"I don't understand," Judith said.

"Bancroft did not die of natural causes. Someone killed him."

"Are you certain?" she asked.

"There was never any doubt."

Judith drew a deep breath. "So I owe a common street criminal for delivering the justice that society would never have given me."

"That is certainly one way of looking at it," Lucas said.

Judith raised her chin. "I hope he died in pain."

"He did. I promise you, he knew fear before he knew death."

Judith nodded once. A great calm settled on her. She looked both weary and relieved. "Thank you, Lucas. You have given me a fine gift today, one I will always be grateful for, but Beth and Tony must never know about Bancroft."

"They will not hear of him from me," he said. "I give you my word. But I have known Beth and Tony all of their lives. I am convinced that they are quite capable of dealing with the truth. In my opinion, they have a right to it. And knowing those two, sooner or later they will discover it, in any event. It would be best if they heard it from you first.

Evangeline looked at Judith. "I agree. Beth and Tony are very impressive, very admirable young people. They are strong enough to handle the facts of their birth. As Lucas said, they have a right to those facts. They will understand why you did what you did."

Judith sighed. "You know the truth, as well, don't you? You are aware that Beth and Tony are not my husband's offspring."

"Lucas said nothing on the subject but my intuition told me that might be the case," Evangeline said. "It explained so much, you see."

Judith was quiet for a long moment. Then she took a deep breath. "Perhaps you are both correct." She looked at Lucas. "You are right when you say that Beth and Tony are strong. What is more, they owe much of their inner strength and character to you. I can see that now."

"Do not discount your own courage and your determination to protect your children, Judith," Lucas said. "Beth and Tony received a great deal of their strong will and character from you."

Judith gave Evangeline a tremulous smile. "Thank you for encouraging me to speak to Lucas today. I feel as if a crushing weight has been lifted from my heart."

She went out into the hall and closed the door very quietly behind her.

Evangeline looked at Lucas. "Obviously you were able to reassure her."

"I did my best. But she has spent nearly twenty years working her nerves into this state. It may take time for her to accept that I have no interest in avenging myself on her and certainly not by depriving Beth and Tony of what is theirs by right."

"For her part, as a young woman she must have felt hopelessly trapped with no way out."

"When did you deduce the truth?" Lucas asked.

"Almost immediately. As I told Judith, it explained much about the past."

"Your intuition is better than mine, at least in this matter. I had always been certain that she was pregnant when she married my father but I assumed that she had a lover who, for some reason, could not marry her. It took me much longer to realize that she had been raped." Lucas picked up the sterling silver letter opener and balanced it on two fingers. "Her attacker was an older, married man who moved in society."

"I'm astonished that she confided such a secret to you."

"She told me the truth today but I actually stumbled across it five years ago. I picked up some old rumors in the course of a case I was investigating. A young prostitute had been badly abused and nearly killed by a gentleman client. She was not the first. The brothel madam asked my acquaintance at Scotland Yard to investigate. He'd had his suspicions of Bancroft for years but there was nothing he could do because of Bancroft's status in society."

"So your friend at the Yard asked you to look into the matter?"

"Yes. I broke into Bancroft's library and found his journals. He had very carefully recorded the details of what he called his conquests. He did not bother to list the prostitutes he had abused. But the names and descriptions of the women he considered respectable were all there. Over the years any number of governesses, hired companions and young women from families that had no social power had fallen victim to him."

"You found Judith's name on the list?"

"Yes."

Evangeline made a small fist. "I am glad you were able to assure her that he died by violent means."

Lucas raised his brows. "That sounds a bit bloodthirsty, Miss Ames."

"Yes, it does, doesn't it? It was the fact that there was no justice for her all those years ago, to say nothing of the trauma she experienced and the price she paid that has been the real source of her inner turmoil all along, not you and your talent. She fixed on you as the source of her fear because she sensed that you knew her most closely held secret."

Lucas set the letter opener down with great care. "I did not tell her everything about Bancroft's death."

"You told her enough. The important thing for Judith is that Bancroft paid for what he did to her. There was no need to tell her that you are the one who was responsible for his death."

Lucas stilled. "You guessed that, as well?"

"I know you. I know what you would have done after you found Judith's name on the list."

"I made sure that Bancroft understood at the end exactly why he was going to die. He had some difficulty grasping the fact that I would kill him because of what he had done to a woman years earlier."

Evangeline walked to Lucas and put her arms around him. "You explained things to Bancroft, I trust?"

Lucas folded her close against his heart. "I told him that he had committed a crime against my family and that he was going to pay the price."

"Of course," Evangeline said.

Thirty-eight

The dark, seething energy struck Beatrice's senses like a wave of icy water. She caught her breath and stopped just inside the front hall of the town house. She stared at the foot of the stairs.

"Clarissa," she said. Shock tightened her voice to a mere whisper.

"What is it?" Clarissa closed the front door of the town house and looked at her. "You sense something? What's wrong?"

"He was here." Beatrice turned quickly to face her. "Right here in our house."

"Who was here?"

"The actor, Garrett Willoughby. This is the same energy I sensed in his dressing room not more than an hour ago."

The old man sweeping the floor of the theater had demanded a sizable bribe in exchange for allowing them into Willoughby's dressing room, but Mrs. Flint and Mrs. Marsh had made it clear that money was no object in the investigation.

"He must have been watching this house," Clarissa said. "He would have seen our housekeeper leave to visit her sister earlier this morning. He waited until we left and then he broke in."

Rage and panic arced through Beatrice, bringing back memories of her dreadful time in Dr. Fleming's Academy of the Occult. She suppressed the past with an effort of will and forced herself to stay focused on the immediate threat.

"He was searching this place while we were asking after him at the theater this morning," she said.

"So much for the story that he sailed for America in search of new opportunities," Clarissa said. "But what did he hope to find here? He obviously knows that Evangeline is in Little Dixby. He sent Hobson there to murder her at the cottage."

"He must have hoped to find something he could use against Evangeline."

"But what could that be?"

"I don't know," Beatrice said. "But we must find out."

A great sense of urgency was beating at her. She whirled around, grasped handfuls of her skirts and flew up the staircase. Clarissa followed her.

"For heaven's sake, have a care," Clarissa said. "He may still be in the house."

Beatrice elevated her senses and shook her head. "No, he is gone now."

They stopped on the landing and looked down the hallway. Beatrice saw the telltale traces of energy on the doorknobs.

"He was searching for Evangeline's room," she said. "He found it. He left the door open."

They walked quickly to the open door and looked into the bedroom. There was no sign that anything had been disturbed. The bed was still neatly made. The wardrobe and the drawers in the small writing desk were closed.

"He was here," Beatrice said. "I can sense it. He searched this room, I think, but what was he looking for? What did he find?"

"He was looking for her secrets," Clarissa said.

Beatrice did not question that assessment. Clarissa knew more than most people did about secrets and how they could be used against a woman. She had, after all, been obliged to invent a new life, indeed an entire new identity, for herself.

"Well, he would not have found Evie's greatest secrets," Beatrice said. Relief cascaded through her. "I'm sure she was not so foolish as to set them down in her journal. In any event, she took her journal with her."

Clarissa walked to the desk and started opening drawers. She stopped when she saw Evangeline's small, neatly organized file of correspondence.

"He found something useful here," she said.

"But Evie has very few correspondents." Beatrice hurried across the room. "She has no family or friends, except us."

"That does not mean that she doesn't send and receive letters." Clarissa reached into the file and plucked out a small handful of papers. She spread them out on the desk. "Here is her correspondence dealing with the rental of the cottage in Little Dixby, for example. There is also a note from her dressmaker informing her that her new gown is finished and ready to be delivered."

Beatrice flipped through some more papers. "I remember this note from the bookshop in Oxford Street letting her know that the new novel she requested had arrived."

There were several more letters of a similar nature but Beatrice knew when they found the correspondence that mattered. The dark currents of energy seething on the pages were unmistakable. Clarissa sensed it at the same time.

"This is what he needed," she said. "He found her vulnerable spot."

"He chose his part well," Beatrice said grimly.

Clarissa looked at the papers in Beatrice's hands. "We must send a telegram to Evie at once."

Thirty-nine

Evangeline was in her bedroom, working on the next cliff-hanger ending and taking advantage of the peaceful atmosphere of the nearly empty house. Lucas, Stone, Beth and Tony were at work in the gardens, using Chester's map to identify the locations of the three crystals.

Quick footsteps sounded in the hall. Molly appeared in the doorway. She was alight with excitement.

"There's a Mr. Guthrie to see you, Miss Ames."

"Guthrie? My publisher?" Evangeline put down her pen, unable to believe her ears. She felt a sudden fluttering sensation in her stomach. "He's here? In this house?"

"Yes, yes, that's him." Evangeline sprang to her feet. "He said he is staying at one of the inns in town. Asked if you got his telegram advising you of his arrival."

"No, indeed, I did not."

"I expect Mr. Applewhite's bicycle broke down again."

"Did Mr. Mayhew bring him from town in his cab?"

"No, miss, I expect Mr. Guthrie walked."

"Never mind. The important thing is that Mr. Guthrie is here. Let me think, we can't put him in the library. Those vines on the windows make most people nervous. Please show him into the parlor. It's on the sunny side of the house."

"Yes, miss. You'll be wanting tea?"

"Yes, yes, of course, and some of your wonderful little cakes, as well. Perhaps I can persuade him to stay for dinner. No, wait, that might not be such a good idea. He would have to be driven home through the woods and that forest can be unnerving after dark."

Molly stepped back into the hall. "I'll go prepare the tea tray."

"Thank you, Molly."

Evangeline hesitated in front of the wardrobe. She was wearing one of her more comfortable day dresses, a simple, dark blue gown. There was no elaborate draping and only one petticoat. The urge to change into a more fashionable gown was overwhelming but she dared not keep Guthrie waiting.

She contented herself with repinning a few stray strands of hair and fluffing up the scarf she had used to fill in the neckline of the gown. Taking a deep breath to compose herself, she went out into the hall and down the stairs.

A moment later she swept through the parlor doorway and paused. The man standing at the window had his back to her. His hair was gray and his coat was cut in the staid, conservative fashion that one expected middle-aged gentlemen to wear. He gripped a walking stick in one hand.

A whisper of intuition aroused her senses. There was something wrong with Guthrie's hair. She was suddenly quite sure that he was wearing a wig. He certainly would not be the first bald-headed man to do so, she thought. Men were entitled to their small vanities.

But the obvious explanation did not satisfy her intuition. She suppressed her unease and summoned a welcoming smile.

"Mr. Guthrie," she said. "How kind of you to call. I'm so sorry I did not receive your telegram. But fortunately you found me at home today."

"It is fortunate, indeed, Miss Ames." Guthrie turned around. "You have already put me to a great deal of trouble. I would not have been pleased if you had made things even more difficult."

Evangeline's insides went ice-cold. Now she could see Guthrie's right hand. It was that of a man who was nowhere near middle-aged and there was a pistol in it. The initial shock stole her breath for a few seconds.

"You are not Mr. Guthrie," she said. "I should have paid attention to what my senses were trying to tell me."

"I have no idea what you're talking about but, no, I'm not your publisher. My name is—"

"Garrett Willoughby, Douglas Mason's brother."

Garrett's eyes hardened. "I'm impressed, Miss Ames. You're very quick, aren't you? My brother did say that you are far too smart for your own good."

"People are searching for you."

"Yes, I know." Garrett pulled a slip of paper out of his pocket. "This was intended for you. It is from a Miss Slate advising you that she and her friend do not believe that I am on my way to America in search of new theatrical opportunities. They suspect that I may, in fact, be on the train to Little Dixby and that I am disguised as your publisher. She was right. When I found the letters from Guthrie and the contract in your desk drawer, I knew that he was the one person you would see without question."

"How did you intercept the telegram?"

"I was concerned that there would be some in London who would not believe that I had sailed for America. I took the precaution of calling in at the local telegraph office on my way here this afternoon to inquire about messages for a visitor who was staying at Crystal Gardens. When I discovered that one had just come in, I offered to deliver it as I was on my way out here." He motioned toward the door with the gun. "We are leaving now."

Evangeline edged back out into the hall. "You cannot possibly hope to escape. Lucas Sebastian will hunt you down."

"You are wrong, Miss Ames. Sebastian is a soft, pampered man of the upper classes. I cut my teeth on the streets of London robbing men who were far more dangerous than he could ever imagine."

"You don't know him very well, do you?"

"Never met the man and I hope to keep it that way. But just to be sure, I rented a horse and a small, closed carriage from the livery stable in town. It is waiting just out of sight down the lane. You and I are going to take a short journey. Short for you, I should say. *Move, you murderous bitch.*"

Evangeline edged out into the hall. The silence of the big house seethed around her. Garrett prodded her toward the front door.

"Outside," he ordered. "If you scream, you will die here and now."

She opened the front door and moved out onto the step. "You are being very foolish, Mr. Willoughby. If you had any sense, you would run for your life while you can."

"Don't waste your breath trying to frighten me." Garrett followed her outside and closed the door. He motioned with the gun again. "Quickly now, into the trees at the edge of the drive."

Evangeline walked into the thick woods that bordered the cobblestone drive. Garrett was directly behind her. The woods closed around them, cutting off much of the view of the big house.

"Where do you intend to take me?" she asked quietly.

"Somewhere private. With luck it will take Sebastian and the others days to find your body in this forest, if they ever find it at all. By then I will, indeed, be on my way to America."

"Why should I walk another step?"

"For the same reason that so many prisoners walk obediently to their doom. As long as you are alive you have some faint, flickering hope of escape or of being able to plead for your life. And as it happens, I do have some questions for you."

"You want to know how your brother died, don't you? You don't really believe that he fell down those stairs but you don't understand how I could have overcome him."

"I know bloody well he didn't fall and break his neck." Garrett's voice shivered with the force of his fury. "He went there that day to kill you. He was enraged because you had ruined the scheme to marry the Rutherford heiress. He told me that it was your fault that he was exposed as a fraud. He said that it was as if you were haunting him."

"Oddly enough I thought he was the one haunting me. I could scarcely believe my eyes when I saw him that first day on the Rutherford case. I know he did not recognize me. When did he realize who I was?"

"He watched Lady Rutherford's house for a time after his proposal had been rejected. He wanted to know how the old lady had discovered that he was a fraud. When he saw you leave with your suitcase in hand, he became suspicious. He said you no longer walked or acted like a hired companion. There was something familiar about you, he said."

"He followed me back to the agency."

"When you emerged without your wig and spectacles, he recognized you instantly."

Evangeline saw the horse and a small carriage through the trees.

"So he set his trap," she said.

"What did you do to my brother that day?"

"Why should I tell you?" Evangeline stopped and turned around. "As soon as I answer your question you will kill me."

"Not here, not unless you make it necessary." Garrett smiled. "Who knows? Perhaps if you answer my questions, I'll give you a sporting chance. Let you make a run for it."

"I doubt it."

Garrett's eyes flashed with rage. "Get into the carriage."

"No," Evangeline said.

Garrett raised the pistol as though to strike her with the handle. "You'll do as you're damn well told, you murdering little bitch, or you will suffer a great deal before you die."

Dark energy howled through the woods. The horse flung its head in panic and lurched forward, dragging the carriage down the lane.

"What is that?" Shocked, Garrett spun around in a circle, searching for the source of the nightmarish energy. "What is happening?"

"This is the end of the hunt for you," Evangeline said.

Garrett froze when he saw Lucas a short distance away, moving through the trees toward him. There was a shiver of movement in the undergrowth on the right. Stone materialized.

"One thing is for certain," Lucas said. His eyes burned with icy fire. "I am not in a sporting mood."

"Bastard." Garrett grabbed Evangeline as she attempted to move out of reach. He wrapped his arm around her throat and dragged her back against his chest. "Where did you come from?"

"Let her go," Lucas said quietly.

"Stop whatever it is that you're doing to me or I'll kill her now, I swear it."

Lucas looked at Evangeline. "Are you all right?"

"I will be soon," she said.

She had the physical contact she needed. She clutched Garrett's arm with both hands and sought the strongest currents of his aura, his life force. Cautiously she started to dampen them. She had learned from the experience of healing Lucas, she reminded herself. She did not have to kill Garrett in order to stop him. All she had to do was render him unconscious.

"W-what's happening to me?" Garrett tightened his hold on Evangeline.

"It's the energy of this place," Lucas said. "Haven't you heard the local legends? These woods are dangerous. Some say they're haunted."

"No," Garrett choked. He reeled away from Evangeline.

When she lost contact with him she lost her ability to manipulate his aura. But Lucas took control. More waves of fierce energy swelled in the atmosphere.

Garrett staggered, clawed at horrors only he could see and frantically tried to aim the pistol at Evangeline.

"This is your fault," he gasped. "All of it. Your fault."

"Get away from him, Evangeline," Lucas said quietly.

She was already moving well beyond Garrett's reach. But he was no longer paying any attention to her. He was lost in the storm of nightmares that had engulfed him. Horror replaced the rage in his eyes.

He put the pistol to his temple and pulled the trigger.

Forty

I know it's too soon to be certain of success," Lucas said, "but it feels different out here, as if the energy is less intense."

"I can feel it, too." Evangeline heightened her senses. "The overheated sensation is dying down. The currents appear to be returning to whatever is normal for this place."

She and Lucas were gathered on the terrace with Beth and Tony. They were surveying the night-shrouded gardens. Earlier the local authorities had been summoned to deal with Willoughby's body. Lucas had provided a short, extremely edited version of events that had not included any mention of attempted murder, just a sad case of suicide.

Everyone had been shocked, but if the policeman and the undertaker wondered why an out-of-work actor had come all the way to Crystal Gardens to take his own life, they were too polite—and too intimidated by Lucas—to inquire. It was common knowledge, after all, that actors were a temperamental lot, given to exaggerated moods, both high and low.

Molly had prepared a light supper that had included what she called a restorative curry-flavored soup and her astonishing salmon-and-leek pie. She claimed both were good for the nerves. Evangeline was not sure about the curative powers of the soup and the pie but she was starting to grow calmer, although she suspected she would not sleep well that night. The sight of Garrett Willoughby's bullet-shattered skull had brought back vivid memories of her father's suicide.

"Tony and I don't have your sensitivity to the paranormal," Beth said. "But we are also aware of the change in the atmosphere."

"The gardens don't seem quite so luminous," Tony observed. "There is still an uncanny sensation out here, but it's not as strong as it was before we dug up the crystals."

"Look at the surface of the gazebo pond," Beth said. "Last night it was like a mirror reflecting the moonlight. But it is dimmer this evening."

Evangeline studied the pond with her senses elevated. It was definitely less ominous. "You're right. There is still energy in the water but it no longer feels so threatening."

Lucas moved to stand beside her, just brushing against her arm. She wanted to turn to him and take comfort from his strength. But this was hardly the time or place for such intimacy. Indeed, she thought, there might never be another opportunity to lose herself in Lucas's arms. The grand adventure was concluded. In the morning they would have to discuss the most discreet way to end their false engagement.

"Tony, you and Beth were right about those crystals," Lucas said. "They were enhancing the natural energy of the gardens, enhancing and reinforcing the power of the spring."

"The problem was that the oscillating pattern of the currents was becoming unstable," Tony said. "Dangerously so. Uncle Chester knew something was wrong but he didn't understand that the crystals were the problem. He was convinced that the powers of the Vision Pool had intensified in some fashion."

"That was why he was so excited to find a woman who could access the chamber," Lucas said. "The question now is: What the devil do we do with those damn crystals?"

"We could always haul them to the coast and drop them into the sea," Beth suggested.

Tony's brow furrowed. "I don't think they should be destroyed. Their paranormal properties could have great value at some time in the future. I would like the opportunity to study them."

"I'm not sure that's a good idea," Lucas said.

"According to Uncle Chester's papers, he found the crystals in a shop that sold mostly fraudulent antiquities," Tony said. "Evidently they had been sitting around in a crate for years without causing any problem. It was only when he inserted them into the ground here at the abbey that they started to resonate in a dangerous manner."

"If you do keep them, they will need to be secured," Evangeline warned. "There will always be others like Chester Sebastian who will be searching for crystals and stones reputed to have paranormal properties. The last thing we need now is for some mad scientist to get hold of them."

"True," Lucas said. "But Tony has a point, the crystals might prove important someday. It might be wise to hang on to them until we can learn more about them."

Beth looked quizzical. "Where do you suggest storing them?"

Lucas looked at the still-luminous foliage. "It strikes me that for the foreseeable future, Crystal Gardens is as secure a hiding place as any. I'll commission a steel box, a safe, to hold them." He looked at Tony. "Will that do?"

"Yes, I'm sure steel will be more than adequate to contain the energy." Tony pursed his lips. "But it might be best to have the interior of the safe lined with glass as an added precaution. If my theories of paranormal energy are correct, those materials have insulating properties as well."

"All right," Lucas said. "That settles it. We'll keep the crystals, at least for now."

Beth glanced at him. "But if you keep the stones here at the abbey, you cannot sell the place. Someone will have to reside here permanently to keep an eye on the crystals and the grounds."

"As it happens, I have decided that it is time I had a country house," Lucas announced.

They all looked at him.

Tony recovered first. "The devil you say. Since when have you been interested in country life?"

"Since I decided to marry and start a family," Lucas said. "Everyone knows that the countryside is a healthier environment for children than the city with its smoke and dust."

Tony and Beth switched their attention to Evangeline. Beth smiled.

"Yes, of course," she said. "Crystal Gardens will make an excellent country residence for the two of you."

Evangeline was speechless. Lucas was digging the hole deeper and deeper, she thought. The more he embroidered their fictional future, the harder it would be to end the false engagement. She caught his eye, frantically trying to send a silent message, but he was oblivious.

"When Evangeline and I are in London, Stone will be here to look after things," he continued.

"Why will Mr. Stone be here?" Beth asked.

"He has informed me that he plans to marry Molly, who has decided to open a tea shop in Little Dixby," Lucas said. He smiled at their startled expressions. "I will provide financing for the tea shop, which, from what I know of Molly, will no doubt be very successful. I have a certain talent for identifying excellent investments, you know."

In spite of her panic, Evangeline experienced a rush of delight. "That's wonderful news. Molly will be so thrilled."

"And as for Stone, he will be happy as long as he is with Molly," Lucas said. "I expect Tony will also be spending a fair amount of time here because he will be conducting research on the crystals. I suggest that he consult with a certain Horace Tolliver, who has a great interest in the science of the paranormal."

Tony grinned. "I will do that. You may depend on seeing a great deal of me in the future. I would very much like to study the paranormal properties of the gardens, as well."

Lucas looked at Beth. "If you do decide to marry Mr. Rushton, I am quite sure he will have some interest in the antiquities here at the abbey. You will both be welcome."

Beth smiled. "As usual, you have come up with a plan to solve all of our problems."

"Not all of them," Lucas said. He looked at Evangeline. "There is still one more problem to be sorted out. If you and Tony will be so good as to leave us, I will attempt to do so."

Tony frowned. "Why must we leave?"

"Because we must," Beth said. "Come with me, Tony. Now."

"I don't see why—" He stopped because she had taken hold of his arm and was propelling him off the terrace and back into the house. He glanced back at Evangeline and Lucas, who had not moved. "Right," he said. "I should jot down my notes regarding the extraction of the crystals today. Wouldn't want to forget the details."

"Exactly," Beth said.

She and Tony disappeared into the house and closed the door.

Evangeline found herself alone with Lucas.

"You have made a great many plans for everyone," she said. "But there is one thing you did not consider."

He moved to stand in front of her and cupped her face in his hands. She was very conscious of the intimate energy of his aura. It whispered to her senses and lifted her spirits. He smiled.

"What is it that I have not considered?" he asked.

"If you make Crystal Gardens your home, what will become of your consulting work? Surely you will not give it up?"

"No," he said. He stroked his thumbs along the line of her jaw. His eyes heated. "I don't think I could give it up altogether even if I wished to do so. You understand that better than anyone."

"Yes," she said.

"But I am asked to consult only a few times a year and London is not that far away by train. In any event, I intend to keep the town house. It will be convenient for those times when we are in London."

"Yes, of course, I should have remembered the train schedule." Actually, she could not seem to think clearly about anything at the moment. Her emotions were in chaos. . . . *When we are in London.*

"You see, I am hoping to have a consulting partner in the future," Lucas said.

She felt blindsided. "What do you mean?"

"It would be very useful to have a partner who has a talent for finding that which is lost."

It was as if all the air had gone out of the night. But she did not need to breathe, she thought. She could live quite nicely on the energy that enveloped both of them.

"I was under the impression that you worked alone," she said.

"I have done so all these years because until you came into my life I never met a woman I could ask to share the burden of knowing the things I know, of seeing the things I see. But you know me for what I am and you do not turn away. You know the beast in me but you are not afraid."

"Of course I am not afraid of you, Lucas." She grasped the lapels of his coat. "Since when did you begin writing melodrama? Good grief, there is no beast inside you. There is a strong, powerful, courageous man who would give his life, if necessary, to protect those in his charge."

Wicked laughter gleamed in his eyes. "Excellent. You are romanticizing me again. I must convince you to marry me before you discover that I am not suited to play the part of the hero."

"Ah, but you are my hero." She smiled and stood on tiptoe to brush her lips across his. "I recognized you the first day I met you. I would very much like to be your partner in your investigations as well as in every other way."

His amusement was transformed as if by magic into a dark, deep need. He caught her hand and kissed her palm.

"I love you, Evangeline, I have since that first day when we met in the bookshop. That night when I found you running for your life in my garden, I knew that I had to find a way to protect you and make you mine. I am not a normal man and I will never be able to offer you a normal life. But I will give you all that I have, all of my love and all of my trust. My heart is in your hands."

Joy swept through her.

"I will guard it well," she vowed. "I love you, Lucas. I always will love you. By now it should be obvious that I am no more normal than you are. But as any author can tell you, normal is not terribly interesting."

He laughed. The sound rang out across the gardens, riding a wave of energy. He pulled her into his arms and kissed her. She responded, as she knew she would for the rest of her life, matching him in heat and energy and the promise of enduring love.

She did not need her psychical intuition to know that it was a promise they would both keep.

Crystal Gardens glowed around them in the moonlit night.

Forty-one

The wedding was held in the Day Garden. Evangeline worried that the location might not yet be entirely safe. Only a month had passed since the crystals had been dug out of the ground, after all. But Tony and Beth and their new colleague, Horace Tolliver, assured her that none of the guests would fall victim to a rogue rose or carnivorous creepers.

A fence, however, was erected around the black water pond in front of the gazebo. *Just to be on the safe side*, Tony had explained. There would, after all, be small children present as the entire Gillingham family had been invited.

There were few, if any, whispered remarks on the matter of the couple's scandalously short engagement. There were a number of reasons for the lack of gossip. The first was that it was obvious to one and all that the bride and groom were deeply in love.

The second reason for so much discretion was equally straightforward: No one wanted to risk bringing the wrath of the new master of Crystal Gardens down on his or her head. It was understood that Lucas Sebastian would not hesitate to avenge even the tiniest offense to his lady's honor.

The summer sun shone on a large crowd that included Judith, Lucas's aunt Florence, Tony and Beth and several other members of the Sebastian family. Tony was best man. Beatrice and Clarissa served as bridesmaids.

Mrs. Flint and Mrs. Marsh, the middle-aged proprietors of the hired companion agency in Lantern Street, sat in the front row on the bride's side of the aisle. Throughout the ceremony they sniffed and dabbed discreetly at their eyes with small linen hankies.

"They were weeping because they knew that they had lost one of their best inquiry agents," Clarissa told Evangeline later. "They know it will be hard to replace you."

"We reminded them that you and Mr. Sebastian would be available for occasional consulting work," Beatrice added. "They, of course, assured us that the agency would not be involved in any more cases of murder. It sounds as if life will be quite boring for Clarissa and me from now on, but there you have it."

Following the ceremony the bride and groom and the guests enjoyed an elaborate wedding feast orchestrated by Molly. The crowd was impressed. The long table set up on the terrace was festively decorated. The dishes included a salmon-and-leek pie, a variety of roasted meats and foul, blancmange, lobster salad, a selection of summer fruits topped with whipped cream, ices and jellies.

At the head of the table there was a spectacular wedding cake trimmed with astonishingly realistic roses. Evangeline knew a moment of panic when she made to cut the cake and noticed the flowers.

"*Molly.* Not *those* roses."

Molly leaned close and lowered her voice. "They're sugar roses, ma'am. Don't worry, I didn't pluck them from the garden."

Lucas and Evangeline spent their wedding night in the ruins of the Roman bath deep in the heart of the Night Garden. If the location struck some as an unusual choice for the start of a honeymoon, no one was foolish enough to remark upon that, either. Nor did anyone comment when Lucas was seen hauling a stack of cushions, pillows and fresh bed linens into the maze the day before the wedding.

It was now a matter of local pride that the new master and mistress of Crystal Gardens were not what anyone would call an ordinary couple. No one could expect them to spend their wedding night in the ordinary fashion.

THE ENERGY in the second pool chamber was good.

Lucas picked up the bottle of champagne that he had just opened and filled two glasses. He carried the glasses to the edge of the sparkling pool where Evangeline sat, her dainty feet dangling in the water. She had changed into a nightgown. Her hair was tumbled around her shoulders and her eyes were filled with the endless mysteries that he knew he would be exploring for the rest of his life.

He handed her one of the glasses and sat down beside her. He had removed his boots and his shirt was open but he was still wearing his trousers. He rolled up the bottom edges of the pants and put his own feet into the pool.

"Congratulations, Mrs. Sebastian," he said.

"On my marriage, do you mean?" Her eyes warmed. "Thank you, Mr. Sebastian. As it happens, I am quite pleased myself."

"I was referring to your remarkable success with the publication of yet another chapter of *Winterscar Hall*." He raised his glass in a small toast. "You did it—you actually managed to convince your readers that the man they had assumed was the villain of your novel is now the hero. Only a very fine writer, indeed, could have pulled off that clever twist."

She smiled and took a sip of the champagne. "Thank you. I must admit, I was fortunate enough to be inspired by none other than my very own husband."

"Who is always happy to be of service."

"That," she said, "will be very convenient."

He touched her cheek, leaned over and kissed her.

"I love you, Evangeline."

"I love you, Lucas."

A fierce joy welled up inside him. He set his glass aside and put hers down beside it.

He gathered her into his arms and kissed her.

The effervescent waters of the ancient pool sparked and flashed, reflecting the energy of love.

FROM

THE LOST NIGHT

BY

Jayne Castle

A NOTE FROM JAYNE

Welcome to Rainshadow Island on the world of Harmony.

In the Rainshadow novels you will meet the passionate men and women who are drawn to this remote island in the Amber Sea. You will also get to know their friends and neighbors in the small town of Shadow Bay.

Everyone on Rainshadow has a past; everyone has secrets. But none of those secrets are as dangerous as the ancient mystery concealed inside the paranormal fence that guards the forbidden portion of the island known as the Preserve.

The secrets of the Preserve have been locked away for centuries. But now something dangerous is stirring. . . .

One

You belong to me," the vampire said. "Soon you will understand that you are meant to be my bride. No matter what happens to me in this place, I will escape and I will come for you."

Marcus Lancaster's voice was rich, compelling and resonant, the voice of an opera singer or the ultimate con man. He accompanied the words with a sly whisper of compelling energy that shivered with promise. *I can fulfill your deepest desires.*

Rachel Bonner did not doubt for a moment that he truly did want her but she was certain it was not because he had fallen in love with her. Lancaster was one of the monsters. That crowd didn't have the capacity to love. They were inclined, however, to be obsessive in their desires and, therefore, quite dangerous.

"I knew this was a waste of time." Rachel gathered up her notepad and pen and got to her feet. The silvery charms attached to her bracelet shivered and clashed lightly.

"You cannot run from me, my beloved," Lancaster said. He reached up with one well-manicured hand and touched the ear stud in his left ear. The small item of jewelry was made of black metal and set with a stone that was the color of rain.

The gesture was casual—made in an absent manner, as if Lancaster was not aware of what he was doing. But the hair on the back of Rachel's neck stirred. A chill of intuition raised goose bumps on her arms. Her palms went cold.

Lancaster wore another piece of jewelry, too, a discreet signet ring engraved with the image of a mythical Old World beast, a griffin.

She had shut down her senses so she wouldn't have to view Lancaster's aura, but there were traces of his energy on the table and everything else that he had touched in the room. She could not abide the way he was watching her. She had to get out of there.

She looked at the one-way mirror set into the wall as she went toward the door and raised her voice a little to make sure her unseen audience could hear her.

"That's it, Dr. Oakford—I'm finished here. There's nothing I can do with this one."

She did not have to see the faces of Dr. Ian Oakford and the other members of the clinic staff who were observing the therapy session to know that they were all reacting with shock and outrage. Ditching a patient the way she had just done was extremely unprofessional. But she no longer cared. She'd had enough of Oakford and his team, enough of their research, enough of trying to fit into the mainstream world of clinical para-psychology.

A woman—at least one who had been raised in a Harmonic Enlightenment community—could take only so much. Her parents and her instructors at the Academy were right. She was not cut out for mainstream life.

Most people would not have known Lancaster for what he was. Tall, blond, blue-eyed and handsome in a slick, distinguished way, he was a natural-born predator who moved easily among his prey. But the dark side of Rachel's talent for aura healing was the ability to see the monsters and recognize them for what they were.

Lancaster had made a tidy fortune in the financial world. But a few days ago he had shocked his associates and his clients when he had voluntarily committed himself to the Chapman Clinic. He claimed to be plagued with severe para-psych trauma induced by the death of his wife several months earlier. His symptoms consisted of nightmares and dangerous delusions—precisely the severe symptoms required for someone to be admitted to Dr. Oakford's new research program at the clinic.

She opened the door, stepped out into the hall and signaled to the waiting orderly.

"You can take Mr. Lancaster back to his room, Carl," she said. "We're finished."

"Yes, ma'am."

Carl moved into the therapy room.

"Time to go, Mr. Lancaster," he said in the soothing, upbeat tone he used with all the patients.

Lancaster chuckled. "I think I make Miss Bonner nervous, Carl."

He got to his feet with leisurely grace, as though he were still dressed in the elegant silver-gray suit and white tie that he had been wearing when he walked into the clinic. Credit where credit was due, Rachel thought. Lancaster managed to make the baggy shirt and trousers that were standard issue for all patients look like resort casual attire.

"Do you think she's afraid of me, Carl?" Lancaster infused his mellifluous words with just the right tincture of regret. "The last thing I want to do is frighten her."

"No, Mr. Lancaster, I'm sure Rachel isn't afraid of you," Carl said. "She has no reason to be afraid of you, now, does she?"

"An excellent question, Carl. One that only Rachel can answer."

Rachel ignored both of them. The tiny stones set into her charms were starting to brighten. That was not a good sign because she was not consciously heating the crystals. They were reacting to her anxiety, a strong indication that her current state of psychical awareness and control was anything but harmonically tuned.

This was it, she thought. Lancaster was the last straw. She was going to hand in her resignation. The money was good at the clinic and the work provided the illusion that, in spite of what everyone back home said, she could make a place for herself in the mainstream world. But she had not signed on to deal with monsters like Marcus Lancaster. Nor was he the only one enrolled in the research trial. There was a very good reason why the patients in Oakford's project were housed in a locked ward.

She was an aura healer. She needed to use her talents in a positive way.

According to mainstream theories of para-psychology, energy-sucking psychic vampires were a myth—the stuff of horror novels and scary movies. But Rachel had met a few in her time and she knew the truth. The monsters were real. The good news was that most of them were relatively weak. They tended to pursue careers as con men, cult leaders and politicians. They preyed on the emotionally vulnerable and the gullible.

Nobody denied that such low-level human predators existed, but few thought of them as vampires or monsters. Psychology textbooks, therapists and clinicians had invented more politically correct terms to describe them. The diagnostic descriptions often involved the phrase *personality disorder*, or para-sociopath. But the ancients back in the Old World had got it right, Rachel thought. So had the philosophers who had founded the Harmonic Enlightenment movement and established the Principles of Harmonic Enlightenment. The correct description for the Marcus Lancasters of the world was *evil*. When that particular attribute was coupled with some paranormal talent, you got psychic vampire.

The question that was worrying her the most was why Lancaster was attracted to her. She knew it was not love or even simple lust that had made him fixate on her out of all the members of the clinic staff. She had learned at the Academy that it was the prospect of controlling others that fascinated the monsters. By the nature of her own psychic ability and training, she possessed a high degree of immunity to their talents. But she suspected her immunity was the very quality that had drawn Lancaster's attention. She was a challenge to him. Seducing and controlling her would affirm his own power.

The problem for the creeps was that they were incapable of achieving any degree of inner harmony. They spent their lives trying to fill the dead zones on their spectrums. No Ponzi scheme was ever lucrative enough, no cult was ever large enough, no business empire was ever sufficiently profitable, no position on the academic or political ladder was imbued with enough power to content a vampire.

And for the subset of vicious monsters who were drawn to death and violence, no amount of torture and killing could satisfy the bloodlust.

But monsters had dreams, too, Rachel thought. Evidently Marcus Lancaster had concluded that controlling her would fulfill some of his own dark fantasies.

Ian Oakford was waiting for her at the end of the hall. Last month, when she had met him, she had done a little fantasizing of her own. Ian was an intelligent, good-looking man with a very buff build and a lot of stylishly cut brown hair. He was endowed with the strong-jawed, trust-me-I'm-a-doctor presence that the patients and most of his female staff found appealing. Rachel was convinced that he could have had a lucrative second career as an actor playing a doctor in pharmaceutical commercials.

Not that Ian wasn't already doing very well for himself. He was still young by the standards of the profession, but his talent for parapsychology, combined with a lot of drive and ambition, had taken him far. Six months ago he had been appointed director of the new research wing of the Chapman Clinic. The funding from drug companies had quickly followed. He had several clinical trials in various stages of progress.

At that moment, however, Ian did not exhibit the kind, reassuring air that people liked in those engaged in the healing professions. Behind the lenses of his designer glasses his gray eyes glittered with anger. His square jaw was rigid.

"What do you think you're doing, walking out of a therapy session like that?" he demanded.

His voice was tight but controlled. Ian prided himself on never expressing extremes of emotions of any kind. He viewed such displays as a symptom of instability in the aura. He was right, of course, at least according to the Principles, and she had admired him for his self-mastery. But she did not need her talent to tell her that he was furious. She didn't blame him. He had taken a huge risk bringing her onto his research team. Her professional failings reflected badly on his judgment.

She braced herself for the inevitable. This was it, the end of her first really good job in the mainstream world. Her parents would breathe a sigh of relief. They had warned her about the difficulties she would encounter when she left the Academy and the Community.

"Marcus Lancaster is not experiencing severe para-trauma, Dr. Oakford," she said quietly. "He's faking it. He's incapable of feeling any sense of loss unless it affects his bottom line or threatens his personal safety. A dead wife wouldn't cut it, trust me, not unless her death cost him financially, which, according to what I found online, was not the case. Just the opposite. He inherited a lot of money when she died."

"You're wrong. No one could fake those night sweats and hallucinations."

"He is," she said simply. "And you and the others here at the clinic are buying his act."

"Why would a man in Lancaster's position pretend to have such a severe mental illness? It could destroy him financially and socially. No one in his right mind would voluntarily commit himself for treatment in a para-psych hospital the way Lancaster did unless he truly feared for his sanity."

"I have no idea why he committed himself voluntarily," Rachel said. "You could ask him but I can tell you right now he'll lie through his fangs."

"Fangs?"

"Sorry, teeth. As I was saying, I don't have any idea why he went to so much trouble to get into your research project, but if I were you, I'd watch out for a lawsuit somewhere down the road."

"Lawsuit?"

"I suspect that Lancaster has a long history of financial cons and schemes," she said. "Maybe he's got a plan for proving that he was a victim of unethical research practices. Who knows? I can't begin to guess his objectives, but I can promise you that there is nothing you or I or modern para-pharmaceuticals can do for him. We can't fix the monsters."

"I have warned you before that we do not use terms like *monsters* and *vampires* in this clinic. I realize you're not a professional, Miss Bonner, but that is no excuse for unprofessional language."

"Yes, Doctor."

"There are no such things as human monsters. How many times do I have to explain to you that Lancaster suffers from para-psych trauma complicated by an underlying instability of his para-senses?" Ian must have realized that his voice was rising. He regained control immediately. "I did not hire you to diagnose my patients. Your sole responsibility is to identify the erratic currents in their auras so that their disorders can be treated by a qualified therapist, and appropriate prescriptions can be written."

"I understand," she said.

Behind Ian, Helen Nelson and Adrian Evans, the two members of the staff who had been observing the session with Oakford walked quietly away in the opposite direction. They knew what was going to happen next, Rachel thought. They were on their way to spread the gossip.

Just before the pair turned the corner Helen glanced back and gave Rachel a sympathetic look. Rachel managed a wan smile in return. She was keenly aware that most of the professional staff at the clinic viewed her with disapproval and, in some cases, outright hostility. Helen had been one of the kinder people on the research team. She had gone so far as to invite Rachel to join her for lunch in the company cafeteria a few times. In return Rachel had done free aura readings at a birthday party for one of Helen's friends. There had been a lot of white wine and canapés that night. Rachel had known full well that she was there as the entertainment for the evening. But she had hoped that it was the first step in building a circle of friends outside the Community, another step toward mainstreaming.

She knew now that she was never going to be accepted at the clinic. She had done her best to blend in, but pinning her hair into a tight bun and donning dark-framed, serious glasses and a white lab coat couldn't hide the truth. Everyone at Chapman was well aware that she was not a real para-psychologist. She wasn't even a licensed therapist. In addition, she qualified as a curiosity, especially among the men on the staff, because she had been raised in a Harmonic Enlightenment community.

She had discovered early on that there were a lot of myths and misunderstandings in the mainstream world concerning the Harmonically Enlightened lifestyle and a number of them revolved around sex. The one aspect of her attempt at mainstreaming that had appeared promising at first was her social life. Men had lined up to invite her out on dates at the tearoom and, later, here at the clinic. But the whirlwind of dating had dissipated rapidly after she had been forced to make it clear that women who lived by the Principles were not necessarily inclined to hop into bed whenever the opportunity arose.

Until a couple of weeks ago she had been making her living selling tea and giving aura readings every Wednesday and Saturday at the Crystal Rainbow Tearoom in the Old Quarter. She had been trying to recover her sense of inner balance following the disturbing events that had occurred on her last trip to Rainshadow Island.

Oakford had found her in the Crystal Rainbow. Why he had wandered into the tearoom that day, she had never discovered. It was not his kind of place. But a quick glance at his aura had warned her that he had some real talent. Her first thought was that he had found it amusing to watch her do the readings. A lot of people treated aura readings as a form of fortune-telling—a parlor trick that was not to be taken seriously.

But Oakford had been serious. He had ordered a cup of tea, sat down at a small table in the corner and quietly observed her work for nearly an hour. In the end he had been convinced that she was a natural—a talent who could not only read auras but also diagnose disorders of the para-senses. He had concluded that she would be useful to him at the clinic and promptly dazzled her with the promise of a high salary and—more important—a respectable opportunity to practice her healing abilities.

He had said nothing about the monsters.

"Here's the problem, Dr. Oakford," she said. "Lancaster does not present with a simple instability of the aura." She was rather proud of the *does not present* line. It sounded clinical, she thought, very professional. "There's a whole chunk of the normal spectrum missing in his energy field. Think flatlined."

"That's not possible," Ian snapped. "If his aura was flatlined, he'd be dead."

"Not his entire aura. But there is a blank section on his spectrum. It's like someone shut down the lights in that region."

"I would remind you, Miss Bonner, that it is your job—indeed, the mission of this clinic—to turn on those lights for our patients."

"Okay, maybe the light thing was a bad analogy. Let me try another approach. In the old days, people would have said Lancaster was soulless. That was always a big element in the traditional vampire myth, you know. Today most laypeople would tell you that Lancaster lacks anything resembling a conscience."

"This is a para-psychiatric clinic, Miss Bonner," Ian said. It sounded as if he had his teeth clenched. "We do not deal in matters of religion or philosophy. We are focused on using modern science to diagnose and heal illnesses of the para-senses."

"And a worthy goal that is," she said quickly. "I'm all for it. In fact, I was thrilled when you asked me to come to work here. I've always felt I had a calling to do this kind of work. Oh, wait, that sounds sort of religious or philosophical, doesn't it? I mean, if my life had taken a different direction, I might have had your job."

Ian's eyes hardened. "Think so?"

Okay, that had been a tactical mistake.

"Well, no, probably not," she admitted. "I wasn't born for upper management."

Another poor choice of words, she realized.

Ian flushed a dark red. Alarmed, she rushed to calm the gathering storm.

"I'm more of an entrepreneur," she explained. "I could never do the kind of work that you do. What I'm trying to tell you is that I can't fix Marcus Lancaster or anyone else like him."

"In that case," Ian said evenly, "your services are no longer needed here at the Chapman Clinic. You've got fifteen minutes to clear out your desk. A member of the security staff will escort you to the door."

Although she knew an escort to the door was standard procedure when someone got fired, it hurt to know that Ian did not trust her.

"Afraid I'll steal some paper clips or a list of your drug company clients on my way out?" she asked.

Ian shook his head and exhaled heavily. "I'm sorry about this, Rachel. I really believed that you would be an asset to my team."

She concentrated her talent. The charms on her bracelet clashed lightly on her wrist, generating just enough ultralight to allow her to view Ian's energy field. Ian was angry but he was also experiencing genuine disappointment and regret. He had taken a chance on her, hoping that she might give him an edge in the highly competitive world of para-psych drug research, and she had failed him.

She heard Carl and Marcus Lancaster in the hall behind her. She did not turn around but she could feel the monster's energy.

"Isn't she lovely, Carl?" Lancaster asked. "Miss Bonner is going to be my bride, you know. The voices tell me that she's my perfect match. We have so much in common."

"Congratulations," Carl said. "Be sure to send me an invitation to the wedding."

"I'll do that," Lancaster said, sounding pleased.

"Meanwhile, it's time for lunch."

"Yes, of course," Lancaster said. "Do you suppose there will be quiche and perhaps a nice white wine at lunch today? I haven't had a decent meal since I arrived here."

"This is Wednesday," Carl said. "That means meat loaf."

"I really don't like meat loaf," Lancaster said. "But I will tolerate anything so long as I can be near my beloved. Her radiance lightens my aura like a fine champagne."

"No wine at lunch, either," Carl said.

"I was afraid of that," Lancaster said.

Carl guided him along the hallway.

"Damn it, Rachel, whatever you did to Lancaster in that therapy session has worsened his condition," Ian said. He kept his voice low but it was plain that he was not just angry—he was concerned for his patient.

Rachel shuddered but she did not turn around. She listened to the retreating footsteps, suddenly very glad to know that in fifteen minutes she would be out of the building and far away from the clinic.

"I know you don't want to hear this," she whispered back, "but Lancaster is deliberately acting crazy. His aura is very stable—scary stable, in fact. He is in full control of himself and his talent. He's a full-on psi-path and he's dangerous, sir."

"You're wrong," Ian said. "There is definitely instability in Lancaster's aura. He is an ideal candidate for the drug trial that I am conducting."

"Right." She clutched her notebook to her breasts. She really needed to get out of the clinic. She fought the suddenly overwhelming urge to run. "If you'll excuse me, I'll go pack up my office." She started to move around him and paused. "I do have one piece of advice for you, although you probably won't take it."

Ian narrowed his eyes. "What?"

"Do not believe anything Marcus Lancaster says."

"If you have any proof that he's lying, now would be a real good time to provide it," Ian said, his expression fierce.

She tried to come up with something, anything that would impress Ian.

"His ear stud," she said.

Ian blinked. "What about it? The crystal isn't tuned amber. It can't be used to generate energy. That was checked out when he was admitted. The patients are not allowed to possess amber. And it's certainly not gem quality. It's just a cold, decorative stone of some kind."

She took a deep breath. "Here's the thing, sir: I've seen stones like it before. Also, you should know that Lancaster doesn't need amber or charged crystal to use his para-senses. He's a natural. I think he has a mid-level talent for psychic hypnosis but that's not my point."

"Ridiculous. There is no such talent."

"I didn't expect you to believe that, but think about this, sir: Why would a guy who wears designer suits and watches that probably cost more than the entire city-state budget wear a cheap ear stud?"

"Probably because it has sentimental value," Ian snapped, exasperated.

"Trust me, there isn't an ounce of sentiment in Marcus Lancaster."

"What makes you think that you are qualified to offer an opinion on Lancaster's para-psych profile?" Ian said. "You were selling tea and giving aura-readings when I found you at the Crystal Rainbow."

"Yes, I was, and I think I'll go back to that career. I don't seem to be cut out for clinical work—or for the mainstream world, come to that."

She tightened her grip on her notebook and stepped around Ian.

"Rachel—"

Surprised by the hesitation in his voice, she paused and turned back.

"Yes?" she said.

"Even though you were technically here on probation, I'll see to it that you receive two weeks' severance pay," Ian said quietly.

"Thanks. I appreciate that. I spent a fortune on new clothes for this job. I'll be paying off the credit card for a while."

"I suppose you'll be going back to the Crystal Rainbow Tearoom?"

"No," she said. "I think it's time for Plan B."

"You're going to return to the Harmonic Enlightenment Academy?"

"No. The truth is, I don't belong there, either. Ever heard of Rainshadow Island?"

"No," Ian said.

"Not many people have. It's one of the islands in the Amber Sea. It's not even on most maps. My great-aunts ran a bookshop and café there for a couple of decades. Several months ago they retired and moved to the desert. They left Shadow Bay Books to me. I've just let the shop sit, closed up, until I could decide what to do with it. In the back of my mind the shop was my fallback plan in case things didn't work out for me here in Frequency City. Good thing I didn't sell it."

She started walking again, heading toward her office.

"One more thing," Ian said.

She paused and turned back to face him again. "What now?"

"You said you'd seen stones like the one in Lancaster's ear stud."

"Yes."

"Where?"

"On Rainshadow Island. As far as anyone knows, that's the only place they have ever been found. They're called rainstones."

She hurried away down the hall to the tiny office that had been allocated to her. Two months ago, when she had accepted the position at the clinic, she had been so excited at having her very own office she had taken dozens of photos of the small, spare space and e-mailed them to everyone in the family. She shook her head at the naive memory. As if an office were proof that she had found her place in the world.

"I should have known this wasn't going to work out," she said into the silence. "Not like I wasn't warned."

It took ten minutes, not fifteen, to gather up her personal possessions and dump them into a cardboard box. Carl was waiting at the door. He looked unhappy.

"I'm really sorry about this, Miss Bonner," he said. "It's been nice having you here. The patients all like you. So do I. Things seem more cheerful and sunnier here when you're around."

She smiled. "Thank you, Carl, but Dr. Oakford is right. It's best that I leave. I don't belong here."

Carl cleared his throat. "I don't suppose you happen to have any more of that tea that you blended for me, do you?"

"Not here in the office, but I'll mix up another batch and send it to you."

Carl brightened. "Thanks, I appreciate that."

Five minutes later she was alone on the street, the cardboard box containing her things tucked under one arm, her purse slung over her shoulder. The low, dark clouds opened up as she walked quickly toward the bus stop. Naturally she would get caught in the rain without an umbrella today, she thought. Some days were just flat-out unharmonic from start to finish.

The cold, sleeting rain plastered her tightly pinned hair to her head and soaked her new, low-heeled black pumps. The shoes would be ruined. Not that it mattered, she told herself. No one wore black low-heeled pumps on Rainshadow. Boots—athletic shoes and sandals were the norm there. And she just happened to own a new pair of boots.

She waited for the bus, chilled to the bone but aware that she felt a lot better now that she was away from the Chapman Clinic.

She would survive the rain and the loss of the job. What mattered was that she would never again find herself alone in a therapy room with Marcus Lancaster. Because she was quite certain it was no coincidence that he had manipulated the situation so that they had wound up together today. If she remained on the staff at the clinic he would manipulate things to ensure that there would be more such encounters. She knew that as surely as she knew the Principles.

Another shiver of apprehension swept through her. Rainshadow was Plan B, but the thought of returning to the island made her uneasy. Something had happened to her the last time she was—something unnerving. Twelve hours of her life had vanished.

She had gone into a psychic fugue late one afternoon and wandered into the forbidden territory of the Preserve. Somehow she had not only survived the night in the dangerous woods, she had done what most people who knew the island considered almost impossible—she had managed to find her way out of the Preserve.

She had emerged at dawn the following morning but she had no memories of the night.

She had, however, collected some souvenirs along the way—dark dreams that now haunted her sleep, the faint memory of ethereal music being played somewhere in the night and a handful of rainstones.